FOR THE

For the

Lilli

Elaine Ellis

With Love

Elaine 🧡

ELAINE ELLIS

Copyright © 2020 Elaine Ellis
All rights reserved.
ISBN:9798641611839

ELAINE ELLIS

FOR THE LOVE OF LILLI

For Jessica, Sophia and Rupert with love -
you bring me such joy.

FOR THE LOVE OF LILLI

ACKNOWLEDGMENTS

Huge thanks to my editors Lorena and Delphine, from Daniel Goldsmith Associates, for their insights and patience and for helping to craft the finished work.

Thanks also to Richie, from More Visual Limited, for his creative artwork on the book's cover.

And finally, not forgetting the people of Nice who unknowingly provided the background research and for generally being cool!

ELAINE ELLIS

CHAPTER 1

As Lilli hid under her bed, screened from the outside world by her little bed's pink valence, she hummed a tune to herself, quietly, from her favourite movie Frozen with her hands cupped over her ears. She had mastered this art of blocking out the sound of her father's rages and had almost perfected it, but not quite. She wanted to 'Let it go' and cry, but even at the tender age of six she knew it would be stupid, a word her mummy didn't like her using, and only upset her mummy.

Lilli wished her mummy would join her like she often did during her father's many, shouty business calls. Katarina would brush Lilli's long blonde hair to soothe her daughter's anxiety. Shouty described exactly how her father spoke, on the phone and when talking to her mummy.

Lilli understood very little of her father's native tongue, but it didn't take a genius to work out that whoever was on the other end of the call was obviously in trouble with him. What her father didn't realise was that Lilli would never learn Estonian because she thought it was a very angry language and hated the sound of it. She only ever heard it being shouted, all the time. Her mummy always spoke to her in English. To Lilli it was a soft, gentle language, just like her mummy.

Katarina was in the kitchen, wishing she could go to her

daughter, knowing exactly where she would be hiding, but Erik was wandering around on his mobile phone in a foul temper. She tried to calm him by offering him a coffee, but he knocked the cup out of her hand as he pushed passed her through the kitchen. She flinched as the hot liquid splashed onto her bare arm but didn't make a sound.

If she had uttered even a decibel of pain, he would have turned on her with his sadistic grin. Instead she put her arm under the cold running water from the tap, then took a sponge from the sink and wiped the remains of coffee off the kitchen tiles. Luckily the cup hadn't broken so job done in seconds, as if the incident had never happened. She knew to keep a very low profile while he ranted at the caller. Erik was always on edge when a new shipment arrived in the country until safely in its designated destination.

Erik was finalising arrangements with his associates, but something had upset him. Katarina listened at a distance. She could have been at their local corner shop four doors away and still would have heard him, so she didn't need to put herself in danger whilst eavesdropping. It seemed that one of the items from the new consignment was defective. Katarina's heart sank. It could mean one of three things: sickness, injury or death. She strained to look around the doorframe to see Erik's body language. Katarina recognised the smile on his face, exuding pure evil. He had calmed down and told the caller that they had two for the price of one; he was ecstatic. She heard the Estonian word 'rase' and realised what he had meant. One of the objects must be pregnant. That wouldn't bother Erik, he'd wait until the baby was born and sell it for more than he would get for the girl. Katarina shivered. She was frightened for the girls who had been seized from their homes, bundled into containers and had endured hours in darkness not knowing their fate. She had been one of those girls. She and five other girls were lined up in front of Erik, tears of fear running down her cheeks, her naivety and innocence were that of a young sixteen-year-old snatched from the security of her family.

She saw in his eyes a sinister look she couldn't put into words. He was staring only at her. She had beautiful blonde hair and eyes a piercing blue and was the youngest of the six girls. He told the other five to go with their captors, and Katarina to follow him. She realised once she was taken to his house that she was to be his. That was seven years ago, and although a nightmare in itself, she had been blessed with an enchanting daughter who was her whole life.

Those poor girls would be scared and homesick but as usual, there was nothing Katarina could do. Erik was always very careful not to reveal the destination of each package. Katarina sneaked passed the sitting room door where Erik was looking out of the window, talking in a calmer voice, having averted a problem and she tiptoed up the stairs to Lilli's bedroom.

She sat crossed legged on the floor next to Lilli's bed and whispered…

"Lilliana, come and give mummy a big cuddle please." Lilli popped out from under her bed and snuggled into her mother's protective arms. Katarina rocked her until Lilli pushed slightly away to see her mother's eyes. They were as blue as her own and remarkably dry and pink. Lilli relaxed back into her mother's cuddle in the knowledge that her mother hadn't been the brunt of her father's rage, that time.

Lilli was not a normal six-year-old, she'd had to grow up fast for self-preservation. Although Erik had never laid a hand on his Little Angel, as he called her, he came very close at times when Lilli had disobeyed him. His main quarrel with the little girl was over her stubbornness to learn Estonian, only speaking and acknowledging conversations in English.

Katarina wondered why he had never bothered to ask his daughter the reason she didn't want to learn the language of her ancestors. Perhaps he knew the answer, she often considered, and was ashamed of his own life choices, but that would mean he had to have a conscience.

After a few minutes Katarina heard the front door slam. She left it for a few more before she gently held Lilli's head, kissed her forehead and lifted her to her feet.

She stood up next to her daughter and held her hand. As they walked down the stairs Lilli's grip was very tight. She was still apprehensive but gave nothing away in her bright smile.

"What would you like for lunch Lilli?" Katarina asked her daughter with the normality of a mother in any home. Lilli's grip loosened, and Katarina inwardly smiled. The process normally took longer, but Lilli was happier this time because her mummy had no red marks, blood or tears. Katarina had pulled down her cardigan sleeve on her way up the stairs to cover the very angry small red scald developing on her arm.

"Beans on toast please." She beamed up at her mother, who was smiling. Katarina knew it was Lilli's least favourite snack but had to smile at the thoughtfulness of her little girl. Beans on toast was the quickest and easiest of meals.

"I was thinking of making a mulgipuder."
She turned to her daughter and saw the excitement on her face. "You can help me if you like." Lilli nodded her head enthusiastically. It was her favourite Estonian dish consisting of mashed potatoes and barley, covered in a delicious sauce with lots of bacon.

It was very simple to prepare and would be ready in no time, or perhaps just a little longer with Lilli's help, thought Katarina with a smile. She knew that Lilli may not like her native tongue, but she loved the recipes that came from her wonderful maternal grandmother. One day Katarina hoped she would be able to let Lilli's grandmother cook for her granddaughter, in person. She shook her head and pushed her yearning to be back with her family aside. Until she became a British Citizen and had legal status in the country she was abducted to, Erik had told her that she could not leave Britain without fear of arrest. Lilli was born in England, but there was no record of her birth. Erik had managed, illegally, to have documents drawn-up in Estonia to register her birth there. Katarina knew that when Lilli reached seven, the age Estonian children started school, Erik would whisk her away to his family in Estonia and Katarina would never see her again. She urgently needed a plan, and soon.

* * *

Emily was unhappy.

It was not because she had put on weight, which was inevitable after her sister's wedding weekend.

It was not because her elderly relatives had said, "don't worry Emily, it'll be your turn next," which made her feel like an old maid. The truth being she was only 14 months older than her sister.

It was not because she hadn't 'got off' with the Best Man as tradition dictated - Luke had looked quite fit in his cravat and tails.

It was not because she was missing her ex, Harry, who'd been offered a dream job abroad and taken it.

Emily Fitzgerald was unhappy because she had found her first grey pubic hair. The world as she knew it was at an end.

Gone were the parties, girls' holidays abroad, music festivals and flirting. Those halcyon days were now behind her. At thirty-one years old she had become a woman.

"For goodness sake Emm, you have dark brown hair. It's a common fact that dark haired people get grey hairs earlier than fair haired people." Chloe had spent the longest 20 minutes she could remember trying to cheer her best friend up.

"I know CC, but it doesn't make it any easier. You're just so lucky being blonde." Emm pouted. Chloe quickly picked up her phone and managed to capture the moment.

"Look how stupid you look!" She passed her phone over to Emm who took one look at the photo and burst out laughing. Chloe Collins, known as CC to her friends, had a medical degree and had already done her foundation training. She was now on the last year of her six-year speciality training to become a consultant psychiatrist. She and Emm had grown up together as neighbours and best friends. CC could also, as of the last weekend, claim a tenuous kinship to Emm, as her brother James had just married Emm's sister Stephanie.

"If you're that bothered, pluck it out, or pop into a chemist and buy some dye." Emm knew CC would not understand. The old adage 'blondes have more fun' was beginning to make sense.

"I'm sorry CC. I think I'm suffering from ante-climax-ism, or whatever the psycho term is." CC smiled. Her best friend had finally snapped out of her mood.

"So, what are you going to wear to Kate's birthday on Friday? Hopefully knickers so no one can see your decrepitude!" Both girls were laughing so hard they were getting stares from the coffee shop clientele. Crisis over, it was time to go. "Let's go shopping and see what bargains we can find." Retail therapy worked on dark brown-haired and blonde-haired girls alike.

CC had arranged to meet Emm at the coffee shop because she had something to tell her and it was too much of a rush first thing in the morning, both trying to get out of their flat door around the same time. Unfortunately, due to Emm's unstable emotions, she decided to keep it to herself until a more opportune moment. She had learned very early in her course that timing was very crucial to a good outcome. CC's problem was to tell her best friend her news before Kate's birthday party that weekend.

***

"Oh no, it's my mother again." Emm looked at the screen of her phone after the third time of ringing. She had been trying on a rather flattering dress for the party.

"You'll have to answer it. You know she'll just keep ringing until you do." CC was right, but Emm knew exactly what her mother wanted, and she really didn't want to go back to Nice with her.

"Why is my life so complicated?" She sighed, took a deep breath, put a fake smile on her face just to get herself psyched up, and answered the phone. "Hello Mother. Can I ring you back later? I'm in the changing room at Harvey Nicks, and before you tell me I'm spending too much money, they have a sale on."

CC was used to Emm's brusqueness with her mother and didn't blame her after what Caroline had put her family through.

"I only wanted to see if you'd changed your mind about coming home with me this weekend. Nico would be so pleased to see you. You know he loves you as much as I do, darling." Her mother's toy boy Nicolas, loved everyone, he was French. After Caroline got no response she carried on. "I'll ring you this evening then darling, when you have more time. À bientôt Emily, Mwah." Emm put her phone back into her bag rather guiltily. She knew she had punished her mother enough for leaving her, her sister and her father, but it didn't make it easier when she kept ramming her boyfriend, Nico, down her throat every time she called.

"My advice is buy the dress, it looks so good on you, and then we'll pop to the Champagne bar and get legless." Emm couldn't stop herself. She burst out laughing and hugged her best friend. CC realised she had lost another opportunity of telling Emm her secret. She was running out of time, but the moment still wasn't right.

* * *

Caroline knew she deserved the cold shoulder from both her girls but hoped time would heal the rift. She'd had a fling with a young opera singer, Nicolas, while on holiday with her mother in the South of France and did not go home. Her daughters stayed in London with their father, Michael, and took a long time forgiving her. They did forgive her, eventually, but only because their father seemed very happy without her. Both Emm and her sister Stephanie secretly thought their father had a girlfriend. He hadn't told them, but he'd changed his aftershave and his hairstyle.

Neither daughter ever knew where he was, when normally he would text or call them if he was going 'out of town'. The other odd thing was that he was dressing more casually, sometimes turning up for meetings without a tie. To the girls the unusual behaviour was a dead give-away he was either going through the male menopause, or he had a woman. Both Emm and Stephanie hoped it was the latter.

Emm's mother, Caroline, lived in Nice with her boyfriend Nicolas Janvier who was the same age as Emm. He was the son and grandson of Parfumeurs, from the renowned Parfumerie House Janvier in Grasse, Alpes-Maritime and the great grandson of the bass operatic singer Marcel Janvier who was famous throughout the world, singing at the Royal Opera House, Covent Garden, Milan's La Scala, Paris Opera and the New York Metropolitan Opera during the first quarter of the twentieth century. The Janvier family were very proud that Nico had inherited his great grandfather's voice.

Caroline was staying in England to enjoy a few weeks with her mother and family after coming over for the wedding of her daughter Stephanie. She had decided, quite rightly, to leave Nico in France. He had to be in Paris for a guest appearance in Verdi's Rigoletto at the Opéra Bastille. It was beyond his wildest dreams to perform in the same opera and in the same city as his great grandfather. He could not and would not miss the opportunity for anyone. Caroline was due to go back to the South of France the week after the wedding and was hoping Emm would go with her for a holiday. There was plenty of room in their luxury apartment on Boulevard Victor Hugo in the Musician's Quarter in central Nice and also at the family villa in Grasse. The Janvier family adored Caroline.

Emm's loyalty was to her father. He had been conspicuous by his absence from the office since the wedding, presumably keeping a very low profile until his ex-wife had gone back to France, so she was needed at the office until he returned. With Stephanie away as well, it left the office with only a few staff members. Discretion was the biggest part of her job. It was also the most exasperating. She met so many famous people but couldn't tell a soul, not even CC, who respected her position, but could normally get it out of Emm. Her father owned an upmarket property rental business in Chelsea, called Fitzgerald & Partners. Their clientele came from all over the world. The clients she personally dealt with were usually recording artists, actors and sports celebrities, the perks of being the boss's daughter. She really loved her job. Not only did she get to meet famous people, but also, she got to see around the most spectacular penthouses and apartments with views all over London.

With her father nowhere to be seen and her sister in Italy on her honeymoon, Emm felt abandoned. If she was honest, she had to admit she was missing Harry. She couldn't blame him taking the job, working for hedge fund multi-millionaire businessman and entrepreneur Patrick Robertshaw, who had homes in England, Monaco and umpteen places dotted about the Pacific Ocean. Harry was like a boy scout with his arms covered in merit badges when he heard he'd got the job. It was only supposed to be for a three-month period crewing Patrick's new Sunseeker Super Yacht from Poole to Monaco, picking up the family and extra crew, and cruising to the Bahamas for the winter.

Three months later Emm got the dreaded phone call from Harry that Patrick wanted to keep him on as a gofer, indefinitely. Patrick needed cars and boats rehomed on a whim and he liked Harry. Emm and Harry tried to keep their relationship going by phone calls and Facetime when he had Wi-Fi, but it didn't work. At the beginning Harry had promised that he'd keep working for Patrick until he'd made enough money to buy a house and afford a wonderful wedding for Emm. He knew in his heart though that he didn't want to get tied down for a long time yet, and he enjoyed the job, what chap wouldn't? So, the phone calls and Facetime dwindled from daily to once a week, to once every so often, until they finally stopped. Emm had moved on. Occasionally Emm got a text from Harry, asking how she was. They also kept a casual contact on Facebook and Instagram where they could see where they both were and whom they both were with and how much they were enjoying their lives. Emm did get a little jealous when she saw the great places Harry visited, but she kept telling herself that he'd grow up one day and want to settle down, and maybe, just maybe she may be available.

Emm left work early on Friday to get herself ready for Kate's birthday party. CC wasn't at their flat. She had left a note to say she'd meet Emm at Kate's. Not unusual in itself, but Emm felt CC had been keeping her distance the last few days. What was she hiding? Emm didn't have time to worry. She had to shower, straighten her hair and get her evening make-up on. All very time-consuming and to help the proceedings along she poured herself a nice glass of chilled white wine. The taxi arrived bang on time, so she told the driver on the intercom that she'd be down in a jiffy.

She grabbed the bottle of Whispering Angel, much favoured by the Beckhams she'd read, in the gift bag for Kate, and with one last quick look in the mirror, happily she locked the door and left. She was pleased with the result of the last two hours of titivation.

Kate's birthday party was at her parents' town house in Chelsea. Luckily, she had invited most of the neighbours.

"Emm, you made it. I thought you'd be flitting off to France after the wedding. So glad you could come." Emm handed Kate the present. "Ooo, thank you. I think I may have to hide this bottle. I'm only offering cheap plonk from Sainsbury's to these philistines!" They both smiled at each other. Kate was such a lovely girl. She totally understood Emm. After all, her father had run off with her mother's personal trainer a year ago. Luckily Kate's mother, who had assumed her trainer was a lesbian, put it down to his mid-life crisis and forgave him when he came back grovelling for forgiveness after only two weeks. It also helped that he bought her a nice little run-around, a new 911 Porsche Carrera S, and an apartment in Torriggia, on the water's edge of Lake Como in Italy, ironically where they'd honeymooned. "Drinks are on the side and CC is waiting for you in the garden." It was a courtyard, to be truthful, but with the Wisteria climbing over the walls and numerous potted plants and clever lighting, it looked like a garden. Emm made her way through the patio doors but stopped in the doorway. CC was in an embrace with a man. Emm tried to see who it was but CC was all over him and all that was visible were his legs. Not wanting to be a voyeur she decided to get herself a drink first.

She backed away as surreptitiously as she could, but just as she was about to turn the man came up for breath.
It was Luke. Emm's mouth dropped open and her fists clenched. Why hadn't she told her? So that was what CC was hiding. Her best friend had 'got off' with the Best Man. She felt stupid opening her heart up to her best friend when said friend kept secrets from her. It wasn't that Emm wanted Luke. She knew in her heart she wasn't really over Harry. It was the secrecy that made her feel betrayed.
Before CC had even noticed Emm was at the party, she left. On the way home in the taxi she started to feel very childish. It was supposed to be Kate's day. She couldn't go back though, that would look worse. She got her phone out of her bag and rung her mother. Perhaps a few days away would smooth things over.
She packed the few things she needed. She had quite a wardrobe full in her room at her mother's apartment in France. Luckily CC did not return to their flat that evening. Emm left for Nice the next day with her mother.

***

Harry Hart loved his job. He travelled all over the world. His salary was piling up nicely in his bank account due to the fact that everything he needed was available on a charge account. The only thing missing in his life was a woman, namely Emily. He missed her more than he thought he would. He had women throwing themselves at him when he was driving around in a Porsche, Bentley, Ferrari, and a rather striking yellow Aston Martin, or cruising on the Sunseeker or playing on the Jet Ski, but they were shallow girls with ideas of marrying someone rich. Unfortunately, all the cars and boats were not his.

He was living the Playboy lifestyle, but it was a very lonely and fake existence. He checked his phone to see where Emm was as he had a few days in the U.K. and thought he might be able to catch up with her. He'd seen her sister Stephanie had got married the other weekend and thought how beautiful Emm looked in her bridesmaid's dress. That was when he realised he missed her the most. She was stunning and real, not like the girls who seem to attach themselves to him, the gold-diggers and party girls. Emm was Emm. Normal, clever, beautiful, fun and she had been all his. That was until Patrick Robertshaw entered his life.

The advert looked appealing. It had been posted in Motorboat and Yachting Magazine. Ironically, Harry had been sitting waiting for Emily to finish work at her office and browsed through the magazines on the coffee table. The particular magazine captured his attention with a Majestic 155 Sunseeker on the cover. He turned the pages and was drawn to a small item underneath an advertisement page for Robertshaw Investments. The first line had him hooked: 'Fast cars, speedboats, sun, sea, global travel. Have you three months to spare? If you're over twenty-five and have a clean driving and ICC licence, please send CV to the address below or email if you have any queries to: Patrick@robertshawinvestments.com'

Harry couldn't believe the advert. It was a dream job that he had all the necessary qualifications to apply. He had a clean driving licence. He was thirty-two. He had an ICC licence, to give it its full name International Certificate for Operators of Pleasure Craft, from when he had worked at the local marina in Poole delivering boats to France and Spain. He applied that day.

Within five working days he had an interview at Patrick's home in Winchester and once Eleanor, Patrick's wife, had met him it was a done deal.

Telling Emm was the most difficult part. To Harry three months would fly by and he'd be back rich enough, he hoped, to propose to her and settle down. But to quote dear old Robert Burns - the best-laid plans of mice and men often go awry - was so true. They tried to keep their relationship alive by social media, but it wasn't easy due to time differences and signal strengths. Harry hung on to the fact that three months wasn't that long, and he'd make it up to Emm as soon as it was over. His first job was to crew Patrick's brand new Sunseeker from its manufacturing yard in Poole to Monaco, where Patrick had a mooring in the marina and an apartment. His next job was to employ a crew, which with Harry's contacts in Poole, he managed with no problem, to help him cruise the family down to the Bahamas for the winter.

Unfortunately, Harry was too good at his job and had made himself indispensable to the Robertshaws. Three months turned into six, then a year had gone. He got the occasional text and he sent the occasional iMessage on Facebook after seeing something funny Emm had posted, but both of them realised they had to move on.

Seeing the photos of Stephanie's wedding on Facebook and Instagram had brought it all back. He had lost so much by leaving Emm behind. He sighed, typical, Emm, was in France just 'up the road' from where he had just left, as he'd been in Monaco. He was off again in a few days as Patrick had decided to stay in Monaco for a while and wanted his Aston Martin brought down from Winchester.

Harry wondered if he'd catch up with Emm before she left France. He hadn't time to worry about it though. He had a ferry to book, car to service, paperwork to finalise and he needed a haircut. He'd check where she was once he'd got back to Monaco.

CHAPTER 2

Emm arrived in Nice late that evening with her mother, where Nico greeted them at the airport.

"Ma chérie Caro, tu m'as manqué." He embraced her and kissed her on both cheeks.

"I have missed you too, my love." Caroline said and moved away so Nico could welcome Emm. Traditional salutations over, they went to find Nico's car. Emm tolerated Nico but still felt it awkward when he embraced her mother, Nico being Emm's age. She realised the French were more adaptable, when Nico's parents took her to the château in Grasse the next day to show her some of their latest range of perfume, she saw that the family genuinely loved her mother. She decided to take a leaf out of the French's open book and begin to enjoy Nico's company. All the way back from Grasse to Nice Nico was telling Caroline how "incroyablement sensationnel" the opera had been. He was proud of himself for holding it together at such a prestigious engagement. He knew there was a lot of pressure on him to do well for his ancestor's sake, but he also wanted to do well for himself.

"I'm so proud of you Nico, I just wish I could have been there to hear you." Caroline had been torn but knew if she had any chance to make it up to her girls she had to be at her daughter's wedding.

"'ow could a mother miss 'er own daughter's wedding day? Ce n'est pas un problème, ma chérie." He took her hand, keeping his eyes on the road, and kissed it. Even Emm thought it a very romantic gesture.

"It is to be on the television in a few weeks so we can watch it together." Caroline just stared at him and smiled. It started to dawn on Emm they really loved each other. Wasn't love funny? You couldn't choose whom you fell in love with. It made her feel guilty at the way she'd treated her mother. The more she thought about it the more she realised she'd done the same to her best friend. She'd ring CC as soon as she was alone.

It was getting late by the time they got back to Nice. Nico went to park the car in the underground car park and let the girls out at the front door of the apartment block. Caroline wanted to check the post box and she always felt safer using the front door rather than entering by the basement.

The commissionaire, François, opened the door for the girls.

"A bonjour Madame Fitzgerald, et Mademoiselle Emily." He did a little bow. Everyone loved François.

"Merçi François." Caroline gave him a huge smile, making François blush. He quickly turned to Emm.

"Mademoiselle Emily you have a visitor. I 'ope you don't mind, but I let 'er into your apartment." He noticed both women looking at each other, puzzled. "It is your friend Mademoiselle Chloe." Emm smiled at François.

"Ah! Merçi François. Mother, I'm going up to see her, okay?" Caroline was searching for her post box key.

"Of course, darling. I'll be up in a minute."

François had read the situation and took out the master key from behind his concierge's desk. Emm went towards the lift with a knowing grin. François was obviously used to her mother's scattiness.

CC heard the lift stop and waited with the apartment door ajar until whoever it was got out. It was Emm. CC ran towards the lift and almost pushed Emm back into it. CC had been crying and threw her arms around Emm's neck.

"I'm so sorry Emm. I've been such a fool. Our friendship is too important to me to ruin it with a silly little boy." Emm noted that the date hadn't gone well. "I did try to tell you all week, but the time never seemed right. Please forgive me." She looked into her friend's eyes and realised that Emm was trying not to laugh. CC looked puzzled.

"I was about to phone you and apologise to you for acting so precious." They hugged each other and Emm steered CC into the apartment. Caroline followed closely behind and was pleased to see the friends had made-up.

Caroline poured the girls a drink while they talked about the infamous Luke. Nico had joined them and was fascinated by the animation of the British girls. He'd always assumed that they were quiet and refined. He watched too many old English movies when he met Caroline, to improve his English.

"All evening, between mauling and groping with the occasional kiss thrown in, he kept asking me questions about you!" Nico and Caroline thought it funny. Emm couldn't see the funny side.

"Yuk. Please tell me he didn't get any information

from you." CC shook her head. "Good. He sounds like stalker material. Yuk." Emm felt like having a shower. The whole situation had made her feel uncomfortable. "I never liked him anyway." The girls laughed. Hopefully that was the last Emm had to hear about lame Luke.

"I've got an idea. Why don't we go to Cannes tomorrow and mingle with the celebrities? The Film Festival is in full swing at the moment, so we're bound to find one or two film stars to take home with us." CC laughed, but it was a brilliant idea.

"Yes please. I'm on the lookout for an attractive actor who could sweep me off my feet and carry me into the sunset." The girls were falling about giggling. Caroline loved watching them. It reminded her of the old days when they would be up in Emily's bedroom whispering and giggling about teachers, boys and probably mothers!

"I wish I could come with you both, but I 'ave a very serious rehearsal tomorrow and 'ave to be on my best form." Nico looked sad. "I 'ave the next day off though. Perhaps you two could escort me to the jazz club around the corner?" Emm felt sorry for Nico. He was still so young, but his profession needed one hundred per cent dedication.

"Quelle bonne idée, Nico. We'll look forward to that." Emm went over to him and kissed his cheek. Caroline smiled and tried not to shed a tear. She had wanted the two of them to get on and it looked like they were now friends. She hoped it would mean that Emily would visit more frequently.

"Well, if you're in Cannes tomorrow, I shall book my favourite restaurant for you and you can run a tab, on me. Chez Astoux et Brun, it's just a few minutes from the

Palais des Festivals just off the Boulevard de la Croisette." Emm was nodding her head.

"I know the one, on the corner?" Nico smiled as she had remembered it was the first meal they had together on her first visit with her sister to meet him. "It has the most delicious seafood CC. You'll love it. Thank you, Nico, I'm sorry you can't come." Nico shrugged.

"I will be looking forward to our evening of jazz at Shapko." He winked at Emm. "My good friend Frédéric will be playing. 'e is looking forward to meeting la jolie fille of Caro."

He looked at Caroline and smiled. She smiled back at Nico. Emm wasn't stupid. She realised they were trying to set her up with Frédéric. She'd save judgement until she had met him. Maybe it was what she needed a little French dalliance, la passion s'il vous plait!

The girls left for Cannes the next morning. They were excited to see as many film stars as they could. They had both charged their phones for selfies and CC had put a small selfie stick in her bag. If Zac Efron or Colin Farrell wanted to photo bomb their selfie, they wouldn't mind a bit. Emm was rather hoping for a glimpse of Benedict Cumberbatch herself.

"Where to first? We can go straight to the Palais des Festival, or walk up to it along the Boulevard de la Croisette?" Emm rather liked window-shopping. "I think we should walk along La Croisette and take some photos of ourselves outside Chanel or Christian Dior. Oo, and Cartier. If we hang around long enough, we're bound to see someone famous coming out." Emm laughed at her friend. CC was like an excited child. It was probably what Emm loved about CC the most. CC was always the serious, logical one. That was until you took her away from her books and academia. Emm looked at her watch.

"That's a plan then. We have time to kill before lunch and we've missed the morning showings. If we get to the restaurant when the table's booked for..." she checked her phone for the message Nico had sent her, "1.15 p.m. that gives us a good hour and a half to have a coffee and walk along the Boulevard looking rich and important." The girls linked arms and walked from Cannes station into town with their sunglasses in place generating an air of stardom.

As the girls got nearer to the restaurant the atmosphere changed. There were people everywhere, standing on anything with height just straining to get a view of someone famous. The Paparazzi were all around, snapping pictures of everyone who looked remotely important in case they missed someone.
The girls were in their element, having practiced all the way along the Boulevard de La Croisette, they beamed at each camera pointed at them, posing as models and giggling until they reached the door to Chez Astoux et Brun. It was not one of the smarter restaurants, but those in the know knew it was renowned for its seafood and was extremely popular with the locals - a glowing accolade for any French restaurant. Emm decided to keep her sunglasses on during her entrance into the restaurant. She thought it would keep the clientele guessing for a while.

"Emm, you won't be able to read the menu with those on." CC ever the logical one, but Emm ignored her; she was having fun.

"Bonjour Mademoiselle, avez-vous une reservation, s'il vous plait?" The Maître d' had automatically gone to Emm with her important sunglasses look. Emm looked at CC to see if she had got the point of the exercise.

"Okay, keep them on if you think they make you look famous." Emm smiled and turned back to the waiter.

"Nous avons une reservation au nom Janvier." The maître d' immediately turned and directed them to the bar area.

"Ah, Mademoiselle Fitzgerald?" Emm nodded. "Please would you sit 'ere while I make your table ready for you." He looked up at the barman. "Le champagne pour la famille Janvier, Guillaume." The maître d' scurried off barking orders to the waiters. Nico had just gone right up there in Emm's estimation.

"Wow, is Nico royalty or something?" CC was also impressed.

"You're funny CC. Have you ever heard of the French revolution? Remember all the heads they chopped off? Most of them were royalty or at least royalists. Which makes this country a republic and a democracy as they vote in their presidents, but not a monarchy. But in answer to your question..."

"I've forgotten what I asked now." They both laughed. "I can't concentrate, I think I'm in love." CC was staring at Guillaume, the barman. He had bouncy blonde shoulder length hair, scraped off his face, occasionally by his hand. He was putting the ice bucket into a stand so it could be taken over to their table and then filled the flutes expertly.

"Hate to burst your love bubble CC, but he's gay."

Emm whispered. CC looked Guillaume up and down.

"I don't care. I think he's adorable." For a clever person, Emm had to admit, CC had abnormal limitations to
human perception. Probably a career as a consultant psychiatrist may be a tad mad for her, but Emm wouldn't tell her, after all, CC had been studying for years and years. Guillaume walked up to them both with their champagne. Emm took off her sunglasses when he put a flute of champagne in front of her. She tried to get her eyes into focus so she didn't spill it. She looked round the restaurant until she could see properly. She caught sight of a man sitting alone in the corner. She blinked a couple of times and looked again.

"OMG CC. Look." Emm nodded towards the man. CC followed Emm's eyes and expected to see someone famous.

"OMG Emm, it's your dad." The barmen thought English girls must have a secret alphabetical code.
Emm wondered if her mother had told him where they were. She hoped he wasn't checking up on her. Logic kicked in. Michael would never have spoken to Caroline, especially about Emm, unless it was an emergency. Emm got up and walked to her father's table, followed very closely by CC. Michael looked over to the 'Toilettes' and then caught sight of his daughter. Emm's answer was in his face. He looked as shocked as the girls. They were nearing Michael's table when CC tapped Emm on her shoulder and pulled her back. Emm turned around to ask CC what on earth she was doing.

"Look." CC was pointing to the woman who had just come out of the 'Toilettes'. Both girls stood on the spot with their mouths wide open in shock.

The woman walked up to Michael, pecked him on the cheek and in a beautiful sultry French accent whispered,

"À bientôt, mon chér." She bent down and kissed him. As she walked towards the restaurant door most of the clients were trying not to stare but failed. She blew Michael a kiss as she left the restaurant.
Michael got up and beckoned the Maître d' to bring the girls drinks to his table. He put his arm around his daughter and steered her to her seat.

"You two can close your mouths now, it's not the most attractive of looks." He was laughing and trying to calm them down. He had a lot of explaining to do and needed them to be discreet. Guillaume brought their champagne over to their table and put the ice bucket beside Michael.

"Merçi Guillaume. Well you girls are certainly living it up. I must be paying you too much Emily." He laughed at his own joke. Emm couldn't help smiling. Her father was looking so… so… cool! She couldn't think of another adjective that would describe her father at that moment. His normally unruly hair was cut short leaving a fringe flicked over to the side. He was wearing denim jeans - Emm had never seen her father in denim before. She had to admit it did suit his long slim legs. Topped off with a very expensive white designer polo shirt. She decided her first description was correct - her father was looking cool.

"I knew you had a girlfriend, but Claudia Pasqualle, Dad?" Michael nodded. "I don't believe it. A Hollywood actress dating my father." She picked up her flute and downed a whole glass of champagne at once.

"Again Emily, not attractive." He was teasing her.

"Oh Dad, you are such a dark horse. Why on earth didn't you tell me, or Stephanie for that matter, about Claudia and your clandestine affair?"

"Claudia wanted me to when she was in the office one day and you were on the telephone. She so wanted to meet you then, but I thought it was too soon. Then with Stephanie's wedding and Claudia's filming, there didn't seem to be an opportunity. We've had to be so careful. I love you with all my heart Emily, but even you have to admit you aren't the best person at keeping secrets, are you?" CC nodded in agreement, making Emm poke her tongue out at her friend.

Before Emm could open her mouth again Michael put his finger up to his lips. "I know you probably have a lot of questions to ask me, but I need to explain something to you both, and you have to listen." The maître d' came over and filled the girls flutes again. He then filled Michael's wine glass.

"Would the ladies like to see a menu, Monsieur?" CC had to admit she was starving but wanted to hear all about the film star that had just kissed her brother's father-in-law.

"Can you give us five minutes Jean-Pierre? I will signal when they are ready." The maître d' nodded and backed away.

"Where was I? Oh yes. To answer your first question, Claudia and I have been together for quite a while now. She came into the office last year looking for an apartment close to where they were filming on Hampstead Heath. I took her round a few that were available for the time she needed it. She didn't know many people in England except other actors and she just wanted to relax and play the tourist. So, I offered to give her a quick sight-seeing tour of the important attractions."

"You are one of them Dad, obviously." The girls laughed and so did Michael.

"Very good Emily. Anyway, this has to stay a secret. If the papers got hold of it our lives will be turned upside down. Luckily the public only see me as Claudia's agent, so at least we can be seen enjoying lunch together. She introduced me as Mr Jones, her agent, at a press conference a few weeks ago. It seemed the only way to be out together in France without tongues wagging. Claudia wants more than anything to tell the world about our relationship, but I want to keep it private for a bit longer so we can enjoy the anonymity as a couple. I hope you understand." Emm smiled. "Obviously she didn't use my real name as the French have already heard of the Fitzgerald name through your mother's shenanigans." His eyebrow went up and he grinned.

"Our lips are sealed." They both gestured zipping their lips and throwing away the key. "But when can we meet her?"

"As soon as we're back in London, where people don't recognize her in civvies."

"I can't quite picture Claudia Pasqualle in tracksuit bottoms and a hoodie." They were all laughing.

"Exactly. She can walk about without too much hassle. I'm not sure that will be possible once this film is out, but we'll enjoy the freedom while it lasts." He nodded towards Jean-Pierre who had been hovering attentively at a distance. The maître d' came over with the menus for the girls. They placed their order and sat back to savour the champagne. Michael was so pleased to see Emily; with Stephanie married he worried about her.

Harry was the perfect match; it was a shame he hadn't stuck around. Michael had to admit that if he had been offered that job, before he was married, he would have taken it too. He couldn't fault the lad. He listened to the girls chattering about what they had done and realised that they hadn't seen the real Cannes. They'd seen the fake, tourist bits, but not the heart of the city. "When you have both finished your golden bream, perhaps I could take you for a little sight-seeing tour of Cannes."

"Aren't you going to watch Claudia's film?" Now her father was dating an A list film star the need to watch minor celebrities sashaying along the red carpet had lost its appeal.

"I've already been to the private viewing and really don't need to go again." He yawned, jokingly. "I'd much rather have fun with you girls and look at the architecture and views of Cannes Old Town." CC nodded. She would rather look at the views than stand hoping to get a glance of someone she'd recognise. It had lost its attraction. Emm nodded too. "That's settled then. I will show you the real Cannes, but only if I have your solemn promise that you tell nobody," he looked at Emm, "especially your mother, about Claudia, until we are ready to 'tell the world' as Claudia shouts, often!" The girls agreed and sealed their pact with a rather light and fluffy crème brûlée. Michael settled the bill and they left with CC waving goodbye to Guillaume who blew her a kiss a little too theatrically back. Emm was right about him. CC left with a little scepticism where Guillaume was concerned and even less confidence in her ability to attract men. They navigated past all the crowds into the side streets. They followed Michael up, what Emm called, a mountain, but was only a hill, to the views from the Musée de la

Castra. When they saw the sights, they agreed it was well worth the trek. The scenes were panoramic, three hundred and sixty degrees of Cannes from one spot.

From the city to the coast and further, it was truly spectacular.

Michael was watching the time and asked the girls if they'd like tea before they left for Nice. He was so English, Emm wondered if he would cope if Claudia wanted him to move to France or even Hollywood with her. They walked along the back streets of Cannes, empty compared to the seafront. Michael took them to a small tea rooms where they tucked into the patisseries and gateaux, all agreeing how delicious they were.

"I hate to spoil the party, darling, but I have to get changed for this evening's reception and after party." He looked at his watch. "I have to escort Claudia as her agent. Once the press has got all the photos they need, and interviews are over, security gets the paparazzi out and the pretence is put on hold and all the stars can become normal human beings again." It sounded exhausting to Emm, keeping up a charade like that.

"You can't hold her hand or cuddle?" Michael shook his head.

"Claudia describes it like being a mannequin on show, having to keep a permanent smile on her face and her hands off me! But at least once the press has gone we can relax and enjoy the evening." Emm started to feel sorry for her father. He had been through so much after her mother's desertion that he deserved to be happy more than anyone. Hopefully once they had told the world their secret, he and Claudia could live a reasonably normal life. "Come on you two. I've just got time to see you both to the station. I'm not having you walk alone with all these temptations on route. Best shops, famous actors, to name but two. No, I definitely need to see you safely on board your train back to Nice." Emm knew her father too well. She hugged her father and smiled up at him.

"We walk around London most evenings, remember? We are girls of the millennium and certainly do not need a chaperone. But if you want our company for a little longer, that's fine." Michael knew he'd been rumbled, but in a funny way he'd missed his daughter's companionship and even his humdrum life. He was pleased to be with her for a little longer.

At the station he waved the girls off and turned back to his complicated life, with a little more reassurance. A weight had been lifted from his shoulders now he knew he had his daughter's blessing. He checked behind him as he walked along the back streets; he took a step forward and jumped in the air, clicking his heels to the side. He checked again and was relieved that no one had seen him. He then walked sedately, like a proper English gentleman, back to his hotel.

* * *

Katarina had been shopping with Lilli and was walking towards their front door when she noticed the postman.

"Good morning, have you anything for us today?" She smiled brightly at him. He checked the small pile he had wrapped in an elastic band in his hand and nodded. He pulled out an envelope which seemed unusually large and stiff. She recognised the postmark and shuddered.

"What's the matter Mummy? Is it one of those letters that makes Daddy angry?" Lilli put her hand on her mother's arm and smiled up at her. Katarina managed to shake off her sudden fear and smiled down at her daughter.

"I haven't a clue darling, until I open it."
The postman took out his ePOD and held the screen close to Katarina for her signature. Katarina put down her shopping bag and used her fingernail to write her name on the device. The postman handed her the package.

"Thank you. Have a good day." The postman smiled at Katarina and Lilli then walked off to the next house whistling to himself. Lilli giggled.

"What has tickled you Lilli?" Katarina took out her front door key and picked up her shopping bag.

"Can't you hear what the postman is whistling?" Katarina stopped and listened. She too giggled. The postman looked back and winked at Lilli. Lilli waved and followed her mummy into the house, humming the tune to 'Postman Pat' in sync with the postman. She would have whistled the tune if she could, but she still hadn't mastered the technique.

"Pop upstairs and wash your hands, Lilli. Then you can come down and help me with the cakes you wanted to make." Lilli rushed up the stairs impatiently. She had made her mother buy a packet of cake mix for individual cakes with unicorn rice paper stickers to put on top of the icing. Katarina always let Lilli experiment with food dyes to make them a little more interesting. It was one of Lilli's favourite treats with the end result of eating them being as much fun as the making of them. While Lilli was upstairs Katarina carefully opened the package. She wanted to be able to seal it so Erik wouldn't realise she'd opened it. It was sealed down with tape and clips. It was impossible to open it surreptitiously, so she had to be brave and just rip it open. It was as she thought, Lilliana's Estonian passport. Recently Erik had been threatening her with Lilli's trip to Estonia to visit his family.

Katarina was a very intelligent woman and knew that the visit was long term and she had not been included in the trip. She looked at her watch. Erik would be back for his lunch any time, so she had to make a quick decision. She had nothing ready for the emergency that had been thrust upon her and was cross with herself. She needed twenty-four hours. She could hear Lilli at the top of the stairs, so her brain had to work quickly. She took the package into the kitchen and hid it in a cupboard. She chose the one Erik would be least likely to open, if any, the utility one with all the cleaning products in. She'd hide it better when she knew exactly where he was and how much time she had.

"Can we make the cakes now please Mummy. Look, I've washed my hands." She showed her mother the palms of her hands and beamed with pride. It was one job that Lilli knew she did well – that and cleaning her teeth.

"Well done Lilli. Yes of course you can make the cakes. I need you to be a very grown up girl though Lilli." Lilli looked at her mother and took hold of her mother's hand. Whenever her mother used that phrase she had to listen and obey. It would mean that her father would not get upset. "You have to keep a secret Lilli." Lilli nodded. "I don't want your father worrying, so we mustn't mention the letter that I had to sign for. Do you understand Lilli?" Lilli let go of her mother's hand and nodded.

"What letter?" She giggled. Katarina loved her so much. Luckily Lilli was as bright as a button and would do as she was told. "Do I have to wash my hands again now I've held yours?" Katarina smiled and shook her head.

"No Lilli, you'll be alright. We'll use a mixer to mix the ingredients and you can scrape the bowl with a spoon to lick afterwards." Katarina put the oven on to warm while Lilli opened the box with the pretty pictures of buns with unicorns on the top.

CHAPTER 3

Emm and CC got back to Nice in time to change before they all went out to dinner. Luckily, they had no time to be quizzed by Caroline or Nico about their day, as they would have lost their reservation. The restaurant was in the Cours Saleya. During the day there was an abundance of flowers and vegetables, but in the evenings the whole marketplace was taken over by the restaurants on either side. Nico had chosen a typical French bistro owned by a distant family member. It was small and friendly. The choice on the menu was small and Emm noticed a sentence at the bottom that fascinated her. "Toute la nourriture dans cet établissment provient humainement."

"Nico, the bottom of the menu, does that mean the food here is humanely sourced? In other words, organic?" Nico nodded.

"Yes, at last we French have gone au naturel." He found his description amusing. "A double entendre." CC laughed. Emm was still thinking.

"Next time Steph is visiting you must take her to this restaurant." Emm hadn't seen many organic restaurants advertised, which was hard for her sister. She had become a semi-vegetarian recently, only eating organic meat, having watched a documentary about factory farming. She had almost persuaded her sister to join her, but Emm loved her meat too much. Although even Emm had to admit she goes to the supermarket organic counters more often now. She had been looking up organic farming on the internet and it made her think a lot more carefully about what she wanted to put inside her body.

"Does that mean Steph would eat meat from here?" Caroline hadn't a clue why her younger daughter had changed her diet. "I just assumed it was because she wanted to get into her wedding dress that she had become a vegetarian."

Emm needed to change the subject. She was cross that her mother knew so little about her sister's life. Luckily the waiter broke the ensuing impasse.
They ordered their food and Caroline couldn't wait any longer.

"So, how was Cannes?" Emm looked at CC and grinned.

"Brilliant. We had a lovely lunch. Thank you, Nico, for booking it for us, but we met a very kind gentleman who paid the bill for us. He was on his own and wanted company. An Englishman abroad, you could say." CC was blushing, and her eyes were almost bulging at Emm playing with fire.

"Oh darling, bit risky wasn't it? Did you get his name?" Emm looked at CC, enjoying her friend's unease.

"Yes, he was called Mr Jones. Nice man but seemed lonely so we spent the afternoon sight-seeing with him." CC couldn't believe Emm was being so truthful. Caroline wasn't stupid. Come on CC, she urged herself to talk, anything to get Emm off the subject of Mr Jones.

"I think I prefer Nice. Cannes is very pretentious with its ridiculously expensive shops on the main boulevard, you could be anywhere in the world with a beach. Nice, on the other hand, seems to have that quaint French feel to it." CC was smiling at Nico as she talked, trying to ignore Emm's eyes boring into her.

"You're so right, CC. Nice 'as character, it 'as culture and Nice 'as soul."
Nico was almost standing up. Caroline offered him a glass of wine and he relaxed.

"As you can hear CC, the French are very passionate about their country. That was one of the reasons that made me stay in France at the beginning." She looked at Nico with a slight grin, she was trying to hide, on her face. It hadn't been missed on Nico.

"And the other reason mon chérie?!" He leant over and she kissed him on his cheek. He positively beamed with delight. Emm was staring at CC, cross she had completely changed the subject and managed to get Nico animated on the wonders of Nice. One nil to CC. Emm decided to wind her up a little more. She was enjoying the evening.

"We saw Claudia Pasqualle in Cannes. She was at our restaurant." CC had had enough. She kicked Emm under the table and gave her a scowling look. It was people's lives she was playing with after all, and she had promised her father she'd be discreet. CC just thought she'd remind her of that fact. Emm smiled at CC and stopped talking.

"Claudia Pasqualle is one of the true actresses of 'er day. I think she is like your Audrey 'epburn. She 'as style, sophistication and maturity beyond 'er years." Again, Caroline poured him a little more wine and handed it to him. Emm wondered if it was a code they had between them to quieten him down when he got excited.

"The French are also very passionate about their film stars, a little like the Americans. I suppose it's because they have no royal family to be proud of." Caroline had to admit she did miss her own country. In a perfect world she could have taken Nico home with her and they could have lived happily ever after. She was brought back to Nice by her daughter who coughed.

"Emily calling Mother… Come in Mother!" Caroline realised Emm had been talking.

"Sorry darling, you were saying?" Caroline sighed. She would love to share her inner thoughts with her daughter, but she had hurt her with her actions and had to tread gently where France and Nico were concerned.

"I was asking how old Claudia Pasqualle is?" Emm needed to know more about Claudia, especially what other people thought of her.

"She looks like she's in her early forties, but I'm not sure if she's had any work done." Caroline couldn't help herself. It was times like those that she felt her age. Nico was positively in love with Claudia Pasqualle. She knew she was being silly, but insecurity occasionally got the better of her. Their food had arrived, and Nico was busy tucking in to a very tender, rare fillet steak. Had he been paying attention to his Caro he would have seen a problem and hugged her, but Caroline knew that the French were also passionate about good food, so she would have to wait for any comfort from him.

Emm was feeling naughty. She had spotted her mother's jealousy and decided to have fun.

"Claudia looked very natural close up. She didn't seem to have any Botox holes, or facelift scars. Did you see any CC?" CC was fed up trying to stop her.

She just shrugged and got on with her beef bourguignon.

"How close did you get to this woman?" Oh dear, Emm noticed the tone of her mother's voice and thought perhaps she'd gone too far. She should have taken CC's silent advice. Now her mother was upset. From famous admired actress, Claudia had become 'this woman'. Emm looked at CC for support. CC couldn't let her down.

"So, Nico, where is this jazz club you're taking us to?" Nico had just finished his steak and was pecking at his fries.

"It is the jazz club in Nice. Shapko is just up there." He pointed further up the road from the restaurant they were in. "It is our favourite night spot, isn't it Caro?" Caroline looked at him and smiled, half-heartedly. "Are you ok mon amour? Were your scallops good?" Nico had mistaken Caroline's mood to be food orientated.

"No Nico chéri, the scallops were délicieux." Nico kissed her on the cheek. It brightened her spirit. "You girls are going to love Frédéric. He is so talented on the keyboard. He is one of Nico's best friends. If he is playing tonight you're in for a treat." Nico nodded. He stretched over and gave Caroline another kiss and a hug. For the first time Emm was pleased watching them. She looked at CC who returned a knowing eyebrow raised look. Okay, thought Emm, CC was right. She had to behave for the rest of the night. That was two nil to CC.

The bouncer on the door recognised Caroline and Nico and let them all in, much to the annoyance of the queue that was forming outside. Emm realised why it had a one in one out policy, as the place was so small. The stage the band was playing on was immediately in front of them as they went in the door. There were tables behind the stage, full of jazz lovers. They were ushered up the stairs to a balcony with the best view and were seated at a small table with a reserved sign. Looking over the railings they could see the band and a small dance floor. If anyone was having problems seeing anything, as the tables were two deep with sofas on the outside wall, the club had fitted an enormous TV over where the band was playing so everyone could see what was going on downstairs and didn't miss anything.

Nico caught Frédéric's eye while he was changing his music. Frédéric gave the five-minute sign with his hand and went straight into the next piece. It was a phenomenal place. They drank the house special, which was 'French 75', or known in France simply as Soixante Quinze. Nico told the girls it was a mixture of Champagne, Gin, lemon juice and sugar, with difficulty due to the amplified music. He used a great deal of gestures and a little mime but managed to get it across. The girls couldn't stop laughing. It reminded Emm of the good old days at Christmas when the whole family played charades. She took another slurp of the delicious cocktail and felt better again.

Frédéric came up to meet them after his set had finished. Luckily the backing track that had been left on was a lot more tolerant on the ears for conversation to be spoken, not shouted. Caroline was feeling old.

Introductions over Frédéric pushed himself between CC and Emm.

"Je suis très heureux que vous soyez venu ici ce soir, Chloé." Chloe hadn't a clue what he was saying, but she loved the way he said her name.

"Je don't parlez Français, sorry." Frédéric laughed.

"You're funny. I love girls that 'ave a sense of 'umour. I said that I was very 'appy that you have come here tonight. You are very beautiful Chloé." Chloe felt herself blush. Was Frédéric gay she wondered? She was never that lucky. He was the most attractive man she had talked to in a long while. Frédéric was facing CC and over his shoulder she could see Emm putting a thumb up to her. Did that mean he wasn't gay, or just that she's given her blessing for CC to see what the conversation led to? She wasn't sure but didn't have time to think. Over-analysing was not conducive to spontaneity.

"Are you enjoying the music?" He looked concerned. Most artists were quite insecure when it came to their ability, although Frédéric didn't need to be, Chloe thought he was extremely good.

"I'm loving it. I especially loved your rendition of Day Breaks. You've changed it slightly from the Norah Jones version, but I liked what you did with it." Frédéric beamed.

"Do you play the piano?" Chloe grimaced. She was no way in his league.

"I struggled through piano forte Grade Four when there were two Debussy pieces. I couldn't even get my head round them, let alone my fingers." Frédéric burst out laughing. Hopefully that was a good sign. She remembered at the beginning of their conversation he said he loved a girl with a sense of humour. "They were Arabesque, which I did ok on, but it was Clair de Lune that I stumbled on with all those fast, crazy arpeggios. I'm convinced that Debussy knew that every piece he wrote would be used for kids taking their piano exams, so made them very hard." Again, Frédéric roared with laughter.

"But Debussy is my favourite compositeur." Oh dear, thought Chloe, had she offended him? He started laughing again. Was he pulling her leg? She thought she better carry on.

"I do like Debussy's music. One day I had hoped to master Danse Bonhémienne but gave up piano and played lacrosse on Saturdays instead." Frédéric was laughing so hard he missed the signal from his band to get back to his keyboard. Nico got his attention and pointed to the saxophonist who was frantically waving at him.

"I'm sorry beautiful, funny lady, but I 'ave to go. Please stay 'ere until I 'ave finished my last set? Promise?" CC nodded. Frédéric took her hand and kissed it. "À bientôt. I will see you later." He winked at her and left.

"OMG CC, you've done it." CC wondered what she'd done. "You've only gone and pulled the most eligible Frenchman this side of Paris." CC could feel herself blushing again. Unfortunately, the live music started, and she didn't hear the rest. She was happy and content with leaving their conversation until she had had time to digest exactly what had just happened.

Little did she know that Emm was very happy too. If her mother had thought she was just going to run after the first man who showed her affection, she had another think coming. Caroline was inwardly seething. She had arranged the meeting on purpose, so Emily would fall for Frédéric and then she would want to stay in France and marry him and live happily ever after. She gestured to Nico that she had a headache and was going to go home. Nico got up to go with her.

"No." She shouted. "I'll be fine on my own. Just make sure the girls get home safely." Nico nodded and kissed her. She waved to the girls and mouthed, "I'll see you in the morning. Goodnight." They shouted goodnight back, but she was already on her way to the stairs. The girls were enjoying themselves too much to worry or even notice what her problem was. They were happy that Nico was allowed to stay and play though. Nico crouched down and shouted in Emm's ear that he'd be back in a moment. Emm assumed he needed the little boys' room and paid little attention.

Nico ran down the stairs and into the street catching up with Caroline.

"Caro, wait, are you okay?" Caroline turned to see Nico, his arms outstretched, enveloping her as he reached her. He felt Caroline's body tremble and realised she was crying. He pushed her gently away, so he could see her face. "Caro, what is the matter? Are you in pain?" She shook her head and felt a little silly. He was not supposed to see her like that. She knew she was being stupid and utterly selfish, but she had missed her daughter so much and had given up a lot for her own self-indulgence.

"No, my darling, I'm not in any physical pain. My pain comes from my heart. I had put too much hope in Emily finding her prince charming and living in France forever. Frédéric was that hope, but he only has eyes for Chloe tonight." She looked at Nico who was smiling.

"I need not tell you, ma chérie, you cannot 'elp 'oo you fall in love with. It was not meant to be. Emily, I feel, still 'as 'er 'eart set on another." Caroline nodded. For a young man, she thought, Nico is very worldly.

"You're right, mon chéri. I was being selectively blind. Emily has not got over Harry and I wouldn't be surprised if they still end up together. They were soulmates and their love was real." Caroline smiled. She could live with Emily back with Harry and happy. She looked at her watch. "Off you go back to the girls. I don't want them walking back to the apartment alone."

"I will go, but I'd rather walk you 'ome. Je t'aime ma chèrie." He pulled her close and kissed her passionately. "I'm your soulmate forever." He turned and walked back to the club. Caroline was feeling better. Nico was right, she could not find love for Emily, that was Emily's job. But she could steer her in the right direction. She'd have a word with her in the morning to see if she'd heard from Harry recently. With a new strategy she may get to see her daughter more often, and who knows, grandchildren too.

After a few more cocktails Frédéric had joined the girls again.

"Have you finished for the night now?" Chloe needed to go back to the apartment soon. She had to get back to London the next day. Skiving was not an option with all the work that had to be done by the end of the month. Having spent years getting to the position she was in, she didn't want to stumble at the last hurdle. She explained to Frédéric how her speciality training in psychiatry was going and that she had to get home, as her finals were only three weeks away. "I need to empty my head of everything that has happened while I've been in France and get back to studying." Frédéric looked sad. "When I've finished my exams, I'll have lots of time to come back and have fun." He smiled. "I wish I could have done the year again though." She went close to Frédéric so only he could hear. "I could have done my whole thesis on Emm's family, on their behaviour alone." She didn't think she was being disloyal to her friend – after all, Emm was the one who had suggested it. Frédéric took CC's mobile phone off her and asked her for her passcode. CC put her thumb on the button and the screen came on. Frédéric went into her contacts and touched 'add'. He put his phone number and email address into the phone and put his name as Frédéric, surname, Besotted. "How do you pronounce your surname?" Asked Chloe innocently. Frédéric laughed again.

"The same way you would in English. It is 'ow I feel about you!" CC felt silly.

"Thank you Frédéric. Would you like my number?" Frédéric had been busy on her phone.

"I 'ave your number and email address. I sent it to myself from your phone." He winked at her. "May I come to London when you 'ave finished your exams?" CC's heart was racing.

"Yes please," was all she could manage as a pair of masterful lips homed in on hers.

Chloe couldn't stop talking all the way back to the apartment. Emm was so pleased for her. CC had been working so hard for so many years that she almost missed out on ever getting a boyfriend and Frédéric was just right for her in so many ways; he was kind, considerate and above all romantically French, yes, thought Emm, just right for her best friend.

She was too excited to sleep so Emm Googled Claudia and they had a shock.

"She is of French aristocracy." Emm told CC excitedly. "Her father Albert was a Count." She read on. "He had died a few years previously leaving the family château in the protection of his son, Laurent. That must be Claudia's brother." She needed to read more. "The château is in the north of Avignon in Sauveterre." She turned the screen towards CC and pointed to the pictures of the château and its grounds. She continued reading. "The château itself is now a hotel with magnificent gardens. It has an extensive vineyard, which is open to the public for wine tasting and tours." Emm thought it looked very romantic. Rapunzel came to her mind when she saw the turrets.

"Well, she certainly isn't after my father for his money!" Neither of them thought she was, but it still sounded humorous.

"Have you decided if you're coming back with me or staying out here?" Emm thought about it for a few seconds. She nodded to CC and opened up the airline page and booked her flight back to Gatwick.

"With my father gallivanting around the South of France I think one of us should get back to the office." They both laughed at the fact they were being the grown-ups, for a change.

In the morning Emm promised her mother she'd be back very soon.

"I've really had fun, Mum." She kissed her mother on the cheek. "I have to get back or my desk will be covered in so many queries that I will be working every weekend until Christmas." A slight exaggeration but she didn't want to tell her mother the real reason, that her father was AWOL in France and so she had to man the fort, as it were, until he returned.

Caroline didn't know the true reason for Emily's rush to get back home but was grateful that she had made a feasible excuse and not just left with a 'goodbye, see you soon' response to her, like on numerous occasions in the past. For the first time in ages Caroline believed that her daughter's heart was thawing and the big freeze she had shown her mother over the last few years was melting. She decided not to push her luck in asking about her daughter's love life but perhaps on the next visit she would get even closer to the daughter she loved with all her heart and was so desperate for her forgiveness. She'd keep the tears for her pillow and the guilt at bay, with the help of Nico's empathy and his infinite love for her.

Nico drove them to the airport and said he hoped he'd see more of them both. It was 'plus amusant' when they visited. CC didn't tell Emm, but she felt that Nico wasn't as happy as he would have them believe. She had a feeling that Caroline's insecurities were wearing him down. Nico loved her but how long can you keep reassuring someone of that fact? She wished she could sit them both down and thrash it out with them. She knew that was the answer, but she wasn't qualified yet and it needed to be a stranger anyway. She was looking forward to starting her career. She hoped, no, felt that she'd be good at it, time would tell.

***

Having been back in London for twenty-four hours everything seemed dull, including the weather for the beginning of June. It was heavy and thundery and Emm had a headache. She was trying to look in her father's files for a lease in the name of Claudia Pasqualle or even Claudia Jones. It was worth a shot, but she couldn't find one in the office files, so she decided it must be on her father's private computer. She didn't have the password for that, understandably, so she'd have to wait for her father to come back from his sojourn. She hadn't heard from him since they had met in Cannes, so hadn't a clue when he'd be back en Angleterre. In the meantime, she looked up all the reviews for Claudia's latest movie that had been filmed in France and London. It was a British production with National Lottery funding and was having great reviews even from the American film critics. The French director of the film won the Palme d'Or award at the Cannes Film Festival and Claudia and Matt Pride were both nominees for best actress and actor.

Emm hoped she would get to meet Matt Pride as she thought he was rather fit. He had been in a movie with Sean Penn recently and was covered in sweat and blood in what had been a white t-shirt and her heartbeat rose to a dangerous level.

She was disturbed from her reverie by a tap on her shoulder. She was surprised to see her father who was obviously back from France, tanned and relaxed looking. She got up from her chair and hugged him. She had so many questions for him.

"I still can't believe you were able to keep such a massive secret from me and Steph. You do realise that we had sussed you had a girlfriend, don't you?" Michael just smiled. He knew exactly what she meant. When he had become serious with Claudia, he metamorphosed from being a divorcé to a man about town. He changed his hairstyle to suit his new life – Claudia little by little made him into a modern man. She'd bought him aftershave and cologne that the old Michael would have thought was for youngsters. She made him buy clothing that flattered his handsome physique. He was now rather fond of the new Michael Fitzgerald.

"I like to keep you girls on your toes." He was grinning. Emm suddenly realised that her father actually looked ten years younger than his age. Claudia was definitely good for him. Thinking of Claudia, she decided to ask him straight out.

"Where is the lease for Claudia Pasqualle? I just wondered which apartment she was in." Michael laughed and tapped his nose. "Oh Daddy, come on, tell me. From purely an emergency point of view, I should know where you are."

"Good try. You should know by now that it isn't as simple as looking for Claudia Pasqualle." He was winking at her. She thought he was being very infuriating but decided to play his game.

"Ok then, what is the equivalent name in French to Smith or Jones?" Her father clapped his hands. Chip off the old block, he thought.

"There you go. Thinking outside the box. If it were Smith in England it would probably be Martin in France as the first most popular name. But if it were Jones in England as the second most popular name, it would be Bernard in France." Before he had finished his explanation Emm had already logged into the office leasing documents.

"Eureka. Claudia Bernard. Oh my goodness, she has that Penthouse in St. John's Wood. It's the one I've always wanted to view but was never allowed to. You said it was a security thing and the owners only gave you access." She was frowning at her father. He found it amusing but tried to look serious.

"I was the only person at the office that the owners trusted. They didn't mean to offend any of the staff, but they were adamant about access. But of course, as a guest of the tenant," he winked at her, "they cannot object." It took a moment before it dawned on Emm that she was getting an invitation to the apartment, albeit cryptically.

"You mean… when?" He smiled. He was just glad that Emm wanted to meet Claudia. She was the love of his life and wanted his girls to love her too.

"Tomorrow night. Claudia has invited some close friends of ours, and you and CC. It's a shame Stephanie and James aren't back from their honeymoon yet. I'd like them to meet Claudia too. Never mind, we'll surprise her when she gets home." While Michael was talking, Emm was collecting her handbag and logging off her computer. "Where are you going? You couldn't have been here more than an hour. Have you got a viewing?" Michael looked at his watch. It was eleven thirty, too early for lunch and too late for coffee.

"How long do you think it takes to sort out an outfit for a celebrity gathering? I really needed a week Father, not twenty-four hours' notice. Men!" With that Emm turned her back and marched out of the office. Michael stifled a laugh, that was his girl!

CHAPTER 4

Sobs wracked her body as she pleaded with the French receptionist behind the desk for a cabin. The receptionist was being very sympathetic.

"I'm sorry madam, but we are full to capacity today. We 'ave no cabins available. You can 'ave two reclining seats on Deck five if that 'elps?" The woman holding the child was almost distraught. She put her child down and appealed to the receptionist in a quiet voice, but still in vain.

"Per'aps if I take your name, I can call you over the public address system if we 'ave a cancellation or a no show. You can 'ave first refusal as you 'ave a young child. No more can I do, je suis désolé Madam." The receptionist waited for the young woman to give her name.

"Please understand I cannot have my name for the whole ship to hear. Can I just give you my mobile number?" The young woman pleaded.

"It is against our policy to call members of the public on their telephones." The receptionist shrugged and looked sad. She was prevented from helping by the ship's rules. Katarina looked dejected and turned to find Lilli gone.

Harry got on the ferry in Portsmouth for the evening crossing to Cherbourg, France. He manoeuvred the sunburst-yellow Aston Martin into the garage deck and made sure it was secure before walking up the three flights of stairs to the bar. He had popped in to grab a quick glass of port, as he knew it settled his stomach, just in case the crossing wasn't calm. As he sat in the bar the boat started to move out of the harbour. He took off his watch and changed the time to an hour ahead, a habit of his. He drank his port quickly and decided to put his overnight holdall into his cabin before going back down to have a meal. On his way down the stairs from the cabin deck he noticed a small disturbance at the information desk. There he saw a young woman crying, holding a small child, strangely both in hooded jackets. He walked over to the Duty-Free boutique that was still closed and took out a magazine to check the price of their rum. He didn't need any but thought it a good idea to have his favourite brand available when he wanted some.

A little girl in a hooded jacket wandered over to Harry and smiled at him.

"Hello there, what's your name?" The little girl looked over to see her mother still talking to the French lady and decided she wanted a friend.

"Hello. I'm Lilliana. What's your name?" Harry bent down slightly to tell her without having to shout and scare her.

"Harry." He put out his hand. "How do you do, Lilliana." Lilliana shook his hand.

"How do you do, Harry." They both laughed at their politeness. Harry noticed the young woman who had been so upset at the Reception Desk hurrying over to them. She had seen a man talking gently to Lilli.

"I'm so sorry. I hope she hasn't been pestering

you." The young woman grabbed Lilliana's hand. "Lilliana, what have I told you? You're to stay by my side and not move. I really don't want to lose you."
She hugged Lilliana and picked her up.

"She wasn't bothering me at all." Harry stood up and offered to shake her hand. Before he could introduce himself, Lilliana did it for him.

"His name is Harry, Mummy." The woman managed to smile. Harry shook her hand. She was very young to be the mother of Lilliana, he thought. Oddly she also had an accent, which Lilliana hadn't.

"Hello Harry. My name is Katarina, and you have met my daughter already I see." Her whole face lit up when she smiled at Lilliana. Harry wanted to keep the smile on her face, if he could.

"Mummy, I'm very hungry." Lilli whined.

"I know darling, but we have to wait until we are at Cousin Maria's."

"But you said we wouldn't get there until tomorrow, and I'm hungry now." Harry looked at Lilliana. She couldn't be older than five or six, how can a child not eat for a day? He had to step in.

"Please let me help you. You're obviously in trouble. I was about to go to the cafeteria for a quick bite to eat. I would be very honoured if you would both join me." He smiled at Katarina. Something was making her trust him. "Here, let me help you with your bags." Harry picked up the rucksacks and pulled a case along behind him.

"Okay, thank you." She followed him to the self-service restaurant and he gave her a tray. She put Lilliana down and they all chose what they wanted. Lilliana found a table where she could watch the sea and they sat down and ate.

"Is there anything else I can do to help you both?" Harry smiled at her. He had to try and make her relax, even if it was only for Lilliana's sake. They hadn't even taken their jackets off. They must both be roasting.

"I'm sure you're wondering why I have no money, and I'm so anxious to get a cabin. You deserve an explanation." She looked at her sated daughter who had curled up with her head in her mother's lap. Katarina could tell by her child's breathing that she was already asleep. In whispers she tried to explain what had put them in such a desperate predicament. She knew she was taking a risk, but Harry had very kind eyes. That, and she had little choice if she wanted to get out of sight and keep her daughter safe. "I'm originally from Estonia. I was forcibly taken from my home and brought to England to work as a cleaner. I was never allowed out on my own and was told I'd be put in prison for being in England illegally if the police caught me. I was terrified. I was only sixteen. The man in charge of all of us girls…" Harry looked shocked.

"There were more than just you?" Katarina nodded. She carried on.

"He is called Erik. He is a nasty bully. He gave me a proposition as he liked me and told me he'd look after me and let me live with him if I married him." She looked up at Harry's angry face. She mistook it for disgust. "I was young and naïve and knew if I didn't agree he would beat me or worse I would end up in a brothel with some of the other girls." She checked Lilliana was still asleep and continued in a quieter voice. "He raped me on the first night of my arrival at his house, but I was too scared to tell anyone. Erik took my Estonian passport and he managed to get a marriage certificate from Estonia in our names. I later found out that while he was in Estonia he had paid a girl that looked like me to marry him and he forged my signature. When he got home he had my new Estonian passport in my married name. He seemed to leave me alone after that, as long as I kept the house clean and cooked for him." Harry couldn't believe that this was going on in England in the twenty first century. It was tantamount to slavery.

He wanted to stop her talking and make things better for her, all at once. But he knew that it was better to let her tell him everything. He may be the first and only person she had told. He would not rob her of the brave achievement that she would feel getting it all out and having someone listen. She took a deep breath and carried on. "I noticed that I was pregnant a few months later. I tried to hide it from him. I overheard another shipment of girls were on their way and he was organising where they would put them. He was high up in the gang of traffickers. Is that the right term?" Harry nodded. He didn't want to interrupt. She continued. "I knew my life was in danger as a new batch was on its way and I thought he may want a younger model." She looked up at Harry and tried to smile at her own joke – she had just turned seventeen.

He looked back with caring eyes, so she carried on. "I decided the safest thing was to tell him I was pregnant with his baby. Erik treated me very well until Lilliana was born. He was devoted to Lilli. For the last six years I have been secretly learning English and studying hard to get my British citizenship. Lilli only speaks English and it infuriates her father that she does not want to learn

Estonian. Erik had recently applied for an Estonian passport for Lilli and wanted to take her to Estonia to visit his family. I did not want him taking her there.

I know he needs to get her there before she is seven, to start her in the Estonian school system. He will keep her there living with his family, who are all in the trafficking trade. I would not be allowed to see her again. While he was out yesterday, finding positions for some new girls due in today, an official letter from Estonia arrived in the post. It was Lilli's Estonian passport. I realised it was time to escape. I hid her passport yesterday with mine hoping he'd not realise it had arrived. I packed a few things in my rucksack and hid the passports in the pocket. I put enough clothes for Lilli to carry in her rucksack too. I waited until this morning when Erik had a meeting and packed the rest of my things, got Lilli ready and we left the house before Erik got back. We have been hiding around the corner from our house, at Gunwharf Quays Shopping Centre, most of the day, but we had to risk walking to the docks to catch the ferry to France." Harry knew exactly where that was. He wanted to tell her his shoes had come from that outlet centre, but it wasn't the time. He listened on. "I knew he would have noticed us gone so I tried to disguise ourselves in case he had people searching on all transport leaving Portsmouth." Harry had to smile, caringly. "You don't believe me?" Katarina wouldn't have believed her either. It sounded inconceivable that a woman would put herself through so much and not left sooner.

"Of course I believe you. I wasn't smiling at that. What I was smiling at was your attempt at disguise. It is hot; summer is in full swing and you two are in baking jackets with hoods. You're so conspicuous and actually draw people's attention rather than blend in." She realised he was right. She laughed. "That's better. It's nice to see you laughing. After all you have been through, you're one very incredible woman." Katarina knew she had chosen the right person to help her. "I overheard that you need a cabin." Katarina nodded. "I hope I'm not being too forward, but I have a cabin with four berths, and I only need one. You're very welcome to share it with me." Katarina was quietly crying.

"Thank you. You're too kind." Harry really didn't know what he was getting himself into, but he was a sucker for a woman in tears.

"Stay here for a moment while I pop to the Duty-Free shop, it should be open by now. I think, after all that, we deserve a drink. I'll buy a bottle of wine and we can drink it in the cabin once we've settled Lilliana down." Katarina nodded and thanked him. She would be glad to get out of the public view.

Harry was back minutes later with a bottle and two pairs of sunglasses and a couple of caps. "How's that for a disguise. You'll fit in perfectly as an English girl on holiday." Katarina laughed again. They took Lilliana up to the cabin and sat on the opposite bunk sipping wine and thinking of the next plan of action.

Unfortunately she had no money except what she had in her bag, probably about £20. Harry insisted on giving her some Euros. He knew he had around 300€ in his wallet, he told her he would give her the money. It would be easy enough to get more out from an ATM on his way down to the Riviera.

"You will need it if you have to travel. It should get you both a train or a coach to… you haven't told me where you're going."

"I'm trying to get down to my cousin's farm near Girona, in Spain. She will let us stay there. Erik doesn't know who she is, so he won't find us there." Katarina hoped. But she was still sure she would be followed as soon as she left the boat.

"I would offer to give you a lift, but I only have a two-seater car. I will give you my mobile number though, in case I can help with anything." He felt useless. He really wanted to help Katarina and her little girl, but his hands were tied. Stupid car. Why hadn't his boss asked for the Bentley? He knew why, Monaco had narrow, steep roads and the Aston Martin was fun to drive.

"I'm so grateful to you Harry. You're such a kind man. I haven't met many. Thank you for everything." She smiled at him and then couldn't stop herself yawning. "I need to go to sleep. Lilli and I have a big day ahead of us. The beginning of a new life." Harry was happy for the first time since meeting Katarina. She sounded positive at last. He had so much admiration for her. He felt so guilty having lived the life he had especially over the last year.

"Come on, let's get some sleep. You'll need all your energy in the morning with that journey ahead of you." Katarina settled down on the lower bunk opposite Lilli. Harry went up the ladder above Lilliana. Once the light went out Lilliana was still sleeping soundly, but Katarina was too scared to sleep. She quietly went up the ladder to Harry's bunk and lay next to him.

"What are you doing? Neither of us will get any sleep with you up here. It's stifling and there's no room to move." He heard her sobs and put his arms around her and held her tight. What an awful life she'd had. She could

only be around twenty-two or twenty-three years old herself. He wished he could have been more help. He had five days to get the car down to Monaco as he'd left England earlier than he needed so he could do a little sight-seeing on the way, but the mode of transport he had was of no use to Katarina and her daughter.
Her body relaxed and he could tell she was asleep as her breathing had slowed down. Harry managed to free his arm and shuffle down the bed. He dangled his legs off the side of the bunk and dropped down to the floor. If he was going to be alert enough to drive on the French roads, he needed to get some sleep. He ducked into the bed opposite Lilliana and fell asleep almost immediately.

Harry woke with a start. All too soon the purser was banging on all the cabin doors. He looked at his watch. It was 5.50 a.m. local time. That meant it was only 4.50 a.m. by his body clock. He looked across and saw Lilliana sleeping deeply through the wake-up call. He popped in the shower to get himself ready for the day. When he'd finished and dressed, as quietly as possible, he whispered to Katarina in the top bunk.

"Time to get up if you want any breakfast." He didn't see any sign of movement so nudged her pillow gently. Still no sign of life, he pulled back the duvet a little and saw the top of something that wasn't in any shape or form a head. He pulled the duvet right down and found a rucksack. He turned to the window and opened the curtain. There was just enough light in the sky to see a note on the little table between the bunks. He put on the small light over the table and picked up the note. He noticed there were two pieces of paper together, next to two passports and his wallet. He was sure he'd left his passport and wallet in his jacket pocket. He read the top one first.

Dear Harry,

You are the kindest man I have ever met in my life. I know I can trust you with my baby's life. Please can you look after my Lilliana and get her safely to my cousin Maria's farm in Spain. On her own she has more chance of getting there, as I know Erik's henchmen will follow me.

I will throw my phone into the sea as I have remembered they could track me on it. When I buy a new one, I will send you Maria's exact address. I have your number from your business card in your wallet. I also took 100€ which I promise I will give you back as soon as I can. I'm so sorry to involve you Harry. I want to thank you from the bottom of my heart for all you have done already for us. Please look after my little girl.

Thank you again

Katarina

Harry put the note back on the table and read the one underneath.

To whom it may concern,

I give my permission KATARINA ESKOLA, Estonian passport number:

1283450. Date of birth: 09.02.1996

for my daughter LILLIANA ESKOLA, Estonian passport number:

1423490. Date of birth: 10.04.2013

to travel with her uncle, HARRY HART, passport number: 8009265542 Date of birth: 09.11.1986

to France and Spain on holiday.

She had signed the letter and given her address as Harry's, which she had copied from his business card.

"Bloody hell." Harry couldn't believe what he'd committed himself to. But he took one look at the sleeping Lilliana and knew he had to think of the child and her safety. He suppressed a laugh at his next thought.

'Young Harry has finally grown up'!
He had no idea what to do with a child, a female child at that. His first thought was breakfast. They would miss it if he didn't get her up soon. He couldn't risk going down and leaving her to wake up alone. He decided to wake her.

"Where's my Mummy?" she asked, rubbing her eyes. Harry thought it best to tell her the truth, his first mistake.

"She's gone to find her cousin Maria and asked me to take you to them in my fun car." Unfortunately, it backfired on him. Lilliana started crying for her mother. Harry got her clothes out of the bag her mother had left. It was still chilly outside at that time in the morning, so he found trousers and a t-shirt, to go with her hoody, rather than a dress. "Be a good girl and put these on for me. I'll go and get you something to eat. I'll be as quick as I can. Okay?" To his surprise Lilliana just nodded. She sniffed back her tears and tried to stop crying and got out of the bunk obediently. Harry had no time to think about the reason why Lilliana had complied so readily but knew in his heart that the child had learned not to question an adult. He rushed down to the cafeteria and grabbed a couple of croissants and a couple of bottles of water. He could stop at the services to get her more once they had started on their journey. When he'd got back to the cabin Lilliana was dressed and had made her bunk up. Harry had to smile. What a good girl she was. He gave her one of the croissants and they sat and ate them until the public address system announced that drivers could return to their cars. Harry playfully brushed the crumbs off himself and Lilliana in the hope he could make her understand that he was a good guy and grabbed their bags. With a quick check round that nothing had been forgotten, wallet, letters and both passports safely in his bag, they made their way down to the parking deck. Harry realised that the seat belt would probably strangle Lilliana as she was so small. He took a small towel and an old rug from the boot and folded the rug, covering it with the towel onto the passenger seat. He put Lilliana onto the seat and pulled down the seat belt, but that didn't work. He adjusted the seat belt from the side and made the shoulder strap lower; luckily that worked. But Lilliana's neck looked pinched.

He slipped the towel off the rug and wrapped it around the belt, so it fit comfortably on her shoulder, and softly on her skin. Job done he went around to the back and checked he'd closed the boot properly, then got in the car. Although his charge was a little higher in the seat, so if she stretched she could see out, from outside she would not be seen, putting Harry's mind at rest.

Lilliana was quite excited by the time they got into the car.

"Yellow is actually my favourite colour Harry. Did you know that?" She looked at her new best friend.

"Well I do now Lilliana." He smiled at her.

"If we are going to be friends, Harry, you can call me Lilli. All my best friends call me Lilli." Harry nodded. That's what he'd call her then. It was less of a mouthful anyway. It also hadn't gone unnoticed that Lilli was already at ease with Harry. Perhaps he could make the trip fun for her. It will be a learning curve for them both. Harry had to learn how to look after a six-year-old little girl, and Lilli had to learn how to trust another grown-up that wasn't her mother. The car in front of him drove off and Harry followed. He drove slowly around the disembarkation area in the hope he'd see Katarina, but he didn't. What he did spot sent a shiver through him. There, parked at the end of the gangway, was a black Mercedes with English registration plates, fully tinted windows and two menacing looking men standing by the car, smoking and staring up towards the pedestrian ramp from the boat. Harry had his fears re-established. Katarina had made a good decision by splitting up from her young daughter. It would have been a dead give-away if they had left the boat as mother and little girl. He drove out onto the open road to the dual carriageway and the beginning of a very long journey.

What was he going to do to amuse a six-year-old girl? Almost to answer his question Lilli took out an iPad from her rucksack and started playing a game. Harry didn't know how long that would keep her amused, but he thought he'd better get on as far as he could whilst she was happy and occupied. Harry would normally be listening to his iTunes blaring his Drake playlist from the Bang & Olufsen 3D premium sound system, curtesy of Aston Martin, but he concluded that most of the tracks were probably not suitable for a six-year-old. He fiddled with the stations on the radio and found a local one playing a mixture of mainly English and American hits interrupted by annoying French adverts. He thought it would alleviate his boredom, but unfortunately not. What a complete waste of the terrific sound system, was going through his mind. It was the major thing he looked forward to, apart from the driving itself, when using the car – that and the looks of admiration he got from both sexes. He looked out at his surroundings, keeping one eye on the road. He sighed as all he could see were fields and trees. As there was nothing else to do his mind wandered and it occurred to him that all the dilapidated, half brick walls and collapsed roofs, that the animals seemed to gather in, were originally farmhouses. If he stretched and looked further into the distance over the fields, he could see relatively new, larger ones. It seemed a good idea to him making use of the old buildings instead of knocking them down completely. He thought there would bound to be an issue if this happened in England with 'Health and Safety'. Looking ahead on the motorway he came to the conclusion that most of the derelict buildings would have been too close to the road to live in, once the motorway had been made, so that was probably why the new ones had been built over the other side of the fields. His mind was relaxed looking at the serene views of cows munching on the grass, and maze swaying in the light breeze. He thought it must be very rewarding being a farmer, working outside in the fresh air. Hard work he could see, but very gratifying. Real life, not like the fantasy world he lived in. He looked over at Lilli, who had dropped off to sleep.

For the first time in his life he thought that he might like a Lilli, one day.

One and a half hours later, nearing the town of Avranches, Harry had almost forgotten Lilli was in the car with him, until she spoke for the first time since leaving the boat.

"Harry, I need the toilet." He looked over at her

and she had switched her iPad off. "Brilliant timing Lilli. I was going to stop in this town for coffee anyway. Just hold on for a few minutes, okay?" Lilli nodded and looked out of the window as best she could. She was too low for a good view. Harry looked over at her. He knew she was struggling to see out, but the advantage of that was that no one outside could see her. He looked like he was travelling alone and that suited him if they were being followed.

He wondered if he was getting paranoid but seeing the black Mercedes had heightened his senses and erring on the side of caution was probably a good idea.
He drove into the town, as inconspicuously as you could in a very loud, yellow sports car. Luckily the attention he was getting was from the men with smiles. All men were boys where cars were concerned. He pulled up outside a bar advertising 'Le petit déjeuner 3€'.
Harry helped Lilli out of the car, as the door was too heavy for her to open. They went inside. Lilli found the toilet and Harry ordered an Orangina for Lilli and an espresso for himself. He needed to keep alert. He also ordered two ham and cheese baguettes. Lilli came back from the toilet, wiping her hands on her trousers.

"I love that kind of bread." Lilli smiled up at Harry. He had cut hers in half, as it was big enough for an adult, and wrapped half into a napkin for her to have later when she was hungry again. He put the other half in front of her. He kept looking over his shoulder into the street. He didn't want to stay too long and needed to get back on the road.

"Harry, will we be seeing Mummy soon?" Lilli looked at Harry pleadingly whilst enjoying her baguette.

"Soon, Lilli, soon." He smiled at the little girl.

He'd said the right thing, even if it was a lie – he was learning from his mistakes. She had crumbs everywhere and he needed to get those off her before she got in the newly valeted Aston Martin.

"I need the loo now. I'm going to ask the waitress to look after you until I get back. Let's play a game." Lilli was listening avidly and nodded. "Well, in front of other people you have to call me Uncle Harry, okay?" He hadn't a clue if that would work, but it would be a lot easier if Lilli was seen as his niece.

In as grown-up a voice as a six-year-old could speak, and for Lilli a quiet one, she responded.

"You should say you want me to be a very grown up girl, then I know it's a secret game, Harry. Sorry, I mean Uncle Harry." She screwed up her face as she tried to wink. Harry laughed.

"By George, I think she's got it!" Lilli looked at him and smiled. She would get used to Harry quoting lines from old movies. It was one of his and Emm's things. Oh, how he could do with her there right now, he thought.

Harry popped to the loo, while the waitress watched Lilli for him and by the time he got back she had brushed all the crumbs off Lilli. "Thank you so much. My niece is a bit of a messy eater." Harry wanted to try it out. The waitress smiled at him.

"You are 'er 'ero, apparently, Uncle 'arry. She 'as told me you are going to Spain to meet 'er mummy. Safe journey, monsieur." He was relieved that their first encounter as uncle and niece had gone to plan. Looking at Lilli it was quite possible to get away with being seen as relations. Harry's hair was white as a child and had settled into a fair to blonde colour in adulthood, depending on the amount of sunshine bleaching occurred. Of course, in his job he had more blonde streaks than fair. He'd just had his hair cut before he left England, so Lilli had the edge there. His eyes were almost as blue as Lilli's too. Lilli was slight in figure as was her mother. Again, due to Harry's job, he stayed fit and ate very healthily so his fat index was low. Looking alike definitely helped with the plan.

He felt in England there would have been more questions asked but thank goodness the waitress was just happy to have helped Lilli with her crumbs. He put a large tip on the plate and got Lilli back into the car. He pinged up the sat nav and decided on the route to the next stop.

"Uncle Harry, my iPad needs charging." Harry checked to see what model it was and took out the wire from the glove compartment and plugged one end into the USB port and the other into Lilli's iPad. Luckily the lead was long enough for her to continue playing while it charged, to Harry's great relief. He put Perpignan into his sat nav. Eight and a half hours came up. No way was a six-year-old going to survive that, no matter how well behaved she was. He needed to head for Spain in the hope that he'd hear from Katarina with an address.

He put in a few stops on the sat nav, so it would take them on the coast road. He thought that would be more fun for Lilli, but also keep them off the main obvious route to Spain.

"We'll be by the seaside at lunchtime Lilli. Shall we buy a bucket and spade?" Lilli looked up from her game she was playing.

"Oo, yes please. Can we swim too?" Harry had to be tough. He really didn't want to stay too long in one place.

"We'll see Lilli. Perhaps we will have time to paddle, definitely." She smiled and went back to her game. Harry was learning that if you take something away from a child, you give them something else in exchange. He went back to his planning. He worked out that by lunchtime they could be in La Rochelle. It would be full of tourists and had a beach. No one would pay any attention to a man and child. After staying a while there stretching their legs and eating a spot of lunch, they could travel for a few more hours and stay in Bordeaux for the night. They should be safe in a large city. He quickly looked for a hotel with private parking. No way was he going to leave the Aston Martin out on the road. He found one and booked a family room for one night.

They drove on down to La Rochelle. Lilli was an exceptional child. Harry thought girls chatted and were noisy, but Lilli sat and played on her iPad, stretched up high to look out of the window at the scenery and slept. Lilliana was definitely not a normal six-year-old little girl. Harry came to that conclusion very early on. She had lived with a tyrant for all of her life, so he realised that she knew she was safer being seen but not heard. Self-preservation probably taught her that, at a very young age. He hoped Katarina could find somewhere where they both could be happy.
Every so often Lilli would look up at Harry and ask a question. Normally they were related to the journey, 'are we nearly there yet Harry?', or the one Harry dreaded, 'will I see Mummy soon Harry?', or just a question about Harry himself that she had just thought of, 'have you got a girlfriend Harry?' was one such question. Harry answered

all the questions with positive answers to keep her happy He made most of them up and lied a little for the others. She spoke just enough to alleviate the monotony but little enough as not to be annoying. Another trick she must have learnt during early childhood. He was already growing very fond of Lilli.

He made excellent progress and was nearing La Rochelle when the fuel light came on. He had dropped his guard and pulled into the next motorway services without looking around. As he pulled up, he looked in his rear-view mirror and noticed a black Mercedes behind him. Getting nearer, although he couldn't see the registration plate, he automatically checked the driver was on the right-hand side of the car. Harry tried not to panic. Plenty of English, black Mercedes owners drove around Europe. As the black car broke away and weaved through the petrol pumps erratically, Harry could see the passenger was one of the men from the boat.

He quickly looked at Lilli who was playing some game on her tablet, that involved puppies and dog bones. He grabbed the cap he had bought her on the ferry and put it on her head. Luckily, he'd put her in jeans and a plain red t-shirt. He twisted her hair up and pushed it under the cap. He hoped she would be mistaken for a boy. Even her trainers were unisex. He had noticed she had pink shoes in her rucksack but hadn't worn them with her jeans. How can a six-year-old be so fashion conscious? His answer was that she was a girl.

"Sorry Lilli, but we need to keep the sun off your face as I don't have any cream." Lilli looked up from her game.

"Ok Harry. Do I look pretty?" Harry smiled at her

and nodded. Sometimes there was no mistaking her gender. All girls want to look pretty, even when they became women, he knew that from experience.

"You look cool. All the French girls wear caps and they are the prettiest girls in the world, apart from you." He winked at her. She giggled. Harry checked in his rear-view mirror and the Mercedes had gone. He had taken his eye off the ball again. Where the hell was it? He looked around and spotted it by the café services. Fortunately, the petrol pump had a 'pay at the pump' facility. Harry filled the car as quickly as he could and jumped back in. He had to decide whether to go over to the services with Lilli in disguise or push on to La Rochelle, a quarter of an hour down the road. Lilli had been three and a half hours since her last toilet stop. Harry knew she'd drunk a bottle of Orangina and had been sipping from the bottle of water in the cup holder. She must need the toilet. He couldn't let her go into the services with those goons in there. He'd pull out of the petrol station and take the slip road back onto the motorway. As he pulled away from the pump, Lilli looked up from her iPad.

"Harry? I need the toilet, nooow." She was wriggling and even Harry knew what that meant. Harry didn't know whether to be pleased that he hadn't reached the motorway or be worried that he now had to stop at the café services.

"OK Lilli, we'll pop to the toilets." Talking of toilets had made Harry realise he needed to relieve himself too. They drove over and parked as far from the Mercedes as possible. Harry looked for another entrance and found one to the side of the café itself, and parked. He took Lilli's hand and walked as nonchalantly as he could, in the hope that if anyone looked at him, he'd look like a normal father taking his child to the toilets. He stopped outside the one with the silhouette of a man on. Even Lilli knew what that meant.

"Harry, I'm a girl. I can't go in there." She was pulling him towards the silhouette of a lady. "I have to go in this one." She pointed up at the picture. "Look, that one has a dress on." Harry nodded.

"Okay Lilli, in you go. Don't talk to anyone. I'll be out here when you have finished." Lilli nodded and pushed open the door into the Ladies toilet where there were many cubicles to choose from.

Harry wondered if he had time to pop into the Gents. He made a split-second decision as Lilli would be occupied for a few minutes which meant he would know exactly where she was. He pushed open the door of the Gents and firstly noticed the line of other men relieving themselves at the public urinal. It was obviously busier as it was getting towards lunchtime. He checked the few cubicles and found one vacant. He went in and was as quick as he could be. After washing his hands, he could feel moisture on his trousers. He was angry with himself for being so careless. The tap had gushed quite fiercely, and the basins were not shaped like bowls, but were more like worktops with small channels collecting the running water. He made a note that the channels can fail, and he had to be a little more careful next time. He went to the blow-dryers to try and dry his trousers, but they were also very modern and were ones that only hands can enter. They did not blow in any other direction. He looked across at the old fashion paper towel machine and was pleased to see there were some in the container. He was aware that he was taking too long, so he pushed a handful into his pocket to use once back in the car and left the toilets. Lilli wasn't outside the ladies, so he wasn't sure if she'd wandered off or just hadn't finished. A woman came out and Harry tried to look around her to see if he could see Lilli. He got a very scornful look from the woman. He had to make her realise he was not a pervert.

"Excusez-moi Madame, mais parlez-vous Anglais?" The woman signalled to the man behind Harry. Harry turned and saw a man of the same age as the woman, holding a handbag. Luckily, he gathered that it was her husband.

"My wife speaks no English, Monsieur. Can I 'elp?" Harry sighed with relief, that could have been very awkward.

"My little niece went into the toilet on her own. She was wearing a cap and jeans. I just need to know if she is still in there." The gentlemen translated what Harry said, to his wife. She started pointing towards the front entrance.

"Mais non. La petite fille a quitté appellant 'Maman, Maman'." Harry didn't wait for the translation.

"Merçi. Monsieur Dame." He nodded at them both and rushed off to the front entrance to find Lilli. He understood more French than he could speak. She must have seen her mother, or what she had thought was her mother. Harry's heart was racing. He had a tightness in his chest. Was that what a heart attack felt like, he wondered. He'd try the front first and if she wasn't there, he'd go through the café to check that entrance and the car. He hadn't forgotten about the black Mercedes, but he knew he had to find Lilli as soon as possible.

She must be so scared, he thought. The automatic doors opened in front of him and a very sad, little girl walked in. She spotted Harry and rushed into his arms, with Harry scooping her up off the ground. She was beside herself with sadness and panic. Harry held her very tightly and left the building. He noted that the Mercedes had disappeared. He walked to their car wanting to get her inside before she attracted too much attention. By the time he'd walked around the outside of the café and opened the car door, her sobbing had stopped, and she was just left with involuntary shuddering of breath intake. Harry's heart was breaking. He held her more tightly and gently rocked her. He wasn't sure why he was rocking her, but it just felt natural. Eventually she looked up at Harry.

"I thought I saw Mummy, Harry. But it wasn't. Then I couldn't find you. I was scared. I'm sorry Harry." She was about to cry again when Harry smiled at her.

"Well what a clever girl you are, Lilli. Coming back inside. That was very grown-up of you. I'm very glad to see you. I missed you." She looked at Harry's face and laughed. He was pulling the sides of his mouth down as if he was about to cry, but then he grinned.

"I wasn't that long, Harry. You didn't have time to miss me." She smiled and hugged him again.

If only she knew how long it felt to Harry, she'd understand how Harry had really felt. As he was putting her in the car the lady and gentleman from the toilets approached. The lady went over to Harry and touched his arm.

"Tout est bon, Monsieur, n'est pas?" Harry nodded.

"Yes, Madame, all is good. Merçi bien." She went back over to her husband who looked up at Harry.

"I remember the days our little ones would get lost. I think it took years off my life. Bon chance, Monsieur." He smiled at Harry and Harry knew exactly what he meant.

He drove onto the slip road and was back on the motorway in no time. He had totally forgotten about his wet trousers up until that point. A cold feeling penetrated his thighs. He glanced down and noticed they were almost dry. The French sunshine had helped.

He looked over to Lilli who was watching something on her iPad with her headphones on.

"What game are you playing now Lilli?" She looked up at Harry and laughed.

"I'm not playing a game, silly, I'm watching Dora the Explorer's World Adventure. I'm in France and learning words I might need. Do you want to watch it too?" Harry shook his head. He looked over and noticed the YouTube logo. Think Harry, think. If she hadn't got Wi-Fi how was she watching YouTube? His mind was in overdrive. Katarina had got rid of her phone because she knew Erik could track it, what she forgot was that Lilliana's iPad had the same resource. If it was Erik's iPad he could go into the 'Find' app on his phone. It was so obvious. How would the thugs have known which route they had taken from the ferry? They could have gone via Paris or across land to Clermont-Ferrand and Béziers down to Spain. The route Harry had taken was the most indirect route. He looked at his rear-view mirror and wondered if he was just being over suspicious. How would they be sure which car was emitting the signal, especially as the Aston Martin had Monaco plates. He'd just have to be very careful not to give away the fact he was carrying a fugitive.

He felt he was in a James Bond movie, driving an Aston Martin through France, rescuing a damsel in distress. Although the damsel was a six-year-old little girl and the Aston Martin hadn't been given to him by the British government and didn't have gadgets that would see off any black Mercedes with two villainous thugs.

CHAPTER 5

They arrived in La Rochelle and Harry managed to park the car in the market square opposite a restaurant. They were able to get a table inside by the window. Harry wanted to watch the road and Patrick's car, but he needed them to be out of sight. He ordered an omelette for himself and Lilli had asked for spaghetti Bolognese. While they waited for their food Harry needed to get the iPad's location disabled.

"Can I have a look at your iPad please Lilli?" Lilli handed it to him. There was a sim card in the side, just as he thought. The iPad was keeping Lilli entertained on the journey and had worked wonderfully well so he couldn't get rid of it, although he'd have happily thrown it into the sea. He'd have to do the next best thing until he had a tool to remove the card. He had to make sure 'Find my iPad' was not functioning. He went into Lilli's iCloud settings and tried to turn off 'Find my iPad'. It then asked for her Apple ID password.

"Lilli, do you know your password for this iPad?" Lilli shook her head.

"No Harry, Mummy always does that sort of thing. She took it off the beginning, so I could go straight into my programs, but she wouldn't let me know her password in case I bought something by mistake in my games." She laughed. It was obviously a private joke between mother and daughter. I'll fix it when we get to the hotel later. It would probably be better if you turn it off for now." Lilli took it back with a smile.

"I was bored with Dora anyway. It's for kids and I'm nearly seven." That told him. He knew by her passport that she'd only been six for a few months.

After lunch Harry drove further along the road and took Lilli down to the beach. He could keep an eye on the road and the car while she played. He hoped she hadn't remembered the promised bucket and spade. The shorter the time spent in one place the better.

"Will you come in the sea with me Harry?" Harry shrugged – he needed to stay alert.

"We'll see Lilli." Lilli looked at him.

"What does that mean, yes or no Harry?" Harry forgot a child's rule of logic.

"It means we'll see." Lilli laughed.

"That's what Mummy says it means too. But I know when she says it, it really means yes." She looked up at Harry and smiled. Cheeky, thought Harry, but had to smile at her humour.

He let her change into a skirt so she could paddle. She was having a lovely time, while Harry watched her diligently. He called her back after a while and dried her feet and they wandered around the seafront shops, keeping an eye on the car and the road. She had toiletries in her bag and clothes, but he wanted to keep her happy so he bought her a fluffy stuffed dog that she had fallen in love with when she first saw it. He didn't want to push their luck, so having bought some sweets too they made their way back to the car. No sign of the black Mercedes, they set off on their final journey of the day, to Bordeaux.

By chance traffic was light and the trip only took two and a half hours and Lilli had slept most of the way. He noted that after food and playtime Lilli's eyes were having difficulty staying open. He risked her turning the iPad on for short blasts when she woke. He thought it would have been mean not to.

The hotel car park was behind the building itself and had large gates so could not be seen from the road. Perfect, thought Harry. The bedroom had a large double bed and two small beds at the other end of the room. It had an en suite bathroom and a separate toilet. Harry had a shower while Lilli watched French television. When Harry had finished, he filled a bath for Lilli. He put clean underwear from her bag into the bathroom and told her to take her time in the bubbles. He also thought about the safety of the small child in his care and took the key out of the bathroom door. The last thing he needed was for her to lock herself in and him having to call a gendarme for help.

"Try to explain that one Harry Hart!" He said quietly to himself. Lilli was singing the same song she had been humming most of the journey and to Harry's surprise, he had been humming it too. He also heard through the door that she was word perfect. Listening to the words he could only imagine what that little girl had been through and how the song had helped her escape into a land of fantasy and security for just a few moments. Lilli's vulnerability made Harry just want to wrap her up in cotton wool and keep her from any harm.

"For God's sake Harry Hart, pull yourself together." He took a big breath and let it out slowly. His eyes glanced onto Lilli's bed where her iPad was re-charging. He had an idea, and fingers crossed, he could alleviate some of the danger. He looked around the bedroom suite.

By the window was a rather splendid French bureau. He went over to it and opened the middle drawer.
In it was a folder with hotel information. By that were laundry bags and an inventory pad and pencil. He shut the drawer and decided to check the three smaller drawers to the side of the old bureau. He was in luck with the first one. In it was a shoe cleaner sponge, and to his delight a sewing kit. He took it out and opened it. There were four needles all threaded with different coloured cotton. There was also a large safety pin, which to Harry looked a little too thick for the task. He took out one of the needles from the pouch and went over to the iPad. Turning it on its side he pushed the needle into the hole that was keeping the sim card in its slot and out popped the card holder. He removed the card and bent it to ruin the chip. Relief made him sit down for a moment while he replaced the empty sim card holder and put the needle back into the pouch – after all, he had a six-year-old in his charge and wasn't sure what mayhem could unfold with a sewing kit and a kid.
Harry wondered what to do next. He was on his way to Spain with no address to go to, with a little girl. If her mother didn't make contact he could be left with the child forever. He didn't know anyone in France who could help.

"Yes, I do!" He had a light bulb moment, Emm's mother. He would text Emm and ask her to help him. He wrote a text. *"Hello Emm, how are you? Just wondered if you were in France? Need your help actually. Please ring me. Love Harry."* Should he ring her? He'd take Lilli to dinner first and if Emm hadn't replied by the time they got back he'd wait until Lilli was asleep and then ring Emm for help. Lilli came out of the bathroom with soaking wet hair and a bathrobe on that was swamping her. Harry had to focus on Lilli. She looked frightened.

"Sorry Uncle Harry. I didn't mean to get my hair wet, but I slipped, and it wasn't my fault, honest." Harry scooped her up laughing. Lilli breathed a sigh of relief. She thought she was in trouble. Harry took her back into the bathroom and found the hairdryer, which was attached to the bathroom wall, so he sat her on the marble top next to the basin and brushed her hair with the hairdryer at a distance so as not to burn Lilli's delicate skin. They were both ready to go down to dinner within half an hour. Harry was surprised at how easy it was over dinner, they enjoyed each other's company. Lilli was very advanced for her age, Harry thought. Not that he knew much about six-year-olds, but he knew he wasn't so chatty at that age, maybe it was a girl thing he wondered.

* * *

CC took the evening off from her studies and she and Emm decided to wear long summer dresses. A car had picked them up and they met Michael in the foyer of the apartment block at St. John's Wood, having been let in by the twenty-four-hour concierge. Emm could see why that apartment had been ideal for Claudia, as it was just ten minutes by car to the filming location on Hampstead Heath. On the books the apartment was £7,000 per week. It had five bedrooms and unrivalled views from the vast outdoor entertainment space. Outside was set out on several terraces accessed from the living room and two of the bedrooms above.

Claudia opened her door and hugged them both.

"'ow very lovely to meet you both in person. Emm, you're the image of your father, beautiful." Emm wasn't too sure she wanted to look like a man, and she wasn't sure her father would want to be called beautiful, but Claudia was French and theatrical, so she'd let the description slide.

"Thank you…., you're very kind." Emm didn't even know what to call her.

"So formal. I love the English. Your father was the same when I first met 'im, but I loosened 'im up." She turned to Michael, who Emm swore was blushing. "Now you girls need a drink." She ushered them to the bar in the living room and got the man behind the bar to get them a glass of champagne each. "Merçi Mathieu." She turned to the girls conspiratorially. "'e is my man Friday, as you say in England. Michael knows 'e's safe." She tapped her nose. "'e is wonderfully gay." She turned back to Mathieu who had obviously heard her. Mathieu tossed his head in the air with his mouth wide open in mock distress, then turned smiling to Claudia and blew her a very exaggerated kiss. Emm knew the party was going to be great fun.

Claudia escorted them onto the lower terrace. There they saw Matt Pride and again the mouths gaping - Michael had to laugh. Michael had been with these people during the nine months of filming and saw them as normal people doing a job. His daughter and her best friend were still very starry eyed. The girls had chosen their outfits well. Nearly all the women were wearing long, flowing chiffon dresses, ideal for a summer's evening outside.

"Can I say you two have done me proud this evening. You both look lovely." Michael kissed Emm and

CC on both their cheeks.

"OH, my goodness Daddy, this French thing must be catching. You never kiss except at bedtime." She turned to CC. "He really is in love." The girls were laughing, but Michael wasn't offended. He was glad he had a new lease of life and was enjoying every moment. "By the way, what do we call Claudia?" Michael looked at her and was puzzled.

"What is wrong with, oh let me see." He was rubbing his chin in thought. "I know, Claudia?" He was getting the last laugh.

"Oh, ha ha, very funny. Will she mind first names so soon?" Michael realised that they were all too English.

"Of course she won't mind. It's her name." Just as he'd said it Claudia came up behind him. She had Matt Pride in tow.

"Emm, CC, meet Matt." Both the girls giggled. Michael decided it was time he disappeared. He grabbed Claudia's hand and wandered off to leave his daughter and her friend make idiots of themselves.

As Emm was talking to Matt Pride, trying to get to know the man not the character, her phone pinged. She apologised and quickly looked to see who it was. Harry's name was on an unopened message. What could he want? She excused herself and let CC take over the conversation. Matt wasn't enjoying CC's company as much as Emm's. He had heard CC was studying to be a psychiatrist and was trying to watch everything he said. He had been analysed on numerous occasions and didn't like it.

What he didn't realise was that CC wasn't enjoying his company either. She had been chatting to Frédéric all afternoon and was falling madly in love with him. Frédéric was a handsome, honest, wonderful, romantic, real man – Matt seemed fake. If it wasn't for his looks and fame he'd be just another boring man with shallow ideals. Basically, he'd like any girl who idolised him and would jump into bed with him. Harsh CC, she thought, but true.

Emm opened the message:

"Hello Emm, how are you? Just wondered if you were in France? Need your help actually. Please ring me. Love Harry."

CC turned to Emm and asked her whom the text was from.

"Harry. He sounds odd. I haven't heard from him in ages." She showed CC the text. "What do you think?" CC read the text a second time.

"I think he needs your help." CC smiled at Emm. "That's my professional opinion." Emm laughed. It really didn't need a nearly qualified psychiatrist to tell her that.

"I know what he says, I meant what should I do about it?" CC had to be tactful. She knew Emm still loved Harry, but if Harry was using her and then she didn't see him again for months, that was unfair to Emm. It had taken her a long time to get over Harry the first time, and CC didn't honestly think she had got over him yet.

"My advice is to enjoy the party and text him in the morning to see what he wants. Hopefully by then whatever he needed help with will have been sorted. If it was that urgent, I'm sure he would phone you." Emm nodded. That seemed like good advice. "But please can we move on to someone with a few more human qualities than the empty shell of Matt Pride. Just goes to show how you get taken in by good looks and remarkable scripts." The girls linked arms and headed back into the bar, laughing together. Leaving Matt standing on the terrace wondering why they had both walked away from what could have been the best evening of their lives.

* * *

Lilli started yawning, it was time for bed. After Harry had a coffee, he carried her from the dining room up to their bedroom. He managed to put her pyjamas on with her help and settled her down with her new stuffed dog.

"Have you thought of a name for him yet?" Harry tucked him up beside Lilli.

"Well, we are in France and the capital of France is Paris. So, I think I'll call him Paris. It'll make me remember you forever, Harry, and our road trip." She reached up and kissed Harry on his cheek and hugged him. "You will be my friend forever, won't you Harry?" God, this girl really knows how to make a man a quivering wreck, Harry could swear he had something stuck in his throat. He swallowed and took a deep breath.

"I will Lilli, I promise." He settled her back down and turned off her bedside light. His lamp was so far away that it was just a dim glow - enough to get him undressed and into bed without stumbling over anything. "Goodnight Lilli. Sleep tight."

"Don't let the bedbugs bite." She giggled as she turned over and snuggled down with Paris. He went into the bathroom and got himself ready for bed. As he came out he checked on Lilli.

She was dead to the world. Paris had fallen on the floor. He picked him up and tucked him in, back by her side. He looked at her for a moment and wondered if the fact she hadn't mentioned her mother since they arrived at the hotel was down to fear of the answer or comfort in Harry's presence. Either wasn't natural, it worried Harry.

He had to contact Katarina as soon as possible and get the two of them back together.

He tiptoed over to his bed and grabbed his phone off the bedside table. He was about to ring Emm when he noticed a missed call and a text from a number the phone hadn't recognised. It was from Katarina.

"Hi Harry, it is Katarina. I tried to ring earlier, but I think you may have been eating." Harry turned his phone over and realised, out of habit, he had put it on silent whilst in the restaurant. He shook his head, frustrated with himself for not keeping an eye on it. He turned it back and looked at the screen for the rest of the message. *"I have the address of my cousin Maria."* She had written the name of a farm, in a town just off the main route to Girona. *"She said she would have Lilli until I get there. I'm on my way but it is taking a long time as I'm trying to avoid the main routes."* If only she realised that they were following Lilli not her, but he didn't want to worry her, so he kept that to himself. She asked how Lilli was and apologised again for dumping her off on him and taking his money.

He pressed the phone number and got the unavailable tone. She had either switched it off or was out of signal. He texted her back immediately to put her mind at rest, hoping that once she was back in signal, she would relax a little. *"Hi Katarina. Please do not worry about the money or leaving Lilli with me. We are having great fun on our journey to Maria's. You just take care and arrive in Girona safely, whenever you can. Harry."* He waited to see if she was writing a text back. Nothing happened so he put the phone close to him in case she eventually answered and snuggled down in his bed. He had a long drive again ahead of him and he hadn't had the best sleep the previous night. He debated whether to ring Emm. He just wanted to hear her voice.

He wondered why she hadn't replied to his text earlier.
He checked on his Facebook page to see if she had posted anything recently. There was his answer. Emm and CC had posted a selfie of them both at a penthouse in St John's Wood with the evening view over London, with the caption - 'This is living the 'high' life', and a laughing emoji.
They both looked so happy. Perhaps he'd ring her the next day, he didn't want to ruin her night out. He checked his watch; it was only 9.30 pm. He couldn't remember the last time he was in bed at that time. Probably about Lilli's age, he thought. But he was tired, and he'd keep Lilli awake if he put the tv on, so he put his head on his pillow and dreamt of happier times with Emm in his life. He fell into such a deep sleep that he didn't hear or feel the text message come in minutes later:
"Thank you, Harry. God bless you. Katarina."

What did wake him sent shivers through his body. There was a thudding noise coming from somewhere in the corridor outside their room. Harry recognised it as someone trying to boot a door open. He was out of his bed and over to Lilli's without taking a breath.

"Lilli. Wake-up." Lilli sat up immediately. Harry realised she was wide awake. "Did that noise wake you?" Lilli nodded. She looked so scared. "Right, up you get. We're going to play a game." Harry remembered the last time he wanted her to listen and obey. "I want you to be a very grown up girl."

"Oo, is it a secret game?" Harry nodded. Lilli looked excited.

"Bring Paris with you and come over to my bed."

Lilli did as she was told, without question, a useful art she had learned. Harry glanced out of the window.

Parked along the road from the hotel was a black Mercedes with English number plates. In some degree Harry felt justified for his moment of paranoia, but panic was setting in rapidly. He rushed over to his bed and grabbed the duvet, turning it around so the long length was hanging over the bed, he threw it back on. He made the bed look dishevelled by throwing the pillows randomly over the bed.

"Right Lilli, we're going to hide under the bed and not make a sound, okay?" Lilli nodded. "If anyone talks, we ignore them like we are not here." She nodded again. "The prize is a bag full of sweeties for both of us, if they go away again and don't find us." Lilli nodded and cuddled Paris.

"This game is called 'hide and seek' Paris. You have to be very quiet and make sure they don't find us. Then we've won, haven't we Harry." Harry patted Paris on the head.

"That's it Lilli. I'm sure Paris will be good at it too." He lay Lilli down under the bed with Paris in her arms and picked up the phone to call reception.

They answered in seconds, relieving Harry's stress level very slightly.

"Bonsoir Monsieur 'art, can I 'elp you?" The receptionist sounded efficient.

"I can hear two men trying to get into our room. Please call the Gendarmerie." He heard the receptionist draw breath.

"I will call the Police Nationale immediately Monsieur. Stay in your room. Do not open the door." The phone clicked. Harry was in too much of a panic to argue with the woman, but the civil police were not exactly the force he meant. He needed to Gendarmerie Nationale, the heavies. The perpetrators were not your average thieves, but he couldn't tell her that. Harry put the phone back in the holder, turned off his lamp and shuffled under the bed, snuggling up to Lilli. He put his arm around her and waited. He didn't have long to wait. After three thuds the door flew open. He waited to see feet pass the bed, but there weren't any. After what seemed like an eternity, but was probably a couple of minutes, there were another two thuds, much louder than the last, and light came into their room with the door banging on the side wall. Harry realised the first thuds were over the corridor and the next was next door. They didn't know which room they were in so were trying them all. There were only four rooms that side of the staircase, so they didn't do badly, he smiled to himself at his sarcasm. His mind was on overload. Why did it matter which door they got open first, they were in his room. He took a very quiet deep breath and held Lilli a little tighter. Lilli squeezed his arm and put her other hand over Paris's mouth. She was so scared she wasn't sure whether to scream or giggle, but decided silence was the answer.

Harry could see two sets of large feet walking over to Lilli's bed, and on to the bathroom. The men started talking in a foreign language that Harry didn't recognise, but thought it had to be either Russian or Estonian. Harry strained his ears; he was sure he could hear a siren coming from the window. It was, and the thugs had heard it too. Harry could tell because their conversation was getting more agitated and they ran to the window to see if the police car was stopping outside the hotel. The siren was very loud and instead of fading into the distance it stayed outside. Harry's heart was beating quickly. He hoped they couldn't hear it. He held Lilli as tightly as he could without hurting her. The two men shouted at each other and ran to the bedroom door. They were gone in seconds.

"Are you okay Lilli?" Harry kept it to a whisper, just in case. Lilli nodded, luckily Harry could feel her head going up and down. "You and Paris are brilliant at this game. I think we've all won a box of sweeties each, don't you Lilli?" He felt Lilli's head move up and down again. He was so thankful that she obeyed his every word. She had obviously done this before, he thought, how very sad for her. He daren't tell her she could talk until he was absolutely sure they weren't coming back.

"Monsieur 'art, are you okay?" A woman's voice called from the door. Harry recognised it as the receptionists. Harry and Lilli managed to wriggle out from under the bed.

"Yes, thank you Madam. Did the police catch the intruders?" The receptionist was helping Lilli up." She shook her head.

"Non, Monsieur. They ran out and knocked the policeman to the ground and ran off. By the time 'e got back on his feet they were gone." Harry's stress level had started rising.

"Right Lilli, go and put all your things in your rucksack. We will have to get back in the car." He was trying not to frighten Lilli, but they needed to get far away from Bordeaux.

"Pardon Monsieur 'art but you can't take a little girl off at this time of night. 'ow about moving to our sister 'otel, over the road? You can leave your car here until the morning. No one can get into it Monsieur, we

'ave regular security patrols with dogs".
She was selling it. Harry looked over at Lilli who had curled up on her bed with Paris. He had to make a decision that would be best for Lilli.

"Thank you, Madame. We will move over the road, if that's okay." The receptionist smiled and nodded. She turned to leave.

"I will phone our other 'otel and make a reservation for you. I will send Walter up for your luggage. Come down when you're ready." She took a look at the damage to the door. "You were lucky they did not find you Monsieur." She walked off shaking her head.
Harry went over to put Lilli's things into her rucksack and grabbed their toiletries from the bathroom. As he came out his heart skipped a beat. Standing at the open doorway was a very stunned looking policeman.

"Monsieur…" He looked at his notebook. "art?" Harry nodded. Who else would he be? He didn't have a great deal of confidence in this local French bobby.

"Could you tell me who those men were and why they were 'ere?" Harry had to think very quickly. He didn't want to reveal too much so decided to go down the innocent route.

"I haven't a clue. The only thing I can think of is that they were after my car keys." He took them out of his pocket and showed them to the policeman. He looked at them puzzled. Then his eyebrows went up and he had solved the case all by himself.

"Ah, I understand Monsieur. It is an Aston Martin, Oui? They were probably going to take it to sell. I expect it is worth quite a lot, n'est ce pas?" Harry nodded his head and smiled. "Well Monsieur they will not get it.

We will keep an eye on the car park throughout the night." Harry wondered if he should mention that it was being guarded by dogs. He thought the poor policeman had been through enough for one day. He could see a bruise developing on his cheek bone.

There was a knock on the open door. It was a porter having come for the luggage. Harry pushed his overnight stuff into his holdall and handed it to the lad.

"I will leave you to get on Monsieur. If you 'ave any more trouble tonight, please ring this number." He handed Harry a card. "We will come immediately. Bon nuit Monsieur." He looked again at the notebook. "'art. Au revoir." He left. Harry wondered if he was slightly concussed or if he was just in over his head as a police officer.

* * *

"I think that's the farmhouse, Marek. It's the only one next door to your sister-in-law's farm, so it must be the right one." Jakob was quite pleased with himself having found the village of Kändliku on Google Maps on his new phone. Marek's old Mercedes did not have sat nav. He'd hoped Erik would get him a new car, since he did so much running around for him, but Erik was mean. Even worse now his wife and daughter were missing, to the point that Marek and Jakob were trying to keep a low profile. But they got a call from Erik earlier that day, and so they had driven for three hours across Estonia to get to this place.

"We'll give it a try. Anything to find Katarina and Lilliana just to get Erik off our backs. Have you got your story straight? You're from Rapla Parish okay Jakob?" Jakob nodded. Marek knew Jakob had more confidence than he had to pull off a role of a government employee.

Marek's ears were still ringing from the earlier phone call from his brother.

It was a long shot, but Erik had told him that he thought if they could find Katarina's cousin Maria, they may find his wife and daughter. Maria and Katarina were still in contact, Eric had remembered, from an innocent conversation with Lilli a while ago.

They pulled up at the top of a path leading to the farmhouse. They wanted to see the lie of the land before they were seen.

As the two approached the farmhouse there was a woman washing her windows on a rickety pair of steps. Marek saw his opportunity and ran over to keep the steps still for her.

"You must be careful, madam. These steps are very dangerous. Here, let me do that for you." He helped her down and took a dry cloth up the steps and wiped the moisture of the windows until they shined. Jakob could see the woman was a little overwhelmed by the intrusion and immediately went into character.

"Good morning madam. We are from Rapla Parish and want to know whether you need help for the harvest later this year. We have men needing jobs and we will pay them for you. It is an initiative sent from the government to make people work for their benefits. You have probably heard about it on the news?" Anna shook her head but wanted to hear more. The farm was getting too much for her and her husband Nikoli, so help would be good. Jakob could see he was reeling her in.

"Shall we go inside and have a coffee and discuss how many people you can use and for how long you would need them?" Anna nodded and beckoned them

both to follow her inside. Jakob winked at Marek and they followed the woman into her sitting room/kitchen.
Marek got out a notebook and pencil to look more official.

"So, you're Anna Olesk?" Anna nodded. "And your husband is Nikoli Olesk?" Anna nodded again. "And you have a daughter Maria Olesk?" Anna shook her head.

"No, Maria is now Maria Kõiv. She married Karl Kõiv from Märjamaa Parish." As she was talking, she had put the coffee pot on the stove and had got out three cups. Jakob looked out of the window to see if Nikoli was about.

"Your husband still works on the farm?" He saw no sign of him. Anna nodded.

"He works too hard. I keep telling him that he must take it easy, but he is stubborn. He does need help." She placed the coffee cups on the central table and the men sat down.

"Do Maria and Karl help you on the farm?" Marek had to be patient and ask the questions as if he was trying to help the woman and her husband.

"No. They are living in Spain. They have their own farm there. We have only each other here to work this farm." Marek thought it time to hook her into the charade before Nikoli decided he wanted a cup of coffee.

"Well I think you qualify for help." He turned to Jakob who nodded his head in agreement. Anna looked so pleased that she clapped her hands. "Of course, it will not be right away. But I can assure you nearer harvest time you should have plenty of helpers. I must also make sure you don't worry by reiterating that the government pay them, so you do not have to give them anything except perhaps a meal?" Anna thought that a very wonderful

proposition and immediately agreed to their terms.
Jakob got up and took a photo off a sideboard.

"What a beautiful young lady. Is this your daughter?" Anna nodded with a smile. "I can see the likeness." Anna was being flattered but loved every minute of it. "You say she and her husband have a farm in Spain. That must be challenging with the heat there. What do they grow?" Marek looked at Jakob with respect. Very cleverly done, he thought.

"They keep organic cattle. Their farm is very well known in their area of Girona as they supply organic milk and cheese to the local community." She was so proud of their achievement, but she missed her daughter dearly. She had hoped one day that they would come back and take over the Olesk Farm. But these two men had saved the year's harvest so she'd wait to see what the next year would bring and be happy with that.

Marek and Jakob thanked her for the coffee and told her that someone from the parish would be contacting her in the next few weeks. Anna shut the farm door behind them all and rushed off to find her husband with the good news.

"I better ring Erik before we start back to our village. England is two hours behind us he has ample time to get his Russian minions on the job. He'll be waiting for our call and for once I don't mind obliging him as we have good news. Well done Jacob." They high-fived each other.

"So, Bogdan and Yegor need to look for an organic farm near Girona in the name of Kõiv. Good luck in finding Lilliana, brother." Erik had to get hold of Bogdan and sort the mess out.

"Good work Marek. I will tell you the outcome when I have given Bogdan and Yegor the information. They are on a mission to a hotel in France where Lilliana's iPad last pinged, this evening. I'm not expecting miracles with those two. Surely even they can't cock-up the job of finding my Lilliana with the address in front of them. We have the upper hand with no suspicions from the Kõiv family." But even as Erik said it, he knew that both the Russians had more muscle than brain. He kept them on because they were cheap and didn't mind carrying out any task thrown at them. The one advantage of their lacking in brainpower was that they couldn't see the consequences of their actions before any assignment.

* * *

Having failed at their task, Bogdan and Yegor were worried.

"I'll ring the boss and get it out of the way." Bogdan got out his phone. Yegor decided to go into the tabac they had parked outside so he didn't hear his boss's rage. He needed cigarettes anyway. He signalled to Bogdan if he needed anything from the shop. "Earplugs if they've got them." Yegor turned away grinning. By the time he got back Bogdan had finished his call and was looking to see where they had to go next.

"You okay?" Yegor lit his cigarette and offered one to Bogdan.

"I told him we must have only just missed Lilli at the hotel. I said we checked all the rooms we had time to do, but there was no sign of Lilli. I said we sent a policeman flying, which made him calm down a bit. He's told us to go to Girona and look for an organic farm."

"What the fuck is an organic farm?" Yegor had heard of it but didn't know what the difference was to a normal farm.

"How the hell do I know. But that's what we're looking for." Bogdan was on the internet looking for a shop in Girona selling local organic products that would be open in the early hours. But most of the shops were shut by 9.00 pm. He couldn't believe his luck. "I've found a petrol station that sells organic stuff that's open 24hrs." He put it into the sat nav. "Right, let's get going." He filled Yegor in on the rest of his phone call with the boss. "Erik told us to go and find out if Katarina was at the farm with Lilliana. If they weren't there we have to find out where they were. If that wasn't possible then we have to make sure there was no farm for Katarina to hide in." Yegor's eyes flashed, he did love a good fire. "Erik isn't thinking straight. He sounded drunk. He reckons Katarina would go home if she had nowhere else to go with Lilli." He shook his head. He would hate to be Katarina when Erik finally catches up with her. Bogdan shivered at the thought. But that wasn't his problem, he needed to get this job done, or he'd be dead before he had time to feel sorry for anyone.

They arrived at the petrol station just after 2.30 a.m., but the door was locked, and the pumps were on an automatic card only system. Bogdan looked in to see if anyone was about. Yegor had gone around the back. Suddenly Bogdan saw movement in the shop. He banged on the door to get their attention. It was dark, but the security lights were just bright enough to make out it was a male form. As the person got closer to the door Bogdan saw it was Yegor eating some kind of pastry.

"Open the fucking door you moron." Yegor laughed. He put the whole pastry in his mouth and checked the door. He shook his head at Bogdan and pointed to the rear of the shop. Bogdan walked around and found a door at the back wide open. His first thought was how handy Yegor was. He went in and tried to find some light switches. Yegor had been looking through the stock of milk cartons with his phone torch and came across one with the farm name on.

"Hey, Bogdan, are we looking for an Estonian name?" Bogdan thought hard then remembered the name Erik gave him.

"Yeh, Kõiv." Bogdan had given up looking for the light switches and joined Yegor. "Look. This carton has the Koiv Farm written as the supplier. There's an address too." Bogdan took it off Yegor, who grunted and picked up another one, opened it and drunk it.

"Come on, let's get out of here before an alarm goes off." Bogdan was already out of the shop. They ran back to the car and got in just as a blue light flashed onto the forecourt.

A policeman got out shining a torch at them. "I knew it. I bet it had a silent alarm." Bogdan started the car and revved up towards the policeman. Yegor was laughing as the policeman jumped out of the way. Suddenly there was gunfire. Both men kept their heads down and Bogdan drove off into the darkness. They needed to look for the address, but the more pressing problem was the policeman who would be behind them shortly. Bogdan noticed a round-a- bout ahead. He knew blue lights would be catching up behind and had to think quickly. He saw four roads off and decided to take the third.

The policeman wouldn't have seen which one he had

taken so he turned off his lights and drove into a driveway a few houses down from the turn-off. Yegor was about to get out.

"Stay in the car you idiot. You'll put the light on." Yegor took his hand off the door handle.

"How long do we have to wait?" Yegor wished he hadn't drunk a whole carton of milk, he was bursting.

"I don't know." Bogdan opened his window. There wasn't a sound. "Give me the carton. I need to see which way we have to go." Yegor got his phone out and put the torch app on with his hand over it. Bogdan could just make out the farm address and put it into the Sat nav. *"Continue along the road- turn left at the junction into Carrer Santa Margarita."* The sat nav told him.

"That was bloody lucky." Bogdan turned on the engine and reversed out of the random driveway. Yegor realised that Bogdan was not going to stop so he made use of the empty carton. Bogdan looked over at him.
"You peasant." He was not amused but Yegor was too relieved to care. Bogdan drove straight to the farmhouse in a small village called Vilobí d'Onyar, about a quarter of an hour from the centre of Girona.

Bogdan and Yegor knocked at the farmhouse door just after 3 o'clock in the morning, when most people were at their least defensive. A man eventually answered the door, rubbing his eyes.

"Sorry to bother you mate. Are you Karl Kõiv?" Karl had to get up in two hours, to help milk the cows. He was not happy having been woken earlier than necessary. Aggressively, taking advantage of the half-asleep farmer, they pushed him in and asked him where Maria was.

He was wide awake by the time he had been thrown into his armchair. All his senses were heightened, and he needed to warn Maria to escape. He assumed they were burglars, but they seemed too aggressive to be after money. Suddenly it all added up. These men were looking for Katarina and Lilliana. They must be working for Erik Eskola. Karl was scared for the safety of his wife. In the loudest possible voice he could summon, he shouted.

"I do not know a Maria. I think you have the wrong house." The bluff did not work. Bogdan thrust his fist into Karl's face.

"We'll try again. Where is Maria?" Karl looked at Bogdan and saw a malicious smile on his face. He was enjoying the assault. Once again, through what he assumed was a broken jaw, he managed to shout a warning to Maria.

"No Maria lives here. You have the wrong…." Before he could finish his sentence, another violent round of punches were rained on his face. This time he was out cold.

Maria heard Karl shouting loudly that he didn't know a Maria. Having spoken to her cousin Katarina the day before, she realised he was warning her to escape. She then heard the unmistakable sound of a fist onto flesh. That was her husband they were beating up. She was shocked into stillness, her hand in her mouth to stop her crying out to her husband. Again, she heard Karl denying any knowledge of a Maria living in that house. She shook herself out of her daze and at last took heed from her husband's warning. She had to get help. She had no chance against at least two attackers that she could hear were downstairs. The only way to help Karl was to get herself out of the house and raise the alarm. She grabbed her dressing gown from the inside of the bedroom door and put on her slippers. Quietly she pushed the already open window wide enough for her to climb out. Carefully and as quietly as she could, she managed to get one leg out onto the roof of the single storied kitchen and eased the other leg to join it. It was dark with only the moon to light her way. That was helpful for not being seen, but not a lot of use for her to see where she was going.

She decided the safe way would be on all fours, so crouching she managed to get to the end of the kitchen roof and could feel the small porch at the back door. Holding on to the gutter she managed to swing herself over onto the angled porch roof and slid down, stopping at the edge with another gutter to hang on to.

She lowered herself down to the ground with her hands holding on to the metal gutter and praying it took her weight. She was a small woman, but she knew how long that gutter had been there. With a small drop to the ground she was safely down. Suddenly she realised, in her rush, she hadn't taken her phone with her.

There was no way she would make it back up. She had to think. Juan or Jorges had to be in the stable block. One of them would have had to be on duty for the early milking. She ran as fast as she could past the orange grove towards the staff quarters. It wasn't as difficult as she thought it would be in the moonlight as the security lights were on in the milking shed and they lit the way for her. She arrived panting at the farmhand cottages. She banged on the door, she thought she was far enough away from the main farmhouse that she wouldn't be heard. There was no answer. She just wanted to cry.

As she began to think there was no way she was going to

get any help, she heard the sound of a bolt from the other side of the door. It opened and Juan was standing on the step, dishevelled and half asleep.

"Maria, what is the matter?" Maria pushed him into the cottage and shut the door.

"It is Karl. Some men are beating him up. We must get help Juan. Phone the Policía. Quick, please be quick." Juan knew it was not the time to ask who was beating his boss up. Questions could come later. He ran up to his bedroom and grabbed his mobile. He telephoned the Policía and told them the address and that his boss was being beaten up by unknown assailants, so they probably would need paramedics too. By the time he got back downstairs, Maria had gone.

Maria couldn't wait. She had done all she could by alerting the emergency services and hoping they would arrive quickly. She needed to see what she could do for Karl. The men could have gone so she wanted to check. The nearer she got to the farmhouse, the obvious it was that the men hadn't left. She crept around to the front of the house and hid in the bushes near the road and waited for the help to arrive.

Yegor checked up the stairs of the one bedroomed farm cottage. He came down shaking his head. Bogdan held Karl, who had regained consciousness, while Yegor took his turn throwing punches on him, asking between each strike where Maria was. Karl, again, lost consciousness.

"You moron. How are we going to get information out of him now? He's bloody dead." Yegor checked Karl's pulse.

"No, he isn't." Bogdan shook his head.

"We can't wait all night for him to come around. He wouldn't tell us anyway. Time to carry out the boss's next instruction." Bogdan, in control as usual, went outside to find something that would burn down the farmhouse. He shouted from the front door.

"Come on and help me, you cretin. I don't think this guy will be running after us." Yegor checked Karl again, but with no sign of life he left him slumped in the chair and ran out to help his brother. Yegor found a petrol chain saw. Bogdan had gone around to the back and saw a gas canister, in a wooden lean-to, attached to the kitchen stove through the back wall. He pulled the hose off its jubilee clip attaching it to the stove and tugged it through the wall into the lean-to. He then poured some of the petrol from the chain saw, he'd grabbed from Yegor, around the canister. He trickled the remainder of the petrol along a pathway from the lean-to until he thought he'd gone far enough for them to get away before the explosion.

Leaving Karl unconscious, he set the trail of petrol alight with his lighter and they both ran back to the road and into the Mercedes and sped off sending gravel flying.

From the front of the cottage Maria could see them driving away, and worried about her husband, she rushed into the cottage at the same time as the explosion ripped through the building. Maria ended up near the road. There was no sign of Karl. He hadn't got out.

The Carro de Bomberos arrived shortly after the Policía and the Ambulancia. Maria was drifting in and out of consciousness. She saw Juan talking to the Policía. He was distressed, and the officer had his hand on his shoulder. She followed his gaze and saw the Paramédico shake his head over the blackened body they had just removed from the building. Maria knew in her heart that Karl was gone. She could hear herself wailing but could do nothing to mute the sound. The Paramédico put a mask over her nose and she went into a dark, quiet, peaceful place.

***

Harry must have gone straight off to sleep in his new bed, because the next thing he heard was his alarm.

He turned off the alarm and popped into the bathroom, carefully passing the sleeping Lilli. When he was dressed he needed to make everything sound normal for Lilli after the trauma of the night before. He woke her up.

"We should be seeing your mummy today; you better get up so we can have some breakfast before we get going again." Harry felt a little mean but telling Lilli the truth was probably not the way to go with a child, he'd learnt that from the day before. The truth being he hadn't a clue where Katarina was, or how long it would take her to travel down to Spain.

Harry watched as Lilli went into the bathroom to dress herself and clean her teeth. She was such a good girl, he sighed to himself. He knew it could have been a lot worse if Lilli had been a little brat. They both went down to breakfast in their new hotel. The hotel staff couldn't have been more helpful, piling their table baskets with as much as they could fit in. One of the things that Harry liked about travelling in France was the breakfasts. Having tucked into croissants with homemade strawberry jam, pain au chocolat, fresh fruit salad and topped off with local yoghurt, they were ready to get going.

They stood at the reception desk with their bags and

waited for the receptionist so Harry could settle the bill.
A Large man came out of the office behind reception, followed by a policeman.

"Ah, Monsieur 'art. Please accept our apologies for the..." He coughed to work out how to say that wouldn't admit fault. He didn't want a lawsuit. "Inconvenience of the evening. Our 'otel offer you and your daughter your room and breakfast on the 'ouse." He did a little bow. Harry managed to keep a straight face.

"Well, that is extremely kind of you. Come on Lilli, let's get to the car and off to Spain." Lilli looked up at Harry.

"Okay Daddy." With that she managed to screw her face up and attempt a wink. Harry had to bite his lip or he would have laughed. They turned to leave but were stopped by the policeman.

"Monsieur? Pardon, but just to tell you that we watched your magnificent car all evening and nobody came near it." The policeman smiled.

"Thank you and all your colleagues, Monsieur. We will be off now. Au revoir." Harry practically pushed Lilli out of the hotel in case the policeman wanted to come with them for a little test drive.

Harry had no choice but to get going. He checked the road up and down, with no sign of the Mercedes. He drove slowly up to the barrier, it opened for him and they were off.

Harry was going to split the journey again and planned two and a half hours driving in the morning probably lunching just outside Toulouse, using the services café, saving time by not getting off the motorway, putting them in Girona by teatime.

"Are we there yet, Harry?" Harry looked at the sat nav to see exactly where they were and was pleasantly surprised to see they were further on than he had expected.

"We will be having lunch in about ten minutes Lilli." Lilli seemed happy with his answer and stretched to look out of the window. "Harry, we're by the sea again." Harry just nodded. He had to concentrate as the sat nav was showing him the slip road off the motorway was just ahead.

He hoped the cameras had not clocked some of the speeds he had driven, but he blamed the car. Keeping to the French speed limit almost stalled a car of that calibre. He enjoyed the German roads best, they had sensible speed limits, but he was sure the medical profession would not agree. Lilli had been a little fidgety and annoying with her questions about where her mother was and how long until they stop and were they nearly there yet! Harry had to remember that Lilli was a six-year-old little girl who had been thrust into his car and just wanted to know where her mummy was. So did Harry! His patience was being tested whenever Lilli was bored, but he'd managed to keep her occupied by a mammoth game of I Spy and a classic alphabet game from his younger days travelling with his parents, 'I packed my bag and in it I put a…' They had both been laughing most of the way through the car games and time had passed quickly.

They arrived in Narbonne for lunch and had less than two hours to the end destination. Harry decided to treat Lilli, as it may be the last time he got the chance. He left the motorway so they could have lunch on the quay and

FOR THE LOVE OF LILLI

Harry introduced Lilli to Moules-frites. To his surprise she loved the mussels. He wasn't sure children were allowed them but then realised that French children had probably been eating them all their lives. He was enjoying Lilli's company, thankful that she took after her mother not her father.

For someone he had only just met, he had a lot of respect for Katarina. To put her own life in danger for the sake of her child was incredible.

He understood why, having been with Lilli for only a couple of days - but would he do the same? He looked over at the little girl enjoying her ice cream dessert and he realised he probably would. He kept looking out of the window checking to see if the black Mercedes was about. He knew he was in just as much danger having seen the two thugs. He had to keep alert as Katarina had entrusted the most important thing in her world to him, Lilli.

After lunch they decided to take a wander around the marina. He pointed out all the boats and the countries they were from. Lilli said she'd love to go on a boat one day, but Harry told her there wasn't time that day.

"Will there be time tomorrow Harry?" Harry didn't have a clue what tomorrow held for Lilli. He shook his head and noticed her bottom lip quivering. He couldn't tell Lilli the truth so had to stall her.

"We'll see Lilli, we'll see." Lilli smiled. Harry felt guilty and needed to explain to Lilli. "We may not be near water tomorrow though, but one day Lilli I promise to take you out on a boat and I never break my promises." She squealed with delight. Harry had always wanted a boat of his own, perhaps not the size of his boss's, but a Sunseeker would be his dream boat.

His grandmother, God rest her soul, always told him that without dreams there were no goals. It was only when he left the affluence of his home that he realised what she had been talking about. They set off on the last part of their adventure, as Harry had called it to Lilli.

He put the address that Katarina had given him into the sat nav, checked all around, and with no sign of a black Mercedes with English plates, off they went.

Half an hour into their last leg they reached the border into Spain at the Catalan frontier. The passport security cubicles were empty, but there were French and Spanish police on either side. Harry realised that although border control had been abolished in 2010 the governments of both countries were aware of the increased threat from terrorism. The police were evident, but not confrontational. Or so he thought…

As he drove the car through one of the empty border posts two Spanish policemen decided to do a spot check on the yellow Aston Martin. One of the border policemen waved for Harry to slow down, while the other walked around to Lilli's side of the car. Lilli was engrossed in a computer game and hadn't noticed the policeman staring in at her. Harry stopped the car as the first man had put his hand up. Harry opened his window and the policeman spoke to him in English.

"You have a nice car señor. Is it yours?" Harry swallowed hard. The car details didn't worry him. The paperwork was up to date in the glove compartment. It was the other officer staring at Lilli that made him nervous.

"No, it is my boss's. I'm delivering it to him." Harry reached over to the glove compartment and took out the insurance documents, his driving licence, and a legal document in English, French and Spanish from Patrick giving Harry permission to drive the vehicle, which Patrick had put in all his cars for such an eventuality. The policeman glanced at the documentation, without actually reading any. After a few minutes his colleague joined him. They spoke for a moment without Harry being able to make out what they were saying. The first officer turned back to Harry.

"The child is yours?" Lilli could see Harry was having a bit of trouble talking to the men in uniform, so she decided to speak for herself.

"Hello, my name is Lilliana, and this is my uncle, Harry. We're going to see my Mummy in a minute." She smiled at the policemen. The little girl impressed Harry as she sounded so confident, but he had to take control.

"I have our passports if you would like to see them." He knew he had Katarina's letters, but didn't want to make a big deal out of the situation. He'd wait to be asked. The first policeman smiled.

"So señor, what speed can you get out of this clásico car?" Harry wondered if it was a trick question. He racked his brain for the highest speed limit on Spanish roads. He knew it had recently gone up by 10 kilometres per hour to 130 on motorways, although less in wet weather.

"On the motorways, in dry weather, I can reach 130 kilometres per hour." The policemen laughed.

"Bueno, señor. Now tell us the speed you have actually got the car up to, let's say, on a private road." They had guessed Harry's response was erring on the side of caution. It suddenly dawned on Harry that these men were not bothered about Lilli, nor who the car belonged to, just about the actual car. Harry smiled at them.

"On a track day I have actually managed to get 150 per hour out of her, which is just over," he looks down at the speedo, "240 kilometres per hour. Probably could have got at least 175 miles an hour out of it, but it's not my car and I didn't want to break it." The policemen were laughing hard and nodding. The first policeman waved him on. Harry started the car and revved it a few times for them. He then put his foot down and drove off, noting in the rear-view mirror that he had made two policemen's day. One had his phone out and Harry could guarantee he had it on video mode to show his colleagues later. The sound alone would be phenomenal if you were not used to it. Harry glanced over to Lilli, who was smiling back at him.

"You were very good talking to those men, Lilli. Well done." Lilli was still smiling. "What's so funny?"

"I think that those men in uniform like yellow too Harry." Harry couldn't help loving that little girl. He smiled at her as his heartbeat had almost got back to normal and envied the innocence of a six-year-old.

An hour later the sat nav lady told him to turn into the next road and he had reached his destination.

"Harry, are we there yet?" Lilli was beginning to understand that when the lady said that it normally meant they could stop.

"Just around this next corner, Lilli, and we should be at Maria's." Harry turned the corner and immediately spotted the fire engines. The firemen seemed to be dampening down the remains of a building that must have been the farmhouse. He pulled up a little way from the scene and told Lilli to stay in the car. He went over to a man, holding a dog on a lead, watching the firemen.

"Excuse me, do you speak English?" The man shook his head.

"Anglès? No." The man hadn't taken his eyes off the smouldering ruin.

Harry dug deep into his memory of school Spanish classes. "Dónde está la señora de la casa?" Luckily, he understood.

"Maria està a l'hospital. Karl ha mort." He shook his head and looked at the ground. Harry knew what he meant, but it wasn't the Spanish he'd learnt at school. He needed to find out more.

"Hablas español? Maria, gravemente?" Harry needed him to speak Spanish. He couldn't remember how to ask 'how bad is she?'

"Dolent molt dolent." He shook his head again. With pride he looked up at Harry and said, "Parlo Català," and walked his dog on down the road. Harry had then realised he had offended the man. He was a local, so he must have been speaking Catalan not Spanish. That was why Harry couldn't understand what he had said.

Maria was in the hospital and Harry thought he said bad, very bad and Karl was dead. That must be Maria's husband he realised. Katarina was wrong, Erik did know she had a cousin in Spain after all. The reality of what was happening was finally sinking in. He was out of sight of his car and sunk to the ground with his head in his hands. He wanted to get back in the car and just keep driving away from the nightmare. But the fact kicked in that he was all Lilli had in the world at that moment. After a few deep breaths he got up and walked slowly back to the car.

The first thing he knew was that he had to get the car away from the area. If the murdering heavies had realised they had lost the tracking source, then the Aston Martin was the only common denominator in the whole chain of events from the ferry. Not a car to blend in very well he knew.
He was right; Bogdan and Yegor had been told by Erik to keep a distance but watch if anyone stopped there for a period of time and make a note of the car.

"You better phone Erik, that Yellow Aston Martin was on the ferry. I bet that guy over there knows something about his daughter." Bogdan was pointing at Harry who was walking back to the car. He was pleased they had taken Erik's advice and had sat in view of the remains of the farmhouse.

"Your turn to phone the boss," Bogdan smirked.
Yegor phoned Erik.

"Hey Boss, you were right. We have our eyes on a yellow Aston Martin. It has Monaco number plates, but we aren't near enough to make it out." Yegor shut his eyes and he'd his breath.

"Okay. You two follow the Aston Martin. Don't lose it." A chill ran through Yegor's body. He knew what would happen to them both if they messed it up again, just by the tone of Erik's last instruction.

* * *

Harry needed to get out of Spain. He'd head for Monaco and get rid of the car. If he could get hold of Emm he and Lilli could stay at her mother's place in Nice, Caroline willing, until things had quietened down. He'd try ringing her when Lilli was asleep as there was no need to frighten her. He had to tell Katarina too, that whatever she did she mustn't visit her cousin. He worried that the Russians were probably waiting at the hospital for her. He rang the number the text message had come from but got a Spanish woman saying "El número que está intentando no está disponible". That worried Harry. Did it mean the phone was broken? Did it mean it was switched off? He'd leave a text for her to ring him and hope she was just out of signal, nothing worse.

"Katarina, do not go to your cousin. Ring me as soon as you can. Harry." He wanted to warn her, but not leave any incriminating evidence on the phone. He could have given her the address in Monaco, but if the phone got into the wrong hands, he would be jeopardising Lilli's safety. He'd ring her later and perhaps she could speak to Lilli. He got back in the car and started the engine. Lilli looked up from a game she had been playing. He gave her a smile and turned the car around and drove off, away from the devastation of what looked like was once a charming farmhouse. Surprisingly Lilli didn't talk. He couldn't understand why she wasn't bombarding him with questions, especially about the fire engines, and where her mother and aunt were. He preferred it when she was chatting away. He knew she had seen the burnt-out building, but was it a child's coping mechanism, her own survival, that stopped her asking anything? He wondered if she was in shock and didn't want to know the answer. How odd that in such a short time he seemed to be feeling fatherly towards Lilli.

CHAPTER 6

Katarina had made good progress. The most difficult part of the journey for her was finding a lift from the ferry so she didn't have to walk off the disembarkation ramp and be found straight away. After writing two notes, in the light of the cabin's shower room, she left Harry and Lilli asleep and made her way to the drivers' lounge to ask if anyone was going to Spain, and if so, could they give her a lift. There were a couple going to Portugal and a few to Spain but none of them were insured to take passengers. She was about to leave with tears in her eyes when a concerned Scotsman, not surprisingly called Jock by his fellow drivers, stopped her. Although they called him Jock, his real name was Robbie, he told her. He got her a coffee and sat her down and asked her exactly where she had to go and why. As quickly as she could she explained that she was meeting her daughter in Girona and had to stay off the main transport routes as her alcoholic, cruel husband had sent out men to get her and take them both home. Robbie nodded his head in understanding and didn't judge. His own father drank and Robbie used to get the brunt of his rage.

"They will be watching the coach and rail links so I thought if I could get into a lorry I'd be safer." She told him that a kind man was taking Lilliana separately down in his car.

"He is called Harry and is very good with Lilliana.

The problem is that his car has only two seats. I want Lilliana to be safe, so it is better that I travel alone."

"Is Harry a nice man?" Robbie wondered if it would be better to take Lilliana and her mother together. Katarina nodded.

"I'm a good reader of people and I would say that Harry is a decent man. I already know you are." Robbie was flattered.

"Well, it's your lucky day. I have to deliver furniture to a villa in Murcia for a couple retiring down there from Salisbury. I'm licenced to take them as passengers, but they realised they'd need their car down there, and as they are taking their dog too, they decided to drive down themselves." He spread his map out on the table. "If I change my route from Bordeaux following the east coast instead of going through Madrid, I could stop and drop you off in Girona. Unfortunately, it would have to be at the services, but you should easily get a lift into town from there." She looked so pleased. He calculated that it would only take an hour or two longer, but he had three days to make it down to Murcia.

He couldn't unload until the family got there, they had the keys, so had plenty of time free. She was so grateful. She grabbed a baguette, spread it with honey and wrapped it up to eat once they were on their way. Just in case she was being watched on board, Robbie put his Hi-Viz jacket on her which swamped her, but not even her own mother would recognise her in it. She took the cap out of her holdall that Harry had given her, and it finished off her ensemble perfectly.

"No offence, but you look like a wee daffodil growing in Seaton Park in Aberdeen. Come on, we can go down to the garage deck before the car drivers are allowed." Katarina wasn't offended in the least. In fact, it was the first time she felt positive about getting away. She mustn't drop her guard though. Going down to the garage deck before the car drivers was a good idea and Robbie led the way taking her to his furniture removal lorry that had been outside on a ramp. He helped her up into the cabin, it was very high, and she settled down and looked around it while Robbie checked the outside of the lorry for sea damage. It was like a little home from home. There was a curtain behind her and as she pulled it back slightly she could see a bed. There were photos everywhere of two little girls and a woman. There were a few with just the girls and a soppy looking black Labrador. Above the bed was a big picture of Robbie cuddling, she assumed, his wife, with the two girls entwined around them and the Labrador at their feet. They were all laughing, the dog seemed to be smiling too. He was obviously a family man. She knew she had judged him well.

"Are you comfortable? It's a long journey to be sitting down so you need to have everything in the right place. Can you see out okay? I can put your seat up if you like." Robbie slammed his cab door and fiddled with some instruments.

"No, I'm fine thank you." She could just see out, but that worked in her favour, as it would look like Robbie was on his own. "I'm sorry to be a bother, but is there anywhere on route to buy a cheap pay-as-you-go mobile phone? I had to throw mine into the sea because I knew Erik could track it and I must keep in contact with Harry to check on Lilli." Robbie knew that the services around Nantes on the way down to Bordeaux would be one of the biggest en route and had shops. He hoped she would find one there.

He had to stay on the motorways and would rather not go into towns with his lorry. Katarina understood, and she managed to get a phone when they stopped for coffee at Nantes services as he predicted.

They chatted most of the way. Robbie enjoyed the company and Katarina enjoyed Robbie's sense of humour and friendliness. She had a little trouble with his accent, but Robbie found it funny and taught her a few Scottish phrases to help her understand the dialects. She had him in stitches when she was rolling her r's during the phrase 'round the rugged rock the ragged rascal ran'. Katarina had almost forgotten her worries, almost, but not enough to relax. Once she was back with her little girl and they were safe in a new life then they could enjoy living again, like normal people, like Harry and Robbie. She was only twenty-three and deserved a better life. She kept looking at the photos around Robbie's cabin and envied his wife, Hannah, that Robbie couldn't stop talking about.

"How long do you think it will take us to get to Girona?" She was anxious to see Lilliana. Robbie had to explain to Katarina that due to his tachograph he had to stop frequently. Every four and a half hours of driving meant he had to stop for forty-five minutes, and he was only allowed to drive for nine hours in any one day.

"I will have to stop overnight at Bordeaux. We should be there around bedtime. There is a Formule 1 Hotel at the services, so I'll park there, and you can get a room for the night." He noticed Katarina looked worried. Robbie wanted to pay for her but didn't want to hurt her pride.

"I'm happy to stay in here tonight." Robbie knew

she was lying. He had to word his next sentence perfectly.

"Again, it's your lucky day. I have an expense account. I run all accommodation through expenses, so the clients pay for my room. You can have it with pleasure. I normally kip down in the cabin; it reminds me of home on long-haul trips." Katarina looked at him. He was lying, she knew it, but it would be rude for her not to accept his generosity and she had spent all her money on a phone.

"Okay, thank you Robbie." She smiled at him and he blushed. He had a mop of red hair, and his skin was pale and freckly. There was no hiding the blushing!
Frequently en-route Katarina tried to ring
Harry to see how Lilli was, but as Robbie pointed out, the French motorways went through the countryside of France more often than towns, so the signal for mobile phones was bad.
It was getting late and she knew they would not be stopping for a while, but she wanted to catch Harry while Lilli was awake. She took out her new phone and saw a few bars on the display. She hoped it was enough to connect. They were on the outskirts of Bordeaux, so the signal would be getting stronger eventually, but she didn't want to wait. She entered his phone number into her empty address book under 'Harry' and pressed call. After a few rings it was being diverted into his voice mail, so she hung-up. She looked at her watch and thought they most probably would be eating somewhere, and his phone may have been in his pocket, so he wouldn't hear the ring. More scenarios were playing in her head, but Robbie had been watching Katarina's facial expressions and wanted to reassure her.

"I bet they are having a lovely meal somewhere. Why don't you text this Harry, and let him know you now have a phone?" Katarina looked up at Robbie and smiled.

"You're a mind reader. I was thinking the same." She decided to text him her cousin's address in case she couldn't get through later and also apologise for dumping Lilli off with him and for taking his money. She knew he had offered it to her, but it was very rude of her just to take it but then emergencies overrode manners. She also asked him if he would give Lilli a big cuddle and a kiss from her. She sighed and put her phone away. No more could she do. "How do you cope with not seeing your family for days at a time?" It hadn't even been twenty-four hours and Katarina's heart was breaking.

Robbie chose his words carefully. If he was honest, he didn't cope that well. He missed his family so much every time he crossed the Channel, but he spoke to them as often as he could. Luckily, he limited his periods away to no more than four days at a time and tried to be home most weekends.

"If I'm truthful I miss them every minute - I just have to compartmentalise my thoughts. If I think about them I get sad, so I'm not concentrating on my driving. I have to focus on the few days ahead of me, and then I know I'm nearer the time I'll be seeing them. Most of my trips are this way, so I know that if I leave on a Monday, I'll be home by Thursday or Friday. That means I get the whole weekend at home. Now both my girls are at school I feel I get the best of them at weekends." He thought of his little girls running to the door when he got home and smiled. He sniggered aloud. "I just remembered getting home on Friday last week and was bowled over by

Humphrey, the dog." Katarina laughed. She pictured the sight in her head.

When they arrived at the services' hotel in Bordeaux later that night, Robbie told her he'd knock on her door to get her up when he was leaving. Katarina decided it was time to try to contact Harry again. She pressed his name, but nothing happened. She looked at the top of the screen and noticed there were no bars. The signal in the middle of nowhere was rubbish. She realised they were obviously further from Bordeaux than the name of the services led one to believe. Tears were running down her cheeks, but she tried to hide them from Robbie, who had been so kind to her. She knew her problem was that she had got herself hopeful of talking to her little girl and it wasn't going to happen that night.

Robbie decided to get himself a room too. For the sake of 40€ he wanted the cab to smell better than it usually did in the morning after he had slept there all night. He paid the receptionist for them both that evening so they could leave early in the morning.

By the time he knocked on Katarina's door, the next morning, he had his hands full of croissants and paper cups of coffee. They sat on a bench behind the lorry and had breakfast.

They made good headway that day, until they got to the border of France with Spain. Unfortunately, the border patrol picked on his lorry, and a couple more with British number plates. He would understand on the way back because of migrants hiding in the lorries, but it was just the luck of the draw on the way out. The police asked for Robbie's tachograph readings. They then made him drive over the scales. Katarina got out and went over to the toilets. The longer she was out in the open the more worried she got. She could see the lorry from the doorway and stayed there until Robbie motioned to her that all was ok. The weight matched his documentation. Thankfully they did not want to search through the truck so within fifteen minutes they were off again.

"A few years ago you were rarely stopped, but because of all the problems with terrorists and migrants the police and customs have got jittery." He looked serious. "Understandably too, it was a lorry that had killed so many people in Nice." He shook his head. She totally understood the need for vigilance.

When they got to Girona it was late afternoon. Robbie pulled into the service area to fill his lorry with diesel. He helped Katarina out of the cabin.

"Thank you for everything Robbie. Hannah is a very lucky lady." She stretched up and kissed his cheek.

"No, I thank you for the company. It is normally very boring driving on my own, and I have to admit, this has been anything but boring." He smiled at her. He wanted to give her a big hug, but she may misconstrue his Scottish geniality and warmth.

"Call me gallant, old fashioned or even just chivalrous, but I'd really like to know when you're safely back with your daughter. I'll be passing this was on my way back in a day or two, so if you need me just ring." He took her phone and put in his number. "But anyway, let me know how you get on lassie. Goodbye, and take care." He gave her back her phone and squeezed her hand.

"Bye Robbie. Drive carefully." She turned and walked towards the service area shop. She didn't look back. She had to be strong. She brushed away a tear from her cheek and quickened her pace. What a good man Robbie had been, she knew she would never forget him. Robbie watched her go until she was out of sight. Life truly was a bitch at times, he thought. He wished her all the luck and happiness she deserved.

Katarina went into the services shop and tried to find a lift into town. She sat outside on a bench with a coffee in her hand when an empty taxi pulled up and the driver rushed into the shop. He came out holding a small cup of espresso and a newspaper. Katarina was desperate so she would have to make a move. She went over to the taxi driver who was sipping his coffee and reading his El País newspaper. Her Spanish language skills were limited to hello and goodbye and thank you. She'd have to hope he spoke, or at least understood English.

"Excuse me, do you speak English?" Her fingers were crossed behind her back. The taxi driver looked up and put his paper down. "Yes, a little. Can I help you?" Phew she thought and sighed with relief.

"I need to go to an address in Girona, I wondered if you could take me." She showed him the address she had typed on her phone. He looked at his watch.

"Give me five minutes and I will take you." She thanked him and waited back on the seat. He went into the café, when he'd finished his coffee, and came out a few minutes later wiping his hands on his trousers.

He beckoned her over and opened the car door for her. She gave him the address again and he drove them off the motorway via the toll.

On arriving at the farmhouse Katarina gasped as it was obvious it had burnt to the ground. The fire engines were there dampening the whole area so as to save the orange trees and the outbuildings. The taxi driver could see how distressed Katarina was and got out to talk to the firemen. He came back and said the lady of the house was at the local hospital but unfortunately the man was dead.

"They are family?" Katarina went very white and nodded. He thought she was going to faint. "Are you okay? You want to go to the hospital?" Katarina nodded again. She couldn't find words. She felt numb. He got back into the taxi and drove off to the Hospital Universitari de Girona, he'd thought it was the nearest and therefore the most obvious destination of the patient. Katarina noticed the meter going as fast as the speedometer, but she was beyond caring. The bastard must have known about her cousin living there. How did he know? She only knew it was in Girona but didn't even know the actual address until she phoned her mother. But it was obvious the fire was too much of a coincidence.

The taxi driver pulled up outside the hospital and helped Katarina out. She opened her bag and hoped she had enough left to pay him. Tears were streaming down her eyes and she was shaking. The taxi driver put his hand on hers. She looked up and he shook his head.

"Go." He said nodding his head in the direction of the front doors. "Good luck." He smiled at her and went back into his taxi. How wonderfully kind he was, Katarina was so grateful, she shouted 'gracias' to him as he pulled away. He waved his hand and drove off. She went in through the automatic doors and asked at the reception if there was a patient recently brought in, in the name of Maria Kõiv. The receptionist typed in the name and told Katarina that the lady was in intensive care. Was she a relative?

"Yes, I'm her cousin." The receptionist gave her a small plan of the hospital and showed her where the 'Intensiva Crítica y Unidades' was.

Katarina thanked her and went towards the lifts. She got in but as the door was closing a hand stopped it and pulled it open. The face staring at her furiously was Erik's. How on earth did he get there so quickly? The door shut before she had time to get out.

"Hello my love. Fancy seeing you here." Erik was taunting her. She kept quiet. If he had found Lilliana he would have been long gone. Inside she felt relief, but it would be short lived once she knew what he had in store for her. "I take it you have seen that Yegor and Bogdan had found Maria's farm?" Katarina knew it would have been the two Sokolov brothers, or as she called them the Russian Mafia. "I assumed you would want to visit your cousin in hospital, so I thought I would find you here." His voice changed and became very intimidating. "Where is my Lilliana?" Katarina honestly didn't know, so she shrugged her shoulders and shook her head. It enraged Erik to the point that she was aware of a sharp pain, then nothing else, just oblivion.

With Bogdan and Yegor following the Aston Martin, Erik had decided to wait at the hospital in case Katarina risked visiting her cousin, and it had paid off. Erik had managed to knock Katarina out between the second and third floor. The lift opened on the third floor and he spotted a nurse in the corridor. He shouted urgently as the nurse walked by.

"Help, please. We need a wheelchair." He jammed his foot in the lift, so it didn't shut. The nurse rushed into a side room and wheeled one out for him. Thank goodness she spoke English. His Spanish was nonexistent apart from the obvious pleasantries.

"Do you need any help señor?" The nurse went to pick Katarina up.

"No, thank you, she has just fainted." He needed the nurse to keep her distance so she didn't see the wound on Katarina's head was bleeding. "I just need to get her outside for some fresh air. Thank you." He pulled the wheelchair into the lift and pressed the ground floor button. The nurse was too busy to give it another thought. He managed to pull Katarina onto the chair while the lift went down and wheeled her out into the car park and to the rental car. He clumsily lifted her into the passenger seat and fixed her seat belt around her. Katarina was aware of the smell first, the sickly, sweet, overpowering smell of Erik's aftershave. She kept her eyes closed due to years of abuse. Playing 'dead' bought her time to assess the situation she was in and formulate an escape strategy accordingly.

Erik had had plenty of time to plan the abduction during his flight over. He was going to put her in the boot but forgot about the extreme temperature compared to England. He walked round to the driver's side, not paying attention to Katarina, who felt it safer to keep her unconscious charade up until there was a chance of getting away. She felt too woozy to try at that moment, but she hoped she'd be able to if another opportunity presented itself soon. What she did have the presence of mind to do was to take her phone out of her pocket and slip it in her knickers. She'd had years of practice with subterfuge living with Erik, and it was working to her benefit. Erik got into the car and looked over at an unconscious Katarina. There was obvious evidence of a head wound with blood dripping down her left temple and on over her cheek and jaw. A stain was showing on her jacket. He rifled through her bag to see if he could find anything to mop it up with, and also to see if she had a phone. He found a pair of knickers that would do and wiped the blood off her face as best as he could, but no sign of a phone. He leant over and checked her pockets. Maybe she had thrown it away and didn't have money for a new one. He had to get on and find his daughter. He telephoned Bogdan to check where they were.

"We are following the yellow Aston Martin, like you told us to. We couldn't get close enough to see if Lilliana was in it. We are heading along the A9 just going past Narbonne, but we are afraid we may lose him. That car is very fast." Bogdan looked at Yegor and they both felt anxious. No one got on the wrong side of Erik. The problem was that they had lost the yellow Aston Martin around Narbonne, nearly half an hour earlier. They were hoping to find it when it had to stop for fuel. They felt sure it would be continuing along the A9 that meant it was either heading for the A8 and the Mediterranean coastline or the A7 to Paris. Taking into consideration that the yellow Aston Martin had Monaco number plates, the Mediterranean route was a logical option. They were going to bluff it with Erik until they either found it or they'd catch the next flight to Russia, never to be seen again.

It was nearly dark by the time the Aston Martin got to Beziers. Harry parked the car in the hotel car park he had booked the previous day, thinking he'd be alone and on his way to Monaco. He'd thought he may have to wait for Katarina to arrive at the farmhouse, and so didn't plan to go too far that night. Just as well as things had turned out, he thought. He carried a sleeping Lilli into the hotel. They had stopped for tea on the way, but Harry just wanted to get out of Spain. Lilli was sound asleep, so Harry decided he could risk the phone call.

He tried to ring Emm. She was not picking up. He left her a text too.

"Emm, I really need your help. It is a life or death situation. That's no exaggeration. Please call me. Harry." Harry had never been dramatic. Hopefully Emm would realise it was totally out of character and get back to him as soon as possible. With all options exhausted and himself too, he went to bed.

Harry was woken-up by the insistent ring from his mobile phone. He saw it was Emm. It was nine in the morning - he must have been tired. He looked over and could see Lilli still fast asleep on the twin bed next to his.

"Hi Harry, what's the urgency? What life or death situation have you got yourself into?" Harry tried to explain about meeting this woman on the ferry. It sounded so far-fetched how could anyone believe him.

"So, let me get this straight. This woman left her six-year-old little girl with a complete stranger and then disappeared. Does the child have any of your DNA in her?" He could hear Emm laugh.

"Oh, ha ha. Emm it isn't funny." He then explained about the thugs and the burnt-out farmhouse with Lilli's mother's cousin in the hospital. "I have to get rid of this car as soon as possible and I'm hoping I can leave Lilli with your mum while I go to Monaco to deliver it." Emm told him she'd phone her mother and couldn't see a problem.

"But then what are you going to do? How are you going to find the mother?" Harry was wondering the same thing.

"I'm hoping that she'll get my text and ring me so I can organise something. That's if the Russians haven't got her already." Harry checked to make sure Lilli was still asleep. He realised his agitation was making his voice go louder.

"Well stop chatting to me and get that little girl to safety with my mother, I'll ring her and make sure she's home. If she isn't François will let you in. In the meantime, get off the phone, I have a plane to catch." He could hear her laughing in the background before she hung up. He had to admit just hearing Emm's voice had a calming effect on him. It was like a weight had been taken off his mind. He hadn't been able to share the epic journey that it had turned out to be, with anyone. At least with Emm on board, and her family in the area, he had a better chance of looking after Lilli and help with finding Katarina. He woke Lilli gently and got her up.

She popped into the bathroom to dress and clean her teeth as if it was an ordinary day. She had got used to the routine and Harry noticed that children liked routine. He was learning a lot from the little girl. Hopefully it would come in useful when he and … he wanted to say Emm, were thinking of having their own family. He was already thinking more and more about what he had thrown away. He was looking forward to seeing her very soon.

After breakfast they drove for a few hours and stopped at Aix-en-Provence as a treat for Lilli. Harry had been there on numerous occasions and knew she would love it. As they pulled up at the end of the road Lilli spotted the treat

Harry had been talking about. There in front of them was a two-tiered merry-go-round. Lilli squealed with joy and ran up the steps to the big girls' seats. Harry couldn't resist and took photos of the little girl laughing and waving to him. He wanted something to show her mother.
They had lunch in a crêperie which Lilli adored.

"Pancakes are my favourite thing ever. Did you know that Harry?" Harry couldn't help but smile.

"I do now, Lilli." They laughed. "And as you have eaten all your savoury one, would you like another with ice cream and chocolate sauce for pudding." Lilli squealed with happiness. Harry noted that little girls did a lot of squealing.

"Yes please, Harry. Am I allowed?" Harry nodded and signalled the waitress. Harry knew if the day before was anything to go by, Lilli would have an afternoon nap after a big lunch. True to form, the little girl slept most of the two hours it took from Aix to Nice.

***

Bogdan and Yegor were ecstatic. Their plan had worked. They had travelled from early dawn and had made the decision to continue on the A8 towards Cannes. Bogdan, being the scholar of the two, (he had, at least, gone on into upper-secondary school whereas Yegor left school at fifteen) had roughly calculated, with fuel consumption, mileage and guesswork thrown in, when the Aston Martin would need to stop for fuel. Totally by chance, while they were debating whether to pull into the Cannes service area, a yellow Aston Martin overtook them. Both patted each other on the back. While they were being so self-absorbed, they nearly lost the car again, but luckily the traffic slowed down at the airport turnoff giving them a chance to catch up.

The phone rang while they were keeping the car in their view, without getting too close.

"Where are you now?" It was Erik. He was tired and angry. He had tried to sleep in a motorway car park, having tied a conscious Katarina up, but was woken by the traffic. Katarina had needed the toilet, but Erik made her squat by the side of the car, still attached to the door handle by rope. He let her sit in the car while he went over to some bushes to relieve himself, with his eye never off her. She had managed to take the phone out of its hiding place and had turned it on, on silent. She felt a vibration and took a quick look. A message from Harry, *Katarina, do not go to your cousin. Ring me as soon as you can. Harry.'* She'd try to ring him if she got a chance later. The phone went back into its hiding place.

They were now on the Côte d'Azur. Erik continued talking to Bogdan, "I have just passed the sign to Antibes."

"We are near the turn off for the airport at Nice. They are in front of us. We are keeping our distance so we don't spook them." Bogdan sighed. Thank goodness they had caught up with it.

"Okay, let me know where they stop. Keep on their tail. Give me the registration number, I'll see who it belongs to and get an address, just in case you two numbskulls lose it." Bogdan was so glad they had found the car. He wouldn't have been able to bluff that one.

"It's a Monaco registration, PR 1." Erik hung up with not even a thank you. Bogdan really didn't like working for Erik. Yegor looked worried.

"Boggy, I need the toilet." Bogdan took his eyes off the road and looked at his brother, and saw he was in considerable discomfort.

"Well you'll have to wait. I'm not risking losing them again. It's your own fault eating that baguette for breakfast. It has been in the car since the ferry crossing. What was in it? Oh yes, tuna and egg." Yegor moaned and bent forward. Bogdan looked back onto the road. "Shit, where are they? Yegor, where have they gone?" Yegor stared at the road ahead. The yellow Aston Martin was no longer in front of them. "We are dead Yegor."

* * *

Harry and Lilli arrived in Nice and Harry parked the car outside Caroline's apartment block. He would get the car into the underground car park as soon as he'd got Lilli safely inside. He walked up to the front door with Lilli behind him. Before he had time to ring for attention François had opened the door.

"Bonjour Monsieur 'arry. Good to see you." Harry smiled at François. He was chuffed that he remembered him.

"Bonjour François. You're looking well." Harry turned to pull Lilli in. "This is Lilliana, my best friend." Lilli put her hand out to shake François' hand.

"How do you do?" She was so cute, Harry just wanted to hug her.

"Bonjour Mademoiselle Lilliana. Welcome to Nice." Lilli turned to Harry and giggled.

"Am I really a mademoiselle, Harry?" He nodded. "I've always wanted to be a mademoiselle."

"Harry, lovely to see you." Caroline had got out of the lift just as Harry looked up from his conversation with Lilli, as if by telepathy. François had signalled her on her intercom as soon as the yellow Aston Martin had pulled up. She went over to him and the traditional salutations took place. Lilli thought it was funny.

"All that kissing, it spreads germs you know." François tried to stifle a laugh. Caroline turned to her.

"Ah, so this is Lilliana. How do you do Lilliana?" Lilli put out her hand. Caroline ignored it and hugged her. Lilli would have preferred the handshake; Caroline's perfume was rather overpowering. Lilli coughed and choked fanning her hand over her face a little more dramatically than was polite. François tried even harder not to laugh. It was more than his job was worth, but that little girl was a breath of fresh air. "Come on upstairs, Nico is waiting for you. He wants to help if he can." Caroline linked Harry's arm. Harry beckoned Lilli to follow them.

"That's very kind Caroline. A fluent French speaker will definitely come in handy. Can you keep an eye on the car please François, I'll move it in a minute?" François could look at the car all day. To him it was a fine piece of engineering.

"I can park it for you if you would like, Monsieur 'arry?" Harry smiled.

"Good one François, but no, thank you anyway." Harry tried not to laugh at François' dejected face. He unlinked Caroline's grip and went over to shake François' hand. François was very grateful for the 5€ note. He tipped his cap and went to stand where he could see the car without any obstruction.
Nico was waiting up in the flat. He shook Harry's hand and Lilli's and made them sit down.

"Do you want to put the yellow beast into the underground car park 'arry?" Harry shook his head. Nico had obviously looked out of the window when they had arrived. Harry checked to see where Lilli had gone. She was out of earshot.

"No thank you Nico. I think it would be better if I get it to Monaco as soon as possible. The idiots that have been following us only have the car to recognise us by. Not the subtlest of cars to do covert operations in, you have to agree." Nico laughed. It wasn't a laughing matter, but it needed to be put into perspective, or they would all just hide and leave it to someone else to fix. If Nico was honest, it was the most exciting thing that had happened to him in a while.

"Ok. I will follow in my car to Monaco and then I can bring you back. It shouldn't take us more than forty minutes to get there, perhaps a little longer to come back as we'll hit the rush hour traffic." Harry looked at his watch. He needed to get back before Lilli's bedtime.

"What about Lilli? She'll want to come with me." Caroline had just come back into the room. She'd been showing Lilli her room and let her play with some old clothes of hers. She remembered from her daughters that children, especially little girls, loved to dress up.

"Lilliana and I are best friends." Harry felt betrayed, but was secretly happy that Lilli had settled in. "We have a date at Galleries Lafayette, for some serious clothes shopping." Caroline had noticed that Lilli had the clothes she was wearing and a few items that were dirty in her bag. She knew the best way to a little girl's heart was through her wardrobe, no matter what the age.

"Well if that's settled can I suggest we get going? We may even beat the rush hour if we get off now." Nico was right. Harry gave him the address in Monaco in case they got split up and they left after Harry had kissed Lilli goodbye.

"I know you'll be good for Caroline. I promise I'll be back to tuck you in, okay?" Lilli nodded. She trusted Harry. He was one of the good guys, her mummy said.

"Harry, can we play I Spy when you get back, pleeeease?" Lilli elongated the word for emphasis and effect.

"We'll see Lilli, we'll see." Lilli smiled knowingly. Harry left with a grin on his face too. Lilli had a delightful way about her that he knew he couldn't say 'no'; he'd be playing I Spy on his return!

CHAPTER 7

Emm had packed a small holdall and been online to book a flight from Gatwick to Nice. There was one early that morning, so she was kicking herself she didn't ring Harry the night before. The next available flight was at 5 o'clock that afternoon. With the hour change she should be there by 6 o'clock French time. Depending on how long the passport queue was, and with only hand luggage, she should be out of the airport within fifteen minutes. If she then walked up onto the main road, she could book an Uber on her phone app, and be at the apartment within ten minutes, traffic willing.

All these plans were whirling around her head at great speed, so much so that she nearly missed her Tube stop. She rushed up the stairs into the daylight and got to the office somewhat flustered. Her father was at his desk looking worse than she did.

"Morning Daddy. I'm afraid I need a favour." Michael looked up and tried to smile but at that point nothing in his body was doing what his brain was telling it. "Oh dear. What time did you get to bed? Brilliant party though, wasn't it." Michael tried to nod but again his internal wiring system failed him. Emm knew exactly what her father needed. She rushed off to the kitchen just next to her office. Someone had been in early - the coffee jug was full and another filling nicely. She poured one for her father and one for herself. She should have had a hangover too, but it was funny what a shock did to the system. She took the coffee in to her father and left him to drink it and sober up before she pestered him again. Back at her office she checked her emails and messages. There was one from her mother. She and Nico were quite excited about their visitors arriving sometime that afternoon. Somehow Emm felt her mother had missed the significance of why Harry was bringing a little girl to stay.

"Oh darling, this is just such fun. It'll be like old times. I'll take the little girl shopping for some pretty clothes. Does she speak English? Never mind, it won't matter. How long will they be staying? It'll be so nice to see Harry again, won't it? Hope you can get here soon. Nico and I can babysit if you and Harry want to go out." Emm stopped reading that message and went on to read some work-related ones. Her mother was playing Cupid. She couldn't do subtle, but for some reason Emm didn't mind, she had missed Harry too.

You don't just stop loving someone when all they had done was grow up, move on, and make plans that hadn't included you. But they had included her, she knew he was doing it all so he could come back and afford the best for her. It was Emm that couldn't wait. Being celibate in London at the age of thirty-something would be tantamount to joining a convent. She bet he hadn't been a monk. Girls must have thrown themselves at his tanned, muscular body. She could have waited for him. There hadn't been anyone since. What an idiot she'd been. It suddenly dawned on her that he phoned her for help. He'd been in France for most of the year, he must have met a woman or two, but he phoned her. Maybe there was hope. Maybe he'd missed her. Maybe he still loved her.

Maybe…

"So, what is the favour?" Michael was at her office door, jolting her out of her reverie. She snapped out of it and shuffled some papers.

"Ah, yes. I need to pop over to Nice this afternoon for a few days, again." She was about to apologise when Michael came in and sat in front of her desk.

"Is it your mother? Is she okay?" Emm found her father's concern very honourable. She realised that Claudia had restored his self-esteem and his faith in women.

"No, Mum's fine. It's a long story, but Harry is in trouble and I'm going down to help him with a child he has…" 'picked up' sounded wrong, "been put in charge of." Michael looked totally puzzled. Emm started from the beginning, it was the best way to help her father understand. Michael did understand but was worried about what Emm was getting herself into. He knew better than to show it.

"Well, hopefully there will be a happy ending and you can get back to work." He winked at her. He wasn't pulling the wool over her eyes; she could see he was worried. Michael took out his wallet and found some Euros and gave them to her. "At least they should cover a taxi and perhaps a meal. All that is left to say is 'bon chance'."

"Get you, Father, bi-lingual now!" Michael knew his daughter was pulling his leg. He had been the last person you'd catch speaking anything but English. She was proud of him, but knew it was to impress his girlfriend. That sounded funny too, her dad having a girlfriend. She must remember that 'mum' was still the word, especially in France.

***

Emm tried to get hold of her mother for a lift from the airport, but no joy. She walked past the taxi rank and onto the main road, as she booked an Uber from her phone. It was only a few minutes later that she was being driven along Boulevard René Cassin and felt at home with the Promenade des Anglais on her right and the beautiful relaxing sight of the azure blue Mediterranean Sea.

By the time she got to her mother's apartment she hoped someone would be there. She rang the Concierge's bell and François opened the door for her.

"A bonjour Mademoiselle Emily. How lovely to see you again, so soon." Bless him, thought Emm.

"Merçi François. Is my mother home?" François shook his head.

"Mais non Mademoiselle. She 'as taken little Lilliana to buy some clothes. Such a pretty little girl, est très poli… 'ow do you say?"

"Very polite?" François nodded. "Good, she will get on very well with my mother then." François smiled and nodded, knowingly. "I'm sure they'll be in Galaries Lafayette. That means they will be ages. They won't just be in the children's department." Again, François smiled and nodded, knowingly. Emm found it quite endearing that the concierge of the whole apartment block knew her mother as well as she did, a sign of a good concierge. François went into the lift with direct access to the penthouse and put in his key. On the ride up he wanted to know who the little girl was? Emm wanted to tease him but knowing how the French loved children, it would backfire, as he would be delighted if her mother and Nico adopted a little girl. So, she just said it was a friend's daughter and they were looking after her until she came back. As near the truth as Emm knew herself.

By the time Caroline had returned Emm had unpacked her small suitcase and was making herself a drink in the kitchen.

"Emm, darling, come out and meet Lilliana." Emm walked out into the living area and saw the cutest little girl, completely swamped by bags, but with a massive smile on her face. As Emm walked over to them, Lilli put down all the bags and ran into Emm's arms.

"Hello." Emm said into the head of Lilli. She put her down on the floor. "My name is Emily, what's yours?" She knew her name but wanted to get her to talk.

"I'm Lilliana, but you can call me Lilli. All my best friends call me Lilli. Harry calls me Lilli." She put out her hand to shake Emm's.

"Well, how do you do Lilli? You can call me Emm, that's what Harry calls me." Caroline was surreptitiously taking some of the bags into her own bedroom. Emm knew her mother wouldn't have been able to resist buying a few things for herself. "I see you have been shopping." Emm said it loud enough for her mother to turn and slightly blush, but she had actually been looking at Lilli. Emm knew exactly what she was doing, and it had worked. She smiled at her own impish sense of humour.

"I have the most beautiful dress in my favourite colour. Do you know what my favourite colour is Emm?" Emm had to think what her favourite colour was at six-years-old.

"Could it be yellow by any chance?" Lilli jumped

up and down clapping.

"Yes, you're so clever. Harry said you were very clever too." Did he? Thank you, Harry - she wondered if Harry had said anything else about her.

"Sounds like you and Harry have had a good time together." Lilli looked sad. "What's the matter Lilli? Are you missing your mummy? I'm sure Harry will find her soon." Emm wasn't sure if she was even lost, but she hadn't had much experience talking to a young child.

"I know Harry will find her, he promised. But it's Harry I miss. He is funny. I love Harry, do you love Harry, Emm?" From the mouths of babes, what was she to say?

"Yes Lilli, I love Harry too." Lilli clapped her hands and jumped up and down in delight. She ran behind Emm over to the apartment door.

"Harry, there you are I've missed you." She jumped into his arms. Harry looked at Emm. He had obviously heard what she said and was looking very smug. Emm tried not to blush but it was difficult. Harry put Lilli down and went over to Emm, wanting to pick her up too, but perhaps it was a little too soon.

"Hi Emm. It's really good to see you." He kissed her on her cheek.

"Hello Harry. I'm glad you have survived the trials and tribulations of parenthood." Harry laughed. That was the old Emm, the Emm he fell in love with.

He wanted to admit that he'd missed her, but it was a little soon for that too. Perhaps later, when the danger was over, and Lilli was back safely in her mother's arms. While Harry and Nico brought Emm and Caroline up to date with events, Lilli was entertaining them with her new outfits. She was running into her little room that Caroline had put her in, (it was actually their study, but Lilli was so small, she could lie on Caroline's leather chaise longue and it was as good as a bed for her) and running out with a different ensemble on. She imitated a model wonderfully. They couldn't hold back their amusement. Emm had already fallen in love with Lilli.

"Well she's managed to get into all your hearts by the look of it." Harry pulled Lilli over to him and hugged her. "You're a very lucky little girl Lilli. Have you said thank you to Caroline?" Emm couldn't believe what she was hearing.

"Harry, you're a daddy!" Harry tried not to bite but was actually quite proud of himself. If he ever had children, he'd want them to be just like Lilli.

"Thank you very much for the pretty clothes." Lilli went over to Caroline and planted a big kiss on her cheek. Emm swore she saw her mum's eyes glisten.

"You're very welcome Lilliana." Lilli smiled at her.

"You can call me Lilli. You're my best friend now." The ficklcness of a child, but Harry was pleased that everyone loved Lilli. If he couldn't find her mother, they may be seeing a lot more of her. Lilli disappeared into her room to change.

"While we were on the way back from Monaco I managed to speak to my father." Nico was looking serious. "He has friends in the government and I asked if they were able to trace a missing person by their phone."

"I have Katarina's phone number from a text she sent me. She isn't answering any of my texts or calls, so she either has it on silent or she's dumped it like her last one, so she can't be traced. I'm hoping it's the first option." Harry looked worried. He wondered if she'd got caught before his last warning text had reached her.

"My father is going to get back to me as soon as he's spoken to a few people." He tapped his nose. It seemed very cloak and dagger, Emm reflected. "Now I will go and light the barbecue." That was Caroline's cue to get in the kitchen and take out the meat they had bought for the evening's meal.

Both Nico and Caroline decided it safer to eat in and they could also get Lilli to bed at a reasonable time.

"Is there anything I can do to help?" Harry got up and followed Nico out onto the balcony. Nico pointed to the drinks cooler conveniently by the built-in cooker and barbecue.

"How about opening a chilled bottle of Côte de Provence. The glasses are on the shelf above." Harry considered that an extremely good idea. He took two filled glasses into the kitchen where he found the girls chatting and making sauces and salads.

"A little chilled Côte de Provence for you ladies?"

"Oo, thank you Harry. My favourite. It doesn't have the same 'je ne sais quoi' from Lidl!" Harry laughed as Emm took hers off him. He put the remaining one down by Caroline. Lilli walked into the kitchen.

"What would you like to drink Lilli?" Lilli thought about it.

"Can I have the same as you please Harry?" Emm watched how Harry was going to deal with that one.

"We'll see, Lilli." Lilli giggled. She looked at Harry with puppy-dog eyes. Harry shrugged smiling and nodded. "Okay, mademoiselle. If you'd like to go and sit with Nico outside, I will bring you your drink." Lilli screwed up her face and winked at Harry.

She walked off still imitating a model, although she was

just wearing her jeans and an old t-shirt. She did make them smile. "How anyone could hurt that little girl I don't know. There are some evil bastards in this world." Harry looked so cross. He sighed and turned to Caroline. "Have you any blackcurrant syrup, or juice?"

"I have crème de cassis, but it's not really for children. Oh, hang on, I have some strawberry cordial somewhere." She looked in a cupboard and found it. "How's that?"

"Perfect, thank you. Have you any plastic wine glasses?" Caroline shook her head.

"No. But if it's for Lilli she can have an ordinary one, we have hundreds." Caroline reached up to the glass cupboard and took one out. Harry put in a little cordial then added Badoit sparkling mineral water. He took a sip and found a teaspoon and stirred it. He took another sip and smiled.

"You really have changed Harry, so much attention to detail. This wine you have given me, is it shaken, not stirred?" Emm was enjoying ribbing Harry, just like the old days.

"Ha, bloody ha." Harry went off to give Lilli her 'glass of wine'.

"You still love him, don't you?" Caroline wasn't stupid. She could see the way they both looked at each other. "You should tell him."

"Not exactly the right time, Mother. Let's see how things go with Lilli and her mother. Plenty of time when this situation has been resolved, hopefully with a happy outcome." Caroline nodded. Her daughter was right, but while there was hope for Harry to be back in their lives, she could dream. But for now, she'd drop the subject.

The barbecue was a success. All had eaten their fill and drunk a little more than was necessary, but for Harry it was the first time in days he could let his guard down and enjoy the evening. He looked over to the swing seat and saw little Lilli sound asleep, cuddling Paris.

"I ought to put her to bed. She is such an angel." Harry was exhausted, but Lilli was his responsibility. "I'll be back in a moment." Emm pushed him back down into his seat.

"You've done enough. I'll do it." Emm went over to Lilli and picked her up gently. She caught hold of the stuffed dog and carried her inside.

"It's called Paris, by the way." Harry whispered as loudly as he could to get Emm to hear but not too loud that would wake Lilli. Emm carried Lilli to her little bedroom and laid her on the chaise longue. She managed to slip her jeans off without disturbing her but didn't want to chance anything else. She covered her with the sheet and tucked Paris in beside her. She bent over and kissed her goodnight. She pulled her door to, so they could hear her if she cried or called out.

Harry was waiting for her outside the room. He turned her round to him and couldn't help himself. He pulled her into his arms and kissed her for what seemed like an eternity. When he finally let her go, he looked into her eyes. "I'm sorry I couldn't wait any longer. I have wanted to do that since the moment I saw you standing there with Lilli. I love you Emm, I have loved you all this time. I'm not letting you go again." Emm hadn't had a chance to tell him how she felt. His lips homed straight back on to hers. She thought there was plenty of time for words. Action was what was needed, so she'd go with the flow.

"Harry, I need the toilet." They both burst out laughing at the little voice that had come from behind the door. "I need the toilet, NOW!" Harry opened the door and grabbed Lilli from the chaise longue. He sprinted across the living area and disappeared into the bathroom. At the sight of an extremely anxious looking Harry running past her, Emm was practically wetting herself too! Only she had better control of her bladder, she hoped. She composed herself and went outside to talk to Nico.

"What are the chances that Alain will find someone to help Harry?" Nico looked positive. He knew how many dignitaries his father had in his contact list. Most of them were from local government and the police.

"If anyone can find out what is going on it will be my father. I can assure you of that. French politics, like most countries, relies on donations, and my father is very generous - specifically to the wives, with frequent free perfume samples going their way." Nico smiled. Emm got the message. She helped herself to another glass of Côtes de Provence and sat down next to her mother.

"Thank you for all your help. Poor Harry looks knackered. This parenting lark is tiring." She laughed. Caroline wondered if Emm would ever realise how much it takes out of you when you don't get any help. It was one of the reasons she left her father. He was so busy establishing his little empire that he forgot how difficult it was to bring up two daughters alone.

"Talking of which, how is your father?" That took the wind out of Emm's sails. Where had that come from, she wondered?

"He's fine." Emm was being very guarded with

the news she was dying to tell everybody about her father, but she had promised not to tell a soul, especially not her mother. She had to change the subject. "Hey, Nico, how's Frédéric? He and CC seemed to have hit it off." Nico nodded.

"Yes, I'm afraid 'e 'as fallen in love. 'e 'as gone to London to find a job in a jazz café that asked 'im last year to join them. The job is Frédéric's if CC wants 'im to stay. But 'e is worried it will interfere with 'er studies." Emm wondered when all of that had happened. She only saw CC last night. She hadn't mentioned anything about Frédéric.

"Funny, she didn't say Frédéric was in England when I saw her last night." Emm wondered if CC was starting to keep things from her again.

"I don't think Frédéric 'as told 'er that 'e is there. 'e wants to 'ave everything organised before 'e offers 'er a fait accompli, which I think is the same in English?" Emm nodded.

"Well CC's studies will be over in a few weeks and depending on her results, she can start living again and have a social life. So, if you tell Frédéric to hold on for a little while longer, who knows, it may be the beginning of a beautiful friendship." Harry joined them on the balcony.

"Casablanca, 1942, with Humphrey Bogart and Ingrid Bergman. Last line of the film, Rick says," Harry put on a very bad American accent. "'Louis, I think this is the beginning of a beautiful friendship.'" He took a bow. Emm clapped. "Was I right?" Emm laughed. Harry had caught the tail end of the conversation and assumed they were playing 'name that film', one of their favourite games, back in the day.

"You're a dope sometimes, Harry. We weren't

playing a game. We were discussing CC and her new chap Frédéric." Emm explained who Frédéric was. "It's so romantic. A man has moved to another country and got a job to stay there while he woos the woman he loves." Emm looked all dreamy. "And she doesn't even know." Nico looked serious.

"You must promise not to say anything to CC. It could ruin everything. Promise Emily, please?" Emm couldn't believe it. Not another promise. She was never good in the Girl Guides because she couldn't keep the 'Promise', but she nodded.

"Okay, I promise." Harry could see that she probably meant it, but there was something bothering her. Did CC have a boyfriend in England? Was CC a lesbian and finally come out? What was making Emm so uneasy? He'd get to the bottom of it later. The others had started to clean up, so he collected the empty bottles to put in the recycling chute by the lift.

"We may have a busy day tomorrow, so I think it best if we go to bed. I have some linen I've put on the sofa for you Harry. I hope it is comfortable for you. Goodnight." Caroline waved to them all and went off into her bedroom. Nico followed on behind her, having said goodnight to them both.

"Will you be comfortable on the sofa Harry?" He didn't know if Emm was teasing him.

"I think the sofa will do just nicely, thank you."

"Ok then, I'll see you in the morning. Good night." She was just about to go when Harry grabbed her arm and pulled her down onto the sofa.

"Can I just try it out first?" He drew her into a cuddle and kissed her passionately. Emm could have stayed there all night, but she had to get to bed.

She was late after the party the night before and had got up very early that day. She had to admit that she was tired, but she knew the real reason for her hesitance. Could she let Harry back into her life before he'd proved to her that it was forever? She knew she could, but she had to be strong.

"Loving this as I am Harry, I really need to get some sleep. I think I have jet lag." She giggled. She pushed herself off the sofa and blew him a kiss. "I'll see you in the morning. Let's hope this nightmare will be over by this time tomorrow. Then we can resume where we left off this evening. Night night." She turned and went into her room, shutting the door. Well, that told me, thought Harry. He knew she was right, after all they hadn't seen each other for over a year. It was probably not the best time to renew their acquaintance with so much uncertainty hanging over them. He stripped down to his boxer shorts, and checked on Lilli, who was sleeping soundly with Paris by her side. He went back to the sofa, keeping Lilli's door ajar, he shook out the sheet and pulled it over himself while lying down. The sofa was remarkably comfortable, so much so that Harry was dead to the world before he had time to dream.

CHAPTER 8

Michael stayed at the apartment over night as he was missing his girls and wanted to see Claudia alone, with no one else about. Most evenings Claudia organised gatherings. All good publicity for the movie, but it didn't leave much alone time. The party the other day had been a great success. Emm and CC were in their element and Claudia loved them. Michael had assumed that after that party Claudia would have wanted a quiet night in, but sadly no. When Michael arrived home after work, another was already in full swing. The last guests' left around two in the morning; Michael had retired at midnight.

In the morning he left her asleep and decided the kitchen was in such a mess he'd leave it to the housekeeper and pop out to get their breakfast.

He took the lift down to the ground floor and nodded a good morning to the security chap. He couldn't remember his name. They seemed to change every day. He walked to the local bakery where the smell was enough to believe you had arrived in Heaven. Unfortunately, his pounding head took away a lot of the good karma that was emitting from the smell. He bought croissants, a baguette and two very strong coffees to take-away. He popped into the newsagents and grabbed a Times newspaper and a day-old copy of Le Monde for Claudia. As he was paying, he noticed a batch of Paris Match on the counter, still tied together. He asked if he could have one, and the shopkeeper got out a knife and cut one free. He thought it would be a lovely surprise for Claudia if it mentioned her nomination for the Palme d'Or and reviews of her film.

By the time he'd got back to the apartment the housekeeper had tackled a lot of the debris from the night before and had set the table outside on the balcony with fruit juice and crockery. Claudia wandered out of the bedroom onto the balcony with her sunglasses in place.

"Could you turn the lights down a little, chéri?" Michael didn't feel quite as bad as Claudia.

"I'll ask God to turn the sunshine off for you, but I'm sure he's probably a little occupied at present." She tried to smile. She spotted the coffee and gulped half down before she had even sat on a chair. She dunked a croissant in the last half. Michael loved the French and their idiosyncrasies.

He was beginning to understand why Caroline's indiscretion with Nicolas Janvier had blossomed into a romance. He was feeling the same way about Claudia Pasqualle. He wanted to shout his love for her for all to hear, but he had to respect her wishes. One day, hopefully soon, he could tell the world.

"I'm afraid I have to love you and leave you this morning. I have a client to meet and hopefully to accommodate for the next three months in a very lucrative little residence in Chelsea. Emily will be gutted because it was her appointment and as he used an alias, she wouldn't have realised it is a member of her favourite boy band." Claudia looked concerned.

"Why isn't Emily showing this pop star round the

'ouse? Is she poorly?" Michael shook his head and wished he hadn't.

"No, she's flitted off to France in an emergency, something about her ex-boyfriend and a little girl. Not his. It's too complicated to explain now. I'll tell you all about it this evening. How about I take you out for a nice meal and we can come back here and relax, alone." He emphasised 'alone'. She smiled up at him.

"Je suis désolé, my love. I 'ave been naughty. Tonight is for us, and us alone." She copied him with an emphasised 'alone'. She got up and kissed him. "A bientôt, mon chéri." Michael went off to the office feeling happier.

He arrived with a thumping headache. Where was Emily when he needed her? He hoped she was ok. He went straight to the kitchen and the coffee fairy had been kind to him. He poured himself a cup full, from the new jug, and walked over to Emily's desk. On the top were all her appointments that she had handed over to her father. He found the one he was looking for in the name of Charles Chaplin. The boy had a sense of humour. His real name was Charlie Banks. He had just split up from his band and was branching out as a solo artist and about to record his first album. His recording studio was moments away from the King's Road. Michael had the ideal property for him to view in Chelsea, with his mother, apparently. It was a small town house on Jubilee Place, a quiet street, moments away from the studio. Michael thought he'd have to change the details for other rental properties in the vicinity, for the next three months, to a 'relatively' quiet street. Michael had an apartment close by too but decided to try to get him to take the town house.

Otherwise he knew he'd have no end of noise complaints from people in the other apartments. He could do without that hassle. The town house was a better option with its own front door and thick walls, with the advantage of being an end of terrace.

Charlie's mother immediately fell in love with it. Having walked through a wrought iron gate into a small front garden she felt it was ideal.

"Charlie didn't even have a front garden when he were growing up. You opened' door straight on t' street where we lived." Michael naughtily had visions of Coronation Street.

"Where was that, may I ask?" Charlie had gone inside to explore. He didn't look more than twelve, thought Michael. He had read the file and he was actually nineteen.

"Manchester, can't you tell by me accent?" Michael politely shook his head. There was no mistaking by the flat vowels and the clipped endings that she was from the north. "I've been down 'ere so long I've probably lost most of it." Michael smiled. It was going to be a long appointment.

"Shall we go inside?" He didn't wait for an answer. He moved to the front door and stood aside for her to go in. "May I ask, will you be living here too?" Charlie's mother burst out laughing. He didn't see anything funny in the question, so just smiled.

"Goodness no, love. I have seven children at home, all needin' me. Charlie is me eldest. My Nathan has only just come off boob." She pointed in the direction of her upper body. Michael didn't look. He was feeling a little sick as it was, it didn't need any encouragement.

Not once had he seen Caroline feed either of the girls, it

wasn't necessary. He knew he loved the girls just as much without watching their mealtimes. He took a deep breath and carried on inside, secretly cussing Emily for gallivanting off to France. He was sure her emergency would blend into insignificance on meeting Mrs Banks.

While extolling the virtue of wet floor bathrooms to a couple of philistines, Michael's phone rang. Claudia's name flashed on the screen.

"Please do excuse me. I have to take this call. Look around all you want; I will be outside when you've finished." He was blessing the interruption. Once outside he answered his call. "Hello, my darling, what can I do you for?" He liked to confuse her with silly English.

"I need you to come 'ome chéri, now!" She carried on in French at a rate of knots. "Je suis mortifié de voir dans les journaux que vous et moi avons été découverts." Michael had to calm her down.

"Claudia, can you tell me what has happened, in a language that I can understand." Claudia realised she had been wittering on and Michael hadn't understood a word she'd said. She did that when she was nervous.

"Just please come 'ome. La presse est 'orrible." She hung up. Michael understood the last phrase. It sounded like the excrement had truly hit the cooling system.

He hurried back into the house and told them he had to leave. Charlie wanted to sign the lease, but Michael explained that he'd have to go to the office, and he can do it there after his references had cleared.

"He's a good lad. He probably has more money than you've had hot dinners." Michael just smiled.

"It's normal procedure, Mrs Banks.

Unfortunately, even if Prince Harry himself came to us we'd still have to take up his references." Mrs Banks nodded.

"That's ok then. I'll get him t' office tomorrow. Will that be alright?" Michael nodded and smiled again. It hurt his head, but he didn't want to offend the woman. He locked up the house and waved good-bye to them while they wondered around the outside, with Charlie taking photos on his phone.

He got back to Claudia's apartment in record time. She was still on the balcony, with the latest Paris Match open and she was screaming down the phone in French. She saw him and motioned for him to look at the page she had open.
The headline was in French, but he managed to translate most of it:
Best Actress nominee from this year's Palme D'or, Claudia Pasqualle être passionné, being passionate? avec un homme plus âgé. He didn't need to translate that remark, it was rude. He didn't see himself as an old man at all.
He picked up the magazine and took a good look at the photo. It was an amateur phone photo of Michael with his arm around Claudia's waist. It was difficult to see exactly where they were as it was relatively dark, but it was definitely Cannes and, by what they were wearing, it looked like the after party from the premiere of her film.

Claudia had gone quiet. Her phone call had ended and Michael felt very sorry for the person at the other end. He assumed it was probably poor Brigitte, Claudia's agent.

"So much for security." She shook her head.

Michael wasn't sure what to do. He'd take his lead from Claudia. She sighed, and then got up. "There is only one thing we can do now, chéri. I will get Brigitte to arrange a press conference. We will make our relationship legitimate." She smiled and kissed him. Michael was smiling too, inside and out.

Claudia explained to Michael how she had opened it to see if her publicity photo was in that edition or if it was too soon. Also, if there was an article about the nominations for the Palme d'Or and at least a paragraph of what the critics thought of her film, that would be a bonus.

She had been very pleased with her publicity photo, but then she noticed the headline underneath it.

"Well, you have come out of it with wonderful publicity. I, on the other hand, have been portrayed as a dirty old man." Claudia had to laugh.

"Oh chéri. Don't make me laugh, my 'ead is still throbbing. You 'ave mistranslated the article. Avec un 'omme plus âgé means 'with an older man', not an old man." She laughed again. "Come 'ere and give me a cuddle. I will make you feel better." Michael wasn't going to argue with that. "I wanted to keep it a secret for a little longer to enjoy our relationship without the world knowing. But it is now time to tell my public. I need to organise Brigitte to set up a meeting with the French and English press at the Dorchester as soon as possible. It won't take long before you're recognised so we will be one jump ahead of them." Michael had a couple of concerns.

"I would like to tell the girls before all this is splashed about the papers. I'll ring Stephanie tonight. It's a shame she's not back from her honeymoon yet, but it can't be helped. Emily just needs warning, she's with her mother and I don't envy her when Caroline finds out!" He had to laugh. How funny that they had both fallen madly, deeply in love with French partners.

"I shall organise it for the weekend, is that ok mon chéri?" Michael smiled and nodded. That gave him a couple of days to let everyone know that needed to. "Do you 'ave to go back to the office?" Michael looked at his watch.

There wasn't any point so near lunchtime. He shook his head. Claudia took him by the hand and walked towards their bedroom. It was time to consummate their new social position.

***

In the morning, as promised, Nico's father Alain, arrived at the apartment in Nice. Harry thought he was the epitome of a French gentleman. He was lean, with a straight demeanour, making him taller than he actually was. Emm could see where Nico had got his good looks from. Alain was wearing a white linen suit, with an open-neck blue and white striped shirt. On his feet were brown and beige brogues and he was carrying a white trilby with a brown band. In his jacket's breast pocket was a blue and white handkerchief, matching his shirt. He looked elegant and casual at the same time.

"How do you do Harry. I hear you're the hero of the hour." Alain shook Harry's hand. Harry was appreciative that Alain used the staid English greeting of shaking hands and not the French's normal intimate salutation. In fact, Harry noticed that his French accent wasn't strong at all and his English was perfect.

"I'm not sure I can go as far as saying I'm a hero, at least not until I manage to get mother and child together, safely. But I appreciate the sentiment. Thank you." Emm was very impressed by Harry's humility. The old Harry would have been flaunting his bravado. Her Harry had grown into a very nice young man. Who'd have thought! Emm was being a little harsh in her own opinion. Harry wasn't a show-off - he had just been a young man trying to impress a girl.

"Well, I think I may have some helpful news for you. My good friend Philippe, who is Deputy Minister for the Interior, has contacted the local Police Nationale. They have tracked the phone being used by the young lady to Monaco." Harry and Nico looked at each other.

"You were right, mon ami. Those men were following the Aston Martin. Papa, 'ave they an exact position?" Alain nodded.

"Yes, Port Hercule. Philippe has passed all the information you gave me, about the two men, on to the Monaco criminal police division and they have taken over. The Maritime police divisions have also been put on alert. If it wasn't so serious it would be rather exciting." Alain was now caught up in the moment.

"The other news is that Philippe has heard that Interpol have been watching a human trafficking gang from Estonia and" he checked his phone message to get the name right, "Erik Eskola is on their most wanted list. The two thugs you were talking about may be the Sokolov brothers from Russia. They are wanted in most of Eastern Europe for murder and trafficking. I'm glad the law is closing in on these bad men." Harry suddenly realised that was where Patrick's Sunseeker was moored.

"Nico, Patrick has probably gone to the boat and driven the car there. Alain, if I give you the berth number that Patrick has his boat moored, at Port Hercule, then that could help the police." Alain nodded his head. He took a note of the number and went out of the room to telephone, they assumed, good old Philippe, Deputy Minister of the Interior of France. Harry had to say it in his mind because he wanted to believe that all would be well if the whole French government were on their side.

"Hey, Nico, fancy a trip to Monaco?" Nico looked excited. He nodded to Harry, but the girls did not seem so pleased.

"No Nico, leave it to the professionals, please." Caroline was looking very concerned. It was times like this that it hit her how young Nico actually was. She looked to Emm for support. Emm was on Harry's side.

"Can I come?" Harry shook his head.

"No, it could be dangerous. I just thought since I've seen the two Russians, that we could go onto Patrick's boat and keep watch." Emm felt like stamping her foot. How dare Harry think that a man was any more capable at surveillance than a woman. Women invented surveillance. Many a home had net curtains purely for that reason. She calmed down.

"Harry Hart, you chauvinist. I was thinking that I could be a good decoy, considering no one has seen me. And, when you find Katarina, I'm sure she would prefer a woman there to help her. Especially if she's been injured." Suddenly there was a big squeal from behind the patio door to the balcony. Harry turned automatically as he recognised the squeal.

"Harry, has somebody hurt my mummy?" She ran into his arms and real sobs were coming from her little frame.
Emm had her hands over her mouth, shaking her head.

They had all got so carried away no one had even thought to check where Lilli was. How much had she heard?
Even a six-year-old can understand body language, and theirs had been tense when talking about her mother. Alain came back in and caught sight of Lilli.

"Ah, this is the beautiful Lilliana, I take it." He went over to Harry, who was still clutching Lilli. She had stopped crying and wanted to see who had just called her beautiful. "Hello Mademoiselle. I have a little present for you. Would you like to see it?" Lilli nodded and got off Harry. That fickleness was there again, thought Harry. At least Alain had brought a smile back on Lilli's face. Alain took out a small box from his pocket. He handed it to Lilli. She looked at it and then looked at Harry, as if asking his permission. He nodded and she opened the box. Inside was a small bottle. She carefully opened the bottle and the smell was like fields of lovely flowers. "I was told you were six years old. In France that means you're a full mademoiselle. Do you know what that means?" Lilli shook her head. "It means that you're one step away from being a young lady. You now have to wear perfume, just a little. Here, I'll show you." He took the top off the perfume bottle and joined to the glass stopper was a glass stick. "You pop this stick behind your ears, comme ça? Now you put the top back on, always remember to do that or there will be no perfume left next time you look. Now you go over to Harry and watch what he says." Alain winked at Harry. Lilli went over to Harry as he bent down to smell behind Lilli's ears.

"Wow. You smell delicious Lilli. I'll have to keep an eye on you, or all the little French boys will be chasing you." Lilli giggled.

"They won't catch me though, Harry. Because I'll be in a fast, yellow car." They all laughed. Lilli turned back to Alain. "Thank you very much for my perfume. You can call me Lilli now, as you're my new best friend." Alain bent down and kissed Lilli the French way. Lilli went off to her room, positively beaming. She wanted to put the bottle in her bag. It was the very first time she had been given such a grown-up present and wanted to keep it forever. Once she was out of hearing distance Harry turned to Emm.

"Thinking about what you said, you're absolutely right. Katarina may need your help, if we find her." He sighed. He had to stay positive. "When we find her." He corrected.

Alain knew better than to stop them going. Had he been younger he would have joined them. He also had family and business responsibilities that Nico won't have for quite a while, he hoped.

"You better get off. Be safe. Bon chance." Nico went over and kissed his father.

"Au revoir Papa. We will be careful, I promise." Alain was very proud of his opera-singing son. Perhaps he should tell him more often? It may sound melodramatic at that point in time - he'd wait until they were back and hopefully the ordeal would be over with a happy conclusion.

"Be careful as you go off to war, my darling." Caroline wasn't happy but tried not to show it. Nico went over to Caroline and kissed her. She was opening her mouth to say something else, when he put his finger up to her mouth and shushed her.

"Be brave, ma chérie." He kissed her again and turned away. The irony wasn't lost on Caroline. He went over to the hall table by the door and took his car keys out. Harry and Emm followed Nico, waving good-bye to Alain and Caroline.

"Tell Lilli I'll be back soon, please Caroline." She nodded. Harry didn't want to say good-bye to Lilli. He would have to lie to her about where he was going. He couldn't do that again, so it was better if they just left. Caroline shooed them out of the door to show she was supporting them, but inside she was feeling panic-stricken. Two of the people she loved most in her world were off to who knows what kind of danger.

"It'll probably all be over by the time they get there." Alain reassured Caroline, but he was trying to convince himself too.

CHAPTER 9

They piled into Nico's Renault Sport Mégane R. S. It wasn't exactly comfortable for Emm in the back, but she kept quiet in case they changed their minds about taking her.

"Your father knows an awful lot of influential people Nico." Alain had intrigued Harry. "He also speaks English with only a slight accent. He really is a conundrum." Nico laughed. He'd never heard his father being described as a conundrum before. He must remember to tell his mother; she'd find that very amusing. Most of his family thought Alain was a very see-through, matter-of-fact kind of guy.

"In answer to your first statement, our family go back a very long way in the area and most of my ancestors 'ave been mayors, ministers, and we've probably 'ad royalty in our blood too," he whispers the next remark "but we don't tell anyone because it's 'armful to our 'ealth." He had just done the same as his father.

Considering they were going to a dangerous situation, they all seemed to be relaxed and calm. "And in answer to your second statement, my father spent a lot of 'is young days in London. 'e was at a university there, Imperial College, if I remember correctly? My grandfather made 'im learn more about the chemistry of fragrance so 'e would be an even greater perfumier than Grand-père.

Papa 'as a BSc., but it is a bit of a waste in France." Harry was impressed. "'e didn't want to come back to France, 'e was 'aving a great time in London. My maman eventually went over to bring 'im back." Nico laughed. He loved it when his mother told him the story, especially as she wanted him back to marry her, and didn't trust the English girls, as she knew Frenchmen seemed to be very attractive to them. He thought perhaps it was the accent, or the style, but he insisted his father had none of those qualities - obviously his mother thought otherwise. Nico didn't want to elaborate any further.

They were approaching the tunnel system that took them through the rock that Monte Carlo sat on, and onto the enclosed marina with Monte Carlo and the Pink Palace on one side with the mountains on the other, fronted by the many blocks of flats surrounding the harbour of Monaco. Nico headed for Port Hercule, directly in front of them. Harry telephoned Patrick.

"Hi Patrick. Are you on the boat? Can you call security to let us in to the port? I'm in a blue Mégane." Harry hadn't explained what was going on to his boss. He needed to see him in person. "Thanks, be there in a mo." Patrick was still talking to Harry. "Right, cheers." Harry put his phone in his pocket. "Patrick says we can park next to the Aston Martin in the space allocated to his wife as she's gone to their apartment and taken her car."

Harry directed Nico through the port security. He leant out and said hello to the guard, who recognised Harry and waved them through. They pulled up alongside the Aston Martin and Nico passed his Polo cap to Harry who pulled it over his face just in case the Russian thugs were watching the boat. They got out and walked along the gangplank onto the platform where the Rib was situated. Harry told them he used it for fast getaways if he's followed on board by lots of sexy women. Emm pretended to be annoyed, but she knew he was winding them up. Nico's mouth was wide open. He'd seen lots of boats, but Patrick's was beautiful. He noted it was called the Lady Eleanor.

"Welcome aboard." Patrick was waiting for them on the upper deck. "Come and join me for a drink." Harry led the way explaining what everything was and what everything did. On the first level was the lounge area with sumptuous sofas, a massive television and a bar. It had a dining table with seating for ten people.

"Where's the kitchen?" Emm couldn't see one.

"Downstairs. It's with all the crews' accommodation. That's where I normally sleep when I'm crewing on the boat." Harry moved them on to the stairs, up to the next deck.

"Wow, a hot tub. This is more like a penthouse apartment Harry. It's got another bar too," she was mesmerised as she took in a 360-degree panoramic view from where she was standing, "and a magnificent sea view." Harry laughed. Emm was doing her job very well. Patrick came from behind the bar to meet them.

"Welcome to the Lady Eleanor." He passed the wine glasses around. "You must be Emily?" Good job she was, thought Harry. That could have been tricky. Patrick had seen many photos of Emm. Harry had never stopped talking about her.

"This is Nicolas Janvier, a famous opera singer." Harry couldn't resist teasing Nico.

"Bonjour Monsieur. It is my pleasure to have you aboard. My wife follows the arts and opera is her passion.

She will know you, I bet." He turned to Harry. "To what do I owe you for this pleasure, Harry? You're not due back for a few more days yet." Harry took Patrick aside and explained as best as he could the story from the port in Portsmouth to the port in Monaco. While he was telling Patrick, two rather fit stewards came up from below wearing identical white shorts and white t-shirts, with white deck shoes.

"G'day. Can I get you anything?" Emm was rather taken with the Adonis in front of her. Nico smiled.
"What did you have in mind, um?" Emm wanted to get to know him.

"Lachlan." He extended his hand. "Very much at your service." Harry was watching and wasn't amused.

"Excuse me just a moment Patrick. Oy, you Aussi git, get your hands away from my Sheila." Lachlan swung round and saw who had just shouted at him.

"Harry. Good to see you mate." They shook hands and fake wrestled. They were obviously best of friends. "Davo, Harry's back." Lachlan had shouted over to his mate who was wiping the stair rails. Dave came over to the seating area.

"Harry mate. Where have you been? We've missed you. Especially on poker night, eh Lachlan?" They laughed.

"Well thank you Dave, it's nice to be missed." He got a hug too. Harry introduced his fellow crew members to Emm and Nico.

Patrick wanted to know how he could help Harry. He'd got the gist of what had happened but wasn't quite sure where he came into it. "We need to go to the fly bridge where I can get a good look around the port without being seen." Patrick and Harry disappeared up the stairs to the top deck.

"Can I get you another drink?" Lachlan wanted to know what was going on but didn't think it was his place to ask.

"No thank you, we need to keep a level head." Emm thought she ought to explain a little. "We are here to catch some nasty men who have kidnapped a woman." Lachlan thought it a little far-fetched, but who was he to doubt them. Nico could see the Australian was finding it difficult to believe so thought he'd change the subject.

"How many other crew members are on board?" Lachlan looked at Davo, who was counting on his hands. "There's four of us at the moment. But that's because we are in dock. When we are at sea we normally try to have at least six." Davo was wiping the bar. He didn't want Patrick thinking they were skiving.

"So, is Patrick very into 70's music?" Emm was interested where the boat's name came from. The crewmen looked puzzled. "You know, the Lady Eleanor. It's a classic Lindisfarne." Emm only knew the song because it was on one of her father's own compilation CD of his favourites. Lachlan suddenly clicked.

"No, it's his Sheila's name." Lachlan excused himself and went to find something to do before Patrick came back. Harry was scanning the port with the binoculars. Someone caught his eye at the security gate.

"There are two policemen, at the gate. Oh no, they are heading towards the boat." Patrick took the binoculars off Harry and looked to see what they were doing.

"They're checking out the Aston Martin. I better

go down before they blow your hiding place." Patrick passed the binoculars back to Harry. "Keep a watch in case they are here and get spooked when they see the police. I'll try and get rid of them." Harry watched the whole quay for sudden movement.

Patrick disembarked and walked casually up to the policemen. Harry watched as he talked to them. Patrick seemed to joke with the officers and after a few minutes the police went back to the gate and left the quay entrance. Patrick came back on board and found Harry by the bar talking to Emm and Nico.

"Well that could have been awkward." Patrick poured himself a whiskey. "They wanted to come on board to tell you they had the Mercedes under surveillance over the other side of the quay. Unfortunately, a bloody great Princess is blocking our view." Patrick pointed to the offending boat. Harry had to laugh. It was an in-joke to all Sunseeker owners that Princess motor yachts were inferior. The Princess owners thought the same about Sunseekers. "They have unmarked cars at the gate and the only other way out is by sea and that is being covered by the Marine Police, just outside the harbour entrance. It seems to be a waiting game." Patrick took another large gulp of the whiskey.

"What if Katarina is in the car, unconscious in a foot-well with a blanket over her, or even worse, in the boot of the car. The sun is very hot. She won't survive a waiting game. No, there is no choice we have to get closer to the Mercedes." Harry looked at Nico. He made a wonderful opera singer, but as additional muscle in a situation like this, he would be rubbish.

"Patrick, can we borrow Lachlan and Dave?" Patrick nodded.

"Good idea. It will look less suspicious with a couple of crewmen walking round the marina. Go and get them. I last saw them pretending to look busy by the Rib." Harry had to smile. Patrick wasn't stupid, he saw right through the two 'flaming galahs'. It was his affectionate nickname for them both. Harry had been an avid watcher of Home and Away when he got home from school, and he loved Alf Roberts' expression when talking about a couple of idiots. To him it was typical Australian. Harry went to find Lachlan. He had a soft spot for the man, who had been through an horrendous time years earlier, when his girlfriend, Matilda, had died in his arms. He kept assuring people that he was over it, but Dave and Harry knew otherwise. It was the main reason why Lachlan would not move on. He was more qualified than Harry on boats and could captain his own easily, but he had the ambition knocked out of him. One day, Harry hoped, he'd meet a girl who would give him back his passion for the sea and his vitality for life.

He found the pair of them, as Patrick had crudely said, pretending to polish the Rib. He came back with his fellow crewmen, having brought them up to date with the events unfolding.

"I can't be seen, or I'll give the game away. They don't know you Nico so if you and these two get near to the Mercedes you can come back and tell us how the land lies." Nico was up for it. "As soon as you know what's going on ring me, okay?" Nico nodded to Harry with conviction.

"'ow will I recognise these men?" Nico assumed they wouldn't have badges with 'Villain 1' and 'Villain 2'.

"They are in dark suits, which in this heat look ridiculously out of place and they have no necks." Nico nodded and understood what that meant. Inside Nico was slightly apprehensive, but looking at his minders, Lachlan and Dave, eased his worries a little. Luckily his profession needed his voice, not his limbs. That thought actually made him more anxious.

As Harry watched Nico walk along the quay, followed by the Australians, he said a silent prayer that all would go well. He had faith in his two work mates, but this was not a poker night with friends. For all their fitness and muscle, he hadn't actually ever seen the two of them engage in an unfriendly skirmish.

They knew a Sheila was in danger so he just hoped their basic instincts would kick in and be ready for any situation that was thrown at them.

Suddenly Patrick shouted from the Flybridge. Harry couldn't catch what he was saying and so rushed up the stairs, followed by Emm.

"What's up?" Patrick handed him the binoculars.

"The bloody great Princess is on the move." He was smiling. Hopefully they could get a look at what was going on. Harry spotted Nico with Lachlan and Dave walking nonchalantly towards the mooring the Princess had just vacated. There was the Mercedes.

"There's one, smoking next to the car. I can't see the other one though." He tried to focus the binoculars further, but they were at their limit. "I can't see anyone in the car either. The windows are too dark." Harry felt frustrated. Emm squeezed his free hand. He knew she was there for him and it eased his anxiety, slightly.

It was now a waiting game. Patrick had found two more sets of binoculars, not quite as good as the ones Harry had commandeered, but they would do. Emm and Patrick joined in the wait in quiet observation.

Nico made the Australians wait back a little, where they were able to survey the whole scenario in case Nico got into trouble, while he sauntered passed the Mercedes alone, slowly. He could see one of the Russians smoking in front of the car, staring into the sea. He would love to push him in, but that wouldn't get them anywhere.

As he walked on he saw the other Russian berating, very loudly, a man in a small motorboat. The discussion was getting more heated and the smoking Russian by the car threw his cigarette into the sea and wandered over to see what the commotion was about.

Nico could make out the Frenchman in the small motorboat was saying, "non, pas assez," meaning, 'no, not enough'. The Russian shouting at the Frenchman gestured for his brother to get out some money. Nico assumed they were trying to buy the motorboat from the Frenchman, or at least the man's services, for an escape. He took the chance of getting nearer to the Mercedes while the Russians were occupied.

The windows were heavily tinted making it difficult to see in. He needed to get much closer. Keeping an eye on the Russians, he walked as nonchalantly as he could to the front of the car. He bent down as if to look at something on the ground, there was no obvious sign of anyone sitting in the car. Peering in through the dark tinted windows, Nico strained to see into the passenger foot-well. It was empty, so he crept to the back door and looked in. Nothing in either foot-well, but he could see an overnight bag on the back seat of the car.

He came away and shook his head at Lachlan and Dave, who started walking closer to him, keeping their eyes on the enemy. He walked around to the boot, still checking the position of the two thugs.

"If it wasn't so worrying, I'd be finding the little Frenchman's actions quite hilarious." Dave was looking at the Frenchman gesticulating at the Russians; his arms resembling windmills. "Should we just go and knock the blocks off those two drongos, mate?" Dave was all for action.

"Too much at stake, mate. I'd love to, but if there's a chance a woman is in that boot, we don't want to jeopardise her rescue. Patience, Davo, has never been one of your strong points." Lachlan winked at his shipmate. He lowered his voice; "Just be ready in case the French bloke cocks up." Dave laughed, quietly to himself. Nico walked around to the boot of the car, backwards, so he could check he wasn't being watched. He approached the boot and bent low. He whispered Katarina's name. Lachlan and Dave decided the time was right to shield Nico from view. They stood together pretending to be chatting. Nico tried again, a little louder.

"Katarina, are you in there? I am a friend of 'arry's. We've come to rescue you." They waited for a response. All Nico could hear was his heartbeat. The tension, he considered, was worse than first night nerves. "There, did you hear that?" Lachlan had heard something.

"I'm sure I heard a knock, listen." There was a distinct knock coming from the boot. Nico tried to open it but there wasn't a button to press. He crept around to the driver's side as low as he could and opened the door slightly, feeling relieved the thugs hadn't locked the car.

He pulled the boot catch by the steering wheel and the boot pinged open. It was very fortunate that his father had a Mercedes a few years ago and knew its little quirks. Lachlan and Dave immediately bent down into the boot and managed to lift Katarina out. She looked in a very bad way and barely conscious. Hardly surprising having been shut in a hot and oxygen deprived boot when the outside temperature was no less than thirty-eight degrees centigrade. Lachlan cradled Katarina in his arms and carried her around the quay. His mind was all over the place. Should he take her straight back to the boat for safety, or should he get her to help as soon as he could? He made a decision on looking at her appearance. She was in a bad way.

"I'm going to take her to the port authority offices. They should be able to call an ambulance." He shouted over his shoulder at the other two. He ran as fast as he could, Katarina was extremely light. Lachlan looked at her and felt his heart sink. She was not moving and her eyes were closed. He hurried on, gently calling her name.

"Katarina, Katarina, hang in there, please." He was pleading with her. "You'll be safe in a minute, I promise." He stopped talking and saved his energy to move quicker. He couldn't lose another girl.

"I have to save her; I just have to." He shouted silently in his head. He willed himself to help Katarina in memory of his beloved Matilda. With more willpower than he thought possible, Lachlan was racing along the quay at a rate of knots. From the corner of his eye he could see the cavalry arriving from the marina entrance. It looked like the whole Monaco Police Department was descending on the marina. Dave stayed with Nico as the Russians had seen what was going on by the Mercedes, just as Lachlan was running with a body in his arms. They realised their prisoner had been stolen and were shouting at Nico and Dave, heading towards them looking incredibly hostile. They suddenly stopped. They had also seen the armed officers rapidly making their way towards them. They ran back to the Frenchman's motorboat. Nico turned to see a group of policemen behind him running towards the motorboat.

Bogdan propelled the little French boat owner into his boat aggressively, from his position on the quay side, injuring the poor man's leg. But the Frenchman shuffled along to his seat and held his breath to stop the pain that was searing from his ankle. He didn't have time to feel the intensity before Bogdan and Yegor jumped in behind him

"Take us out to sea, now!" Bogdan was pointing to the marina entrance in case he wasn't understood. The poor Frenchman was looking scared for his life. Bogdan alone was menacing, but with Yegor moving up towards him he didn't argue, he started his engine and pulled away from the quay. If it hadn't been so terrifying the Frenchman would have laughed at the sight of both Bogdan and Yegor falling backwards with the thrust of the engine. Regrettably they took no time at all to steady themselves.

"Faster, garlic breath." Yegor laughed at his brother's humour.   Harry had been watching from the Lady Eleanor and had rushed down to the lower deck and grabbed the Jet Ski from behind the Rib. He knew it would be quicker to get going and easier to manoeuvre than the Rib. He was on the water in record time, Patrick noticed that when the boy was determined, there was no stopping him. He was still the best crew member he'd ever had; he nodded at his own appraisal.

Harry took off and arrived at the first marina exit gap too late. They had already gone through. He had one more chance at the final exit on the other side before the open sea. It was like a chicane on a racetrack, to slow the boats down entering the marina. He had time to get to them before they reached the last opening then out into the Mediterranean Sea.

"Faster you French fool. He's gaining on us." Bogdan was getting irritated at the skipper. "Get this rust bucket out into open waters before you find yourself in a watery grave." Yegor found that funny too. Bogdan swung round at his brother. "Instead of laughing like a jackass, find something to throw at that Jet Ski." Harry had managed to catch up with the motorboat and broadsided them, soaking the occupants. Yegor looked around the deck aimlessly. "Yegor hurry. Find anything that can be thrown at him, now!" Yegor looked around the deck again. Bogdan decided he could get rid of the Jet Skier himself. He pushed the Frenchman aside, took hold of the wheel and aimed the boat directly at the Jet Ski.

"Hard luck mate." Shouted Harry. The Jet Ski was able to manoeuvre far quicker than any motorboat and was now in front of the boat, between them and the harbour entrance. He guided the Jet Ski back along the length of the motorboat. He wanted to keep his distance, but he needed to keep an eye on the skipper in case there was a chance to help him get off. Yegor hadn't been paying attention to events as his mind was on what to throw out of the boat that could stop the maniac on the Jet Ski. As he turned to the stern of the boat he spotted some lobster pots. He thought Bogdan would be pleased if he just used his own initiative, so he threw them out to the side Harry was on, not realising the pots were attached to the stern by rope. Harry had overtaken them and was blocking their path. The Frenchman took the throttle down a few knots so they wouldn't hit the Jet Ski. Bogdan was about to grab the Frenchman and throw him overboard, when all of a sudden, he fell backwards with a jolt.

The boat made an awful noise and was then still. Both Bogdan and Yegor were prone on the deck. The Frenchman got up from of his seat as Harry steered the Jet Ski alongside the boat.

"Monsieur, monsieur, vite, sauter du bateau, rapidement!" Harry shouted urgently. The Frenchman didn't need to be told twice to get off the boat. He limped to the side and jumped. As Harry turned to pick the skipper up, he noticed a rather large bright orange boat entering the marina exit gap with 'Police' written boldly on the side.

Harry skimmed around to the Frenchman and leant over and grabbed the man's arm helping him to the seat behind him. As they pulled away from his boat the Frenchman saluted his motorboat. The boat was taking on water very quickly. He knew he was insured so wasn't that bothered - it was old and needed replacing. As they passed behind the boat they both could see what had caused the sudden stop. The lobster pots and ropes had got tangled in the motorboat's propeller. Rookie mistake thought Harry. The Russian's were debating whether to jump into the water or wait for the police to rescue them. Yegor was frantically baling water out with a bowl he had found.

Bogdan was just looking over at the land, knowing the current would be too strong for him to even contemplate swimming to the quay. He resigned himself to the fact he was going to jail. As the Jet Ski roared off towards the safety of the land, the Frenchman smiled at the just retribution being meted out to his captors. He looked up to Heaven and nodded. God was very quick, he thought. Harry dropped the Frenchman off by the spot his motorboat had been tied. The police were there waiting to help him.

"Merci beaucoup monsieur." The Frenchman knew the current was extremely dangerous at the mouth of the marina, so he wanted to shake Harry's hand for saving him, but Harry just saluted him from a slight distance. It was more than his job was worth to scrape the Jet Ski on the wall.

"Mon plaisir, mate!" Harry waved and left. The Frenchman waved and smiled at his hero. Harry, who knew he'd been speeding in the harbour with his boss watching, drove the Jet Ski slowly back to Patrick's boat. Emm had been watching it all and was smiling too. Harry looked so sexy riding around on the Jet Ski. It was like watching a Bond movie. Patrick was watching the Maritime Police expertly rescuing the thugs before the boat sunk.

"Yay, they've got them." Patrick put the binoculars down and saw Emm looking over his shoulder, petrified. Patrick turned around slowly to see a man standing on his Flybridge with a gun in his hand. In typical British style, Patrick asked politely, "Can I help you?" If she weren't so frightened, Emm would have laughed.

"Where is my Lilliana?" Ah, the penny dropped with them both. This must be the infamous Erik. Patrick knew it wasn't the time to play silly beggars, so didn't say 'who?' but wasn't quite sure how to respond.

Emm, on the other hand, knew exactly how to respond to a bully.

"If you mean that adorable little girl who deserves more than you could ever offer her, she is safe and sound and above all happy." Emm wasn't sure where that came from, but anger seemed to far outweigh fear. Patrick glanced at Emm and took his lead from her positivity.

"Now you have got your answer, please disembark the way you came in." Emm giggled but then realised the situation they were both in. They had a lunatic with a gun pointed at them and they were resorting to humour. If that wasn't British, she didn't know what was. Erik found the whole scenario a charade. He knew they must be scared. He obviously wasn't being taken seriously, so he'd have to up the ante. He couldn't shoot the gun in the air, or the police would come running. He would use the girl to get the answer out of the man.

"You, over here." He said very impolitely to Emm. Emm now knew she had to play along with him, for safety sake. She moved closer to him but stopped short. Over his head she saw Harry quietly waiting at the top of the stairs. He had seen Erik get onto the boat while he was crossing the harbour. Thanking himself for going so slowly, he turned the Jet Ski off before he got too close and managed to manoeuvre it towards its berthing station. He tied it off and jumped on board.

He signalled to Emm to go back towards Patrick. She reversed keeping her eye on Erik. Erik wasn't happy.

"I said over here, NOW." He aimed the gun at Emm but was taken by surprise when Harry came up behind him and cracked him over the head with the oar from the Rig, he had picked up on his way to the Flybridge. Erik lay prone and inert on the deck.

Emm ran into Harry's arms. Patrick kicked the gun over to the other side of the deck, right away from Erik.

He shouted down to a couple of policemen who were standing by the water's edge. With Emm in Harry's arms and Patrick leaning over the side of the boat trying to get the attention of the policemen, Erik, who had just been stunned, had faked unconsciousness for just long enough. He crawled, surreptitiously along the deck with his gun in view. Harry had kept one eye on his prize and noticed the distance the prone assailant had moved. Letting go of Emm, he grabbed the oar back from where it was propped against the instrument panel and headed back towards Eric for a final thwack. Erik caught the movement from his side vision and managed to see Harry grab the oar and decided he really didn't want to hang around for another blow. With as much strength as he could muster, through the pain coming from his first injury, he made it to the top of the stairs and bolted down two and a half flights. He couldn't believe his luck when he noticed the Jet Ski waiting for him. He untied it and accelerated off.

As Harry reached the Bottom of the stairs he recognised the sound of the Jet Ski and shouted at the policemen chatting on the dock. He pointed out to sea and saw one of the officers radioing for assistance. Patrick couldn't believe that a few moments earlier they had the murderer lying on the deck. He shook his head.

"Oh my God, what just happened? If those bloody policemen had been paying attention and not standing there admiring the boats, they would have been able to arrest him and throw the key away." Patrick's head was in his hands when a police officer finally got up to the Flybridge. He took charge of the situation by questioning Harry who had gone back up to check on Emm.

"'Ow did the man escape? Do you usually leave the Jet Ski so anyone can take it?" Harry was about to explain the rush he was in, but Patrick took over.

"I hope you're not accusing our liberator of misconduct. If it wasn't for him we'd have been shot." He pointed at the gun on the deck. The policeman looked embarrassed as he hadn't even noticed it. He picked it up in a polythene bag and walked off down the stairs.
Sirens were blasting out at sea where the Maritime Police were in pursuit of the Jet Ski.

"They won't have to go far." Harry smirked. "I hadn't filled it up with fuel last time I took it out so it's running on fumes now." Patrick went over and patted Harry on the back.

"We'll get him yet. Come on, we deserve a strong drink. Let's leave it to the professionals." Patrick too had a smirk on his face. Just as they were about to go down to the lower deck Harry heard a recognisable Kookaburra impression that always sounded more like an ape to him. It was Lachlan. Patrick went off to meet them. Harry went over to the boat rail where Emm was watching the chase.

"Are you okay?" Emm looked at Harry.

"Apart from my life passing in front of my eyes, I'm just fine. But I think you need to go to the gym. That whack of the oar was feeble, to say the least. I would have knocked him out for a week." Harry took Emm's arm and squeezed her biceps. He cocked his head in sympathy.

Emm couldn't help but grin. He took Emm's hand and she followed him down to the lower deck to welcome back their conquering heroes. Nico rushed onto the boat.

"Did you see us? We took Katarina from right under their noses." He was so thrilled to have been part of the adventure. Of course, he had no idea what had happened back on the Lady Eleanor. Emm smiled at Harry. They'd let Nico have his moment of euphoria. Harry got off the boat and walked towards Katarina. She was feeling better after the port authority medic on duty had put an oxygen mask on her for a while and also cleaned up her head wound. She was able to freshen up and was feeling more human than she had done for a while. She was walking as steadily as she could between Lachlan and Dave. She managed to muster some strength and walked quicker to Harry. He hugged her, but he realised he was hurting her.

"Sorry. How are you feeling?" Stupid question, he thought. She just smiled as she was so happy to be free.

"Thank you all so much for helping me get away from those monsters." Lachlan and Dave patted each other on the back. Patrick introduced himself and welcomed her on board. They managed to get her up to the first deck and Patrick poured her a small glass of brandy while Harry got her comfortable on a sofa.

"I need to see Lilli. Has she been good?" Harry didn't know where to start.

"Not being an expert on children's behaviour, well before this trip anyway, I would say that you have the epitome of an angel on this earth." He smiled while he answered her.

"Absolutely, she's just so cute." Emm had to put Katarina's mind at rest. The experience of caring for a

FOR THE LOVE OF LILLI

little girl for a few days had probably been the best thing ever to happen to Harry, in her opinion.
It had made him into a man.

"I absolutely agree with them both." Nico wanted to put his two euros worth in. "Your problem now is getting 'er back." Katarina looked anxious. Nico realised she'd misunderstood what he meant. "We all love 'er so much, we will not want 'er to go." Katarina understood and smiled.

"Talking of going, we better start thinking about getting back to Caroline's and reunite Lilli with her mother." Harry went over to talk to Patrick behind the bar. "Is it ok for me to have a little longer off, boss? I'm not sure what I can do for Katarina, but she won't want to go back to England I wouldn't think. Not for a while anyway. At least not until Erik is locked away in some dark hole." Patrick nodded.

"I totally agree with you Harry. The police want to interview us all in the morning. Hopefully they'll have some good news about Erik. Until then we need to keep Katarina safe. I take it you haven't told Katarina about Erik's escape?" Harry shook his head. "Probably wise. No need to worry her any more than we need to. She could stay in Monaco, we have plenty of room. Her daughter can go to the International school, it's just there." He pointed to the corner of the port where the Frenchman's motorboat had been moored. "I know Eleanor would be overjoyed to have the company, especially with a child. I wouldn't have to take my wife with us all the time." He winked at Harry, who knew he was only joking. He adored Eleanor and was the one wanting her with him. "It'll give Katarina time, in a safe environment, to work out what she wants to do and where she wants to go, without rushing into anything."

"I'll take her back to Emm's mother's apartment and talk to her once she's seen Lilli. If she likes the idea, when I bring her back tomorrow, she can meet Eleanor." They shook hands and Harry helped Katarina up and they followed Nico down to his car. Katarina thanked everybody, especially Lachlan and Dave.

"Our pleasure. Haven't had that much fun since we lost Harry overboard in the Bahamas last month." Dave was laughing as hard as Lachlan.

"And he thought a shark was chasing him, but it turned out to be a black coral tree." Lachlan had finally relaxed, knowing Katarina would be fine. They were laughing so much that they were in fear of falling into the sea themselves.

"Ignore the flaming galahs, Katarina, they're from Australia." She nodded as if that explained a lot. Harry smiled, he had to admit he did have fun with those Aussies.

Emm had got in the back with Harry, and Katarina was in the more spacious front seat. Nico drove them back to Nice while Katarina filled in the gaps of her journey to Monaco. Understandably the last twenty-four hours were a blur to her. She knew she had been drugged as well as beaten.

"But I have managed to stay alive, that is a bonus, yes?" They half-heartedly laughed. It would have been funnier if she hadn't looked so bruised.

"I'm sorry, but what man could beat a woman?" Nico was shaking his head while biting his lower lip, hard.

"A weak one." Katarina replied.

CHAPTER 10

By the time they got back to the Nice apartment Lilli was asleep. Alain was still there keeping Caroline company. He didn't want to go home before he saw his son home safely. Emm had telephoned her mother to tell her they were on their way back with Katarina. She then texted her to ask if she could get her bedroom made up for Katarina, as she wasn't in a very good way. Emm was happy to sleep on the sofa, with Harry on the floor. She decided to tell Harry about the new sleeping arrangements once Katarina was settled in Emm's bed.
Caroline opened the door to greet them all. Alain had put himself in charge of the drinks. After introducing Katarina to Caroline and Alain, Harry knew Katarina would be desperate to see Lilli. He pushed her door open as quietly as he could.

"I'll try not to wake her up, but I can't promise anything." Katarina was so anxious to hold Lilli in her arms that she knew temptation may be too great. They both stood over a sleeping Lilli and stared at her. Whether it was their breathing, or the light sneaking past her door, or even the smell of her mother near her, who knows, but something woke Lilli.

"Mummy, you're here." She jumped up off the chaise longue and into her mother's arms. Harry could see how much it was hurting Katarina, but she didn't show it to Lilli. "Look Harry, Mummy's here." Harry smiled at Lilli.

"Why don't you sit back down and let your mummy cuddle you. You can tell her all about our trip." Katarina was very grateful to Harry. Lilli unattached herself from her mother and went to the drawers where she had put her perfume.

"Look Mummy. Alain has given me a bottle of perfume, because I'm a real mademoiselle. Did you know that Mummy?" Katarina laughed.

"I think you're definitely a real mademoiselle Lilli." Lilli went back to her mother, who was now sitting on the chaise longue, and cuddled her. Harry thought he'd leave them to catch up on their exploits. "Harry, thank you so much for looking after Lilli. I can never re-pay you for what you have done." Harry shook his head.

"It was actually me that needs to re-pay you for the loan of your daughter. She is such a credit to you Katarina. I'm just glad we have a wonderfully happy ending." He left the room before he got any soppier. Emm was waiting for him outside the room. She looked at his face and wanted to kiss him.

Not really appropriate with her mother staring at them both.

"I'm afraid you have been allocated the floor tonight. I have shot-gunned the sofa." He laughed and put his arm around her and walked with her into the kitchen where drinks were being poured. Nico was explaining everyone's part in the Great Kidnap Rescue and the arrest of the two Russians. Alain looked across at Harry and Emm.

"Harry and I have listened avidly to Nico's version of events, and although they do pick up the important parts, he wasn't there when Harry managed to knock-out Erik and save Patrick and I from being shot." Emm couldn't help herself. Caroline looked horrified so Nico put his arm round her and tried to calm her down. "As you can see, we are all home safe and sound. So chill Mother." Emm sounded far more confident than she felt. It was stupid to blurt the gun thing out in front of her mother, but she was so proud of Harry that she wanted them all to know.

"Well I'm just glad you all got home in one piece." Caroline planted a kiss on Nico's lips. Emm thought 'gross' but didn't say it aloud. She was about to tell them about Erik escaping, but heard Katarina moving about. They had kept that piece of bad news away from her. She was in a bad state and as they were all there protecting her, she didn't need to know, yet.

Katarina eventually came out of Lilli's room, looking tired but happy. Caroline started fussing over her.

"Can I get you a warm drink Katarina? Or did you want to get to bed? You are very welcome to stay here as long as you need to, by the way. Please, relax and enjoy your freedom." Katarina didn't know what she wanted to do. Harry picked up on her indecision. He got up and walked her over to what was Emm's bedroom. He left the door ajar and gently pushed her down to sit on the bed.

"Sorry about that, Caroline can be overpowering at times, but she means well." Harry got a smile out of Katarina.

"She is very kind. You all are very kind." She shook her head with tears in her eyes. "I need to know how Maria is before I can relax." Harry looked on his phone for the number of Girona hospital on the Internet.

He sat by her on the bed and pressed the highlighted number and waited for an answer.

"Hello, do you speak English. Good. Can you tell me how a Maria…?" He looked at Katarina.

"Kõiv."

"Maria Kõiv is please? She was brought in two days ago after a fire." He could hear a keyboard being tapped.

"She is in room 23. I will put you through to the desk on that floor." Harry was about to say thank you when he realised he was already calling the ward. A Spanish female voice answered but spoke far too quickly for Harry to understand. He asked if she spoke English. Fortunately, she did.

"I'm enquiring after the health of Maria Kõiv on behalf of her cousin Katarina Eskola." He grabbed Katarina's hand with his free one and smiled at her. She was so worried he had to try and keep her strong, for Lilli's sake.

"Ah yes, Maria Kõiv. She has just joined us from ICU. That is a good sign. She is still in a lot of pain, but we are keeping that under control. She is resting at the moment as she had a visit from the National Police. We gave them ten minutes only. They are coming back when she is stronger." Harry was going to be very selective in what he told Katarina.

"I don't suppose you know when she will be discharged?" Katarina looked relieved. Discharge meant Maria must be ok.

"She is healing every day. I would hope she could leave within the next week. That is if everything continues without setback. It would probably be a good idea to check again in a few days. We should be able to tell you more by then." Harry thanked her and wished her a good evening. He put his phone in his pocket and stood up to face Katarina.

"They are very happy with Maria. She is out of ICU and on the road to recovery. You can phone them again in a few days and they should be able to tell you when she can leave hospital." Katarina's smile lit up her face. Harry thought he had told her enough. There was no need to worry her unnecessarily.

"Thank you, Harry. That is a weight off my mind." She tried to stifle a yawn, unsuccessfully.

"Come on, time for bed. We can get your belongings tomorrow from the police. I'm sure they will be in the Mercedes, or the car rental Erik was driving. In the meantime, Emm has left you some girlie bits." He pointed at the pile of clothes on a chair, slightly embarrassed. Katarina thought it funny. "I'm glad you find it amusing. Gentlemen don't talk about lady's underwear and things." He grinned. "If you want anything let us know."

"I will. Thank you again and thank everyone out there. I will see you in the morning. Goodnight Harry." She got up and kissed him on the cheek.

He turned and walked out of her room, closing the door behind him.

He found Emm and her mother on the balcony, no sign of Nico or Alain. Caroline noticed him scan the apartment.

"Alain says goodnight, but he had to get back to Veronique. She has been on the phone all day wondering where her son was," Harry realised Veronique was obviously Alain's wife. "Alain didn't want to worry her so

kept telling her he'd be back soon, he was at a rehearsal. He protects her." She sighed. "They are still very much in love after thirty-five years of marriage. Sometimes I wish I had been born in France. The French are far more romantic than the English." Harry had to interrupt.
"Excuse me. On behalf of men of English descent, I'd like to disagree with your last statement. I remember the last birthday present I bought your daughter was a silver and rose gold bangle, which I see she still wears." He pointed at Emm's wrist as she held a glass of wine. Caroline looked too.

"Well, all I can say is that you're an exception. The last present my ex-husband bought me for my birthday was a deep fat fryer." Harry tried not to laugh. Emm didn't look amused. She knew for a fact that her mother had asked for one. It suddenly dawned on her that her father would have the last laugh when the news finally broke on his relationship with a very famous French woman.

As if by telepathy her mobile rang, it was her father.

"I need to answer this, excuse me." She went inside, out of earshot of her mother. "Hi Daddy, how are you?"

"Hello Poppet, I need to tell you something." She heard an intake of breath, which usually meant it was important. "The French tabloids have found out about me and Claudia, so she has decided to have a press conference on Saturday, so the world will know. I'd love it if you could be there for moral support. Stephanie and James should be back on Friday so I'm hoping they'll be there too." Emm could hear the apprehension in her father's voice.

"Of course, I'll be there. Where exactly?"

"The Dorchester Hotel. The Penthouse and Terrace to be exact. Hopefully the weather will be nice and we can do it outside. The backdrop should be good for the photos. Oh dear, I'm beginning to sound like Claudia." He laughed at himself, Emm guessed he was nervous, it was a dead giveaway when he tried to joke.

"I'm sure it will be fine Daddy. Try to enjoy it, if only for Claudia's sake." Michael was so happy his daughter was thinking of his girlfriend. He would enjoy it more if Emily could be there though.

"I should stay here for a few more days, but I shall be on a plane on Friday, I promise." She didn't want to burst his bubble at that moment so decided she'd tell him all about the escapade in France once Saturday was over.

"Take care of yourself and send my love to Claudia. Bye Daddy."

"I will. Take care of you. Oh, and try to keep Paris Match away from your mother until then too. Bye Poppet." Emm put her phone on the worktop and poured herself another drink.

"Going home so soon?" Harry had crept up behind her. "Who's Claudia?" Emm turned to face him.

"She is my father's girlfriend. Mother doesn't know anything about her, so keep shtum and I'll tell you about it later." He nodded conspiratorially.

"I hope they go to bed soon. We'll have to go to Monaco tomorrow to give them our statements, and I'm knackered already." Emm noticed that Harry was looking very drawn. She thought perhaps another drink may help perk him up.

"We can't go to bed until they do." She went over to the kitchen to get a small, strong nightcap. She cam

back and found Harry looking over at the office.
Harry noticed Lilli's bedroom door open. He slowly put his head round the door and couldn't see her in there. He came out and shook his head at Emm. Emm put her finger up to her lips to make him stay quiet. She handed him the drink and walked quietly over to her bedroom and opened the door slightly. There in the bed were mother and daughter fast asleep snuggled up to each other. All was well in Katarina's world. They both backed out of the room and gently shut the door.

"Shot-gun the chaise longue. Goodnight Harry." She giggled all the way back to the study and shut the door. Harry was left staring at the closed door. He tilted his head and downed the drink. That definitely wasn't the ending of the day he had imagined. The only advantage he could see was that he was getting the comfortable sofa instead of the floor, but he was hoping for a more intimate contact than with the sofa cushions.

In the morning Lilli was trying to get Harry up.
"Come on Harry, Paris wants his breakfast." Harry opened one eye to catch a glimpse of the time on his watch. He couldn't believe it was just after nine o'clock. He sat bolt upright to a round of applause. Watching him, out on the balcony, were Emm, Caroline, Katarina and Nico eating their breakfast.

"Sleeping Beauty is awake." Emm found it amusing that everyone had showered, dressed and got breakfast together without Harry stirring.

"Sleeping Beauty was a girl, wasn't she Harry? Does that mean that Emm thinks you're a girl? You're not though are you Harry? Girls don't drive fast cars do they Harry." Lilli went back outside to ask her mother why

Emm had thought that Harry was a girl.

"Emm was being sarcastic Lilli. Do you remember what that means?" Katarina had put Lilli on her lap. She couldn't get enough of her and vowed she would never again let her out of her sight. Lilli shook her head and looked at Emm, who was feeling guilty.

"It was just a joke Lilli. I have to agree with you though, it wasn't funny, and you're right Sleeping Beauty was a girl." Lilli nodded knowingly.

"You should have called him Mr Lazy, you know, from the Mr Men." Emm laughed. That actually wouldn't have suited Harry. He was anything but lazy. Harry walked out onto the balcony and helped himself to a cup of coffee, in his plain grey boxer shorts. "I like the Minions ones best Harry. Why aren't you wearing those?" Harry wondered why Lilli had suddenly become so vocal after the quiet few days he had with her. He realised she was in a happier more secure place, that was why. He knew it was unhealthy the way she had been so compliant. He caught sight of Emm laughing at the idea of the Minions boxer shorts.

"Eleanor bought them for me last Christmas. I didn't like to offend her, so I wear them frequently at work." He winked at her, knowing full well she knew he wouldn't have walked around in Eleanor's company in his boxers… or would he? His facial expression was full of innuendos. Emm was not going to bite.

"On a serious note, you all have to get off to Monaco for your interviews at the Sûreté Publique. I will look after Lilli." Caroline smiled at Lilli who was cuddling into her mother.

"Oh, I thought she could come with us." Katarina held Lilli close.

She knew in her heart that it was a bad idea taking a child into a police station, especially when she knew the trauma of the days before that had to be repeated, would make her distraught.

She didn't want to let Lilli see her so distressed. Caroline was right to offer to have her.

"No, Caroline is right. Lilli would have more fun here than if she had to stay very quiet and still in a boring old office." Harry had seen Katarina's dilemma and wanted Lilli to make the decision. Lilli looked up at Harry.

"But Harry." She whispered, as quietly as possible so as not to offend anyone. "It might be boring here too." Emm looked at the little girl trying to be tactful, and her heart went out to her.

Caroline got up and went over to Lilli and whispered in her ear. Lilli jumped off Katarina's lap and ran to her room. Emm looked cross with her mother. What was the point of upsetting Lilli? She was just a child. She was about to chastise her mother when Lilli came back out of her room with her shoes and little rucksack. She went over to Harry.

"Please could you put these on like you do?" Lilli was beaming at Harry. Harry knew the routine. He put one of her shoes over his big toe.

"But Lilli, they don't fit me." Lilli bent over with laughter, with both hands covering her mouth.

"That's because they're mine, silly." She was giggling while Harry put them on her feet. Katarina knew that Lilli had the best guardian she could have ever imagined. "Are we going now?" She turned and asked Caroline.

"Give me one minute to put my face on and I'll be ready." Caroline disappeared into her bedroom. Nico looked extremely puzzled. Caroline had never only taken one minute to do anything.

"Mummy? I like the face Caroline is wearing now, why does she have to change it?" They all burst out laughing so Emm tried to explain.

"She means she is going to put on some make-up Lilli." Lilli looked stern.

"Then why doesn't she say what she means… said Alice?" Lilli looked at her mother for approval. "I did get that right, didn't I Mummy?" Katarina nodded her head. It was one of their favourite books. Katarina read it to Lilli every bedtime. That now seemed a world away, but what a happier place they were both in now. "That was from Alice in Wonderland, my favourite book." Lilli told everybody. Caroline came back in record time. Nico jokingly looked at his watch.

"Oh, ha ha." Caroline caught the gesture. "When I have something exciting to do, I can be very quick." She winked at Lilli. "Come on Lilli, let's leave them to their boring day. We are going to have so much fun." She winked at Nico, pecked him on the cheek and said goodbye to them all. Clutching Lilli's hand while Lilli blew kisses to her mother and Harry and Emm and Nico, they walked out of the door and were gone.

"All right, I give up, where are they going?" Harry looked at Nico who was grinning.

"My mother and father are about to get an apprentice perfumier for the day. It was my father's idea. My mother was dying to meet Lilli, so 'e suggested that while we were busy today, Caro could take Lilli up to

Grasse and they could spoil 'er. My thoughts are that my parents will be the spoilt ones, she is délicieux Katarina." He smiled over at Katarina, as she was looking a little sad. Katarina smiled, as These people were helping her, she really didn't want to look ungrateful.

"Shall we get off, the sooner we get there the sooner we will be able to put it all behind us." Harry had taken charge. "You girls go and do what you need to do, Nico and I will clear the breakfast things and we'll meet you both at the door in ten minutes." Katarina got up and tried to stack some of the crockery. "We can do that Katarina, go!" He said it with a big smile on his face. She wasn't used to a man doing a woman's task and it felt wrong. But she would go and get ready. It was all so alien to her, but she quite liked it. She took the opportunity to text Robbie.

"Dear Robbie. I'm safe and well and reunited with my beautiful Lilli. Harry has done a wonderful job looking after her." She thought for a moment. There was no need to explain about Girona, especially not in a text message. *"We are staying with friends in Nice and are very happy. I don't know how to thank you, but perhaps when we meet again I can take you out for a meal."* She suddenly thought his wife might see the text and misunderstand. *"It would be great to meet your family too, one day. Give them my love and tell them that they are living with a true hero!"* She read over the message and decided a meal didn't seem enough for all he had done for her. *"Perhaps when Lilly and I are settled, whichever country that may be, you and your family can come and stay with us for a holiday. God bless you dear Robbie. Katarina."* She decided not to add an emoji or any crosses, still aware that it could be misinterpreted. She read it one more time and pressed 'send'.

***

The journey to Monaco was uneventful and pleasantly quick. The traffic at that time in the morning was light. Workers would have got to work, and holidaymakers would only have just finished breakfast.

On the way Katarina explained about the last time she had travelled that road, was it only yesterday? Erik had got a message from one of his gang that they had traced the yellow Aston Martin from its registration plate to a man in Monaco. Bogdan and Yegor had waited outside the Robertshaw's apartment block and when Patrick had left to go to the boat, they followed him. Erik got the call to go to Port Hercule where the car was parked. Katarina said she was taken out of Erik's rental car and put in the boot of the Mercedes for around fifteen minutes, semi-conscious due to drugs and the heavy handedness of the men, before she thankfully heard Nico's voice.

"I 'ave to admit, the ladies like my voice." Nico was trying to break the tension, and it had worked. The atmosphere relaxed almost immediately. Emm knew one of the reasons her mother felt so happy with Nico was the fact that he was not ashamed of showing his gentle side. English men were more reticent about letting their masculine guard down, more's the pity, she thought.

When they arrived at the Public Security building of Monaco they were taken into separate rooms to give their account of the incidents that specifically related to each of them. Harry and Katarina had Spanish detectives in with them as well as the criminal investigation team from Monaco itself. They had to answer questions about the murder of Karl Kõiv and attempted murder of his wife

Maria, in Girona. Patrick was also there to recount the incident on his yacht. Lachlan and Dave had to give statements, but they didn't take long and were back at the boat by coffee time. As custom dictated in Mediterranean countries, they all stopped for lunch.

Patrick invited them to his boat where Eleanor had organised a relaxing buffet with the help of Lachlan and Dave. They had both thought the last place Katarina needed to be was a stuffy restaurant, after the grilling she inevitably would have had all morning. Unfortunately, they had been told that Erik was still at large. The Jet Ski was found abandoned having drifted onto a beach, not far from the port. The tank was empty. Katarina left the police station more positive than she thought she'd be. It was probably because she had so many friends fighting her corner, she was less afraid. She was hoping that Erik had gone back to Estonia and good riddance to him.

They all sat on the lower deck with iced drinks in hand and a pleasant breeze from the Mediterranean Sea keeping them cool.

Patrick took Harry aside and was concerned about Katarina and her future.

"She wants to visit her cousin Maria in Girona as soon as she can. I thought I'd take her tomorrow. Apparently, she is out of ICU but still not good. Perhaps a friendly face may help her recover, who knows?" Harry felt helpless.

"Let me help Harry. I can at least offer you a car to use. What about having Maria moved to the University Hospital in Nice? At least Katarina can visit her any time she wanted without troubling anyone." Harry shook his head.

"I'm not sure Maria has money to pay her hospital bills. Her house has burnt down, and she has lost…" He took a deep breath, as if he had just realised the enormity of the situation, "…everything, including her husband." Patrick had another idea.

"Since I won't get you back to work until all this is sorted out, I had better assist you. How about bringing Lilli and Katarina here tomorrow, with you and Emily and we will sail over to Palamós Marina which, by my calculations, will be about forty-five minutes' drive to Girona hospital. The girls can visit Maria, and we can drive on the twenty minutes to the farm and have a look at the damage. By the time we get back to the hospital it will have given Katarina a good hour with her cousin." Harry nodded in agreement. Harry knew Patrick wasn't offering to help to get Harry back to work quickly - he was just a genuinely nice guy.

"That sounds like a brilliant idea. Thank you, Patrick. I promised to take Lilli on a boat, so that kills two birds at once. Hang on a minute, how come your calculations are so precise? You must have had this idea all along." Patrick was nodding his head. "Well, thank you for thinking of them. Even if you had an ulterior motive." Harry laughed. He knew his boss too well.

"The motive wasn't all me, Eleanor loves the shops in Spain, so I will be killing two birds at once as well. We will drop the girls off and pick them up right outside the door of the hospital and be with them until we get back to the boat, just in case Erik is around." They both companionably shook hands and joined the rest to give them the news.

"So how long will we be away?" Emm had to get

back to London. She was not going to let her father down.

"It'll take a day to get to Palamós, and a day back, with probably a day there. We should be back by Saturday.

Make sure you bring some clothes and a toothbrush." Patrick rather enjoyed playing the Captain. He normally only had crew on board, so it was nice to entertain guests.

"I'm afraid I won't be able to come with you. I have to be in London for Saturday. My father needs me." That sounded so lame, but Emm couldn't divulge the true reason until after the weekend. Harry looked bemused. He knew she had to go back but hoped she could postpone it for such a worthy cause. Emm took a note of Harry's expression and decided he would have to know the truth as soon as the police interviews were over, and they were back in Nice.

"I cannot come either, I'm gutted? Is that the right word? I 'ave an opera to perform at Opéra de Nice, on Saturday and Friday I will be in rehearsals all day. It is so unfair." Emm tried not to laugh. Nico looked like a schoolboy who had just been told he couldn't go out to play because he hadn't finished his homework.

"Well, Katarina, Lilli and I can come, so with less weight we should get there quicker." Harry thought he was funny, nobody else did. He winked at Eleanor and carried the dirty glasses over to the bar and put them in the glass washer under the worktop. Eleanor had missed Harry's cheekiness. He was like the son they never had. She'd miss him when he left their employ, and intuition told her that would be sooner rather than later. She would just enjoy his company while he was still with them.

"Right, they've finished with us three, so it's just Harry and Katarina they want this afternoon. Lachlan can

give you a lift back to the station and we will relax and enjoy the quiet. Ring us when you want a lift back."
Patrick had buzzed Lachlan on the intercom earlier and he was waiting in the Range Rover for them both.

"Thank you so much Mr Robertshaw. I'm not sure how I can ever repay you for your kindness." Katarina had tears in her eyes. Patrick could see how emotional she was. He was sad for someone so young to have so much grief in her life, so the sooner they can help her get back on track, the sooner they will all be happier.

"My repayment will be to see you and Lilli living the life you deserve. By the way, call me Patrick. Now off with you before you see a grown man cry." He laughed just in case she thought he was going to cry.

The afternoon was spent very sedately with Patrick showing Nico the features and electronics of the boat, and Eleanor and Emm lying in the sun talking about Harry. What Emm hadn't realised was that Harry had used Eleanor as his confidante, almost like a mother.

He wanted to ring Emm on numerous occasions, but he kept stopping himself because he knew he was keeping her from getting on with her life. He wasn't ready to put on slippers or mow the lawn on a Sunday.

"Recently things have changed though. I see a young man suddenly maturing to the point of husband material." Eleanor had watched Harry grow. "He enjoys the life he is living, but he knows something is missing. I think you're his missing link. He could have telephoned any of his French friends to help with this chain of events, but he rang you. He trusts you. He loves you." Eleanor poured a crisp cool glass of water and handed it to Emm.

"But the question is, how do you feel about

Harry?" Emm took a long sip of the deliciously cold water.

"To be truthful, Eleanor, I have never stopped loving Harry. I haven't even had a boyfriend since we stopped our close relationship. No one seemed to match up to him. But he was young and impetuous, and I wanted the normal dating, engagement, wedding scenario that I knew I'd never get with him. But I have to say over the last few days I have seen a new Harry, a more grown-up Harry and I like what I've seen. But is he ready to settle? I'm still not sure." Eleanor took Emm's hand and looked her in the eyes.

"My dear, you two are meant for each other. You need to let him have a long leash and gradually it will get shorter and shorter until you won't need it, as he'll be right by your side. It will happen without either of you even noticing. Patrick was an adventurer when I first met him. My father called him a gallivanting dreamer. Not far off the mark either. But I kept an eye on him, went with him to all the places he visited. Packed for him. Made sure he had food, drink and clothing. Made myself indispensable. Now he wouldn't dream of not taking me with him wherever he goes. He wouldn't cope without me." She winked at Emm. "You see they need us more than we need them. The trick is not to let them know that." Emm got it. She nodded and smiled.

It wasn't long before Harry and Katarina returned from their interviews. For the moment they were finished, but they had to be available for court dates and more questions if necessary.

They had been told that the court case would probably be heard in Spain as that was where the murder had taken place, and murder beats human trafficking, so Estonia and England's criminal charges would have to wait until they had been prosecuted in Spain first.

They thanked Patrick and Eleanor for their hospitality and left. Katarina was desperate to see Lilli. She was sure Caroline would have spoilt her, but after what felt like the Spanish Inquisition she just wanted to cuddle up to her little girl. Harry explained on the way home what would happen next, with the court case, but thankfully they wouldn't have to think about it for a while.

CHAPTER 11

Lilli was so excited to see them all. She was talking so quickly no one could decipher a word she was saying.

"Lilli calm down. Let us get in the door and you can tell us all about your day when we've got a glass of wine in our hands." Harry was protecting Katarina again. Emm liked that about him. Lilli followed them into the kitchen where Caroline already had the glasses lined up. Nico started pouring the ice cold Côtes de Provence and they went out onto the balcony to tell Caroline all about their day. Before anyone got a word in Lilli was back with so many bags, she couldn't carry them all, so two were between her teeth. The blessing was she couldn't talk! She put them all down on the table and started handing them out.

"It's not perfume, it's something much better." Nico chuckled. He was glad his father wasn't there to hear that remark. He'd recognised the bags. "It's candies, and I helped to make these ones. There were chocolates too, but Caroline thought they might melt by the time we got home. But aren't these super Mummy. All different colours and the man said I could get a job there whenever I want. He said I'd have to stop eating them all though because I wouldn't make any money." Katarina was laughing so hard it made them all join in. Just the therapy they all needed after such a horrid day.

"Did you go around Nico's house?" Katarina

wanted to calm Lilli down. Asking her questions, that made her think, normally did the trick.

"Yes Mummy. It's called House January and it's huge." She took out a small bottle from her pocket. "I made my own perfume, smell it." She took off the lid and Katarina could smell it before it was thrust under her nose. It was very strong. "The back garden has flowers growing for infinity plus infinity." Katarina made a note to limit Lilli's internet time. "I went into a room where they were all wearing white coats and they called it the chemists. It didn't look a bit like our chemists Mummy. This one just has big bottles and little bottles and all different coloured bottles everywhere. This lady let me use a poppet…" Nico interrupted her for a second.

"Pipette Lilli." Lilli looked up at Nico and was grateful for the correction.

"Pipette, and I took some perfume from a big bottle and put it in mine. I did it five times from different coloured bottles that all smelt of flowers. And a nice man put my name on it and called it Parfum Lilli. See?" She pointed at the label attached to her bottle. "They say perfume funny." She screwed up her nose and tried to say it in French. "Parfum." She had them all in stitches.

"Well it looks like you had a good day. I hope you thanked Caroline for taking you?" Lilli nodded. Katarina looked over at Caroline who was nodding and smiling.

"Good girl. Now can you be a very big girl and take all your things and put them tidily in the room? I'll come in and get you ready for your bath in a moment."

"Ok Mummy. I don't feel tired though." As she was picking up all her bits and pieces she yawned. Katarina couldn't help but smile at her darling daughter, her angel, her life.

"Can you thank Alain and Veronique for letting Lilli go mad in their home. I hope she didn't cause too much chaos? Is that the right word?" Katarina could tell that wasn't the case by Caroline's reaction.

"It is the right word Katarina, but I can assure you, not in this context. Alain and Veronique thanked me for bringing such a ray of sunshine into their, I quote 'musty old lives'. She was a delight, Katarina." Katarina looked pleased.

"Thank you, Caroline. Now I must get her ready for bed. I'm tired and if it's all right with you all I think I may go to bed with Lilli again tonight. She will go off quicker if I hold her." They all knew that Katarina would go off quicker if she was cuddling Lilli, but they nodded understandingly.

"I shall put some sandwiches on a tray for you in case you're a little hungry. I will leave them outside your door with a glass of wine." Caroline smiled at her guest. Katarina thought she had truly made the most wonderful friends.

"Thank you, all of you. Goodnight." She went over and kissed Caroline and hurried to her bedroom before they saw her tears. Caroline got up and Emm followed her into the kitchen to help her make the sandwiches.

"Would you mind awfully if I take Harry out for a quick pizza? I need to get back to London on Friday and he's going off to Spain tomorrow with Patrick so tonight will be my last chance to catch up with him." Caroline practically pushed her out of the door.

"Of course, you must. What a splendid idea. Are you and he an item again?" She had to ask. A mother needed to know these things. It was her dream that Emily and Harry would be back together before Emm disappeared back to London.

"Baby steps, mother, baby steps." Caroline was left wondering what the devil that was supposed to mean. But at least she hadn't said a definite 'no'.

Emm went out onto the balcony and found Nico and Harry staring at the dark Mediterranean Sea and watching people walking along the Promenade des Anglais.

"Harry Hart, how about taking me out for a pizza?" Harry high-fived Nico. "What is that about?" Emm looked suspicious. Harry looked coy so Nico explained.

"'arry was wondering 'ow 'e could convince you to go out for a pizza with 'im tonight. You 'ave just solved 'is problem, n'est-ce pas?" Nico left them alone and went in to find Caroline. It would cheer her up to know that Harry wanted Emm back.

"It's not a date Harry. I just want to explain the reason I'm in a rush to get back to London. It is to do with my father, and walls have ears." She nodded her head in the direction of the patio doors. Harry tapped his nose.

"I understand. It's very hush hush. Get your drift. Wink wink, nudge nudge, say no more." Emm shook her head. He had regressed and it had been going so well.

While they walked down to the Cours Saleya, where Emm's favourite pizzeria was, she realised, as Harry was talking ten to the dozen, that perhaps his demeanour that evening was due to nerves. As ludicrous as it sounded, it was the only reason she could think of after his recent displays of heroism and dependability. It never occurred to her that someone who exudes so much confidence could just be covering up his insecurities. She wondered if she had listened too much to CC. Analysing Harry was probably not one of her best ideas for an evening of relaxation.

"Penny for them." Harry had noticed he'd lost Emm's attention. They had been sitting waiting for their pizzas and Emm had just been staring at him.

"I was just thinking what had happened over the last few days. It's trying to process in my brain." He reached his hand over the table and held hers.

"I'm sorry I involved you in all this Emm. I'm selfish because I was dying for a reason to call you and this cropped up. I've missed you so much." Their pizzas arrived before Emm could respond. "Merçi, can I have some chilli oil please?" The waitress stretched across to the next table and handed Harry the oil. "Merçi." Emm watched him dribble the oil around his pizza without tasting it first. Big mistake, she thought. He took his first mouthful and his eyes nearly popped out of their sockets. He poured a whole glass of water down his throat and wiped his eyes. Emm had tried not to laugh, but she couldn't hold it in any longer.

"A man with a gun doesn't faze you but give you a little chilli oil and you cry like a baby." She was enjoying his discomfort.

"A little chilli oil? I put the bloody bottle on my pizza. You try it." He lifted a wedge up to Emm's mouth. She shook her head.

"I've tried it before, so I know how hot it is." She was still laughing - fortunately Harry had recovered enough to see the funny side too. "I'll order you another one." She went to catch the waitress's attention when Harry stopped her.

"I've got used to it now. It's only the initial mouthful that does that, honest." They carried on eating and laughing. Emm chose her moment to explain about Claudia Pasqualle and her father. "That is the reason I have to get back to London so soon. I would love to stay out here and join you all in Spain, but Dad needs me. Once the press finds out, he's going to need all the family support we can offer him." She put down her knife and reached for Harry's hand over the table. She looked straight into his eyes so she could see he was paying attention.

"Please believe me when I say how important it is for you to keep this information to yourself Harry. On no account must we let my mother know until the time is right. Goodness knows when the right time will be." She shook her head and sighed. "So, if you breathe a word of this, Harry Hart, before it goes public, I will never talk to you again." Harry felt elated that Emm had chosen to confide in him, he would never ruin that trust.

"The old fox. Claudia Pasqualle, wow." He had to tone it down a little, Emm could see he was impressed. "She was stunningly beautiful, in her day." Well retrieved, he thought to himself. He smiled at Emm, who just shook her head slowly. Men, she thought, were just little smutty boys with only one thing on their minds. She was quite pleased that Harry had tried to rein his libido in though. Before they went into the apartment block Harry spun Emm around and kissed her. Emm was aware of two eyes staring at them through the glass doors. She glimpsed up to see François grinning with a thumb up. Emm knew only too well that the French loved lovers.

"Come on, we must get in to bed." Harry giggled.

"Why take it the wrong way? You can be an ass sometimes Harry." She tutted and grabbed his hand to steer him inside.

He stopped her outside the apartment door.

"Is there any chance for us Emm? I've so enjoyed being with you the last few days. I'm a changed man!" He grinned. "But really though, we are meant to be together." She wanted to agree. In her heart she did. She remembered what Eleanor had said to her, so she'd give him a chance.

"The ball is in your court Harry. I will be by your side whenever you need me. I just need you to find the place you want to be first." Harry thought he understood what she was saying but needed to clarify.

"So, if I've understood you correctly, if I find where I want to be and what I want to do, you will come back to me?" Emm nodded. It was what she had been waiting for through most of their on/off relationship – Harry finally realised that he needed to grow up and settle down if he wanted Emm for the long term. Emm secretly had her fingers and toes crossed that Harry would finally enter the adult world with the responsibility and heroism he had shown briefly over the last few days.

"By George, I think he's got it! My Fair Lady 1964." Harry picked her up and kissed her once again.

"I think this is the beginning of a beautiful friendship. Casablanca 1942." They were back in Emm's flat over a year ago, playing their game.

"You can't have that one, we used it the other day." Harry sulked. "Okay, you can have it, this once." Caroline must have heard them. She came to the door as they were walking in.

"You two look like you've had a good time."

Emm knew what her mother was after, but her intentions towards Harry were her own business. She didn't want to be unkind, but she needed Harry to sort himself out before any words like 'boyfriend' or 'going steady' came into any conversation. She had been hurt before but was in control now. She must remember to thank Eleanor when she next saw her. What a wonderful woman she was, there's no wonder Patrick was a billionaire, he was a lucky guy. What was the phrase? 'Behind every man there is a great woman'. Emm had decided to be that woman in Harry's life. She would make him realise that he needed her. Harry was a dreamer; she knew he had an intellectual brain, but he squandered it on fun. She had to rein him in and get him to believe in himself. One day he will thank her for it, she smiled at the thought. She decided he was her next challenge; he was worth it.

* * *

Erik had a very busy night. He had managed to steal an unobtrusive black Renault Mégane with a French number plate from a shopping centre car park at Port de Fontvielle, the next port along from Port Hercule.

He drove to Nice and into the car park of Centre Commercial Nice where he found a few black Méganes to choose from. He found a good match and prized off the number plates and swapped them.

He drove out of the car park in the Mégane from Monaco with the number plates from the Megan in Nice, knowing that the number plate was the last thing people looked at and the owners would probably just drive off unaware, giving him some time. The police will be looking for the wrong stolen car. He had learnt that trick in England when moving girls around the country.

It totally confused the police, just long enough to deliver and run. He had calculated that, as a delaying tactic, it would work even better if he needed to drive into Spain. His thoughts were to get to Maria's hospital and wait. He didn't care about Katarina, he just wanted to get Lilli back to his family in Estonia.

His next port of call, having slept overnight in a beach car park, was Port Hercule. He wanted to check they weren't on the boat. If he could grab Lilli from there, he wouldn't have to drive all the way to Girona. He headed for the Direction Des Ports. He had managed to park the car outside the harbour entrance and walked into the port offices area. By the side of the offices was the refuge area. He opened the recycling bin and found a cardboard box with boat parts pictured on the outside. He straightened out the crushes and put it under his arm. He walked into the reception area.

"Bonjour, puis-je vous aider?" The young girl behind the desk asked Erik.

"Sorry, I don't speak French. But I need to find out the schedule of the Lady Eleanor, for maintenance." The girl nodded and buzzed the door to his left. He walked through into another office with computers and screens everywhere. He was beckoned over to a desk by a woman with a stern face and glasses.

"I hope you speak English." She nodded. "Good. I'm looking for the schedule of the Lady Eleanor as I have parts for the boat." He showed her the box under his arm. She typed in the name of the vessel.

"You're lucky Monsieur. She is leaving for Port De Palamós in Spain this evening. They are still here in their berth." Erik had to think.

"Merçi, Madame." He left the offices deep in

thought. He threw the box back into the recycling bin and walked out of the port to the car. If he went near the boat and got spotted the game was up. The port gates would be closed and the only way out would be the sea. He'd had enough drenching when the Jet Ski started chugging and he realised it was nearly out of fuel. He managed to nurse it to the shore but had to stay soaked for a while as he had no change of clothes with him. He had to dry off before walking into a hotel for a room, but at least credit cards dried off quickly. He looked on Google Maps and saw the drive to Palamós was around six hours. He thought he'd probably have the same problem at that port with security, so he decided to go straight to the hospital. At least he knew his way around there.

He anticipated Katarina wouldn't be there until midmorning having docked first thing. He expected Lilli would go with her, she probably hadn't let her out of her sight since getting back with her. If Katarina was alone he could just grab Lilli, but if they had the men with them, that wouldn't work. He was getting a headache with all the conjecture; he won't know what will happen until he gets there. Time was of the essence, otherwise he'd have to steal another car. He decided to drive first and sleep when he got there. He put the hospital address into the Mégane's sat nav and with six hours-five minutes, showing on the screen, he retraced his route, back the way he had come with Katarina a few days earlier.

* * *

Thursday morning Nico drove Katarina, Lilli and Harry to the port where Patrick and Eleanor were waiting to meet the famous Lilli. They had not been blessed with children themselves. Eleanor had made the decision that neither would be checked medically to see why. She didn't want blame or guilt to weigh either of them down. It was just one of those things that would happen if it was meant to be.

"Thanks for the lift Nico. And break a leg on Saturday." Nico shook Harry's hand.

"Thank goodness you do not know the French equivalent. Not to be said in front of the ladies. It is 'je vous dis merde'." Harry looked puzzled. He checked to see that Lilli had got on board the boat and then asked Nico to explain.

"I thought merde meant 'shit'?" Nico nodded and laughed.

"We are not quite so polite as you English. Bon chance mon ami." He waved and drove off laughing. His first rehearsal was in one hour, so he had no time to lose, he also needed to check his script.

"Ah, this is Lilli. How do you do Lilli, I'm Patrick." Lilli shook Patrick's hand. "And this is my wife Eleanor." Eleanor didn't want to shake her hand. She picked her up and hugged her.

"You're just the prettiest little girl that has ever been on this boat. Do you like milk shake?" Lilli nodded. "Well, come with me to the kitchen, although it's called the galley on the boat, and you can choose the flavour you like best." She carried Lilli to the top of the stairs and let her walk down herself. "We have banana, pineapple, strawberry, vanilla, chocolate..." They were out of earshot.

"You probably won't see those two again for a while. Eleanor is also partial to milk shake herself. Especially when Sonia makes it." Patrick motioned for Katarina to sit down. "Would you like a coffee Katarina?"

She nodded. Patrick pushed a bell by the light switch.

"If Sonia is here does that mean Alberto is too." Patrick smiled and nodded his head slowly at Harry. He knew Harry would be delighted. Alberto and Harry were great friends. Sonia was Alberto's wife. The pair of them on the crew would mean plain sailing and wonderful Spanish food. What Alberto didn't know about boats, wasn't worth knowing. He had taught Harry a great deal in his first few months. Sonia had kept them fed. She was a remarkable cook, considering the size of the on-board kitchen and the amount of people she had to cook for, especially as the Robertshaws were frequent entertainers.

"The reason I got Alberto to crew was because he knows the Spanish coast like no one else I know. I haven't actually moored at Palamós before, so I need him to take charge of the boat." Harry knew that was a wise move. Sonia came up the stairs and immediately saw Harry.

"Harry, you're here. We are going to have such fun, yes?" Harry hugged her. "Does Alberto know you're on board?" Harry was about to say 'no' when a roar came from the other side of the boat. Alberto rushed into the seating area and took Harry off his feet in a bear hug. Patrick tried to look stern but was being ignored so shrugged his shoulders and sat down next to Katarina and waited for the friends to get reacquainted. Katarina was puzzled. These people work for Patrick, but he was enjoying their revelry. Patrick noticed Katarina's confusion.

"If I want any work out of them I usually have to go with the flow until they have finished catching up. When we are at sea, they have a code of conduct that I could never fault, but here in dock they are relaxed."

He raised his voice a tad. "They will calm down soon and we may get that coffee we so desperately want." Sonia looked over at her boss.

"I'm so sorry. I'll get your coffee immediately, boss." She winked at him and left the deck. Katarina looked over at Patrick. He was smiling.

"That was for your benefit. She normally calls me Patrick not boss. Everyone has an important role on this vessel - we all need each other to keep safe. Therefore, I'm not the big cheese here. Alberto knows more than I do about boats, so I bow to his better judgement. How can I put myself above that? We are equal when at sea. On land it is a different matter, they have to call me 'sir'." Harry and Alberto laughed. Alberto tipped his cap and left. Harry joined Katarina and Patrick on the sofas. Patrick checked his watch. "We shall be leaving in twenty minutes. It might be a good idea if you show Katarina to her cabin, so she knows where to go in case she hasn't good sea legs." Harry totally understood. The Mediterranean Sea looked beautiful and blue, but it had a temper that could throw you across the deck if it wanted to. Luckily the sea was calm, but they had to go further out than the coastline and that was where it could be choppy. "We've given Katarina and Lilli the twin room and you've got the blue room." Harry looked shocked.

"Am I not in my usual one downstairs?" Patrick shook his head.

"No, you're not crew on this trip. Eleanor thought it only right that you should be treated like any other guest. I, on the other hand, would have put you below decks where you should be but 'she who must be obeyed'..." Harry smiled.

"Rumpole of the Bailey, circa 1978?" Harry had

taught them his and Emm's game. Patrick had adjusted it to incorporate TV programmes, as he wasn't a great movie buff.

"Correct, anyway we both thought you'd be more comfortable on the upper deck." Harry appreciated their thoughtfulness. He got up and picked up Katarina and Lilli's bags. Sonia had arrived with the coffee. "I'll take these while you have your coffee Katarina and then I'll show you your room." Harry disappeared along the passageway. Lilli came bouncing in with a pink moustache. Eleanor wasn't far behind her.

"Mummy, the kitchen is bigger than ours at home, and the boat is bigger than our house. It's enormous." Katarina smiled. This was an adventure of a lifetime to Lilli. She couldn't believe how lucky she was to have met Harry. "I've seen our bedroom too. It's called a cabin and I have my own bed and a TV and a bathroom and fridge with lots of water in and Eleanor said I can press a button if I'm hungry." Katarina took a deep breath. She could see the ramifications with giving Lilli control of a communication button. Patrick laughed as he was on Katarina's wavelength.

"The button is for emergencies. If you're hungry you can go and find Sonia or ask one of us and we'll get you something with pleasure. And if you're very good, I'll show you my secret sweetie store." Lilli's eyes lit up.

"I'm always very good. I don't like getting told off. I'm a good girl aren't I Mummy." She looked pleadingly at her mother, hoping she'd say the right thing.

"Yes Lilli. Patrick, Lilli is a very good girl." She smiled at him. They were playing a game that could keep Lilli out of danger. Lilli took hold of Patrick's hand.

"When you hear this noise," Patrick pressed something under the bar and a siren went off, Lilli put her hands over her ears. "You must come and find one of us. Then you get a chance to go to the sweetie store. Okay?" Lilli was nodding her head. She liked the sound of that game.

"You're my best friend now. Let's go exploring." Lilli pulled Patrick up off the sofa. He was amused and walked with her over to the bar.

"Give me a few seconds Lilli and I'll be with you." He picked up the intercom. "Hello Alberto. Are Lachlan and Dave back from town yet?" Alberto told him they had just got on board. "We can cast off then. Thank you, Alberto." He put the intercom back on its holder and turned to Lilli. "Would you like to be the captain? We can go up to the Flybridge and you can steer us out of port and off to sea." Lilli's eyes were open so wide and her mouth matched. They both went off to cement their new friendship.

"I'm not sure we should leave those two in charge of the boat." Eleanor laughed. "Lilli is the sweetest little girl I have ever met. You deserve a medal for what you have been through and come out the other side with such a well-adjusted, polite and I have to say adorable little girl. Well done Katarina." Katarina tried not to cry, but she felt a lump in her throat. She remembered Harry saying Eleanor was more like a mother to him than the boss's wife, she now knew what he meant.

"Thank you so much for all your kindness. I just hope Lilli isn't being a pest." Eleanor frowned.

"Patrick and I were never blessed with children, if we had been, I'd have loved a Lilli. The reason Patrick was bribing her to be good, for sweeties, is that we sometimes hit rough seas with very little notice, and we may need to make sure she is sitting in the cabin with you or out here where we can keep an eye on her. We have to lock all the outer doors in bad weather, so we need to know where everyone is." Katarina understood fully. "Now let me show you your room and then you can come up onto the Flybridge and watch us leave port. It's quite exciting, if you like that sort of thing. If you'd rather, you can join me back here for a morning liqueur." She smiled at Katarina.

"That does sound tempting. I think I may have to do that. I'm not sure if I have good sea legs, but I heard from Harry a small port settles the stomach. Thank you, Eleanor." Eleanor laughed.

"Harry needs no excuse to have a port, or a brandy, or a glass of wine. He's just Harry." Katarina noted the affection in her voice. It seems everyone loves Harry. Eleanor took her round to the twin cabin and left her to unpack her clothes and Lilli's. There was a quiet tap on her door. She opened it and there was Lachlan standing with a big grin on his face and a bunch of flowers in his hand.

"Well you're looking better than I last saw you." He handed the flowers to her. "These are for you. Welcome on board the Lady Eleanor. I've just met Lilli. I'm her best friend, apparently. I gave her a lollipop. I hope you don't mind." Katarina put the flowers down and hugged Lachlan.

"Thank you for saving me Lachlan. I will always remember your kindness to me that day." Lachlan blushed.

"Jeez, no worries." He stood back and looked at her. She was beautiful. He hadn't noticed when she was scrunched up in the boot, or while he carried her, she looked so pale he thought she was dead. What a difference a few days had made. "I better get back to work. The vase is secured on the table so won't tip over in bad weather, just don't fill it too high." He winked at her. "I'll see you later for a drink?" Katarina nodded.

"I'll look forward to that." He shut her door and went back to the Flybridge. She sat on the bed and tried to come back down to earth. He was such a kind soul hidden by his brash exterior. She had seen through his armour immediately and wondered if he had been hurt like she had. She hoped she'd get close enough to ask him one day.

* * *

"Emily, if you're leaving early tomorrow, would you come out with me today and have a girlie day? I could book the spa and then we could go to Galeries Lafayette for a little shopping." Emm was in her room trying to text her father. She'd booked her flight back and wanted to know if he could pick her up from Gatwick. The train journey back into town was depressing. She also wanted to talk to him alone. She needed his advice about Harry and wanted to know what his intentions were regarding Claudia and where they were going to live. Would he keep the office? Would she still have a job? They were questions one couldn't ask on the phone. She liked talking directly to people so she could watch their facial expressions and eyes. So much can be misunderstood when reading a message or talking into a phone. Spontaneous reactions cannot be hidden when confronting people face to face.

"I'll be out in a minute. Yes, that sounds like a good idea, book the spa if you like." She'd just finished her text to her father and wondered if she should send one to Harry. She decided to leave it until they had docked in Spain. She would text him from the airport and wish him luck. By her calculations, and by what Harry had told her, they should be in Spain by early morning, about the time she would be waiting in the departure lounge.

She dutifully did the mother/daughter day but had to watch what she said when her father came into the conversation. She knew Caroline would be livid when she heard the news and realised Emm had known and hadn't told her, but her loyalty was still with her father. In fact, if her mother had confided in her and told her not to tell her father a secret, she would have honoured that too. At least it would be over by Sunday. She could take the flack and her mother would get over it.

"Nico said we could pop in and watch a little of his rehearsal to let him know we are back, if you like." Emm thought that a good idea so they slipped into the Opéra de Nice, Caroline waved to the woman behind the ticket booth. She recognised her and waved back. There was already a queue for tickets - the show was in two days' time. Must be popular thought Emm. They went along to the side and through a curtain covering a door. Immediately Caroline beamed, she could hear Nico's aria booming around the grand auditorium. They crouched in and sat on the nearest seats. It was magnificent. Emm wasn't a fan of opera and couldn't understand a word, but the pure magic of one man's voice, and not a large man either, was intense. Nico caught sight of them and sang to them instead of the leading lady, who was not amused. Emm realised where the word Diva came from, she had just seen one in real life.

Emm looked around the vast inside of the opera house. From where they were sitting in the stalls, she could see private boxes one on top of the other all around her, going right up to the ceiling. The ceiling was very high and too dark to make out the artwork but there was a beautiful chandelier hanging from the central dome. When lit it must look wondrous, she thought. The whole hall was draped in luxurious red velvet with gold pillars depicting angels and cherubs. Emm could only imagine how old it all was and the work that must have gone into building and decorating such a magnificent opera house.

After ten minutes the cast seemed to be drifting off the stage. Nico was by their side in no time.

"I need a drink." He kissed them both and hurried them out. They walked across to the nearest bar, called the Bar L'Opéra and had three Campari sodas. "Well 'ave you two ladies 'ad a good day?" Caroline said it was a wonderful day and Emm had to agree. She had bought a new outfit for herself and for her sister for the press conference at The Dorchester. Emm knew Stephanie would not have time to go out and buy anything when she got back from her honeymoon. She had to tell her mother the dresses were for an important meeting they had to go to in London. It was the truth, as her mother would find out very soon. Caroline assumed it was to do with Fitzgerald & Partners. Emm just didn't correct her mother's assumptions.

"My skin is still tingling from the body scrub. Mummy had a mud bath. I wish I had been allowed to take my phone in, it would have been a brilliant picture." Nico wanted to laugh at the image he'd just imagined but didn't want to offend Caroline. He was going to miss Emily around. But the upside was that Caroline was more relaxed when they were alone. Caroline was actually thrilled inside but didn't want to make it obvious. Her estranged daughter, who had practically ignored her since she left England to be with Nico, had just called her by the name she used before her desertion. She hoped it wasn't a slip of the tongue.

"So, when are you coming back to see us?" Nico asked as Caroline seemed to be in her own little world. Emm shook her head and shrugged.

"I've taken a lot of time off work recently. I'm going to have so much on my desk to clear. But I'm sure it won't be too long. Who knows what the future holds?" She left the question in the air. Caroline was listening and had to smile. She was hoping the future held Harry.

CHAPTER 12

Lilli had entertained them that night with her rendition of Rita Ora's 'Your Song'. She had them in stitches when she was dancing around the sofa with Paris in her arms singing 'I'm in love, I'm in love' and 'I don't want to hear bad songs on the floor'." She made up words when she couldn't remember the original, but it was just as entertaining with her own version.
Lachlan came off duty from the Flybridge and went to check on Katarina. She was sitting on a bar stool watching Lilli perform. Harry was sitting on the settee with Eleanor, catching up. Patrick was sorting out the music for Lilli, who wanted to dance to 'anything by Lily Allen.'

"Tell Patrick why you like Lily Allen, Lilli." Katarina was grinning.

"Because she has the same name as me, but she spelt it wrong." Lilli frowned. Patrick tried to keep a straight face, and just nodded in agreement.

"Hello Katarina." Lachlan had snuck behind the bar. "Would you like that drink I promised you?" Katarina turned to face him.

"That would be very pleasant. Thank you, Lachlan." Lachlan noticed she was drinking some white wine Sangria. He poured some more, from the jug on the bar, into her glass and added more fruit. "That looks delicious." She smiled at him.

"When in Rome." She looked a little puzzled.

"We are on our way to Spain, the home of Sangria. Cheers." He decided to pour himself one too.

"Ah, I see. Yes, cheers." Lachlan walked around from the serving side of the bar and joined her on the stool next to her.

"Do you come here often?" Katarina was warming to Lachlan's humour.

"Not as often as you, I think." She winked at him. Lachlan couldn't think of anything to say to her. He felt content by being next to her enjoying looking at her smiling face. He was glad she had come away from her awful life and was still able to enjoy the little things. It took him months, he was thinking, to smile again after losing Tilly, but he didn't have the advantage of a Lilli. He watched the way Katarina was giggling at Lilli's antics, and realised that out of all the women he had known, not one was as brave as the one sitting next to him.

* * *

They docked just after breakfast. The sea crossing hadn't been bad at all.

Patrick had ordered a seven-seater car with a driver to be waiting in the port for them. They were going to drop Katarina and Lilli off at the hospital and Eleanor had offered to go with them so she could take Lilli out exploring while Katarina stayed with Maria for a while. Patrick and Harry were going to go on to the farmhouse to assess the damage and make sure the cows were being looked after. Maria had told Katarina that she had two farm hands. They lived in the outbuildings that hadn't been damaged, so hopefully the livestock were being looked after.

Lachlan had permission to take the yacht and crew down

to Barcelona for the day. He needed to have the deck crane checked out as it kept jamming when they wanted the Rib put into the water. He also wanted to see his Uncle Steve who ran a yacht crewing agency from the Elite Yachting Marina. He'd had cryptic messages from him and needed to see what his uncle really wanted.

They stopped outside the huge building that was Hospital Universitari de Girona Dr Josep Trueta. Named after a revered Catalan nationalist doctor, their driver José told them.

"We'll be back for you girls at around one o'clock. Then we can have a nice lunch in Girona. Lilli and I will go to the famous Ice Cream Shop afterwards. How does that sound?" Lilli squealed. Harry had missed that. He'd never tire of Lilli's enthusiasm for life. It was actually better than any antidepressants. Perhaps he could get Nico's family to bottle it. He kissed Lilli goodbye and got back into the car.

Patrick whispered into Eleanor's ear to be careful and make sure none of them were on their own at any time. Eleanor knew the score and told her husband to stop fretting. He walked over to the car and waved to Eleanor and Katarina. "Right driver, on to the farm address, please." José nodded and drove on.

Katarina remembered with horror the last time she'd entered the lift to the third floor. Hopefully she did not need to go there this time. She went up to the reception desk and asked what room Maria Kõiv was in. The receptionist checked on the computer and told Katarina that she was on the first floor, room 112. She pointed to the lifts. Katarina thanked her. She was not going in the lift again. She'd take the stairs to the first floor.

"Can you come too, Eleanor?" She asked in a whisper as Lilli ran on in front. "I'm a little worried about the state Maria may be in. I do not want to frighten Lilli." Eleanor understood.

"I will keep Lilli occupied while you go in. You can signal me if everything is ok." Katarina smiled and nodded. They had to catch up with Lilli first though.

"Lilli, don't run in a hospital, it is very disrespectful." Lilli slowed down. It was also quite dangerous, but Katarina didn't want to scare her.

Lilli had got quite a bit ahead of them and stopped to see where they were. She turned around to look.

Erik saw his chance. He had been hiding in a janitor's cupboard almost opposite Maria's room and watching from the window in the door. He couldn't believe his luck when he saw his little angel running towards his hiding place. He opened the door slowly and was about to grab Lilli when he heard an English woman's voice.

"Lilli darling, could you help me with these sweeties? They seem to have fallen out of their packet, they're somewhere in my handbag." The magic word got Lilli over to Eleanor as quickly as she could, without being rude. She didn't want her mummy being cross with her.

Erik shut the door frustratedly as he could hear footsteps of more than one person, coming towards Maria's room. He'd wait for another opportunity, once he could see what he was up against.

Katarina looked in the window at her cousin. Maria was sitting up and drinking a glass of water. Katarina opened the door slowly as not to make Maria jump. Maria looked ecstatic seeing her cousin and best friend standing in front of her.

"Katarina, how lovely to see you." Katarina went over to kiss her cousin. She stood back and looked at her. Apart from a gash on her forehead and a very shiny red patch on her cheek that had obviously got burnt, she looked good.

"You are looking well Maria. How are you feeling?" Maria smiled.

"I'm on the mend. I have broken a few ribs and my lung got damaged, but they have been incredible here. I can go home very soon." She looked down and her whole body slumped. "You have heard about Karl?"

"Yes Maria, and I'm so sorry. I will never be able to forgive myself for involving you and your family." Katarina was crying. She promised herself to stay strong and not cry in front of Maria. After all it was Maria who deserved to cry - she was the one who had lost the love of her life.

Maria took hold of her cousin's hand.

"Katarina, you are the one who has suffered the most in the family. I had Karl for seven years as my sweetheart and then husband. We were truly in love. I also had my loving parents around me whenever I wanted them. You have had a murderous gangster keeping you captive from your family for seven years. I know you have a little girl, which we are all grateful for, she must bring you joy Katarina." Maria had said the right thing. Katarina smiled. She wiped away her tears and sat next to her cousin and just held her. It was time for Maria to shed a few tears. After a while Katarina spoke.

"They have caught the bastards responsible. Unfortunately, not Erik yet. But you probably know that." Maria nodded, and sighed. Katarina was angry that Erik was still free, but hopefully not for long.

"Yes, I have been interviewed by the Spanish police and they told me what happened in Monaco. You poor thing, I cannot think of anything worse than being shut in a boot of a car. So dark and hot." Maria had lost her home and her husband, but she was sympathising with her cousin. Katarina admired her cousin's stoicism.

"My friends are off to your farm now. They are going to see what it will take to fix it up. I'm going to help you Maria." Maria shook her head.

"No Katarina. I'm going home to Estonia. I have had a lovely conversation with Mother and Father, and they want to retire. They have been hoodwinked into thinking they were getting help over the harvest time, but my father telephoned Rapla Parish and found out it was all a scam. I will go home and take over their farm. I'm looking forward to it. Would you like to come with me?" Katarina wasn't sure. She would have to think about it and talk to Lilli. Oh dear, Lilli she thought. She went to the door and checked the corridor for Lilli and Eleanor. They were sitting on a bench playing I Spy. Katarina mouthed a 'thank you' to Eleanor and beckoned Lilli over. Lilli walked into the room nervously as she hadn't met Maria before, but had seen all the pictures of her and knew she was her mother's favourite cousin.

"Tere Lilli. On väga tore sind näha." Unfortunately, Maria spoke in Estonian. Lilli looked up at her mother.

"Maria said it is very nice to see you." Lilli smiled at Maria.

"It is very nice to see you too." She spoke very slowly and loudly, and Maria had to laugh.

"I'm sorry, my English is not as good as yours Lilli. But I will try, yes?" Lilli nodded and sat on the edge of her bed. "I have pictures of you Lilli, but it is nice to see you... päris elu?" She looked at Katarina for help.

"Maria means it's nice to see you in real life." Lilli looked over at Maria.

"I thought she meant why isn't Paris with you." Lilli laughed. Maria looked bewildered.

"Lilli has a cuddly dog called Paris. She thought you meant him." Maria laughed and believed languages can be fun, especially for children. She asked Katarina if she was going to teach Lilli Estonian. Katarina shook her head.

"Maybe one day." She took Lilli's hand and helped her off the bed. "Can you go and keep Eleanor company while I talk boringly to our cousin?" Lilli caught the word boringly and skipped to the door.

"Bye bye Maria. Hope you get better soon." She blew her a kiss and went back to sit with Eleanor. She wanted to continue their game of I-spy as Eleanor wasn't very good at it.

"She is a very good-natured child, Katarina. You are very lucky." Katarina had to agree with her and smiled.

"I do not want anything to do with Erik. She will not learn Estonian until she wants to. I cannot go back there, Maria. People we knew betrayed me. I know the police are now arresting those people, but they will not get them all. Erik is very clever and influential. I do not have confidence that it will stop, and I don't want to put Lilli in danger. Maria understood. She had nothing to live for except her own family back in Estonia. Katarina had Lilli. She was the most important person in her life.

"You are right. You deserve happiness Katarina.

I just hope you find it." Maria smiled at her cousin.

"I have very good friends Maria. I trust them with my life and Lilli's. But what can I do for you?" Katarina felt helpless.

"I will put what is left of my farm on the market. The insurance should help keep it going until a buyer comes forward. Karl's body is being released from the Spanish authorities and they are transporting it back to Estonia. As Karl had no family left, my parents and your parents have helped by organising all the necessary documents and coordinating the funeral with my arrival back in Estonia. The firemen said there was nothing worth rescuing from the farm, so all I have to do is get on a plane." Maria's tears were flowing. Katarina grabbed a box of tissues from her bedside cabinet and put them on Maria's lap. "Sorry, it hits me all of a sudden. He was a wonderful man and didn't deserve the ending he got. But I'm strong. I will get the farm in Kändliku running to full potential. Karl taught me so much – I will put my knowledge to good use." She had got Katarina crying too. They hugged each other for comfort. The cousins had been dealt bad hands in life, but things were looking up for them both.

***

As Patrick and Harry approached the farmhouse, it didn't look good. There was no roof left. They walked up the path to where the front door was hanging open on one hinge and into the house.

"The good news is that this building was built to last. The walls are still standing, but obviously the wood has burnt so there is no floor and no ceiling." Patrick looked at Harry. "What we have to work out is how much it will cost to restore against how much it will cost to demolish and re-build?"

Harry shrugged his shoulders. He had no idea what the cost of building materials was. They heard a car stop outside as the builder Patrick had contacted to meet them there, had arrived. He went out and shook his hand. The local builder, Miguel, took a look and sucked in his breath, shaking his head. He pointed out the kitchen wall that had taken the brunt of the blast.

"It is unsafe this side of the building." He shook his head again. "This wall would have to be pinned. My advice, demoler… demolish?" Patrick knew in his heart it was the right thing to do. He was sure Maria would not want to live where her husband had been so brutally murdered. "Let's check the outbuildings." They walked round the farmhouse and behind a row of orange trees to find a beautiful sight.

"Why did they live in that small cottage when they have this surprisingly large stable block?" Harry couldn't understand. The stable block was used for storage. It also had living quarters, he guessed for the farm hands. Miguel went into the main part that was filled with bales of hay and bags of animal feed and old farming equipment. It was huge. It had a loft that was reached by a stone staircase. There was adequate headroom and although old, it had roof windows keeping the upstairs lit.

From the outside the staff accommodation cleverly integrated into the main stable and was on two floors - one bedroom on each floor and a bathroom between on a mezzanine floor. Harry thought it must have been for the stable lads, back in the day. It was obviously being used so he hoped it was for farmhands.

"I think the stable block is better to make into a

farmhouse. It will cost half of rebuilding the old one. You would end up with a good-sized house and still have accommodation for the farmhands. That part could be updated too." Miguel was busy writing things down on his clipboard. "I can give you a rough estimate and it could all be finished in a few months." Patrick shook his hand.

"Thank you, Miguel. I will await your estimate." He handed Miguel his card with all his contact and said goodbye. "Well Harry, what do you think?" Harry was in awe of the building. It was so old and full of character. Just as they were about to leave, a farmhand came over to them.

"Hola." He shook Patrick and Harry's hand. "I'm Juan, I look after the cows. Would you like to see them?" Harry nodded. He was getting into this farming lark. They followed Juan past the stables, along a track, over an unmade road where they came to a modern looking building.

"The cows are milked in here." He pointed to a vast space with machinery either side. "And their food is in here." He slid back a massive door to a large storage area almost the same size as the cow milking area. The building was as big as the stable block. He beckoned them to follow him and took them along a path, obviously recently used by cattle due to the fresh cowpats under foot. At the end of the path, which was also lined with orange trees, they came out into a field. There were acres and acres of grassland. "All organic here. Happy cows." He pointed at a herd close by. "We have been looking after them for Maria. She will come home soon, yes?" Patrick didn't know what to say. Harry smiled at him.

"We're not sure Juan. But someone will make sure you and the cows will be ok." Juan nodded. "Do you live here, in the stable?" Juan nodded again.

"Jorge has upstairs, I have downstairs. I have a wife and two children in the village, but Jorge and I have a rota, so I can stay with my family every few days. I have to go. Jorge will need my help. Adiós." He left them looking around the expanse of grass, while he went back towards the milking block.

"Maria is not going to be able to do this alone. Maybe I could stay and help her manage the place until she sells it. Or maybe I could buy it off her? I wonder if Emm would join me?" Patrick wondered if Harry was talking to him, or just to himself. "I've always liked working outside, farming never occurred to me until now." He turned to Patrick. "What do you think? Would I make a good farmer?" Patrick put his hand on Harry's shoulder.

"Harry, when you put your mind to something it happens. If you want to be a farmer, you will make a very good one. From a totally selfish point of view I would not like to see you go. On the other hand, if I were the one that held you back, Eleanor would never forgive me. Why don't you ask Emily if she wants to be a farmer's wife?" He walked off laughing. Was this what Emm had hinted at? Would she stay with him once Harry had found something he really wanted to do? Almost in answer to his questions a cow came very near to the gate and mooed very loudly. He turned around and stared into her eyes. She rested her nose on the gate.

"Hello Daisy, oh no, hola Lucia." Lucia answered Harry with an elongated "Moooo."

"I'm afraid I'll have to get my Catalan to English

phrase book out if we are going to keep meeting like this, Lucia." He put his hand out and stroked her nose.

"You've made a friend for life there Harry. I think she likes you." Patrick had doubled back to find him. They had to go if they wanted to get the girls into Girona for lunch. "Come on. Let's go and get the girls and you can think about your future over a nice jug of Sangria." Harry liked that idea.

They got into the car and made their way back to Girona Hospital. Patrick looked across to Harry and swore he could hear the cogs in Harry's brain turning. He wanted to help him. "Harry, you know Eleanor and I think of you as family," Harry turned to him and nodded. "Well, if you are serious about this farming business, and I know I'm talking for Eleanor too, we would like to help. I will give you the money you will need to get it up and running to its full potential. Call it a loan if you feel that bad about it, make your fortune from organic produce, and you can pay me back then." Harry turned and hugged him. He had to find the words that would express how loved he felt without it sounding insincere. He took a deep breath.

"Thank you so much and thank Eleanor too. You two have been more like parents to me over the last year than my parents were over my lifetime." Patrick tilted his head and realised that was the first time Harry had mentioned his parents. He assumed he was an orphan and never asked. Harry knew he was going to have to explain his comment. "My father is a judge." Patrick took in a breath.

"You don't mean Sir Rodney Hart is your father?" Harry nodded.

"My mother is a snob. My younger brother is the

golden boy. I used to be the golden boy, but I threw it all away. I have a law degree. I was supposed to take my Masters' and then work towards becoming a fully-fledged Barrister. I took a sabbatical year having worked my socks off for three years and gained a First to please my father. After messing about in boats for most of that year, crewing and thinking, I decided law wasn't for me. I discussed it with my parents and they went mad. Dad is old school. His father was a judge, his grandfather was a judge - you get the gist?" Patrick nodded. "Well, he was furious. My mother was squealing about how on earth she was going to face her golf club ladies with such a failure as a son, she didn't know. Unfortunately, I thought her reaction very amusing and got a clout for disrespecting my mother. I walked out to the resounding voice of The Judge saying 'Do not come back until you've come to your senses'. I met Emm and then you and Eleanor and I haven't looked back since. I haven't felt more secure or happier in my life." Patrick had to hug him.

"You draw up the relevant papers and then Eleanor and I can adopt you legally." Harry laughed. He knew Patrick was joking, after all Harry was in his thirties, but the sentiment was appreciated.

As they reached the entrance to the hospital the girls were standing waiting at the main doors. Patrick got out of the car and went over to Eleanor.

"Everything alright? No uninvited guests?" Eleanor shook her head and walked towards the car, eager to get to the shops. Harry had picked Lilli up and was walking to the car with Katarina.

"How is Maria? Is she getting better?" Katarina nodded.

"She just needs time." Harry understood. He helped both the girls get into the car and walked around to the other side. He stopped and peered back in through the hospital doors. Was he seeing things? Perhaps it was his imagination, but he swore he saw Erik standing by a pillar behind the main doors. He blinked to clear his eyes and looked again. No, it must have been a trick of the light. Patrick came around to see what was worrying Harry.

"Everything okay?" Harry checked the girls were not watching.

"I swear I caught a glimpse of Erik in there. But I can't see him now." He shook his head. "Should I go and look properly?" Patrick looked at the girls, chattering away about the shops in Girona.

"No. If it was him, he'll be long gone now. We'll just stay vigilant though, just in case." Harry agreed. Erik was on his mind so it could have been an illusion. There was no need to worry the girls.

They both got into the car and José drove out of the hospital car park onto the main road. Patrick needed to keep his mind occupied. He asked Katarina how her cousin was.

"She is on the mend, thank you Patrick. But she is very depressed, I think. She wants to go home, back to Estonia to be with her parents. They have a farm and want to retire, so it seems like the best solution. She never wants to go to her farm again. She is putting it on the market." Harry looked at Patrick with excitement registering all over his face. Eleanor caught the look.

"You look very pleased with yourself, Harry?" Patrick would tell her the true reason later, but for now he'd reply for him.

"He wants to be a farmer." Harry nodded. Lilli squealed with excitement and started singing,

"Old Harry Donald had a farm, E-I-E-I-O, and on his farm he had some cows. E-I-E-I-O. With a Moo moo here and a moo moo there..."

"Thank you, Lilli, that's enough now. I'm not sure how much she wants for it Harry, but she wants rid of it as quickly as possible, so you could probably make a deal with her." Katarina wanted the best for her cousin, but the best would be to have her safely back with her family in Estonia.

"I don't want to diddle her Katarina. I will pay the asking price. I'm sure with the insurance money she should get, we could come to an amicable decision on what it is worth." Harry looked at Patrick and smiled. Patrick wanted to make sure Harry realised the seriousness of what he was hoping to take on and wanted to see his response to finalise the agreement in his mind.

"Are you happy to stay in one place? You won't be able to pop off for a few weeks with cows relying on you." Harry looked Patrick in the eye.

"I've never been more serious in my life. I need to settle down if I want the woman I love to be with me. I would hate an office job. I'm an outside man. Name me another job which keeps you in the open air every day of the week." Patrick smiled, knowing deep down that Harry was being sincere. Suddenly Lilli burst into life.

"Postman Pat. He is outside every day, delivering letters to everyone - and what about Mr Bloom, the gardener on CBeebies. He works outside every day to keep the fruit and vegetables watered." Lilli looked at Harry to see if she'd got the right answers.

"Thank you, Lilli. Yes, you're right. A postman works outside, as does a gardener. But this will be a home, a job and a challenge. What woman wouldn't want to join me in this great adventure?" Before Lilli opened her mouth again Harry turned to her. "It was a rhetorical question Lilli." Lilli looked at her mother with a puzzled expression.

"It doesn't need an answer Lilli." Katarina pulled Lilli nearer for a cuddle. "Adults talk differently to children. One day you will understand that not all questions are meant to be answered immediately."

With impeccable timing José had parked outside the restaurant, beside the river in Girona, that Patrick was dying to try. They all got out and Lilli suddenly spied the Ice Cream Shop sign.

"Look Patrick, our shop." Patrick laughed. He wondered how on earth do you keep up with a six-year-old? "We better have some vegetables first though. Mummy always says if I eat my vegetables, I'm allowed a treat. We'll have to eat a lot of vegetables for a treat from that shop, won't we Patrick? That was supposed to be a re…trolical question Patrick." She beamed up at Patrick, hoping she got it right. She took hold of Patrick's hand and they all entered the restaurant, with grins on their faces.

* * *

Michael had been able to collect Emm from Gatwick Airport. He'd been watching her land on his phone app, so timed his arrival to within minutes of her getting through passport control. Security was tight so he knew they'd be onto him if he stayed past the ten minutes allowed for pick-ups.

"Hi Daddy, thank you for this. I seem to have been travelling forever so it's nice just to get into a car with a friendly face." She leant over and kissed him.

"Hello poppet. How's Harry? Did you sort out his problems?" Emm didn't know where to start.

"You'll never believe what we've been through. But we are all safe and well." She noticed her father frowning. It wasn't because he was trying to get off Airport Way onto the M23 when the world and his wife had decided to do the same. She knew she had to explain the shenanigans in the South of France. "Well, it all started when Harry met this woman on the ferry over to Cherbourg." She had his undivided attention and looking at the traffic she knew she had plenty of time before they got into London, so she could start from the beginning.

"So, you and Harry are an item again?" Her father was smiling. Emm couldn't believe her parents. She had been held at gunpoint, could have been killed and all they wanted to know was if she and Harry were getting back together! Emm sighed and shrugged. All lost on her father who was trying to manoeuvre through a traffic jam, nipping down side roads he knew well.

"It's up to Harry. If he finds what he wants to do with his life, and it includes me then I'll think about going back to him." She was trying to sound confident. She wanted Harry back, but not the old Harry. She needed stability and so did he - he just had to find that out for himself.

"My little Emily has grown up." Michael squeezed Emm's knee and glanced at her with a big smile on his face. Emm smiled back. She loved her dad.

Michael had masterfully played London at its own game and had beaten the jams. He was just entering the congestion charge area. He wanted to go into the jeweller's shop in Covent Garden, which was one of Claudia's favourite stores.

"I hope you don't mind darling, but I need to pick up a piece of jewellery I have bought for Claudia and I need it for tomorrow's press conference." Michael sounded nervous. Emm had picked up on it.

"Is it a ring Daddy?" Michael smiled nervously. "Don't tell me you're going to propose to her in the middle of the conference, with the world watching." He nodded. "Good luck with that. I hope she says yes, for your sake." His smile went from his face and turned into a worried frown. "I'm only kidding. Of course she will say yes. She's madly in love with you. A girl can tell these things." Michael took a deep breath.

"I hope you're right. Perhaps I'll leave it until another time. When we are alone." He pulled up outside the jewellers and got out his phone to use his parking app. Emm put her hand on his arm to get his attention.

"I really was joking. Go for it tomorrow Daddy. I'll be there to boost you on." She smiled at him and he leant over and kissed her on the cheek.

"You're right. I will be filled with confidence with you there." He got out of the car and left Emm wondering whether he was being sarcastic. She got out and looked over at her father. For some reason she saw him differently, perhaps a little vulnerable. She realised he really wanted his family behind him for such a nerve-racking event. He pressed the fob to lock the car and turned to Emm. "Come on then, let's check out your father's taste in jewellery." She was looking forward to seeing what he had got Claudia. Anything was better than a deep fat fryer anyway!

The assistant brought out a box from the back room. Cartier had modified the engagement ring to Michael's specifications. As she was opening the box Michael held his breath.

"I was trying to make it as understated as possible. Claudia has never been one for bling or open displays of wealth." Emm wondered whom he was trying to convince. She never doubted Claudia's taste. She was French after all. "It's Cartier's, from their Paris collection, how apt is that." Emm caught her first glimpse of the ring. It was exquisite. Michael picked it up and held it so Emm could see it closely. "It has a .65 carat round brilliant diamond, on a platinum ring. I've just had two small blue sapphires added on either side, can you see? They match Claudia's eyes." He was positively beaming. He was so pleased by the way it had turned out. Emm was jealous. She would love an engagement ring like that.

"It's absolutely beautiful Daddy. Clever you. She's going to love it. I hope it fits." He had a smug look on his face. The assistant took out another ring and put it by the Cartier.

"I put one of her rings on that finger as a joke a while ago, pretending to rehearse when I would actually ask her properly. It fitted so we used it to size this one." Michael settled up with the assistant while Emm wandered down the road to watch a juggler entertain the crowd. She was feeling chuffed that her father had included her in his shopping trip, and his surprise engagement. Stephanie should be back late that night, she'd have so much to tell her, but perhaps she'll leave it until after the press conference. Their father's engagement will be enough to take in after two weeks of sheer bliss, as Stephanie had described her honeymoon to her sister before she left.

On the way back to her flat, thoughts of the future started questions forming in her mind. She had to know if she'd have a job for much longer.

"So, when you marry Claudia, where are you thinking of living?" Michael was expecting that question.

"Well, I think we will be flitting between France, London and California. Not much time for the business I'm afraid. Do you think you could run things without me?" Emm wondered if that was a trick question. Of course she couldn't, at least not with her social life intact. If she forgot about a life, then perhaps she could donate enough time to keeping it going, but she was only thirty-one. If she was really honest, although she loved snooping in other peoples' properties, and checking out the cool penthouses, she hated dealing with people.

"How do I say this without causing offence? I'm afraid it is a resounding 'no' father. Sorry." Michael laughed. "What's so funny?"

"I was only kidding. There is no way you would cope with the likes of Mrs Banks, Charlie Banks' mother." He waited for it to sink in.

"Charlie Banks. Not the Charlie Banks?"

"Well to you he was Charles Chaplin. Your appointment the morning you went off to France. I had to take him and his mother round the townhouse in Chelsea for you. His mother was a character. You'd have loved to have dealt with her." He was laughing even harder at the memory. "As I said, you're not exactly a people person, Emily. Be truthful." Emm nodded in admission. "I'm also sure that Stephanie will have other things on her agenda, like producing my grandchildren, so she won't want the burden of the company. So after much deliberation, I've already put it on the market and had astounding results. Phil Peters from VIP Rentals Kensington is very interested and so is Jenna, from JT Executive Housing, the one you call that awful name…"

"Genitalia!" Her father sighed. Inside he was chuckling, a little. "Well what self-respecting woman with her first name Jenna wouldn't have kept her maiden name when she married a man called Taylor, honestly Dad, come on. She's just asking for trouble." She could see her father trying not to laugh. She smiled at him.

"You're incorrigible." He couldn't really get cross - she had his sense of humour, much to her mother's displeasure. "Anyway, I'm sorry but I have to give you the sack." He laughed at his own joke. Emm didn't find it that amusing. "I'll give you a glowing reference. Have you any idea what you want to do next?" Emm knew exactly what she wanted to do next. She wanted Harry's balls to drop and become an adult, but she won't hold her breath on that score.

"I would love to get married and have lots of babies and live happily ever after. But in the real world I'll just roll up at the Job Centre and see what I can find." She was teasing him. She could get a job by picking up her phone and calling a few people who have been asking for her to work for them, but she wanted to make her father feel a little guilty. "I'll be fine. Anyway, you won't sell it that quickly and they may want to keep me on for a while." That was true, Michael thought. He could add that to the contract. They were nearing Emm's flat.

The only wonderful thing about London traffic was that a five-minute distance could take at least twenty minutes in the traffic. Time enough for a good conversation. Emm suddenly remembered the other news she was going to tell him.

"CC has fallen in love with a musician called Frédéric from a jazz club in Nice. What she doesn't know is that he has now got a job at the Jazz Café in Soho. The stupid thing is, though, he doesn't want her to know because he doesn't want to interrupt her studies. She'll need a therapist herself if she doesn't have some fun soon." Michael agreed. But there was nothing he could do about it at that moment. Later, he thought, they'll take her to the Jazz Café and surprise this Frédéric. For now, he had to think of the present.

"So, you know when to be at the Dorchester?" Emm nodded. "Are you seeing your sister beforehand?" Emm nodded. "Now you will make sure she knows when and where, and also you can tell her about Claudia dying to meet her?" Emm nodded.

"Daddy, chill. Everything will be fine. Steph is looking forward to meeting her and is excited about being in all the world's tabloids." She had spoken to her that morning. She smiled at her father. That did sound like Stephanie - Michael nodded. He was glad Stephanie had found a man who could take his younger daughter on. She had been a nightmare up until James finally asked her out. She seemed to blossom and grow into a wonderful woman from that day.

"Okey doke, see you tomorrow darling. Oh, and Emily?" She had got out of the car and now had to crouch down to look at her father through the window.

"Yes Daddy?" He blew her a kiss.

"Thank you for being so understanding and for coming with me for moral support. I love you, poppet." He drove off before she could love him back. She swore she caught sight of a drop of water cruising down his cheek.

CHAPTER 13

Alberto and Lachlan had docked masterfully at the Elite Yachting Marina, in Barcelona Port. They made Dave stay on board while the mechanics were sorting the crane. Sonia and Alberto walked off into town for a shopping expedition. Lachlan sauntered over to the offices of Aussi Yacht Crew Agency.

"G'day Uncle Stevo. How ya doin'?" Steve got out of his seat and bear hugged his nephew, followed by a manly punch to his arm.

"Lachlan, I've been trying to get you here for days. I'm in trouble mate and I need your help." Lachlan had just relaxed after the last bit of trouble - he didn't need any more for a while. But this was his uncle.

"What's up?" Steve got him to sit down.

"Your granddad is really sick now. I need to go back to Aus to help your grandma get things sorted. It doesn't look good, so I want to go and say goodbye to my old man. Trouble is I could be gone for a while and this place is booming. I don't want to close it, so I thought of you. You know as much about the business as I do. What do you say? Will you take over for me until I get back?" Lachlan had to think about it. It was all quite a shock. He didn't want to go back to Australia as he'd been there at Christmas and said goodbye to his granddad then. Steve was right in that Lachlan was ably qualified to run the business. He was in a tricky position.

If he said no, his uncle would have to close the business he had built up over the years. If he said yes, he'd be tied down to an office job for months. But he was family, and family help family.

"When were you thinking of going?" Steve thought the question sounded optimistic.

"As soon as I can. You can live in my place and treat it as your own. You can either have a salary or just take what you need out of the profits. You'll be in sole charge, your own boss. You'll have Sheila here in case you have problems. As she is my right-hand man, I asked her first, but she feels it'll be too much commitment with her new dog rescue venture. She's happy to stay and help you though."

Lachlan thought that the offer was very generous and wanted to say yes. He knew Sheila would be running the business as usual, so he wouldn't have any problems there. He also knew that Steve's apartment was about fifteen minutes up the coast. He'd been there crashing many a time after a night out in Barcelona. It had three bedrooms, a balcony with a built-in barbeque on it, a must for any proud Australian. It also had a large communal pool, with the added advantage of the beach just over the pedestrian zone, so no cars allowed, paradise, free of charge. Why was he hesitant? He didn't know.

"I'll let you know in the next few days. Is that okay?" Steve got up and hugged him again.

"Thank you mate. Knew I could rely on you." Lachlan felt bad.

"I haven't said yes yet." Steve patted him on the back.

"But you'll do the right thing for your family."

Steve winked at him. Lachlan smiled.

"I'll let you know on Monday. I'll have to discuss it with Patrick. I don't want to leave him high and dry after all he has done for me." Steve grabbed a folder off his desk.

"Got the perfect man for your replacement here." He grinned at Lachlan.

"Okay, I'll put that to him. Now I have to go and check on a jammed deck crane. I'll ring you on Monday. No promises, but I'll see what I can do." Steve was still smiling as he left. After all, Lachlan was his brother's son. Steve knew him better than he knew himself. He'd be back.

With the crane fixed and the boat back at Palamós the crew waited for Patrick and his party to return so they could push-off before it got dark. Alberto had slept all the way from Barcelona so was ready to take them out of port and have first watch. Patrick arrived back with Eleanor and Harry, Katarina and Lilli. They had taken a while because Patrick decided to go back to the hospital to give Maria some good news for a change and Harry discussed with her the sale of the farm. She was very pleased and trusted them to find out a good price for it. She wanted nothing more to do with the property. She never wanted to see it again.

Patrick already had called his solicitor to find out the going rate for the farm including the cows.

He also gave him details of Maria's solicitors and insurance company to see how much Maria was due for repairs etc. and to see if Karl's life was insured. The more they could help Maria the better they would all feel.

Patrick thanked José for his chauffeuring and shook his hand. José thanked Patrick for what he could feel in his palm. Harry hadn't quite perfected subtlety but was learning from the maestro.

The girls were busy getting their shopping bags from the back of the car and Lilli was so excited she wanted to carry her own. Patrick rounded the ladies up and ushered them onto the boat. He wanted to catch the tide.

Harry helped Lilli by taking a few of the bags off her. She had been struggling and dropped a couple.

"Did you leave any clothes for the Spanish girls, Lilli?" Lilli giggled.

"I got some new shoes too, Harry. Do you want to see them?" She stopped and put her bags down to find the one she was looking for. Harry turned and went back towards her.

"Not now Lilli. We have to leave the port before all the water drains away." Lilli giggled again. She couldn't understand how there would be no water left in the sea. As Harry picked up Lilli's remaining bags, he noticed movement from the boat moored next door. It had obviously been for sale for a while as the 'For Sale' board had faded and so had the covers on its Flybridge, so there shouldn't be anyone on it. "Come on Lilli. Let's get you on board." He tried to corral Lilli and all her bags as quickly and safely as possible but could see a figure emerging from the stern of the neighbouring boat. He needed help but didn't want to alarm Lilli. She was just as likely to run and slip into the sea. He looked up and caught sight of the back of Lachlan on the Flybridge watching the tide. An idea came to him and he made the sound of a kookaburra. It worked. Lachlan looked over the side of the boat and saw Harry pointing in the direction of the wintered boat. Lachlan looked to where Harry was pointing and suddenly disappeared.

Just before Lilli was able to get up onto the gangplank, she heard a familiar voice.

"Lilliana, come to Papa." She turned and saw her father bending down with his arms outstretched. Lilli looked at Harry confused and scared. She stood still not knowing what she was supposed to do.

Erik, knowing this would be his last chance, went a little closer and shouted, "Lilli, come here." She turned, dropping her bags, and ran into Harry's arms. Harry threw the bags he was carryon onto the floor and caught Lilli. He ran with her onto the gangplank.

Erik was about to follow when a strong hand grasped his shoulder and swung him round.

"Sorry mate, but mongrels aren't welcome on board." Erik's face went straight into Lachlan's right hook. Eric was motionless on the ground. Harry had managed to get Lilli into Patrick's arms and ran back out to help Lachlan.

"You're too late mate. He's out for the count." Lachlan looked very pleased with himself. Patrick shouted from the deck.

"Don't trust him." Lachlan nodded and sat on Erik unceremoniously. Katarina and Eleanor had come out to see what the commotion was. She took a tearful Lilli from Patrick and carried her back inside, leaving Patrick to telephone the police immediately. Harry picked up all the bags and deposited them onto the gangplank for Eleanor to take inside and went back to keep Lachlan company until the police arrived.

"I have to ask, what the hell was that noise you

startled me with?" Lachlan said, tongue in cheek.

"I'll have you know it was the greater spotted kookaburra toad." Lachlan couldn't help laughing. He felt movement underneath him, so turned and delivered another right hook. He carried on chatting to Harry.

"That's how it's done in Aus. Not with a piece of wood like you Pommies. No wonder you're crap at cricket, you can't even swing a stick." Harry took it on the chin, like a true Brit.

The police arrived within minutes, and there were a lot of them. Two of them helped Lachlan to his feet while another two tied Erik's hands and feet, before moving him. They carried him upside down, rather roughly and tossed him into the back of a police van. Patrick explained to one of the senior officers who Erik was and told him they would be available for interviews once they return to Monaco. He gave him the name of the Monaco and Spanish police officers who were assigned to the case. He turned to his crew.

"Let's get this boat sailing boys and girls. We have a very small window, and I don't fancy staying here for another twenty-four hours." All hands ran to their positions while Harry lifted the gangplank. They were away.

They all went to their respective cabins to get ready for dinner. Katarina had calmed Lilli down and explained that her Daddy had been naughty and had to go home. Eleanor had knocked on their door and brought in all their shopping. Once Lilli had tried on a few items she was back to herself.

Sonia had cooked Paella, with a small portion of plain rice and chicken, in case Lilli didn't like it. Lachlan stayed by the bar to pour the drinks as they arrived in the dining room. The sundeck doors were open as the evening was warm, so they could sit on the outside sofas until they were all there and Sonia could serve the dinner. Lilli arrived first.

"Hello Lachlan, I'm first because I'm the smallest and don't have so much to wash." Lachlan laughed; she really was a pleasure to have on board.

"What would you like to drink, madam?" Lilli wasn't sure she liked being called madam.

"I'm mademoiselle actually Lachlan, didn't you know that?" Lachlan shook his head.

"We are in Spanish waters at the moment, so to be correct you're now a señorita." Lilli squealed with euphoria, a señorita sounded very beautiful to her.

"I like being a señorita, Lachlan. Can you call me that all night? You will be my best friend if you do." Lachlan smiled at her.

"Of course, señorita. And what would señorita like to drink this evening? Perhaps a glass of sangria? All señoritas drink sangria." Lilli nodded with excitement. Lachlan poured a little blackcurrant cordial in a glass and topped it up with lemonade. He then scooped some fruit out from the real sangria jug and set it floating on the top of Lilli's glass, finishing off by putting a long straw in the glass with a paper umbrella and handed it to her. Her eyes lit up. She slurped the drink through the straw.

"It's delicious, thank you Lachlan." She walked over to the sundeck but stopped before going outside. She looked round at Lachlan, "I'll have to wait for Mummy. I'm not allowed outside on my own." She sat on a stool and continued drinking her 'sangria'. Lachlan hadn't seen a child behave quite so well. He was pleased that he'd managed to sit with Katarina the night before, for the promised drink. He was about to call Lilli over when Katarina came in. She checked Lilli was happy and hadn't gone outside and went over to talk to Lachlan.

"Good evening Lachlan. Did you have a pleasant trip? How was your uncle?" Lachlan wanted to tell her about his granddad, but Katarina had her own troubles. It was his job to keep all the guests happy.

"He was chipper, thanks. Now Katarina, what can I get you to drink. Lilli is having a rather refreshing glass of sangria," he winked at Katarina without Lilli seeing, "would you like the same?" Katarina nodded. Lachlan was so caring and considerate.

Patrick came in and noticed Katarina walking onto the balcony with Lilli.

"Wish we could do more for those two. Eleanor wants to adopt Lilli." Patrick smiled at Lachlan while he poured his boss his favourite evening tipple, gin with a dash of tonic and a squeeze of lemon. "How did your day go? I see they've managed to fix the crane."

"Yep, it only took half an hour. Good lads down there." Lachlan wanted to talk to Patrick, but it wasn't the right time. He was relaxed and in evening mode.

"So how was your uncle? Did you find out what he wanted?" Lachlan bit the bullet.

"He needs to go back to Australia - my granddad is dying, and my grandma needs him." Patrick could see there was more. He raised his eyebrows at Lachlan. Okay, Lachlan thought, perhaps this was the time.

"He's asked me to take over the crewing agency for a while. I can live in his place and take out as much money as I need from the bank to run it and live on." Patrick was delighted for him. Lachlan would be great at running a company. He was wasted crewing.

"So why are you being so hesitant? Don't tell me it's because you love working for me." Patrick laughed, and then stopped when he saw Lachlan's face.

"That's one reason. The other is that I'm not cut out for office work. I like being outside on the boats." He shook his head. "And I don't want to leave you in the lurch."

"Firstly, this is a crewing agency, yes? So, there'll be plenty of crew on the books. Secondly, I'm sure it isn't forever. How long did he say he'd be gone?"

"He's not sure, six months, a year?" It didn't sound that long when he said it aloud.

"Even a year is no time at all. Treat it like an adventure. You'll have the time off to play on boats. I take it he has staff?" Lachlan nodded. He knew of two, probably more in the summer months.

"He has an Ozzie Sheila called Sheila. She's his man Friday and wants to stay and help me." Lachlan was almost convincing himself while he explained.

"Well, what are you waiting for? Ring your uncle and put his mind at rest. When he gets back from Australia Lady Eleanor will be waiting for you. She may be a newer version, and perhaps a bit bigger, but we'll be here to welcome you back." Lachlan had seen the brochures lying around and knew Lady Eleanor was going to be bigger and faster by the end of the year! He shook Patrick's hand. Patrick went behind the bar and pushed Lachlan away. "No time like the present."

Lachlan went off to his room to telephone his uncle, before he lost the signal, and his nerve.

"Hello barman. I'd like an Aperol Spritz please."

Eleanor had walked in finding her husband behind the bar. Patrick looked worried.

"Where are the staff when you need them? I chose the wrong night to become a barman!" He laughed. Eleanor took pity on him.

"I've changed my mind barman. A nice cool glass of Prosecco please." Patrick smiled at his wife. What would he do without her?

When Lachlan returned from giving the good news to his uncle, he took advantage of Harry keeping Patrick busy behind the bar and Eleanor showing Lilli how to work the music centre, perhaps for a little more karaoke later. He went out onto the balcony and found Katarina.

"Are you warm enough? I can bring you a blanket if you like." Katarina looked up and shook her head.

"No thank you Lachlan, it is rather pleasant out here." Lachlan sat next to her.

"I'm going back to Barcelona next week to take over my uncle's crewing company while he goes back to Australia. It isn't forever but it'll feel like it there all on my own." He looked out to sea in the direction of Barcelona, or where it would be if they were near enough to see it.

He turned to look at Katarina. "I hope you don't think me forward, but have you and Lilli any idea where you're going to live?" Katarina shook her head. She hadn't thought that far in the future.

"I know where I don't want to live, and that is anywhere where I'd be putting Lilli in danger. So, England and Estonia are out of the question." Katarina knew that with Erik locked up she hadn't completely eradicated the risk of Lilli being taken from her.

"You were going to live in Spain, before… well before the farm incident." He was trying to play it down so as not to dredge it all back into Katarina's memory. She smiled at his concern.

"I was, you're right. The problem is there is nowhere left to stay." Lachlan took her hand into his.

"Katarina, I'm going to be living in a large apartment with three bedrooms, by the beach, all alone. It seems such a waste when you and Lilli have nowhere to live. Would you both do me the honour and move in with me, no strings attached?" Katarina burst out crying. Eleanor spotted her and rushed out to see what was wrong.

"Whatever is the matter Katarina?" Eleanor sat the other side of her and put her arm around her shoulders. As Katarina looked up, Eleanor could see she had mistaken the tears for sadness. They were definitely tears of joy given away by the immense smile she had on her face.

"Lachlan has just offered Lilli and me a home in Spain. I cannot get over the generosity of all of you. I don't know what to say."

"Say yes Mummy, silly." Lilli had followed Eleanor outside. "I can be a señorita there, can't I Lachlan?" Lachlan nodded and grabbed Lilli and threw her in the air, gently. She squealed with joy. Harry came out to see what all the commotion was. Patrick followed with a bottle of beer for Lachlan.

"I take it you have accepted your uncle's proposal?" Lachlan nodded. "Have you also managed to get the company you so needed, so you won't be alone?" Lachlan nodded. Patrick hadn't got where he was today without reading people and evaluating outcomes - inwardly he chuckled but couldn't tell them why, it would ruin the moment. The phrase in his head had come to mind from one of his favourite old BBC farces. "Well, congratulations for your new job, and congratulations to Katarina and Lilli for their new home. Cheers." He handed Lachlan the bottle and they all chinked their drinks.

Katarina took Lilli to their bedroom to help her get ready for bed. Once in her pyjamas Lilli sat on the bed and didn't move, with her arms crossed and a frown on her forehead. Katarina knew that Lilli wasn't happy but didn't know why.

"Okay Lilli, what's the matter?" Lilli turned away from her mother.

"Come on Lilli. I can't make it better until you tell me what's wrong." Katarina thought she was over the Erik issue. She seemed to accept the explanation she had given her. Lilli started to cry. It broke Katarina's heart to hear her daughter so unhappy. She put her arm around her shoulders and drew her nearer. "Are you sad because you're going to miss your Daddy?" To Katarina's surprise Lilli shook her head. She looked up into her mother's eyes.

"No, I'm upset because I'm going to miss Harry. If we go with Lachlan, we won't be able to live with Harry." Katarina was relieved. She could cope with Lilli's little wobble when it wasn't about her father.

"Oh Lilli. You're funny. I thought you liked Lachlan." Lilli sniffed.

"I do. But I like Harry more."

Well, thought Katarina, that told her. Although this was trivial in Katarina's mind, if it wasn't handled correctly, they may not be going to Spain with Lachlan.

"That's because you've been with Harry longer.

When you get to know Lachlan, you will like him as much as Harry. I promise." Lilli looked at her mummy. "And just because we are going to Spain with Lachlan, it doesn't mean we won't see Harry. He's Lachlan's friend too so I'm sure he'll be popping in lots of times." Lilli smiled.

"To see me?" Katarina nodded. "I want to be a señorita, so okay, we'll try Spain." Katarina snuggled up with Lilli until she fell asleep.

After Lilli had gone to bed and dinner had been cleared the party went inside. The wind had picked up on the open sea, so it had turned chilly. Dave had perched himself behind the bar, his favourite place on the boat. Unfortunately, it was his turn on watch next, so he only had an hour to relax. Lachlan had last watch, before Alberto would join him to take them into port, probably around breakfast time.

Lachlan couldn't find Katarina and supposed she had retired with Lilli. He went out to take in the night air before he had to turn in for a few hours' kip ready for his watch in the early hours of the morning. Holding the rail to steady herself, Katarina saw Lachlan and smiled.

"I had to get some air. The boat is rocking a little and I didn't want to lose the delicious paella Sonia had cooked." She looked so vulnerable in the moonlight. His heart missed a beat. He went closer to her and realised she was shivering. He put his arm around her to warm her up.

"Shall I go and get you a blanket?" Katarina cosied into him and a small voice replied.

"No thank you Lachlan, this will do nicely." Lachlan smiled. He had just met this woman and it felt so natural holding her and watching the South of France's coastline glisten from their position, with the moonlight bouncing up and down on the sea. Lachlan thought it must be the most romantic place on earth at that moment. He'd been back and forth from Spain to France on numerous occasions but had never noticed it before. He took a deep breath of air. He felt himself going sentimental and Aussies don't do mushy. "Lachlan tell me why you're hurting inside." Lachlan pulled away slightly so he could look into her eyes.

"Are you some kind of mind reader or something?" He was spooked. Katarina laughed.

"Call it women's intuition. Every so often I have noticed the smile go from your face and you get a haunting look. On the outside you're happy-go-lucky, is that the phrase?" Lachlan nodded. "But I can tell inside you're hiding something. I know what that is like. I have lived that life every day for many years. I had to be so happy for Lilli, but inside I wanted to cry. You and your friends have changed my life and I'm now happy inside. I want to help you Lachlan. Life is so worth living when you're happy." Lachlan had to agree. If he could stop being sad inside, he wouldn't have to put on a front every day. He had thought of Matilda more over the last few days, especially seeing Katarina in the state she was in when they found her. He led Katarina to one of the outside sofas and sat her down. Opening the box on the deck he took out a blanket. He sat up close to her to keep the wind from freezing her to death and wrapped them together.

"You're very astute, Katarina. I'm sad because I miss my girlfriend, Tilly." Katarina wished she hadn't asked. Lachlan carried on explaining. "Tilly and I had been at school together, but we drifted apart when she went to college. We started dating after we met up again at our mate Dylan's twenty-first birthday bash. We had been dating for about six months and we decided to move in together."

He looked out to sea, with memories flooding back, and smiled. "We were so happy. I was working hard to pay the rent and she was studying to become a teacher. She'd have been a bonza teacher too." Katarina didn't want to interrupt him so assumed bonza meant good. Lachlan swallowed hard and carried on. "It all happened so quickly. I got home from work to find her crumpled up on the kitchen floor with her phone in her hand. She was breathing but unconscious. I heard the ambulance siren and went to let them in. She must have telephoned them before she passed out." Katarina noticed he was looking away from her trying to compose himself.

"What had happened to her Lachlan?" She placed her hand gently on his arm.

"By the time we got her to the hospital her appendix had burst. They operated straight away, and I was able to see her in ICU a few hours later. Before the nurse took me to her bed, she told me I was to talk to her as hearing was the last sense to go, but she didn't have long. She looked so crook. She had tubes and monitors everywhere. She was barely conscious but smiled gently when I sat on her bed and cuddled her. She had no strength in her body. She was dying in my arms, and there was nothing I could do about it. I talked to her and told her what an adorable woman she was, inside and out, and that I'd miss her very much. I thanked her for being in my life and told her if she needed to go to sleep then that was okay." He took another deep breath. "She slipped away a few hours later in my arms."

Katarina wanted to say something but was waiting until Lachlan's breathing calmed. He took out a handkerchief and blew his nose, cross with himself for not being able to control his emotions. He turned to Katarina and took her hand. "That's why, when I saw you, I had to get you to the medics and save you. I couldn't help Tilly, but I could help you." Katarina nodded with a warm smile.

"And you did save me Lachlan. You're a very good man. I'm sorry about poor Tilly, but you were there for her. She wasn't alone." Lachlan hadn't thought of that. He was there, and she knew he was there. "And I'm sure she took comfort in that for her last moments on earth."

"That sort of helps, thanks Katarina." She thought he was going to carry on, but there was silence. The best therapy was to talk about what is troubling you, so she needed him to get it all out.

"Did the doctor tell you what had happened to Tilly?" Lachlan inclined his head in thought.

"He explained that nothing could be done. By the time they operated on Tilly she had already gone into septic shock. Her organs were failing, and they weren't sure she'd even survive through the operation. That is one thing I'm thankful for, being able to say goodbye to her." Katarina wanted to put her arm around Lachlan and let him cry on her shoulder. He was barely holding it together. He hadn't told anyone the full details of Tilly's death but felt the need to tell Katarina. "I felt guilty for months afterwards."

Katarina looked at him questioningly wondering why he could have thought it was his fault. Lachlan was nodding.

"I know it wasn't my fault, but I should have hassled her more to go and see the doctor when she first complained of stomachache. She kept telling me it was her period, but her pain seemed much stronger to me. The morning of that day, I found her with a fever. I told her enough was enough and she had to make an appointment. She promised me she would, just after she'd finished some thesis, she had to hand in that arvo. I telephoned her at lunchtime, and she told me she was fine. She had finished her thesis and was going to drop it off on the way to the health centre. She never got there. The thesis was on the kitchen table when I got back from the hospital. I should have taken the day off and driven her to the hospital myself." He shook his head. "But apparently it wouldn't have made any difference. According to the surgeon who came to talk to me before Tilly died, she already had sepsis from the burst appendix, so it was like a ticking bomb." Lachlan was glad he had said all the details out loud. It had convinced him that he could have done no more than he did. He was aware of Katarina gently holding his hand.

He couldn't understand the overwhelming feeling that was enveloping him. It was like a tremendous feeling of guilt and sadness was lifting from his psyche. He took his hand from hers and moved her chin towards him. He kissed her gently on her lips. She melted into his arms and the kiss became passionate. He hoped he wasn't hurting her, as the bruising was still evident. She pulled back and looked at his kind eyes.

"I think we could heal each other Lachlan, don't you?" His answer was to lean forward and kiss her again. The desire for a happier life became obvious to them both.

Patrick had decided to stop off at Nice in Port Lympia the next morning, before mooring in Monaco. Eleanor wanted to catch the Saturday matinee of Nico's opera and she knew Katarina needed to see Caroline to thank her for everything.

"I'll phone Caroline and organise the timing. I know she wants to meet you both." Harry got out his phone.

"Invite them to have coffee on the boat first so we can meet them here." Eleanor thought it better to meet new people in the comfort of a family home and away from prying eyes. Although she saw her home as the house in Winchester, not the apartment in Monaco, or the Lady Eleanor, she had to be adaptable.

"That's a good idea. We can stay for the day before sailing back to Monaco." Patrick had to fill in the charts and telephone Port Lympia for a docking place, so he bid everyone a good night.

Eleanor and Katarina had decided to turn in too, so they could be up nice and early for the docking at Nice. Harry went to find Lachlan and found him wrapped up in a blanket, alone, on the outer deck. He was fast asleep. What Harry couldn't know was that Lachlan was completely relaxed for the first time since that fateful day Matilda passed away. He decided to leave him there and went up to relieve Dave for an hour or so. Lachlan would eventually wake up and realise his watch had started, so Harry thought he'd enjoy his last watch before he became a farmer!

CHAPTER 14

Stephanie arrived at Emm and CC's flat, in Elizabeth Street, just off Buckingham Palace Road, early. She was excited to see her sister and get all the gossip. The night before the newlyweds had arrived home to a surprise party laid-on by CC's parents, Stephanie's new in-laws. It blew Emm's plans of getting her sister up to date with the entire goings on that had happened while she was away in Italy. No one had told her anything apart from a text message from her sister, duplicated by her father in even less detail, to say her presence was required at the Dorchester by two o'clock on Saturday. Michael had tried to ring her but kept going into her voicemail. The news he wanted to tell her could not be left on a voice mail.

"Hello gorgeous girl. How was your honeymoon?" Emm dragged Steph in and sat her on the settee. She took the holdall from her and placed it on a chair. Steph had arrived in comfy clothes, with her smart stuff in the bag.

"Plenty of time for that. Tell me what this big secret is. All I know is from your text." She read it out. "We have to be at the Dorchester in glad rags, for14.00hours. It's something to do with Daddy. Can't tell you in text as too complicated. #goodsurprise #happydaddy." She looked up at her sister with curiosity seeping from her every pore. Emm thought it best to tell her everything.

"Daddy has a girlfriend, as we had rightly guessed. What we didn't know was who she was. She is only Claudia Pasqualle." Emm paused for her sister to cotton on.

"OMG, not the Claudia Pasqualle?" Emm nodded. Her sister shrieked, "OMG Emm. How long has this been going on?" Steph was more excited than hurt, being the last one to know.

"Long enough for Daddy to propose to her today." Steph shrieked again.

"It sounds like someone is strangling a cat in here. Hello sister-in-law. I take it you've heard the news? Hope you've got posh clothes for your photo shoot." CC was winding Steph up. She went into the kitchen to make some coffee and wake up properly. She'd been swotting till very late. "Anyone want a coffee?" Steph had turned to Emm with an enquiring look. Her eyebrows were so high up they couldn't be seen under her fringe.

"I haven't got to that bit yet CC., and yes to the coffee." Steph put her hand up. "Two coffees please. Anyway, because the French press seem to have found out, Claudia is worried that the English won't be far behind. She's holding a press conference at the Dorchester to reveal the identity of her lover, Daddy!" Steph couldn't believe it. But before she could say anything, Emm carried on. "Not only that, but Daddy has decided to choose today to ask her to marry him. In front of the world no less." Steph was flabbergasted. What could she say? Her coffee was put in front of her, and CC joined her on the settee.

"Exciting stuff isn't it?" CC was rather enjoying

the whole scenario. "Now I'm family, can I come?"
She was looking at Emm, but already knew the answer. Emm had promised she could come and mingle but she was not to talk to any of the press. "Oh yes, I forgot, I am." She giggled. Steph was still in a state of euphoria and unable to talk. Although her father was marrying one of the hottest box office actresses, she was just happy that he had a new woman in his life. Gradually the significance of the situation started to creep into her mind and the consequences of her father's decision to marry a film star, and the effect it would have on family life, as she knew it, was keeping her from enjoying the initial excitement.

"You don't look happy Steph. Daddy is, and he hoped we would be too." Steph felt selfish. Emm was right. Her father was obviously really happy probably for the first time since their mother left. It just occurred to her that both of them had gone for French people.

"What is so good about the French, all of a sudden?" She said it with a smile on her face to lighten the mood.

"French men are adorable. I'm madly and passionately in love with a Frenchman, so I'd watch what you say." CC was enjoying winding her sister in law up. Emm hadn't told CC that her adorable Frenchman was literally ten minutes away from their flat, not nine hundred miles away (near as damn it) as she thought.

"How long have I been away? The whole world has gone mad." Steph was dumbfounded. So much had happened over the two weeks she and James had decided to have a social media detox during their honeymoon. Emm brought her sister up to speed about her and CC's unintentional stalking of their father in Cannes, how their mother still knows nothing, and the description of the ring.

"The only thing I haven't told you yet is that we are unemployed too. Daddy is selling the business." Emm waited for a reaction. Steph let out a loud sigh of relief.

"Phew. Thank goodness for that. I was trying to build up the courage to tell him that I wanted to leave. This way we may get some redundancy money?" She winked at her sister. Emm knew Steph's heart wasn't in the job. It was obvious when she arrived late every day and left early. Not a lot of work got done between those times either. She hated talking to strangers on the phone, the main part of her job as the receptionist. Michael had employed her to make sure she had a job, not because of her communicative skills.

"Well you took that information well. Any ideas about what you want to do?" Steph smiled.

"I would like to be a lady of leisure for as long as I can, before James and I start a family. I will talk to my husband about it. That still sounds weird. My husband." She giggled. Emm was glad her sister seemed so happy. CC was up and dressed by the time Emm had told Steph everything.

"Are we going to warn Mother?" Steph thought it only fair. "I worry that as soon as the French press learn of Daddy's name, they will probably flag up the news of his ex-wife living with a famous opera singer in The South of France."

"I hoped it would take longer than a day, but we would have to say something to her tomorrow. Today is all about Daddy." Emm had her fingers crossed that she had time to be complacent.

The girls decided to have breakfast at The Breakfast Club, just around the corner from their flat. The closer they got to the press conference, the more nervous they would be and so probably lunch would be very light.

***

The sunshine in Nice was therapeutic for all Patrick's guests, and coffee on the boat was a very good idea. Everyone was relaxed, and Patrick was entertaining Caroline while Eleanor chatted to Nico about the opera. Harry kept looking at his watch. Taking the extra hour off for British Summer Time, he was trying to calculate when the proverbial excrement would hit the fan. They had a few hours before the press would be invading their space. That would be if any of them managed to put two and two together and realise that the ex-wife of Michael Fitzgerald was co-habiting with the famous opera singer Nicolas Janvier.

Harry wished he could be there, but he knew he'd probably be more useful in Nice, so he can tell Emm what was happening at Camp Caroline!

Lachlan had gone off into town with Katarina and Lilli. He wanted to get them some clothes and toiletries for their stay in Barcelona. Lilli was beyond excited. Although she didn't quite comprehend why she was going to live with Lachlan, she did like him very much. He was kind and made her laugh. He also was very good at piggybacks, which made him her very best friend, at that moment. Patrick had let the rest of the crew have a few hours off to enjoy Nice. He was at a secure marina he had often used, so he was happy to leave the boat unattended if they hadn't got back before his party left. Lunchtime was calling them all into town too. They were going to eat early so Nico could get off to make-up at the opera house.

"Are you going to join Eleanor at the opera this afternoon, Caroline?" Harry wanted to know where she would be every second of the day. He was worried for her safety in a strange way. He knew how the press went in packs and it was quite daunting if you weren't used to it. Having worked for Patrick for a while, he had got used to the swarms, and how to evade them.

"I'm going with Nico's parent's tomorrow evening, so I don't want to ruin the surprise. I've seen quite a few snippets from the rehearsals, but it isn't the same. I haven't seen it all the way through in the right order. It'll be spectacular. You will enjoy it Eleanor. Are you going Patrick?" Patrick couldn't think of anything worse, oh yes he could, the ballet! Before he had time to respond Eleanor helped him out.

"I'm afraid it isn't Patrick's cup of tea. He prefers watching grown men chasing after an oval ball all round a field." She was playing with him - he laughed, but she was right.

They left the boat, but Patrick hung back slightly so he could talk to Harry.

"You seem worried and you keep looking at your watch. Are you expecting someone?" Harry shook his head. He was under oath not to tell anyone, but Patrick wasn't anyone.

"I can't tell you exactly what's worrying me, I've been sworn to secrecy by Emm, but I think the press may be about to pester Caroline on a rather big scale. It may not happen, but if it does it'll be around mid-afternoon today." Patrick grinned. He loved his little spats with the press.

"Intriguing. I don't want you to break your promise, but could it be to do with Emily's father?" Harry nodded. "And could it be something to do with a lady?" Harry nodded again. "Ah, so the lady in question is obviously well known to the press."

"You're bloody good at this game, aren't you Patrick?" They both laughed.

"Well, we will both just have to see how today pans out. If need be, we can make a fast escape on the Lady Eleanor with Caroline. We are getting quite good at this 'rescuing damsels in distress' malarkey!" Patrick put a fatherly arm around Harry and they walked on to catch up with the others.

* * *

The press conference was held in The Dorchester's Penthouse and Terrace. Claudia's agent, Brigitte, decided if the weather was good the Terrace would be ideal for a photo shoot with its views of Mayfair and the whole of London as the backdrop. But as a contingency, due to the English weather, the Penthouse itself was a splendid room too.

Claudia arrived and was taken up to the eighth Floor. She decided, initially, to meet the press alone. Michael, wearing a cream linen suit Claudia had bought with him, and the girls were in The Bar at The Dorchester.

They would join Claudia when they got the nod from Brigitte. Stephanie and Emm were wearing their summer dresses by Tara Jarmon, Paris, from Nice's Galeries Lafayette's sale, and CC was wearing a skirt from Hobbs and a blouse from Whistles she had bought as an alternative for her brother's wedding after party and hadn't worn.

Michael had to admit the girls all looked wonderful, he was very proud of them all. The girls couldn't believe they were in such a famous London landmark. Emm couldn't believe they were in such decadence.

The whole concept was purple, set off by imposing purple glass stalagmites bordering the seating area. The classic luxury seemed to blend elegantly with the modern design. Emm thought it unashamedly indulgent.

Their cocktails were just as indulgent. The girls had ordered Cosmopolitans shaken with ice and served in chilled Martini glasses. Michael had ordered a Cognac, for courage! He went over to talk to the bar manager while the girls were occupied.

The manager got out a couple of bottles of Champagne and Michael chose the Cristal.

"Good choice Daddy!" Emm was behind him. "I take it this is for the toast?" Michael nodded and put his finger to his lips, making sure Emm didn't shout it out. He wouldn't put it past the paparazzi to be one step ahead of them.

"So, half a dozen sir, with another six chilling in case?" Michael nodded to the bar manager. "I'll take them up to the Penthouse now, before we get too busy."

Michael watched as the manager organised his team to take ice and champagne up to the eighth floor. Michael and Emm went back to sit at the bar and await their summons.

Claudia was standing by the Terrace doors, with a light breeze keeping everyone cool. She was not a vain person but needed to get the interviews out of the way before they went out to the Terrace for photographs. She knew the breeze could play havoc with her hair, so she thought it unnecessary to tempt providence and the least time out in the wind the better.

"I will explain why I 'ave brought you all 'ere today, then I will answer appropriate questions. I met my soulmate in London, over a year ago. 'e is an English gentleman called Michael Fitzgerald. I do not know what the future 'olds for me, but I do know that I want Michael by my side, forever." There was a frenzy of questions. Claudia had to point to a person individually to answer their question, or she'd never hear any of them properly. She pointed to a face she recognised, a fellow Frenchwoman.

"Bonjour, Christina, Paris Match. Pouvez-vous nous dire comment…" Claudia held up her hand.

"English please." She wanted to wrong step the journalists, if she could. She needed to keep the upper hand. Having learnt the tricks from being in the public eye for so long. She also wanted to protect Michael from their persistent scrutiny, as much as possible.

"Sorry, Christina, Paris Match. Could you tell us 'ow it feels dating an older man?" Christina stuck her microphone as near to Claudia as she could, without Claudia swallowing it. Claudia pushed it aside.

"What 'as age got to do with love? I love this man, no matter when 'e was born, or where 'e was born. 'e is romantic, generous and kind. Attributes which I admire dearly in 'im."

She pointed to another microphone- she found it difficult to see who was holding it.

"Alastair Huntley-Parsons, Tatler." Claudia was impressed. They really have brought out the elite from the English press. "My readers want to know how your relationship will affect your film career."

"My relationship will not be affecting my film career. Michael is very supportive of my job." She saw no point in furthering that interview. She pointed to another woman journalist.

"Alison Butler, Daily Telegraph. Can you tell us if marriage is on the cards?" Claudia looked straight at the woman.

"I don't know, I 'aven't been asked yet." Some of the journalists laughed. She was getting bored with it now. She signalled Brigitte to get Michael up. She'd take one more question before she suggested going outside for photographs. She pointed to a Frenchman she recognised.

"'ello Claudia. Marcel Debois, Le Monde. Will you be 'aving children?" Claudia was expecting someone to ask that but assumed it would come from a female journalist, not from the chief reporter from a French daily newspaper.

"My acting 'as always come first for me, so I think I may 'ave left that too late." She hoped that would be sufficient. She really didn't want to get into the fact that she could not have children. It was not their business and Michael knew all about her ectopic pregnancy a few years ago. Unfortunately, both her fallopian tubes got damaged. Michael entered the room just in time. "My darling." Claudia rushed over to him and linked his arm. There was a bombardment of flash bulbs. He felt like a film star himself. He whispered in her ear.

"You okay?" She smiled and nodded. He squeezed her hand and smiled at the cameras. Claudia walked slowly with Michael to the outside terrace where the views of London were breath taking. The cameras followed them, along with the journalists. They were trying to get Michael to talk, but Claudia thought they had enough for their appetites and were being a little greedy.

The girls had hung back, but Brigitte helped them through the throng and onto the terrace. They blended in well and hadn't been noticed, the whole point of the exercise. All three girls hadn't realised this little oasis existed in Mayfair.

There was a fountain on the edge of the balcony, with water cascading down the sides into a smaller water feature. Flowers were trailing over small wrought iron gazebos like in a whimsical fairy tale. Emm thought it was so apt for Claudia as it reminded her of an enchanted stage set.

Michael made eye contact with the bar staff and thought 'no time like the present'. He hadn't warned either Claudia or Brigitte, as he needed them both to be startled and totally surprised. The last thing he wanted was to upset Claudia by the press thinking it was a publicity stunt. It was time for his debut!

He took Claudia by the hand and walked her over to the water fountain. There was a cushioned bench by the gazebo where he motioned for her to sit down. He could see the press getting fidgety, not knowing what was happening, but anticipating a headline.

Michael went down on one knee while he was holding Claudia's hand. It was obvious to everyone that Claudia had realised what Michael was doing. He was pleased his plan of total surprise had worked as no way could it have been misconstrued.

He put his hand into his linen jacket pocket and took out the unmistakable shape of a ring box. Claudia took a deep breath and a tear was running down her left cheek. Michael opened the box to reveal the beautiful ring, even more magnificent with the sun making it glisten lustrously in his hand.

"Claudia, voulez-vous me faire le plus grand honneur de devenir ma femme?" Not having a great deal of confidence in his Google Translator, he continued, "In other words, will you do me the greatest honour of becoming my wife?" Claudia had tears running down both sides now, and if Michael had turned slightly, he'd have seen the same emotion showing, no, cascading down Brigitte's cheeks. Claudia swallowed hard so she could be heard.

"Oui, oui, oui. Of course, my darling." He slid the ring onto her finger, while breathing a sigh of relief that she had said yes, and that the ring was a good fit. She fell into his arms as he got off his knee.

There was an explosion of applause, flashes, popping corks and chinking of glasses while Michael embraced his fiancée. Emm could see most of the journalists on their phones. Perhaps she should call her mother to warn her, but it was difficult holding the best Champagne she had ever been allowed to drink and using her phone at the same time. The Champagne won.

"Claudia, Claudia, are you happy?" The journalists had their microphones out again.

"Yes, of course. I just wonder why 'e 'ad taken so long to ask me!" Everyone was laughing. The staff appeared with canapés and the glasses were re-filled generously. What had started as a press conference ended as a party. Brigitte was so happy. She knew she couldn't have arranged a better advertising campaign if she had done it herself.

Michael took Claudia over to meet Stephanie. Emm and CC hugged her before Steph had got back from the canapés. She was so hungry now the nerves had gone.

"You're so beautiful, just like your sister." Claudia kissed her on the cheeks.

"Thank you…um?" Emm wanted to help her sister, this was all very new to her.

"You can call her Claudia." Claudia smiled at Steph.

"Or you could start getting used to calling me step-mother?" Claudia laughed. She knew she was teasing the girls, but it was fun. Emm and Steph laughed too. CC felt left out. Michael put his arm around her and squeezed her gently. She felt much better.

"You need a night out, young lady." He smiled at her. "I have an idea. When we've finished here, we will go around the corner to the Soho Jazz Café and have some more of those cocktails you seem to like." Claudia thought it a brilliant idea.

"I will need to go 'ome and change. I put this on for the cameras." She pointed to the smart daytime royal blue dress with white lace collar, and a small jacket edged in white, to match. "But I need something jazzier for tonight." Claudia really wasn't vain - she just knew what to wear and when to wear it. She was French after all; Steph knew they were fashion masters. Although, she thought to herself, the Italian's were very close behind in the fashion stakes. She hadn't been able to buy anything in Italy on her honeymoon, but she certainly enjoyed looking in the shop windows. The photographers and the journalists were enjoying the Champagne and canapés so much that Claudia thought they had forgotten why they were there. That worked on her side. She beckoned Brigitte over.

"We are going. Say goodbye to the press for me. I 'ave an important engagement tonight, with my family." Michael was ecstatic. Claudia was already assuming the title of family to his girls. They left far more relaxed than they had arrived.

Stephanie went home to tell James they were going out to the Jazz Café that evening and he had to go and change. He didn't look enthralled. She tried to explain to him what Emm had told her about the French musician.

"We are doing it for your sister. She is madly in love with a French pianist called Frédéric and he's moved to London, to be with her. Only she doesn't know yet. He doesn't want to interrupt her studies. How wonderful is that. So romantic." James grabbed her arm and pulled her onto his chair.

"If you want romantic, I'll give you it." He kissed her lustfully.

"That's not romantic." She pushed him away and got up. "That's just lust." He looked scorned. She laughed and on seeing his face she then capitulated. "I can do lust too," she checked her watch, "but you've only got one hour to do it with me." James got up and chased a squealing Stephanie up the stairs.

Emm tried to explain to CC that one night was not going to make her fail her exams.

"In fact, it has been proven that if you have a day off you work harder the next day and retain more." CC shook her head.

"Bollocks. You just made that up." Emm laughed.

"I knew you had. But you're right. I do need a break. It'll be weird listening to jazz though. I miss Frédéric so much.
We've chatted on the phone, but he hasn't Facetimed me in ages." Emm knew the reason why. It would give his position away.

"You can keep your eyes closed all evening and pretend he's playing the keyboard." Emm thought it was a good idea. CC scrunched up her nose. How stupid would she look, at a jazz club, with her eyes closed. No, she'd go anyway but wouldn't stay out too long.

"I don't want to be too late back though. Okay?" Emm agreed, with her fingers crossed behind her back.
 They all met at the bar next door to the Jazz Café. Claudia looked striking. She was wearing the prettiest sleeveless white dress, with a dropped waistline, emphasised with a silky grey ribbon. There was silky grey ribbon round the neck, arms and hem too. Her hair had been gelled down and parted to the side, where normally it flowed onto her shoulders without such precision. She had sandals that crossed over her ankles and tied at the back, with grey ribbon

Emm called it chic.

"Wow, you look fantastic." Steph loved her outfit. "Did you buy that in France?" Claudia shook her head.

"I'm not sure where it was from, but I wore it for a film a few years ago with my friend Leo." CC jumped out of her seat.

"OMG, The Great Gatsby? Of course, you were in that film, I remember now." Claudia had just gone up even further in their estimation. "I loved that film.

You were exceptional."

"Remind me to put you in charge of my fan club." Claudia smiled at CC, she liked her. She was glad they could help her in her love life too. Michael had told her his reason for choosing that café. "So, you must be James, I can tell. You and CC look alike." James stood up and shook her hand. Claudia leant forward and kissed him on both cheeks.

"Thank you, I think. It's very nice to meet you." CC giggled. She didn't often see her brother embarrassed, but he was. Steph protected him.

"He's a little jet-lagged. He'll be fine soon." They all knew that Steph and James had just got back from Italy, so jet lag wasn't the reason for his self-consciousness. But they weren't going to push it. CC and Emm had been exactly the same when they first met the famous movie star called Claudia Pasqualle.

"Well, shall we have a drink here first? I made a reservation for eight o'clock because they get tremendously busy on a Saturday night." Michael had booked a table just to the left of the stage area, up on the balcony. He winked at Emm. She just hoped it didn't backfire.

CHAPTER 15

Patrick and Caroline were walking along the Promenade des Anglais chatting about the benefits of living in a warmer climate than England's. They were in full agreement as the sun was setting over the Mediterranean Sea across the beach in Nice and the temperature dropped to a balmy twenty-eight degrees.

"Would you ever go back to England, to live, Caroline?" She looked into Patrick's eyes to reply.

"This is Nico's world - his life is here. Nico is my world, my life. So, the answer to your question Patrick has to be 'no'." Patrick nodded. He understood exactly what Caroline meant. He had the same relationship with Eleanor, and nothing would part him from her - they would sail to the ends of the earth together. He hated leaving her behind.

Nico and Eleanor returned from the opera to find Harry waiting for them. He looked agitated and Nico went into the kitchen to pour him some wine, Eleanor followed them both.

"'ere, drink this and tell us what the problem is." Nico handed Harry a glass and poured Eleanor and himself one. He motioned for Harry and Eleanor to follow him back to the lounge and to sit down. Harry drew a big breath.

"I've been keeping something from you all. I have

been under oath, so it's not my fault. But for the sake of Caroline I must divulge the news." Nico was becoming very agitated. "Calm down Nico. Nothing has happened yet." Nico got off his seat and took a deep breath, facing Harry.

"What is going to 'appen? Vite, mon ami, dis moi." Harry knew he had to explain everything, and quickly before the crazed Frenchman spilt his wine.

"Emm's father is dating Claudia Pasqualle. She has held a press conference to tell the world, this afternoon, and I think the press has put two and two together as, if I'm not mistaken, there is a paparazzi photographer outside your building." Nico rushed to the window and looked down towards the pavement outside the flats.

"Mon Dieu. There is more than one, mon ami." Harry got up and looked. A small pack was beginning to form outside the foyer. Harry had to process the consequences of Caroline being pounced on and knew he needed to keep her away from the building.

"Right Nico, we need to keep Caroline away. She's with Patrick so perhaps we can get a message to him?" He looked at Eleanor optimistically.

"I'll give him a ring. What shall I say I want?" She was worried Caroline may misunderstand his panic.

"Tell him we are all meeting up at Bar L'Opera for after performance drinks." Harry thought it was far enough away for Caroline not to see the flats, but near enough that they could walk there.

"What about Katarina and Lilli? Where are they?" Nico was on high alert looking out of the window the press was multiplying.

"Katarina and Lilli are back on the boat. She

wanted to get Lilli to have some quiet time. I think she wanted some herself." Harry knew Katarina was being stoic, she was still in a lot of discomfort. "We must alert François not to let anyone with a camera or microphone into the building." Nico nodded and went over to the internal phone which was a direct line to François.

"I'm going to cut them off at the pass. I can't have Caroline just walking into it all." Harry grabbed his phone. He had tried to call Emm, but she hadn't answered. He assumed it was on silent for the press conference and she'd forgotten to put the sound back on. He left a text message. "Have you tried Patrick?" He looked at Eleanor. She nodded.

"It'll be in his pocket. He never hears it in there. He will not put vibrate on, for some unknown reason." She sighed. On numerous occasions she'd wished he could at least feel his phone even if he couldn't hear it. He always muttered that the vibration had felt weird in his trouser pocket and could cause embarrassment. Eleanor always responded with, 'you should be so lucky'! "I think we ought to come with you. There are four routes back to this building. We could each take the three most likely ones and hope we haven't got it wrong." Harry agreed that was a good idea. Nico had come back into the conversation having alerted François and said the road they were less likely to use was the one into town. He hoped Caroline was all shopped out. They would either be coming along the Promenade from the port or the sea front, or from behind the apartment from the Cours Saleya, if they'd stopped for a drink. They took the lift down and told François that they were off to look for Caroline. He was being very vigilant and only people he recognised got into the block.

As Harry walked across the road to the Promenade des Anglais, with the sea on his left, he caught sight of them sauntering along towards him. He turned quickly and could see Nico still on the main road, before turning up the side road leading to the Cours Saleya. Eleanor had obviously already gone further down the road, back to the boat. Harry knew if he shouted Nico would hear, but if he got Nico's attention, he'd be drawing attention to himself and the paparazzi would get suspicious. Had he time to run back to the others first and then catch Patrick and Caroline before they crossed the road? He thought not. He turned to check on Nico, at the same time as Nico turned to look over at him. Phew, thought Harry. He beckoned him and pointed along the seafront. Nico made a thumb's up gesture and walked quickly after Eleanor who hadn't got far along the Promenade towards the port. Harry could forget about them now, he concentrated on getting to Caroline before the press got to her. The press had got agitated. They had been watching events and probably wondered why three people left together but all went in different directions. One of them broke free from the pack and started following Harry. He just hoped that they didn't know what Caroline looked like. As he neared them he looked at Patrick and put the palm of his hand up towards him to alert him to stop, using his body to shield the gesture from anyone behind. He then pointed backwards still with his body covering his movements. Then put both hands up to his face and simulated a camera taking a photo. Patrick looked beyond Harry and caught sight of the photographer. He acknowledged that he totally understood what Harry was saying. Caroline was chatting and looking out to sea, oblivious of the messages that had been fed to them by a layman's semaphore. Patrick steered Caroline over the main road while Harry walked on. She hadn't seen him. The lone cameraman followed Harry. Nico, having reached Eleanor before she'd gone too far, had been watching the scenario play out and caught up with Patrick and Caroline. She was pleased to see them both.

"Hello, did the opera go well? Silly question. I'm sure you were magnificent." Nico took Caroline by the hand and walked her towards the opera house, turning off one road from the apartment and in full view of their front door. Patrick and Eleanor followed them. Nico had engaged Caroline in conversation about mishaps on stage in the hope she would be looking at him, not ahead at the already obvious posse outside their home.

It had worked. By the time they had turned the corner she was oblivious to anything wrong. As they walked along Nico wondered whether he should tell Caroline what had happened, but thought she'd make such a fuss that she would draw attention to them. He decided to wait until they were sitting inside the Bar L'Opera. Nico turned around to Patrick.

"Could you give Harry a call and tell him we'll be in the Bar L'Opera? He knows where it is." Patrick nodded and got out his phone.

Harry had got the message from Patrick and continued for a short while along the Promenade. He assumed he was still being followed but didn't want to make the spy's beginner's mistake of checking. He crossed over the main road and went into the Esplanade Georges Pompidou. He walked through into the back road, which led to the opera house and Bar L'Opera. He quickly turned left instead of right to the bar and slipped into a doorway and waited. Within seconds the man with the cameras around his neck walked out into the road. He looked both left and right and knew he'd lost Harry. He turned back the way he had come.

Unknown to the photographer, Harry was watching his image on the window of the restaurant opposite. He left it a couple of more minutes and felt it safe to carry along Rue Saint-François de Paule to the Bar L'Opera. Checking on another shop front window he noticed Monsieur Cameraman was cleverer than he thought and was back in pursuit. Luckily the road was milling with visitors and a wedding had just taken place at the Mairie, with family and friends photographing the happy couple, spilling out onto the pedestrian zone. He skilfully darted back and forth through the throng of wedding revellers. The bar was just ahead of him, so he managed to slip inside without fear of his annoying shadow seeing him.

"There's Harry." Caroline waved at him so he could see where they were sitting. Nico and Patrick looked at him anxiously. He smiled at them both and nodded surreptitiously and they relaxed. It was clear no one had told Caroline why they were hiding out in a French bar. Harry took a deep breath while he sat at their table. He kept an eye on the entrance, but luckily, to keep the shops cool in the South of France, the proprietors limited the amount of lights they put on.

"Caroline, I need you to stay calm while I tell you something that has been going on in England." Caroline immediately got the wrong end of the stick.

"Emily? What has happened to her?" Harry shook his head. "Not Emily? Stephanie then? Oh, my goodness. Please tell me my girls are alright." Nico held her hand

and squeezed it.

"Caro let 'arry tell you what 'as 'appened, it isn't the girls. They are both good." He smiled at her to calm her. Harry smiled at Nico, silently thanking him.

"It's about Michael." Harry immediately put his hand up to stop Caroline interrupting. "He's dating a famous French actress and," he looked at his watch, "they have held a press conference today to let the world know. The press has already caught on to the fact his ex-wife is dating a famous French opera singer. Unfortunately, they are now waiting outside your apartment probably for an interview to tell them what you think."

"I'll tell them what I think, that it's none of my business, and certainly none of theirs." Caroline took her glass and emptied it in one go. "Who is this actress anyway?"

"Claudia Pasqualle." Nico squeezed her hand again. It will hurt that she is so much younger than her ex-husband, he thought, as it seemed to bother the English much more than the French.

"The little minx. You wait until I see her." Harry looked puzzled.

"Have you already met Claudia? Do you know her then?" Caroline shook her head.

"No, I'm talking about Emily. Don't you remember Nico? Emily and CC came back from their visit to Cannes, and they were full of Claudia Pasqualle. They must have met her with Michael." She suddenly opened her eyes wide in disbelief that her daughter could be so unscrupulous. "Michael must have been the 'stranger' in the restaurant. She's known all along and didn't have the good grace to tell me." Caroline looked extremely hurt.

"In actual fact, Caroline, she was under a solemn promise to Michael not to tell anyone, especially you. If you want to blame anyone, blame your ex. She didn't like keeping it from you, but as you know, you had secrets you told her, and she never broke her promise to you in telling her father." Harry was right.

Caroline's initial reaction was subsiding. "But this isn't helping to decide what to do next. Unless you want to confront the journalists?" Caroline shook her head vehemently, "Then we need to get you to a safe place." Eleanor wanted to help.

"You could come back to Monaco with us, if you like. At least until it dies down a little and something else happens to take them on to another story." Caroline thanked Eleanor, but she didn't want to leave Nico to face it all on his own, and he needed to stay for his evening performance in a few hours.

Suddenly Nico's phone started to ring in his pocket.

"It's Papa. 'ello Papa… Oui, le bar en face de l'opéra. D'accord. À bientôt. 'e's just around the corner. François told 'im we were in 'iding somewhere." Caroline had to smile. Harry looked baffled.

"He must have heard what was going on. I can't believe something this trivial is making such headlines in France." Harry shrugged his shoulders in disbelief.

"Ah my friend. You do not realise the admiration the French put on their film stars. It is almost as 'igh as the American public. They are our royalty. It is like when your Prince 'arry fell in love with an American actress, front page news in every country in the world I think, n'est-ce pas?" Harry had to agree. Although Jodie Whittaker had become the new Dr Who in the UK, something he had been very excited about, he somehow didn't think they'd be that impressed about it in the world's news arena.

"Touché, mon ami!" Harry liked showing off his limited French. He would not tell them that most of his early French was learnt watching Dogtanian and the Three Muskehounds, in his childhood.

"Ah, here you all are." Alain had walked in without being noticed. "Do not worry, I deviated through the flower market. I wasn't followed." He was smiling. He knew he should take it seriously, but after all that had happened recently, he felt this was light relief. Nico got up and kissed his father. "I cannot believe it. Veronique and I were just in the office when Sky News announced Claudia Pasqualle had held a press conference at The Dorchester, England, introducing her new man, Michael Fitzgerald."

"My ex-husband is dating a French film star, a few years his junior, and the world thinks it's newsworthy?" She was more angry than upset. She and Nico got a few mentions in the French press and on French television, France 24 news broadcast, on the day they all found out. That was all.

"I think it may be because he proposed to her at the press conference." As soon as Alain had said it, he realised looking at their faces that they didn't know about that small part.

"Did you know about this Harry? I'm sure Emily would have confided in you." Harry immediately shook his head.

"No Caroline. Emm would have told me if she'd known. How did you know that Michael Fitzgerald was Caroline's ex?" He looked at Alain for an answer.

"Because Emily was in the background with Stephanie. I could not mistake those two beautiful daughters of yours." He turned to Caroline who was pleased with the compliment he had just paid her. Nico looked at his watch.

"I'm sorry, Caro, but I need to go and warm up my vocal cords and change into my costume. What are you going to do?" Nico turned to his father for support.

"Veronique has your bedroom ready. She thinks it will be better to let the whole affair calm down before you go back to your apartment. Nico can come home too, when he's finished his evening performance. We were coming to tomorrow night's performance anyway, so after we check with François, that the paparazzi have gone to pester another poor célébrité, you can go back to your flat." That seemed the best option. Nico kissed Caroline and told her he'd see her later. He decided he could get his friend Philippe to drive his car out of the underground car park and have it waiting outside the backdoor of the opera house. It will then be on the coast road and an easy exit off to Grasse.

Alain took Caroline to where he had parked his car. There was no chance of being shanghaied by the press, as Alain knew the streets like the back of his hand.

"Well, after all that excitement, back to the boat I assume?" Patrick sounded a little deflated. Life was definitely going to be more boring with Harry out of it.

* * *

At eight o'clock Emily walked CC into the Jazz Café, followed by Michael and Claudia, Stephanie and James. They were shown to their table upstairs on the balcony, with a superb view of the stage. They ordered their drinks and two large boards of antipasti to nibble on until they decided what they were going to have for dinner. A young trio were playing the music, with one on drums and cymbals, one playing saxophone and one playing double bass. They were very good, but CC thought they might all still be at college. They seemed very young. She stretched over the table and grabbed the programme to see who they were when Emm suddenly snatched it off her.

"Can I check what time the main act is on? These three will need to go to bed soon. They've probably got school in the morning." Michael roared with laughter. He loved Emily's sense of humour. The fact that it was Sunday the next day didn't ruin it for him. He winked at his elder daughter for being so quick with the programme. Emm was glad someone was on her wavelength. That was one of the best things about Harry - he always knew what Emm was thinking, sometimes before she did herself. Why was she thinking of Harry? She had noticed a few missed texts and calls from him, but she was going to call him in the morning, so she could relax with her father and enjoy the evening. He had obviously tried to get hold of her for Caroline. She didn't need her mother's histrionics to ruin her father's euphoria. She was roused from her thoughts by the applause and cheers. The trio took their bows and the stagehands cleared away their instruments. The antipasti boards arrived with delicious looking cooked meats - Salami, Prosciutto, Bresaola, to name but a few, all displayed inside a border of marinated artichoke hearts, garlic stuffed green olives, roasted red and yellow peppers, with garlic bread slices through the middle of each board.

Emm wondered whether to tell CC that she should lay off

the garlic items, but she was sure Frédéric would be used to it, being French! Emm was thinking whether she should have warned Frédéric. He might have the day off but realised not on a busy Saturday night. Before she could worry any longer, the stagehands were back, she watched them pull out a piano on the right side of the stage. Handy she thought. The musicians came onto the stage to a rapturous applause. They were the resident band. The drummer came out first, bowed and took his seat behind the drums and cymbals. Next the double bass player came out and stood behind his instrument.

The saxophonist came in and bowed and stood in the middle of the stage, followed by the guitarist, who stood next to him behind a microphone stand. Lastly the pianist walked on and got an ecstatic welcome from most of the ladies in the audience. He bowed and took his place behind the piano. Emm looked over at CC, who annoyingly had missed his entrance picking out seeds from a slice of yellow pepper. Emm looked up at her father who just shrugged and grinned. There was plenty of time for her to recognise the pianist. Probably better towards the end rather than the beginning.
The band struck up and the music was incredible. Michael loved jazz, but this was one of the best bands he'd heard in a long time, and he'd been to a jazz funeral in New Orleans!
The evening went by with good food, good music and good company. Most of the conversations involved a great degree of lip-reading, but all of them were having a wonderful time. The band broke off for a ten-minute breather, leaving a looped CD playing old time jazz. Emm wondered whether she should go down and tell Frédéric

they were there, when she felt a tap on her shoulder. She turned to see Frédéric with his finger up to his mouth telling her not to say a word. She smiled and looked at CC filling her glass with water. After four cocktails she felt a little light-headed. She had decided to take the next day off as well and continue refreshed on Monday. There was no way anything would have stayed in her brain with a hangover, and she knew she'd have a thumping one after a day of Champagne and cocktails.

Everyone on the table was holding their breath. Frédéric was standing right behind her. He waited until she'd put her glass of water down and patted her on the shoulder. CC turned to see the love of her life standing right behind her.

"Bonsoir ma chérie, Chloé. Vous êtes très belle." He held her face up and bent over to kiss her. Claudia clapped excitedly. She told the rest of the table what he said.

"'e says CC is very beautiful. 'ow romantic." James just nodded. He thought the French a little too emotional. He looked over at Stephanie and Emily, looking all gooey-eyed and sighed. It was obviously catching. Frédéric took hold of CC's hand and steered her off to meet his band. She waved goodbye without saying a word, only giggling. Emm suddenly missed Harry, and it hit her hard. She was pleased for CC, but she suddenly felt alone. She was surrounded by her family, but it wasn't the same. She snuck off to phone him.

***

Harry had just walked into his cabin when his phone rang. He saw it was Emm.

"Hi Emm. I have so much to tell you, but how

did your day go first?" Harry could hear music in the background.

"Daddy proposed to Claudia at the news conference. She accepted, thank goodness. Now we are celebrating at the Jazz Café. CC has just been taken off by the pianist she met in France called Frédéric. He's one of Nico's friends. He secretly followed her over here. It's so romantic Harry." She stopped for a second. "Harry?"

"Yes Emm."

"I've missed you. Not just the last few days, but in my life. We are meant to be together; you know that don't you?" Harry was euphoric. It was exactly the way he wanted Emm to feel. He decided it was the right time to tell her his plans.

"How would you like to be a milk-maid?" Emm thought Harry was mocking her sentimental outburst. Harry carried on. "Maria has sold me her farm. When I say me, I mean us. We are going to be farmers in Girona. What do you think of that? Before you say anything, I've thought long and hard about it Emm. I'm not an indoorsy person. I would hate being in an office every day. The outbuildings that survived the fire are just in need of a little modernisation. It is so beautiful Emm. So, will you settle down with me?" Emm had had time to process what Harry was saying, while he rambled on. She had no job to worry about. She loved being with Harry. It sounded like an adventure that they could both share.

"I'm not saying 'no' Harry. I need to see it for myself and know a little more about your proposal first. I'll come down next week and we can go over the plans together. How's that?" She heard Harry cheer! He was the happiest man on the earth. "Getting back to today, how has Mother taken the news of Claudia and Dad?"

Harry explained about the paparazzi. He told her Caroline was safely in Grasse with Nico's parents and all was well in Nice.

"And you'll never believe what's happened to Lachlan? He's only fallen hook, line and sinker for Katarina." It was Emm's turned to be astonished.

"How absolutely lovely. What a happy ending that is for her, and for Lilli." Harry told her about Lachlan's uncle and both of them going to Barcelona for a while with Lilli. "So they'll be in Spain as well. How exciting. How far is the farm from them?"

"No more than half-an-hour by train, or just over an hour by car. With the planned renovations we will have plenty of rooms to entertain visitors." Harry wanted to keep plugging the farm.

"What do either of us know about cows, Harry? Apart from the obvious, that they need milking." Harry was glad Emm was asking questions - it meant she was interested. He knew the place would sell itself, so he needed her to see it for herself.

"We won't need to worry about the cows, they are in safe hands with Juan and Jorges. They have been looking after them since Maria and poor Karl bought the farm. We would be taking over the business side of selling organic milk and its products such as organic butter, cream, yoghurt and cheese." Emm was laughing. "What's so funny?"

"Sorry Harry, but you sounded like an infomercial on the joys of natural farming." She stopped taking the mickey. She could hear in Harry's voice that he really wanted this. Inside she was happy that he had finally come around to her way of thinking, but thought it was his own idea. True brilliance, and the end result would mean they could settle down to a life together. "I shall check flight times and I could be in Girona as soon as you want me." Harry was ecstatic. He took a big breath and thought.

"Lachlan and Katarina have to be in Barcelona on Monday. Patrick has already said Dave and I can take them in the Lady Eleanor. What if I ask Alberto to crew with Dave and drop me off too? I can grab a train and meet you in Girona. I'll get a rental place near the farm, so we can take our time and you can meet the builder, Miguel. He has some ideas, but he'll need a woman's input to make it our home." He wondered if he was pushing her too quickly. He didn't want to scare her off. To his astonishment Emm agreed.

"I can just imagine the all-important rooms to you and this Miguel, compared to the essential rooms to me." She was shaking her head and smiling, totally lost on Harry at the other end of a phone. "Ok Harry. Leave it with me. I will get on the Internet as soon as I'm home. Hopefully I can have a few more days off since I'm on notice anyway." She heard Harry take a breath but cut in to explain. "Daddy will be selling the business as soon as he gets a good offer. I'm surplus to requirements." She laughed so Harry knew it was a joke. "I have to say that I hadn't thought of animal husbandry as a career. Would you say it was a promotion from a letting agent?" It was Harry's turn to laugh.

"I have so missed your sense of humour Emm. God, we are going to make brilliant farmers. I've already ordered my wellies on Amazon!" They were both still laughing when their conversation had ended.

Harry left his cabin with an enormous grin on his face. He needed to talk to Patrick about his future.

CHAPTER 16

Monday was too exciting for Lilli. They had sailed back to Barcelona on Sunday and arrived Monday morning for breakfast. Lachlan had organised with his uncle that two new crewmembers would be starting work for Patrick on the Lady Eleanor. Dave was happy because they were Aussies. Patrick also was pleased as they came highly recommended by Lachlan. Eleanor had helped Katarina pack all their belongings, including Paris who Lilli now couldn't sleep without. Eleanor knew Lilli had been through so much for a child to comprehend, a little security found in a stuffed dog was paramount for her well-being, at that time. Hopefully living in a new place with a loving couple that doted on her would help Lilli heal inside where the harm had been done. Eleanor just wanted Lilli to know how smashing she was. Time would tell, she thought. Katarina looked at Eleanor as she put Paris in Lilli's rucksack.

"She is going to miss you Eleanor." Katarina went over and hugged her. "So am I." Eleanor pushed her away slightly, so she could look Katarina in the eyes.

"You, young lady, can start living the life of a girl in love. Enjoy every moment. Lachlan is a good person and loves Lilli as we all do. Patrick and I will still be around. I want to watch your daughter grow up." She hugged Katarina again and walked out of her cabin to find

Patrick. Katarina heard a distinct sniff as Eleanor left. It was astonishing how you could know people for only a few days but feel like you have known them a lifetime. Katarina finished zipping up the rucksacks and grabbed her suitcase, wheeling it to the cabin doorway. She looked back at what had been her home for so little time, but so much had happened in that time that it was probably the happiest home she had lived in.

Patrick had just got off the phone to the British School in Castelldefels near Barcelona. Lilli had an interview there that afternoon and Patrick and Eleanor wanted to go with Katarina and Lilli to see around the school. They had asked Katarina if they could be Lilli's benefactors and take care of all her school fees. Katarina was delighted and couldn't believe their kindness.

Lachlan had to meet with his uncle, and Sheila, to sign bank forms and some legal documents. Sheila, her real name due to her Australian parents' sense of humour, had worked at the office with Steve for many years.

She knew all about the files, the cheeky lads who crewed, the local taxes and all the bank stuff. She had come over from Australia at about the same time as Steve, and Lachlan had thought them an item. But as the years went by it was obvious they were just good friends. Lachlan never asked the question 'why?' he just accepted it. All he knew was that the whole business would not run without that Sheila.

Harry had got a text from Emm who was travelling up to Stansted Airport for the only flight that day near London to Girona. He was excited, as he'd spoken at length with Patrick the evening before about finance and loans to make his dream come true. He'd booked an Airbnb property, a small farmhouse just ten minutes' walk from the Kõiv Farm in Vilobí d'Onyar. He thought it was an ideal rental, to get them used to country living. Emm would be getting a taxi from the airport so he gave her the address and told her he'd meet her there. He thought about it afterwards and realised that her flight didn't get in till late, and he felt happier meeting her at the airport. After all it was only a ten-minute drive from the farm. He decided to hire a car for a few days and surprise her at the airport. They may want to check out the surrounding areas, so it made sense. He said goodbye to everyone when they had all finished their breakfast. Lilli kissed Harry goodbye and asked him when she'd see him again.

"Very soon Lilli. I will only be an hour away from you. If I can persuade Emm to live there, you can come and visit anytime." Lilli thought about what Harry had said.

"If you want Emm to marry you, why don't you buy her something nice? Alain gave me my own perfume. He's now my best friend. If you bought Emm perfume or diamonds she'd be your best friend, then she'd marry you." The child's logic was never far off the mark, thought Harry. Perhaps he could buy her a ring? No, too soon, and it'll look like a bribe. He'd think about what Lilli had said though. Once Emm had seen the property and fallen in love with the venture as he had, perhaps a ring would be the next step.

"Thank you for your excellent advice Lilli. I shall give it some thought. I'd really like Emm to be my best friend." Lilli pouted and frowned. "Of course, she'll never replace you, Lilli. You're my very best friend." Lilli smiled.

She stretched up to hug Harry. He picked her up and spun her round. She squealed with delight. Harry wanted to take her with him but knew he couldn't. He put her down and waved goodbye to her as he left. She waved back, neither cried, but Harry did have to take a very deep breath.

That girl, he thought, would break a lot of hearts once she was a little older, she wasn't doing badly now!

He made his way into Barcelona. He'd decided to catch a train to Girona and rent a car from the station. He'd have most of the day to walk round the farm and chat to Juan and Jorges, before Emm arrived. He wanted to have all the facts to be able to sell the idea to her.

***

"Well, young lady, are you excited about seeing your new school?" Lilli looked at Patrick and sighed. Patrick took it as a negative response and carried on. "You'll be able to go in a school bus with all your new friends. They will all be English, like you. You will learn Spanish and they play tennis there." He was trying to remember what he had read on the website. Lilli pulled his sleeve to get his attention, as he was pondering. He looked down and saw a big smile on her face.

"I'm going to love my new school, thank you Patrick. I was only thinking hard about how to say thank you. Mummy told me that you and Eleanor were going to be my bendyfractors, and I was trying to think of how to say it so I could thank you for being my bendyfractors." She beckoned him down to her level and whispered in his ear. "What is a bendyfractor Patrick?" He grabbed her up into the air and hugged her.

"I'm going to miss you Lilli. But I have a feeling you will be in all our lives for a very long time." He put her down. "Eleanor and I are going to be your be-ne-factors." He pronounced it slowly for her. "It means that we both want to help you by sending you to the best schools and giving you the best education we can." Lilli looked confused. Eleanor had overheard their conversation and knew that Patrick was not particularly used to talking to six-year-olds, boardrooms full of people trying to act like adults, but not actual six-year-olds.

"What Patrick is trying to say to you Lilli is that we want to make you the happiest girl in the world. That means that your mummy and Lachlan can concentrate on playing with you and having lots of fun, while we concentrate on your schooling." Lilli still looked puzzled. "Like reading, writing, maths..." as she said it, she thought that it didn't sound very appealing, she tried a different tack. "and music, painting, swimming, tennis, and I hear they also put on shows. Patrick and I can come and watch you in one." Lilli smiled. She liked the idea of being in a show.

"I think I'm going to like you being my be-ne-factors. Thank you." She turned and walked off to find her mother. Patrick put his arm around his wife and pecked her on the cheek.

"What was that for?" Eleanor knew the answer but wanted to hear him say it.

"Because I love you." Patrick never disappointed her.

* * *

"Where did Emily say she was going, chéri?" Claudia was packing her case. Michael had her told that he was taking Claudia off to France to ask for her hand in marriage from her brother, Laurent. She thought it adorable that he was so old fashioned.

"Somewhere called Vilobi something. It's just outside Girona. Why?" Claudia shook her head. Men weren't very curious, were they? She was dying to see the farm. Emily had come back in from her conversation with Harry full of love for him and the country life. Claudia was intrigued to meet the man who had Emily so smitten.

"I just thought it might be 'elpful if you visited your daughter's future enterprise. She may need a professional viewpoint. 'ow far will they be from us?" She had thought of that very quickly. She had impressed herself. She felt it would be wrong to say she was nosey and wanted to see the farm and meet Harry too.

"It'll be about three and a half hours from Avignon. I take it you would like to go and have a look at this enterprise?" He was smiling at her. He knew all along what she wanted, it was just fun to make her admit it. "I wanted to go and have an inspection…" He turned and winked at her. "Sorry, a look, myself if the truth be known. The last thing I want is Emily squandering all her inheritance, before she even gets it." He was laughing at his own joke. Claudia loved it when he laughed. She wished her friends saw that side of Michael, but he always had that British stiff upper lip look. She would turn him into a Frenchman, she was sure of it, eventually.

* * *

Lachlan was dropped off at the marina for his meeting with his uncle and the rest of the party drove, in a rented Seat, the twenty minutes to the school in Castelldefels. They parked in the car park and were impressed when a lady came out to greet them.

"Mr Robertshaw? And this must be little Lilliana. Welcome to BSB. I'm Mrs Porter, the school secretary.

Please come this way."

They followed her into the very modern and clean building. As children passed them, they all smiled and wished them a 'good afternoon'. Katarina thought how very polite; to her manners were very important. They were taken to an office where Mr Croft was waiting for them. He introduced himself and shook each of their hands. He told them that was in charge of admissions. Mrs Porter ushered them to the chairs in front of the solid wooden desk and they sat down. Lilli sat on her mother's lap.

"I have sincere apologies from the Head, but she's had to dash off to the senior department, a small incident on the sports field. Nothing to worry about, but we have to write everything up." He was rushing his words and wiggling a pencil between his thumb and finger, he had picked up from the desk. Patrick thought him a very nervous man for someone who worked with children, although he had to smile, thinking he probably wasn't before he came to work in a school. Mrs Porter went over to Lilli and took hold of her hand.

"If you'd like to come with me Lilliana, I'll show you where your classroom is. I know all the children want to say hello to you." Lilli looked at her mother, who nodded to her, gently guiding her off her lap.

"Off you go darling. We'll catch up in a minute." Lilli looked at Patrick and then Eleanor. They were all smiling at her. She didn't want to let them down followed Mrs Porter down a corridor. She couldn't help noticing that on the outside of the buildings were big blinds to keep the sun out. She wasn't sure she would get, so she used to people stopping the sun shining. At home she loved playing outside when the sun shone.

By the time Patrick, Eleanor and Katarina had finished all the preliminary information the school needed to enrol Lilli, it was time for the children to have their afternoon break. It was agreed that Lilli would start at the school at the beginning of the following week. She needed to settle into her new life in Spain first. It was only one week away and Katarina was happy to home school her until then as she had done in England. The summer holidays were three weeks later, much earlier than in England. Mrs Porter came back into the room.

"I'm sure you would like to find out how Lilliana has done? If you'd all follow me, I shall take you to her." They shook hands with Mr Croft, who apologised again for the Head's absence.

"It really isn't a problem. It's good she puts the school first. Please give her our regards." Patrick tried to calm the man. "We'll pop in next time we are visiting Lilliana and make ourselves known to her. Goodbye old chap." He shook his hand again and left to catch up with the women.

Katarina was delighted. She could see Lilli playing happily with the other children without a care in the world, looking so adorable in their yellow school sun caps. Eleanor walked up behind her and put her hand on her shoulder.

"I really think you have no problem with Lilli settling in." Katarina nodded. She felt so blessed with such a good girl.

"This is Miss Spencer who will be Lilli's form teacher." Mrs Porter introduced the young lady walking towards them.

"What a friendly girl Lilli is. I can't remember a child coming in and after just one lesson looking like she'd been here most of the year." She went up to Katarina. "Can I just say that I'm looking forward to having your Lilli in my classroom. She seems to brighten the whole class." Katarina was about to say thank you when Lilli saw them all waiting for her.

"I have to go now Holly. Thank you for playing with me, and you George and you Sophie. I've had a lovely time. I hope I see you all again soon." She kissed them all goodbye and walked over to Miss Spencer. "Thank you for lending me your cap." She handed it to Miss Spencer. "I like your classroom very much. Did you know my favourite colour is yellow?" Miss Spencer shook her head.

"I do now though Lilli." Miss Spencer smiled down at Lilli. Lilli suddenly realised why she liked Miss Spencer. She reminded her of Harry. He said that too. "Lilli, you can keep this cap, it's yours now." She handed Lilli the yellow sun cap back. Lilli put it back on.

"Thank you very much Miss Spencer. I think I look cool now." She turned for acknowledgement from Patrick who nodded in agreement.

"You look the bee's knees in it, Lilli." Lilli looked baffled. Eleanor laughed. She put one eyebrow up to Patrick, who gathered Lilli wouldn't understand the idiom. "You look really cool Lilli." Lilli smiled and waved goodbye to all her new friends. Patrick got a smile from Eleanor. The bell rang and the children lined up ready to enter the building for the last lesson of the day. Miss Spencer waved goodbye to Lilli and went off to get her charges back into the classroom.

"Come on then Miss Barcelona, 2035. Let's get you back to Lachlan so he can show you your new home." Lilli looked at Eleanor with a contorted face. Eleanor shrugged and smiled.

"One day you will understand all of Patrick's crazy sayings, I promise." Lilli smiled and took hold of her mother's hand.

They were back picking Lachlan up within half-an-hour, during which Lilli couldn't stop talking about her new school. Patrick had told her that the blinds were to keep the heat of the sun from the classrooms, and caps were for keeping the hot sun off their heads, as the ultraviolet rays could be dangerous on her skin and the sun was much hotter than in England. Eleanor had watched Lilli's puzzled gaze, so explained that the Spanish sun can cause headaches and burnt noses. That was enough for Lilli to make sure she wore a hat all the time in the sunshine.

Lachlan directed Patrick to the apartment by the beach. They could park behind, but in the front of the block was a pedestrian area. Lilli couldn't believe that she was only to cross the pedestrian zone and she'd be in the sea. Warnings were flying at her from everyone. She was beginning to think that they all thought she was stupid. She wasn't three - she was six and a half!

Steve was departing for Australia that evening, so his cases were in the hallway. He was leaving Lachlan his car, so the least Lachlan could do was offer to drive his uncle to the airport. His cleaner had been in and all the three bedrooms were clean with the beds made up. Lilli went out on the balcony and could see the sea. Lachlan was showing Katarina the barbecue.

Patrick and Eleanor needed to get off. Alberto wanted to get out of the marina before dark. They kissed Katarina and Lilli and Eleanor kissed Lachlan.

"You take care of those girls. They need you now Lachlan." He kissed Eleanor back.

"I think I need them just as much. Thank you for all the advice and help you've given me over my time with you, Eleanor." She smiled at him and turned to give Lilli one more hug. Patrick shook Lachlan's hand.

"I'm never too far away, if you need any help with the business, or just advice, just call me Lachlan and I'll be here." Lachlan had a lump in his throat. He was a tough Aussie, for goodness sake.
He pulled himself together and shook Patrick's hand with a little more strength. They followed Patrick and Eleanor out to the car park.

"Look, over there. Is that ours Lachlan?" Lilli had spotted the swimming pool. He nodded. "Wow, can I go in please Mummy?" Katarina looked at her watch. Lilli should really be winding down and getting ready for tea and bed. But she'd had such a fun day - perhaps this once wouldn't do her any harm. She looked at Lachlan to see if he was ok about it.

"I'll tell you what Lilli, let's wave goodbye to Eleanor and Patrick and I might go in with you for a little swim. How's that?" Lilli turned to the car. She didn't want to appear rude.

"Bye bye Eleanor and Patrick. Thank you for having me. See you soon." She spoke rapidly and waved frantically. But not wanting to appear rude she blew them a kiss.

"I think that might be our cue to leave darling."

Eleanor waved back to Lilli as Patrick reversed the car. He opened his window and spoke to Lachlan.

"Remember, any problems, call me." He waved back at them all and drove away.

"You know they'll be fine Patrick, stop worrying." She put her hand on his knee. He took it and squeezed it.

"For a couple who's never had children, we seem to have accumulated rather a lot." They both laughed and drove back the fifteen minutes it took to the marina, laughing and enjoying just being in each other's company.

* * *

Claudia and Michael decided to take the Eurostar that morning from London to Avignon TGV Station. It was about a six-hour journey, but there were no flights from London to Avignon that day, so they took a relaxing train ride.

Claudia was always happy when she went home. She still thought of the château as home.

They had time to kill and Michael wanted to know all about Claudia's childhood in France. Her brother had told him some of the family history, but Michael wanted to hear it from Claudia.

"Well it was an 'appy childhood. I grew up being protected by two wonderful men. My brother was my best friend and my father was my world. Maman died from an illness of the blood when I was too small to remember 'er." She looked out at the passing scenery.

"My father kept 'er memory alive with photos and stories, but it wasn't the same as 'aving 'er there. I think a child needs physical presence, don't you chéri? My brother missed 'er the most, being older. That was probably what made Laurent and I so close."

Michael held Claudia tightly. If it was going to upset her,

he'd rather she didn't tell him about her childhood. He was about to change the subject when she carried on. "I was too young to understand why my mother 'ad suddenly disappeared from our lives, but Laurent and I 'ad love in abundance from our Papa. I also 'ad a lot of cuddles from my big brother. Papa never re-married. Laurent said it was because no one else would replace our mother, but I think 'e was too exhausted looking after two children and a vineyard." She looked at Michael and noticed his very sad face. "Oh, mon chéri, do not be sad. I only remember my life as being 'appy. Laurent and I 'ave only 'appy memories of our years spent growing up in our family château with our wonderful Papa. We were 'is life." Michael felt very touched that Claudia had opened up to him. He wished he could have met her father, he knew he'd have liked him very much, but he had died a few years ago, just short of his seventieth birthday. "Why are you looking so sad chéri?" She kissed his cheek and smiled at him.

"I just wish I could have met him. It would have been a great honour to have asked him for his daughter's hand in marriage." It was Claudia's turn to be sad. She had wished her father had met Michael from the first moment Michael had come into her life. Michael reminded her of her beloved father - so kind and caring.

A car was waiting for them at the station in Avignon, at teatime, to take them to Château Pasqualle. Laurent was pleased to see them both and quickly took Michael away to the large converted stable block, where the wine was made and stored. It had been built originally to keep the horses cool in the Provence sun and sloped down into a vaulted cellar, the cave, where the finished bottled wines were kept in wooden racks, lining the walls.

He wanted Michael to see his new state of the art fermentation vats, with wireless sensors. "They measure the temperature and sugar content of the wine. We used to 'ave to take off the lid to check each vat. This can cause the temperature to change, oxidation and contamination. It also meant we needed to employ extra staff at this time. Now we just check the computer readings. I think my ancestors will be turning in their tombs, n'est ce pas Michel?" Michael felt it endearing that Laurent had already given him his French name.

"I'm impressed, Laurent. It all looks très bon." Laurent slapped him on the back and led him to the tasting table.

"How do you English say, 'the proof of the pudding is in the eating'?" He offered Michael a glass of rich red wine. Michael thought it rude not to taste it. It was delicious. He didn't know whether he was supposed to spit it out, but it was really good, so he swallowed it and took another sip. "Côtes du Rhône at its best, n'est ce pas?" Michael had to agree. He nodded, and his glass was re-filled.

"The twenty-first century agrees with wine making, mon ami." They both chinked their glasses and continued sampling the grapes from the Rhône valley.

Claudia and her sister-in-law, Nathalie, found the two men sitting on upturned barrels, putting the world to rights. The girls knew they would, they always did. It had given them time to plan Claudia's wedding arrangements at the château. Nathalie insisted Claudia spoke English while they were visiting. She was trying to learn to speak it more fluently as most of her guests were American. They walked into the winery through the massive oak doors.

"'ave you asked Laurent yet, chéri?" Michael looked at the vision of his fiancée standing at the entrance of the winery. The setting sun behind her made her whole body look celestial. He blinked a couple of times. "Look at the pair of you. Nathalie 'as made a wonderful supper for you both." She shook her head and turned to leave. Nathalie noticed the grin on her sister-in-law's face. She followed Claudia out, tutting and shaking her head. They walked as far as they could, out of earshot and collapsed laughing. "Did you see the look on Michael's face? 'e was like a little schoolboy 'aving been caught stealing the caretaker's apples." Nathalie thought Claudia was being a little mean to Michael, but it was funny. They knew the boys would be in soon, so made their way back to the château arm in arm. Nathalie had checked her calendar and had only two bookings for the weekend of the wedding.

"They are regular clients, both couples. I will ask Henri at the Cheval Blanc if he has rooms for those dates. We will offer them free board for that weekend for their inconvenience. Ce n'est pas un problem." She made a note in her diary. "Now, we can provide eighteen double rooms and five single rooms for your guests. Michael's girls will be in the family quarters." Nathalie was really talking to herself.

Claudia was looking out of the window at the evening view of the garden and vineyard, with the Rhône River in the distance, glistening in the moonlight. She smiled. She knew her mother and father were watching and were happy for her.

***

Emm landed safely in Girona and walked through passport control, on out to the taxi rank. She jumped a mile when a hand touched her shoulder.

"Hola Señorita, would you like a lift?" She turned and wanted to smack him. Instead she kissed him tenderly.

"Oh Harry. It's such a lovely surprise, you being here. Thank you." He beamed. He was glad he'd picked her up. He grabbed her small case and put it in the boot while she got in the car. He got in the other side just as an airport security person wagged his finger at him and pointed to the sign with 'No Estacionar' and if he was in any doubt of what it meant, there was a big red circle round a big red P with a line through it. To make matters worse, there was an identical one next to it in English. Harry put a thumb's up and drove off as quickly as he could. He wasn't quite sure whether a thumbs up was universal in meaning.

"I'm glad you came Emm. I'm really serious about this. I've had a word with Juan and he and Jorges want to continue working at the farm. At the moment Patrick is paying their wages, he'll get it back once poor Karl's probate has been sorted. Maria is lost without him. She ran the business marvellously, but he did all the finances. I think you're going to love it as much as I do Emm." Well, he hoped.

"You really are eager about being a farmer, aren't you?" She didn't wait for a reply. "I have been looking into organic farming with Steph's help and I'm amazed that all it is doing is going back to years when farming was done exactly the same. There were no nasty pesticides. The animals roamed around fields, copulating and giving birth in the same surroundings, and it was all done by hand." Harry laughed.

"Now who sounds like an infomercial?" Emm knew he was happy, he always bantered with her when he was happy. She was already warming to the idea of being with Harry for the rest of her life, albeit sharing him with a lot of cows. They reached the farmhouse they were staying in by ten o'clock in the evening, which was early for the Spanish. Neither wanted to go out though.

Harry had made some Bolognese sauce before he left for the airport, so he put a pot of water on the range, a must for a farm kitchen, and took out enough spaghetti for them both. Emm unpacked a few things in her bedroom. Harry hadn't presumed she would share his room, which Emm was pleased about. It showed respect for her. She would love things to get back to how they were, but not until she was sure he was serious about changing. As they say, talk is cheap. So far his actions were boding well for a good outcome.

"It's delicious Harry. Who'd have thought Harry Hart was a culinary genius." They sat at the kitchen table with a glass of wine each. He wasn't sure if she was taking the mickey. He had to admit it was one of his best dishes. His repertoire was limited. Lachlan had taught him how to throw things on a barbecue, but they were nothing in comparison to his spaghetti Bolognese. Emm tried to stifle a yawn. "I'm so sorry Harry. I seem to have been partying and travelling for a week. Oh, hang on a minute, I have." She laughed at her own joke. He looked at her and smiled. He had been an idiot leaving her in the first place, for a job. He won't be doing that again, he was sure.

"You get off to bed. I'll clear up and then you will

be fresh in the morning for our meeting with Miguel." She looked confused.

"I thought we were meeting Juan and Jorges." She yawned again. Harry got up and escorted her to her room.

"Miguel is the builder, remember?" She nodded in recognition of the name to the trade. "I managed to get hold of him this afternoon and he's promised to meet us at the farm around eleven o'clock. That gives me enough time to introduce you to the cowhands and show you around the land and buildings. Goodnight beautiful. I love you." He kissed her on the lips. Not entirely passionately, but lovingly. He closed her door behind her, in case he made too much noise while clearing up. He was too excited to sleep anyway. This could be the beginning of their new life together. This time he was determined not to blow it.

CHAPTER 17

Harry and Emm walked to the Kõiv Farm, chatting about what they will need to do. As they got nearer, Emm immediately knew it wasn't far off.

"It must be near; I can smell burnt wood." She sniffed and shook her head. Harry took her hand and slowly walked her around the corner into the road the farmhouse fronted onto. What Emm hadn't realised was that they had been walking around the outside of the farm for a good five minutes. They turned into the front garden and Emm stopped. She wanted to take it all in. The farmhouse must have been idyllic before the bastards burnt it down. She shook her head again. Harry had unclenched her hand and walked ahead into the building. "What a beautiful door." The front door had opened the wrong way, out into the front garden, by the force of the blast. It had been a solid wooden door, probably oak, she thought. It was hanging on for dear life with one hinge. Emm felt it was almost alive, and she wanted to help it. She tried to square it up to the frame, but it was too heavy.

"Be careful, Emm. It could fall off at any time and it's very heavy." Harry went over to her and could see she was feeling distressed. He took her hand and walked her past the door into the living room. "You don't have to come in here Emm. Unfortunately, it isn't worth saving." He looked at her and she had tears in her eyes as she looked over the inside of the once beautiful cottage. He cuddled her and walked her out. "Come on, let me show you the stables." He pulled at her arm, but she stayed put.

"I think we should try and use the door, Harry." Harry nodded. "And I think we should raze the building to the ground and plant some colourful wildflowers where Karl died. Then perhaps grow some organic vegetables all around the front to make the area come back to life. What do you think Harry?" Harry took a deep breath. He tried to speak but his voice was a little wobbly.

"I think you're truly a remarkable woman, Emily Fitzgerald. Now come on, let me show you where we are going to live." She smiled and allowed Harry to pull her towards a row of orange trees. As she walked around them her first impression was 'wow'.

"Oh, my goodness Harry, it's beautiful." It was made of the same stone as the farmhouse. There were plants growing up most of the side. Emm thought they could be Bougainvillea, but the buds hadn't flowered yet. She hoped it was. Harry took her right around the building. At the back was definitely Bougainvillea, flowering beautifully in all its pink and purple glory. She noted the sun full on that side and realised it wouldn't be long before the front plants caught up. Harry took her through a double wooden door, into the main storage area, with animal feed and stalls full of old farming equipment. "They've kept the horse stalls. It's barely been touched for years. Look at the character in here Harry." Harry was busy looking at Emm. She was so enthralled that Harry knew she had fallen in love with the place, just like he had. Emm spotted the stone staircase. "Is it safe to go up?" Harry nodded. Emm walked up the stairs and was in the hayloft. She looked up and was pleased to see the roof high up above her head. Harry knew what she was thinking.

"Plenty of room up here for bedrooms and bathrooms. We would have to put in dormer windows, so we can see out though, unless you fancy standing on the furniture to look out of the skylights every morning." He smiled at her. He could tell she was already picturing how she wanted it.

"If you go back down, carefully, I'll show you where the staff live." Emm hugged the wall as she walked down, very grateful that she had worn flat shoes. She followed Harry out. As they walked to the staff building, Emm was concerned.

"Have you told anyone we are looking around their quarters?" Harry nodded. He'd told Juan that the builder was coming over again, and he'd hopefully be able to modernise their sleeping quarters.

Attached to the stables was a lower building, which seemed to sink into the ground. There was a stone staircase up to the front door, but only about five steps. From the top of the steps she looked down and could see a window starting just below ground level and finishing above. There was a small courtyard at the base of the window, so it had plenty of light. The front door opened onto a mezzanine level with steps up and down. There was a bedroom upstairs and another downstairs, both with tiny basins. On the mezzanine level was a shared bathroom. Emm thought it too small and reckoned incorporating some of the stable block to extend it. She walked back into the courtyard and stared at the stable block.

"Well, what do you think?" Harry looked at

Emm's reactions. Emm took a moment before she answered.

"I think it has great potential." She laughed. Her father would have been proud of her assessment. "I think it already looks like home, with a few tweaks here and there, inside." Harry was beaming - he could relax, she liked it. On cue he could see Miguel walking towards them. He introduced Emm to him and she told him what she would like, starting on the ground floor and working up.

By the time they had got up to the first floor in the stable block, Miguel had gone through most of the paper on his clipboard. Emm had totally taken over the refurbishment of her new home, and Harry didn't mind one bit. "We were thinking of dormer windows. Would they be a problem?" Emm looked at Miguel, who was shaking his head. "Would we need planning permission?" Emm knew they would in England.

"Planning permission, sí. But it will not be a problem. My cousin, he is the mayor." He laughed. "It may cost a little, but he lives a simple life, so a crate of vino would do." Emm did like Miguel. "You want it done soon?" Emm nodded her head. "OK. I send Mr Patrick the estimate, and if he agrees, I will start." Harry was keen to get going as soon as possible.

"So how long do you think this will take you?" Miguel scratched his head.

"If we start on the stables, you could be in within two to three months. If we start on the staff quarters, you could be in there within a month, and then move into the stables when they are ready." Harry hadn't thought of that. But what would Juan and Jorges do? He'd have to ask them. They should be fine about it - after all they would end up having new larger quarters by the autumn.

"What about the demolishing of the old farmhouse?" Emm really wanted that looking less distressing as you entered the farm. Miguel shook his head again.

"That will be no problem. I can get unskilled workers to clear the whole building away, while I get my skilled men on to the refurbishments to the stables." He saw Emm about to speak. "And I have remembered that you would like the front door. We could put it at the side of the stable where you want your kitchen. That would leave the double doors as your front door?" Emm nodded.

Miguel was on the ball - she had faith in him already. "I shall leave you to discuss it between you, while I go and get some figures onto paper for Señor Robertshaw. Adiós." He shook Harry's hand and waved goodbye to Emm.

"So, the next problem is to accommodate the staff." Harry took Emm's hand and led her down the track behind the stables, over the unmade road, which, he had found out, belonged solely to the farm, and in front of them was the cow-milking shed. Compared to the rest of the buildings, it was a relatively modern building - at least a few centuries newer. Harry noticed water gushing out of the doors, he pulled them open to find Juan hosing down the floors. "Hola Juan, com estàs?" Emm looked impressed, but it was short lived. Juan chatted away in Catalan, equally impressed that Harry had asked how he was in Catalan, rather than Spanish.

"Whoa there cowboy!" Juan laughed.
He understood what Harry had said.

"I'm Juan Wayne, sí?" Juan had made a joke too. Emm worried that not a lot of work would be done if those two jokers were working together.

"Hello Juan, I'm Emily. How do you do?" Juan rubbed his hand on his trousers and shook Emm's hand. "Over to you Harry." Now she had got the pair of them back to the serious business, it was up to Harry to be the boss.

"Juan. Miguel would like to renovate your quarters first, so Emm and I can stay there until the main stable work is done. The problem is where can you and Jorges go?" Juan smiled.

"We stay here." He pointed to the milk shed. Harry looked slightly worried. It did not look comfortable in the milking stalls. "I show you, come." He beckoned them to follow him. At the back of the milk shed was a door, which opened into a kitchen. To the side of it was a shower room. "Maria had it put in so we could clean ourselves before we left." He shut the door to the shower room and walked to the back of the kitchen. He opened another door that led into a large outside shed. "This is where the calves are kept after we take them from their mothers. Karl decided to rest the cows this year. We have an organic bull ready for the autumn, waiting to be brought here." Emm shuddered. Those poor cows, she thought. Perhaps she wasn't cut out to be a farmer's wife. "You can't sleep here. This is just a wooden shed. It wouldn't be very comfortable." Harry wasn't happy. If he wanted good workers, he had to make sure they were happy. Juan interrupted him.

"In the summer it gets very hot. Jorges and I normally sleep outside. We will be very happy in here with all the doors open. We would not have far to walk for work either." He laughed at his little joke. Harry shrugged.

"Well if you're both happy, we'll get on with the building work. You should be in your new homes by the autumn." Juan nodded. He said goodbye and went back to his chores. "Now you need to meet the livestock." Harry took Emm's hand and led her along another path lined with orange trees. Emm felt her feet squelching under her. The cows had obviously just gone back into their field. Harry laughed at Emm's face.

"Those wellies are a good idea; I'll get you a matching pair with mine." He grinned. Emm was going to answer but they'd reached the field. The cows were munching on the beautiful green grass, with no pesticides. Harry whistled, expecting them to turn and say hello.

"They are not dogs, Harry. Aren't they beautiful I don't remember seeing a cow this close up in real life. Fleetingly driving past fields, but not stopping. How many fields are there?" There was grass as far as her eyes could see.

"Not entirely sure. I know they move them into each field on a rotating basis, but not sure when." Harry whistled again.

"We have so much to learn. Hopefully Juan and Jorges will help us." Suddenly one of the cows lifted its head. She turned leisurely and walked towards the gate.

"Hola Lucia. Com estàs?" Lucia put her nose on the fence and Harry stroked it.

"Well if I hadn't seen that for myself, I wouldn't have believed it. Harry Hart has pulled a cow." She shrieked with laughter, tears were streaming from her eyes.

"Please Emm. You will frighten Lucia. She's not

used to such displays. It's so unladylike, and Lucia is a lady." Lucia had got bored - she mooed and turned to find a nice spot of unmunched grass. As she went her tail went up in the air and Lucia's bowel emptied in ladylike flat round cowpats. Emm tried not to laugh.

"Such a lady, Harry, I agree." They both looked at each other and giggled. "I think this venture is going to be hard work, mixed with quite a bit of fun. Just remember to buy me those wellies."

Harry took her in his arms and kissed her. Emm was beginning to get used to the closeness again. She felt relaxed and happy and for the first time in a while she was letting her guard down.

Later that day Patrick had received two calls. One from Miguel with an estimated quote and permission to start the work - the other was from the Spanish police with a date for all involved to appear in court in Girona. The first call, he was happy for Miguel to start the work. The second call was much trickier. It wasn't until the following week, but it would bring back all the shocking memories that most of the group had managed to put to the back of their minds. He knew he would have to tell Katarina, but he wasn't looking forward to it. He'd tell Lachlan and he can decide how soon Katarina needed to know. He would also let Harry know, as he was in Girona, he might as well stay there.

The only other witness was Nico. He hoped he didn't have an opera that day. He hadn't a clue how those shows ran. Eleanor walked in on a very anxious husband. He explained his conversation with the solicitor in the case.

"Nico will have to be told first, in case he has to get a substitute in." Eleanor couldn't help but smile. It really wasn't Patrick's thing.

"I think you mean understudy, darling. He doesn't play football." Patrick grinned. He knew exactly what he had said. He found it fun to wind his wife up, just a little. "I'll ring Caroline and mention it. I want to know how things have gone with the paparazzi." Good, thought Patrick, one down, two to go. He called Harry to make sure he extended his rental. He also told him Miguel was starting work anytime.

"Will he want payment up front?" Harry didn't have the ready cash to pay anybody.

"He will, but I'm going to set up an account so he can take enough out for wages and supplies. The rest he can have when you're happy with the result." Harry was very grateful. He knew he would have to pay Patrick back, but at least they could start making money straight away. The cows were still being milked and the shops were still buying it. Emm's other ideas could wait until they were in situ. Patrick agreed it all sounded wonderful and was happy for them both.

The next phone call was to Lachlan's office. Patrick was about to pick up the phone when his work phone buzzed. It was his PA. The news was good, and it couldn't have come at a better time. Eleanor had heard Patrick cheering. She turned back into Patrick's on-board office, the bar!

"What are you so happy about?" Patrick went over to her and spun her around. "How much have you had to drink already?" She loved it when he was so pleased with himself.

"My legal team have found the girl who took Katarina's place at her 'so called' wedding. They have a written statement from her that went before the Estonian

Court this morning. The marriage between Eric and Katarina has been annulled, effective immediately." He grabbed Eleanor again and danced round the bar area. "I need to phone Lachlan and tell him the good news and bad news. Which should I tell him first?" Eleanor thought about it.

"I think you will put a dampener on the good news telling them both. I would recommend you just tell them about the court case. It will be over by this time next week, then you could cheer Katarina up with the good news." He kissed her.

"You're a clever girl. That must be one of the reasons why I love you." He winked at her and picked up the phone. Eleanor went back to their cabin to pack a few bits. She'd had enough of living on the boat for a while. She had persuaded Patrick to move back into the Monaco apartment for a few days. She believed it was so much more civilised to wake up in the same country you went to sleep in.

* * *

Claudia had her way. Michael had driven them down to a wonderful hotel, right by a golf course in Caldes de Malavella, Girona. Claudia knew that would be a big persuading point. It was a ten-minute drive to Emily and Harry's new venture.

"When are you going to telephone your daughter, chéri? I thought it would be a lovely surprise if we invite them out to dinner, then tell them we'll meet them in Girona this evening." Michael wasn't sure Emily would be happily surprised, assuming her father was checking up on her. He'd have to be careful how he worded it.

"Hello poppet. How are things?" He could hear what sounded like banging in the background.

"Very busy Daddy. We are knocking down a house." Emm walked away from Harry who was merrily wielding a mallet. She could hardly hear her father. "Just a minute Daddy, I'm just walking away from the noise." She decided it would be quieter round by the stable block. She was feeling quite at home already. "That's better. Harry has decided he wants to be Fred Dibnah, the demolition guy, today. Tomorrow he's going to try to be Bob the builder. Who knows, by the end of the week he could be Old MacDonald the farmer." Michael could hear her laughing. It made him smile. He hoped it meant that Harry was back in her life for good. She hadn't been the same since he left, although she would deny it.

"I'm glad you're enjoying your new venture. Do I take it that you have given in your notice at the office?" He was teasing her. "Only I need to take you off the payroll."

"Don't you dare yet Daddy. I won't be making any money here for months. I have some surprisingly good ideas though, for organic products. Oh, and you should meet the cows, they are adorable. Harry has a pet one already called Lucia." She suddenly realised how daft that sounded.

"Well, Claudia and I wondered if you two needed a break from it all and could join us for dinner, tonight." Emm tried to calculate how far Avignon was from Girona. She knew her father and Claudia were going to Claudia's family estate, something about asking Claudia's big brother for her hand in marriage. She thought it incredibly romantic, but then again, her father was almost French now.

"We need to be here in the morning for the

builders. That would mean driving there and back in a day just for dinner. Not going to work really." It would have been lovely to change out of work clothes and dress up for dinner. She was beginning to feel like Felicity Kendall in The Good Life, she'd been watching it on Gold. She'd even managed to find a pair of wellies, a little on the large size, but they'd do until she got her own pair.

"Surprise!" It was Claudia. Michael was taking too long to tell her. Claudia had grabbed the phone off him. "We are down the road at, where are we chéri?" Michael took the phone back.

"We are in Caldes de Malavella, ten-minutes down the road from you. We wanted to surprise you, and Claudia is dying to see your farm. Ouch." Claudia threw a cushion at him. "So how about we meet you in Girona for dinner, then tomorrow, if it's ok, we'll pop over to see the farm." Emm was delighted that her father and future stepmother wanted to see their venture.

"Why wait? Come on over now and see it. If you bring your glad rags with you, you can change at our rental cottage. I'll get Harry to text you the address. You could have stayed here too if I'd known."

Michael shook his head, and then realised Emily couldn't see him.

"No darling. The one thing we didn't want was to get in the way. But that is a lovely idea about coming now and changing later. We can share a cab and drop you off on the way back from Girona tonight. Brilliant. We'll see you soon Poppet. Bye." He hung up and turned to Claudia. "I couldn't say I was dying to see their farm. She'd think I wanted to interfere with their plans. I know she'll be able to survey the property and judge soundness. She's my daughter after all." Claudia retrieved the cushion and threw it back at him. "What was that for?" She smiled at him.

"It was because you were getting a little big for your boots, monsieur." He laughed. "Come on, let's get some clothes together. I shouldn't need an 'at or scarf, we are in Spain. I don't think I've filmed anything in Spain. 'opefully I will 'ave a pleasant evening without my fans 'arassing me. Ouch." Michael was laughing, having thrown the cushion back at Claudia.

"I think Mademoiselle is getting a little grand pour votre boots!" She got up and hugged him, pulling him towards the bed. "Perhaps we got into a traffic jam on the way?" Claudia nodded. Optimistically they should make it before dinner, she thought, naughtily…

Michael loved the farm, especially the outbuildings. He could see why they would settle down there. Claudia thought it wonderful. She realised she'd made a big mistake in her footwear, but Emm managed to find an odd pair of wellies, luckily a right and a left boot. Claudia knew they were all laughing at her, but she was enjoying it. She loved Harry and thought he was humorous and caring, just right for Emily. In fact, she may even confide in Michael later that she thought Emily had fallen for the image of her father.

By the time they got to the rental cottage they were all in need of a drink. Michael, with forethought had brought a couple of cases for them from Claudia's family winery. As they were all very hot, he slipped a couple in the 'fridge while they went off to change.

Harry was pouring the delicious cold crisp wine into the glasses he had found in a cupboard when his iPad burst to life. Emm handed it to him and he opened it. It was a Facetime call from Katarina. He clicked the green button and suddenly there was a lovely smile beaming across the wireless network.

"Hello Harry, it's me." Harry was beaming back. Emm put her head into the shot. "Hi Emm." Lilli was talking very quietly. "I'm not really allowed to use Mummy's iPad without asking her. But she and Lachlan are kissing. Yuk. She's going to get so many germs that I think she might have tonsillitis by the morning." Harry and Emm were laughing so much Claudia and Michael came in to see what had tickled them. Emm turned the iPad towards her father.

"This is my daddy Lilli, Michael. Daddy, meet Lilli." Michael saluted her and made her giggle.

"Hello Lilli, we've heard a lot about you. It is so nice to meet you." Claudia leant over Michael's shoulder.

"Bonjour ma petite. I'm Claudia, 'ow do you do." Lilli loved her voice.

"I'm doing very well thank you. Harry?" Harry got back into her view.

"Yes Lilli. What's the matter?" Harry got closer to the screen. "Are you happy?"

"I'm very happy Harry. But I miss you. Daddy Toby and Mummy are always in their room. I don't mind really, but sometimes I want to go swimming and Daddy Toby says in a minute, but his minutes are not the same as mine." Harry tried not to smile. Emm came back into the picture.

"Who is Daddy Toby, Lilli?" Lilli laughed.

"Lachlan, silly. Mummy said that I can call him Daddy Toby until they get married and then I can just call him Daddy. Isn't that brilliant." Emm had to be tactful with her response.

"Darling Lilli, do you think Mummy said Daddy Toby or do you think she may have said Daddy To Be?" Lilli suddenly giggled.

"Well that does make more sense. After all, his name is Lachlan, not Toby. So why did she say Toby?" She was still not completely convinced.

"I think you will find it was her accent, Lilli." Lilli nodded in agreement.

"Harry?" She beckoned Harry to come closer and whispered, "you were right. Emm is very clever, isn't she?" Harry smiled and nodded. While they were still in secret mode, Harry got up with the iPad and explained to the others.

"I'm just going to my room with Lilli, I have something to show her." He held the iPad so they could all see Lilli. Emm smiled at her.

"Bye bye Lilli. See you soon." She blew her a kiss. Lilli blew one back. Claudia leant nearer the screen.

"Au revoir Mademoiselle Lilli." Lilli waved to Claudia.

"I'm a Señorita here. But I do like being a Mademoiselle." Claudia smiled at her.

"Well you will 'ave to come and stay with us in our 'ouse in France. Then you can be a Madmoiselle again. Au revoir ma petite." Claudia blew her a kiss. Lilli caught it and put it to her cheek. She had learnt that from Lachlan. Michael and Lilli waved to each other as Harry walked towards his bedroom. Harry could hear chatting from the kitchen and knew he was alone with Lilli, but just in case he shut his bedroom door.

"I have something to show you and I don't want the others to see. Are you ready?" Lilli was nodding but realised that Harry wasn't watching. He was getting something out of his bedside cupboard.

"I'm ready Harry." She sounded excited. Harry took out a small box and opened it in front of the screen. "Wow Harry, that is beautiful. Who is it for?" She was laughing. She loved teasing Harry.

"Oh ha, ha." He took it out of the box and gave her a closer look. "Do you think she'll like it?" Lilli looked at it and screwed up her face. "Don't you like it?" Harry was worried, until Lilli changed her expression to a huge smile.

"I think she'll love it Harry." Harry put it back in the box and safely put it into its hiding place. "When are you going to ask her to marry you Harry?" Harry scratched his head.

"I'll know when the time is right, but I wanted to show you it first as it was because of you I bought it." Lilli looked puzzled. "Don't you remember?" Lilli suddenly remembered.

"Oh yes. I said Alain had given me some perfume and now he's my best friend. If you want Emm to be your best friend, you should buy her some perfume. Oh, I remember, I also said or diamonds, then she'd marry you." She looked at Harry to see if that was the right answer. Harry was nodding.

"You see, I took your advice. My problem is, will she say yes?" He looked at Lilli for the answer. She screwed up her little face and winked at him.

"We'll see Harry, we'll see." Cheeky and adorable, he knew he'd miss her so much. But she was happy. Eventually Harry came out of his room, with his closed iPad under his arm, looking sad, so Emm went over to him and hugged him.

"We can have her to stay for the summer holidays. I'm sure Lachlan and Katarina would love to have some privacy while they get to know each other better." She had made Harry smile.

Not only because he'd see Lilli more often, but also the fact that Emm had admitted to living at the farm in the future tense.

"What an adorable little girl that is. From what I 'ave been told, I thought she would be very timid and quiet." Harry laughed. No one could describe Lilli as timid or quiet. "Thank goodness she 'asn't been too affected by 'er circumstances." Harry agreed and nodded.

"Come on, the wine is getting warm. Let's drink it before the cab arrives." Michael shared out the glasses and they all chinked them. "To new beginnings." He was sure there would be approval for that toast all around.

The evening was a success too. Claudia announced the date of their wedding in September that year.

"It will be during the grape 'arvest. It is magnificent then. Everyone will love Avignon in the autumn. The people celebrate all the time. It will be incroyable." Michael looked for Emily's reaction. She smiled at him. He was relieved.

"I hope Stephanie and I can be bridesmaids." Claudia looked surprised she had to ask.

"Of course, and of course CC. It will be so much fun." Claudia looked at Harry. "Do you think Katarina would allow Lilli to be my flower girl? She is so adorable. Would that be alright with you all?" Michael and Emm were smiling. Harry knew Katarina would be very happy for Lilli.

"I'm sure Katarina wouldn't mind at all." Claudia wanted to make sure there was no problem.

"I will invite the whole family, Katarina and Toby!" She had everyone laughing. Poor Lilli, if she knew she'd have been embarrassed.

Emm couldn't help asking - "Will there be anyone from your profession there?" Claudia knew Emm would ask.

"Matt Pride will be invited." Harry looked worried.

"Matt Pride the Adonis with the lobotomy." He stopped himself from saying more. He forgot where he was for the moment.

Michael stifled a laugh, knowing exactly what Matt's name was with the male population. There were a few other names he was known by but all detrimental. Suddenly a giggle came from Emm. She had tried to stop it but couldn't.

"I'm sorry Claudia, but he does rather love himself. Trying to hold a conversation with him reminds me of the conversation Harry had with Lucia. Very one sided." Claudia and Michael had met Lucia that day.

"Excuse me. But as soon as I have learnt a little more Catalan, we'll be enjoying many an evening in the moon light, behind the cowshed, with our tête-à-têtes. I bet she will be a lot more scintillating than Matt Pride." They were all laughing. Claudia wasn't offended in the least. She was glad they all had the same opinion of him as she had. He was fine with a script, but ad-lib wasn't his forté.

"I would love Nico to sing at our ceremony too. Do you think he will?" Claudia looked at Emm.

"I'm sure he would love to Claudia. I can ask my mother for you, if you like?" Claudia looked at Michael.

"Would you mind, mon chéri? I would like Caroline to come too." Michael smiled.

"Why not? The more the merrier." Emm watched her father's face, he was genuinely agreeing. Respect, she thought; her father was a legend in his own lifetime.

The car dropped Emm and Harry off on its way back to Michael and Claudia's hotel.

"Are you sure you want me to meet the builder tomorrow? I'm sure you have it all in hand." Michael was honoured that he'd been asked.

"Daddy, I know I'm good, but a second opinion would be valuable." She smiled at him and kissed him. "Bye bye Claudia, see you tomorrow." She blew her a kiss and turned to hug Harry.

As the driver turned the corner, Michael looked back to wave. She was definitely the old Emily, back bantering and happy. He thanked Harry under his breath, for finally seeing sense.

As they got into the cottage Harry could see a missed call on his phone from Patrick. He'd turned it onto silent when he arrived at the restaurant. There was a voice mail. He showed Emm.

"Is it too late to ring him back?" Emm saw the time was coming up to midnight.

"Let's listen to what he says, then we can decide whether to bother him before the morning." He put it on loudspeaker so Emm could hear it.

"Harry, I have very important news to tell you. I won't say what it is, but it will be to your advantage if you ring me when you get this message. Don't worry what time it is, I'll not sleep tonight

anyway. Patrick." They looked at each other.

"If it's another life-time experience that can't be missed, will you take it?" Emm looked despondent. They were very nearly back together, but not quite. Harry grabbed her and whispered into her ear, "I will never make the same mistake as I did last time Emily Fitzgerald. I love you too much to let you go again, ever." He lifted her chin and kissed her lovingly. She felt her body go light. Her heart was racing, and she leant into him for better contact. Their tongues were playing cat and mouse with each other. Harry wanted to carry her off into the bedroom, but he was concerned about the phone call. It could be something urgent for Patrick to say he wouldn't sleep. Deals could collapse, and businesses go under, but it never stopped Patrick Robertshaw sleeping. Emm could feel Harry tensing. She knew he was worried. She gently pushed them apart and looked into his eyes.

"Go on, phone him. You know you won't be able to concentrate on anything else until you have." She said it with a smile. Harry still couldn't work out why he had taken the job instead of the woman. He put it down to immaturity. Funny, he thought, just looking after Lilli for those few days had made him a responsible adult. He'd thank her next time he saw her.

"Patrick, it's Harry. What can I do for you?" He motioned for Emm to sit on his lap. She snuggled into him to hear Patrick talking.

"Harry, good news, well beyond good really." Patrick sounded excited.

"Well spit it out then." Harry knew patience had never been his strong point.

"I've had a call from my solicitor, you know Justin, who has been dealing with the Spanish and French police. Erik Eskola has pleaded guilty to aggravated kidnapping of Katarina, the attempted murder of Emily and yours truly, and accessory to murder of poor Karl. The Sokolov brothers have each pleaded guilty to murder of Karl, attempted murder of Katarina and malicious damage to property. The reason they have pleaded guilty is because they know what charges are awaiting them in Estonia and Russia, and believe it or not, these seemed lesser. Justin told me that their legal representatives have done a deal with them, so they can stay in Spanish prisons and not be sent to Siberia, or wherever the Russians imprison murderers. They obviously prefer the climate here in winter than minus twenty-five degrees centigrade in northern Russia. They will be there for at least twenty-five years and if they are still alive after that they will be sent to Russia to be tried there and probably never see the light of day again." Harry wished Patrick would get to the point. "Anyway, this means that there will be no court prosecutions, in fact no court trial at all. Therefore vis-à-vis, apropos, etc., with regard to our invitation to give evidence, Erik, Yegor and Bogdan have finally done us a favour. We are no longer needed to attend. We are off the hook." Emm was nearly asleep. Why couldn't he have just said they'd pleaded guilty so no trial? She looked at Harry's face - he winked at her. He was obviously thinking the same thing.

"Have you told Katarina the good news?" Harry pecked Emm on the cheek. She smiled at him. She was desperate for their interrupted kiss to continue as soon as possible.

"Not yet. We didn't want to disturb the lovebirds this late. Oh, sorry you two, it's just that your family, and

I wanted to tell you first. Eleanor and I are on our way over to Barcelona to see them in the morning with the news. Lilli has her new school uniform and wants to model it for us. Harry?" Patrick was just checking he still had Harry's attention. He thought the next item of news was far more important.

"I'm still here Patrick."

"Good, because I haven't told you the best news yet." Emm took a deep breath. She looked at her watch and saw it was quarter of an hour past midnight. Could it wait until morning, she wondered? Obviously not, Patrick continued. "The woman Erik had employed to impersonate Katarina for their sham marriage in Estonia has been found. She has signed a written statement that she had done it under duress and that Katarina was not in the country when the 'marriage' took place. The Estonian Court has annulled Erik and Katarina's marriage. She is a free woman. She's free to marry Lachlan now, whenever he asks her!" Patrick was so excited about the news. "I'm going to tell them tomorrow after I've told them about the guilty pleas. I wish you could be there to see Katarina's face Harry. After all, without you none of this would have happened. You're a good lad, Harry. I'm going to miss you. But you take care of that girl. She's a keeper Harry, just like my Eleanor. Night Harry. Take care." The phone went dead. Harry tried to move Emm, but she was so comfortable.

"He could have told you all that in the morning." She yawned.

"I know. I think he's missing me." He looked smug. Emm punched him, gently. "We can't stay here all night, come on, let's go to bed." Emm struggled up off his lap. They had been working hard all day and Emm certainly wasn't used to manual labour. Harry could see how tired she was, so helped her to her room. He was about to leave her when she called him back.

"Harry, can we just finish that kiss please? We were very rudely interrupted earlier and I want to see how it finishes." She giggled as Harry jumped onto the bed.

"Where were we?" Harry put his lips on hers but took them off sharply. "How would you like it if we bought a boat? We could visit everyone much easier down here. I'd call it Lady Emily." Emm liked that, but the last thing on her mind was visiting everyone else, when she had the only person she wanted right there. She surrendered into his embrace and resumed their 'affaire de cœur' where they had left off, over a year ago. The phrase was her mother's description of her liaison with Nico in the early days. She'd told Emily that the English 'love affair' didn't sound so romantic. Emm totally understood what her mother had been trying to tell her, and 'affair of the heart' summed up the feeling Emm was having this time around with Harry.

The next morning Harry woke up first and took a second to realise that Emm was still in the bed next to him. It was the most magnificent feeling and Harry couldn't stop staring at her. She looked so content and beautiful with her long dark hair cascading wildly over her pillow. He wondered if he'd ruin it if he followed his heart. He had a longing he had been suppressing since they had rekindled their relationship. He managed to get out of the bed without disturbing Emm and crept into the kitchen. He took out two glasses and poured a little champagne into them both. He plonked a strawberry in each, without finesse as he was alone, wiping the spill from the glasses with some kitchen roll, and placed them on a tray. He warmed two croissants in the range while he tip-toed into his bedroom to find the box he had hidden. Having taken Lilli's advice, he'd bought a present for Emm for this moment. He went back into the kitchen and took out the warm croissants, filling them both with homemade strawberry jam, kindly supplied by Juan's wife along with a punnet of fresh strawberries and some eggs, and finished off the tray with a small sunflower from the garden.

"Morning, sleepy head." He had opened the bedroom door fully by kicking it. Emm woke up and tried to adjust her eyes to the sunshine that Harry had just flooded into the bedroom by opening the window shutters. He took the tray he'd plonked on the sideboard and carried it to the bedside table. He waited for her to sit up and having judged the timing, he took her hand as he sat on the side of the bed.

"Emm, you are the most wonderful human being I have had the good fortune to have known. I want to apologise for my childish behaviour over the last year or so." Emm was about to speak. Harry stopped her with his finger on her lips. "No, please let me finish or I'll chicken out." Emm just smiled at the new mature man sitting on the bed. "I cannot believe what an arse I have been, nearly losing you for a boy's dream. Nothing would come between us now, I promise. I want to spend the rest of my life with you."

Emm was getting a little worried. Harry seemed to be holding it together, just, but she could see he was very emotional. Her first thought was maybe he was ill and hadn't told her. She was about to tell him that everything was ok. She wanted to spend the rest of her life with him too. But Harry had got off the bed and was kneeling. Emm looked over the side of the bed and could see he was on one knee.

"Emily Fitzgerald, will you please marry me?" Emm couldn't believe what was happening. She was wearing an old t-shirt of Harry's and she hadn't even brushed her teeth. But she had got caught in the moment and jumped off the bed into Harry's arms.

"Yes, I so bloody well will!" She kissed him with every bone and fibre of her being, totally surrendering herself into his embrace. With difficulty Harry managed to get one hand free and took out the little box from its hiding place tucked into the elastic waist band of his boxer shorts. He was able to get her hand and as she stretched back she could see what he was doing. "Harry, it's beautiful." She could see it better as he'd slipped it on her finger. It was slightly loose but could be resized by a local jeweller. The band was of white gold with an intricate small heart shaped diamond in the centre.

"Apparently it is," He changed his voice to a posh English woman's "the epitome of romance and affection, sir. Madam will love it." Emm wanted to laugh, but she was still staring at the most beautiful ring she had ever seen. Although Claudia's came a close second. She noted the tell-tale sign of the egg blue box from her favourite jewellers. He'd done well she thought but wouldn't voice that out aloud. It could sound a trifle condescending, which she did not mean it to sound.

"Harry Hart, you're adorable. I missed you from the day you went off to sea, until the day I saw you again in Nice. I knew I'd never find anyone else who'd match your compassion and generosity. Two things that already made you a man in my eyes. What you did for Lilli and Katarina was the most unselfish act deserving my respect and admiration for ever. I love you so much Harry, it hurts."

She had tears streaming down her cheeks. Harry did the only thing he could think of and gently moved her back onto the bed. Having released her from his arms he stretched across and grabbed the champagne glasses.

"To us both. May we always talk through our problems and go to bed with a kiss each night." Emm took her glass and chinked with Harry's.

"May all our troubles be little ones!" She patted her stomach and smiled.

"You can't be. They need more than 12 hours to swim wherever they have to go!" Emm spluttered her champagne and coughed.

"Oh Harry, it was going so well." She smiled at her fiancé. "I mean when we are ready, not now." Harry knew that's what she meant, but couldn't resist being a boy, just a little bit longer.

The End

Printed in Poland
by Amazon Fulfillment
Poland Sp. z o.o., Wrocław